THE LUCIFER GENOME

A Biogenetics Thriller

GLEN CRANEY
AND
JOHN JETER

BRIGID'S FIRE PRESS

Cover and book design by Glen Craney
Cover Art based on David Boyd's work, reproduced with the permission of Lucinda Boyd and Cassandra Boyd. Image courtesy of Eva Breuer Art Dealer.

Published in the United States

FIRST EDITION

Library of Congress Cataloging-in-Publication Data
Craney, Glen and Jeter, John
The Lucifer Genome: A Biogenetics Thriller

ISBN 978-0-9816484-6-0

1. Political thriller 2. Mystery fiction 3. Genetic engineering-Fiction. 4. Science Fiction. 5. Meteorites-Fiction. 6. Black Stone of Kaaba-Fiction. 7. Cloning-Fiction

Brigid's Fire Press
www.brigidsfire.com

Finding nucleobase compounds not typically found in Earth's biochemistry strongly supports an extraterrestrial origin. ... This finding reveals that meteorites may have been molecular tool kits, providing the essential building blocks for life on Earth.
— Jim Cleaves, chemist
Carnegie Institute of Washington

We are the stuff of stars.
— Carl Sagan

1

Llano County, Texas

Twelve-year-old Jennie Delbert reined up her roan filly and squinted at the snowy horizon above Kingdom Come Ranch. Wondering if the white glare was playing with her eyes, she glanced over at her father to confirm if he also saw the gray plume rising in the distance. He had taught her that reading steam in winter was an essential skill for a rancher, one that could mean the difference between life and death on three thousand acres of bonescape hardscrabble. Meandering steam trails that quickly vanished promised a comfortable herd; and small, isolated tufts warned that one of the calves had likely become lost. But sharp, snorted puffs—disconnected, like those now visible over the drifts ahead—could mean only one thing.

One of the animals was in life-threatening distress.

Galen Delbert, the ranch's foreman, answered his daughter's silent question by lashing his Appaloosa into a gallop over the nearest ridge.

Falling several lengths behind, Jennie pushed her pony to its limit and followed her father into the ravine. She found him kneeling over a downed heifer that was struggling in pain. "What's wrong with it, Pa?"

"It's giving birth too early." He grunted as he reached into the writhing cow's birth canal to feel for the calf. "Bring me the rolled canvas on my saddle."

Jennie delivered the tarp and began collecting driftwood to build a crude shelter against the biting wind. In the corner of her eye, she saw something flash across the auburn sky. She pointed at a star shooting. "Look, Pa! It's like Bethlehem!"

Working feverishly to get the calf out, her father grimaced bitterly at the irony of the celestial coincidence. "I guess all we need now are three wise men. But those seem to be in pretty short supply around here."

Jennie knelt aside the suffering heifer and ran her hand across its side to soothe it. She knew Mr. Cohanim, the owner of the ranch, would dock her father's pay if they lost the calf, and it'd be double the penalty if the mother died, too. Extending her caresses to the heifer's forehead, she gasped. "This is Beccah!"

Her father checked the underside of the mother's ear. He stared in disbelief at the engraved number on the metal vaccination tag. "It ain't possible."

Jennie stood and walked around Beccah, trying to make sense of what was happening. The heifer was a freemartin, a rare female twin of the herd's bull. The only other freemartin born on the ranch had been sold a year ago to a genetic-research laboratory at SMU. Her science teacher at the time had explained to her that doctors prized the rare calves for their stem-cell research because almost all of the freemartin's blood cells were identical to those of its twin brother. And every kid who showcased in 4-H knew that a freemartin was made sterile in the womb by the hormones from its male twin. She looked pointedly at her father, questioning if Beccah had somehow been miraculously impregnated, like the Virgin Mary.

Her father had no time to ponder the troublesome mystery. He rolled the heifer on its other side and finally managed to pull a female calf out by its hind legs. He wiped mucous from the newborn's snorting nose and rubbed its throat to start it breathing. Shocked, he lurched to his feet and took a step back. From head to hooves, the calf looked permanently stained with its mother's blood.

Jennie scooped some snow and tried to wipe the newborn's wet hide, but the bright flame coloring wouldn't come off. "It's all red ... even its eyes."

The calf took a shuddering breath and staggered to its wobbly legs.

Looking shaken, her father pulled a cell phone from his coat pocket and punched in a number. "Sir, it's Galen. I'm down at the west end of Cedar Gulch. There's something here I think you need to see. ... I think it may be. ... Yes, sir. Right away." He pressed the "End" button and looked off into the distance, taking a moment to gather his composure. Then, rousing from his unshared thoughts, he ordered his daughter, "Get the horses."

Jennie whispered a prayer of thanks to God for allowing both heifer and newborn to survive. She petted the disoriented calf, unable to break away from it. "Pa, do you think Mr. Cohanim would sell me this one?"

Her father glared at her. "No!"

"But you promised—"

"Get the damn horses, Jennie! Now!'

Frightened by his outburst, Jennie retrieved his Appaloosa and mounted her pony. Her father climbed to his saddle and lashed off into a gallop. She followed him for a half-mile east until he pulled to a stop.

"I've gotta check the fences over at the Bollulos pen," he told her. "You go on home and tell your momma I'll be back an hour after dusk."

She nodded uncertainly, figuring it was best not to ask why she couldn't come along. After watching her father hurry west, she split off toward home, troubled and confused. She had never seen him so rattled.

Moments after he disappeared over the ridge, she heard a distant whirring behind her. She reined up and looked back toward the *arroyo*.

Mr. Cohanim's helicopter was gliding in from the ranch compound.

Why was her father's boss in such a hurry to see another new addition to the herd? Hundreds of calves were born every year, and he never seemed to care much about them. She had been warned never to get attached to the animals, for they'd all eventually go to slaughter. But she felt an overwhelming urge to hold that red calf again and raise it. She glanced west, toward the dissipating wisps of snow left by her father's horse. If she rode hard, she could make it back to the birthing spot and ask Mr. Cohanim for the newborn, then be home before her father found out.

Rearing her pony around, she retraced her tracks down the ravine and navigated in the dimming dusk light toward the approaching chop of the helicopter's blades. She dismounted and tied her pony to a scrub brush. Sneaking down the gulch, she took care to remain out of sight while climbing to the edge of the bank. As the whirr became louder, she inched her eyes above the ridge.

Mr. Cohanim jumped out of the helicopter and walked anxiously toward the calf and downed heifer. With the rancher was a short, bearded man who wore a flat-brimmed black hat and a black coat whose hem dropped to his shins. Tiny boxes tied to long, spiraling curls of his hair hung below his ears. After bringing his companion to the tarped lean-to, Mr. Cohanim took off his Stetson to shield his eyes against the setting sun's reflection off the drifts. He bent down and ran his hand over every inch of the red calf, examining it as if searching for defects. Apparently satisfied with his inspection, he smiled and nodded to the man in the black hat.

Jennie was about to climb the bank and go ask her father's boss for the gift, but the stranger in black began chanting foreign verses that sounded like a hymn. Startled, she ducked back down below the ravine. The only word she could make out was "Levite."

Where had she heard *that* name before?

Wait, hadn't Pastor Mullens told them in Bible class that the Levites were like a big family of Old Testament priests? Maybe the man in black was giving the calf some sort of birth blessing.

The stranger pulled a knife from his coat pocket. He stretched the calf's neck and cut its throat from ear to ear. The mother heifer bawled as the calf's blood gushed across the snow.

Jennie pressed her gloved hand to her mouth. Blind with grief, she tried to make sense of what she had just witnessed. Did they kill the calf because it was different from the others? She bit harder on her glove to stifle her sobs. Even if the poor thing *was* sickly, she would have nursed it to health.

When the spasming calf finally gurgled its last death throes, Mr. Cohanim turned and signaled a thumbs-up at the helicopter. The pilot stepped out, pulled an iron barrel from the cargo bay, and set it next to the gutted calf. He retracted four metal legs, so that the barrel sat above the ground, and opened the top half, revealing a grill.

How had these men known to bring this equipment from her father's cryptic call? Whatever they were doing, it seemed planned and practiced.

While the heifer continued to caterwaul in protest, the black-clad man lifted the dead calf onto the grate as the ranch owner flicked a lighter to ignite a fire under its bleeding carcass. The flames quickly consumed the calf's dripping flesh and wet hide. When the fire finally eased, Mr. Cohanim pulled a pistol from his holster and shot the distraught heifer point-blank between the eyes.

They killed the mother, too?

Jennie swallowed another sobbing gasp. None of this made any sense. Even if Beccah had, through no fault of her own, given birth to a freakish calf, she could have been spared to try again, or at least been butchered for the meat. Wiping tears, she watched, frightened, as the three men scooped up the burnt ashes of the calf's innards and poured them into a metal canister. They loaded the container onto the helicopter, hopped in, and flew off, leaving the charred remnant of the calf's hide and smoking bones in the snow splattered with Beccah's blood.

2

Mecca, Saudi Arabia

"*Salaam*," the arriving hotel guest whispered to himself, practicing for his check-in greeting. "I am Abdul Baith. May the peace of Allah be with you."

He loved the simple but elegant sound of his new alias. *Servant of the Resurrection*, it meant in Arabic. Had a nice tribal resonance to it, like the thump of an oil derrick pounding out a small fortune with each thrust of its drill bit.

As he threaded his way through the busy lobby of the plush Abraj Al Bait Towers, he looked around and savored the perks of his profession. Had he known he would be lodged in such lavish decadence, he might have tempered his nonnegotiable fee of twenty million pounds British sterling. But he quickly dismissed that whimsical notion of generosity with a cynical snort. Such an offer would have set a bad precedent—and besides, money seemed no object to the anonymous client who was paying him for this heist.

He stepped outside through the lobby's doors and strolled across the heliport that sat adjacent to this garish hotel of seventy-six floors. Above him, the iridescent green clock tower—a knock-off of London's Big Ben—soared into the heavens. It was now four in the morning, yet hordes of Muslim pilgrims, too excited to sleep, were still milling about the balconies and corridors.

This was merely the calm before the storm, he knew. The protocol for the next twenty-four hours would the same he used on all of his assignments. In the next few minutes, the order to proceed would arrive by text message from his intermediary in Beirut. Then, he would move on his target, finish the extraction operation, and be out of the country before the next sundown.

Poached by the stifling nocturnal heat, he retreated to the vast air-conditioned lobby, sobered by the knowledge that his struggle for breath would be much worse in the morning. He strolled casually past an expansive plate-glass window and glanced down at his target. His client, he now realized, had not chosen this hotel for the high thread count of its bed sheets. From such a high vantage point, he could scout the security pattern in the Masjid al Haram, the largest mosque in the world. And just as he had expected, the police cordon being thrown up in the pilgrimage square looked tighter than a sultan's garrote.

He wouldn't have it any other way.

In two hours, that vast open enclosure—the most sacred ground in all of Islam—would be teeming with half-crazed worshippers, including many of these wealthy Arabs around him now. They lodged here in luxury while just a few blocks away, thousands of less fortunate Muslims spent their pitiful savings in preparation for what they hoped would be the most profound spiritual experience of their lives. All across this sprawling city, dozens of cranes raising new construction projects pierced the dazzling nightscape. The sky's panorama reminded him of a black velvet cloth studded with an array of sparkling peridot gems.

And yes, he had stolen his share of those, too.

He dug his fingers into his straining neck muscles, trying to stay alert. This extraction operation promised to be the most difficult he had ever undertaken. Only once before had such a theft been attempted, and the captured perpetrators of that bloody fiasco had paid with their severed heads. Shuddering from jet lag, he motioned for a waiter to bring him a double espresso. A good night's sleep would help, but that was time he could not afford. What was it that umpire had told Ted Williams as the Red Sox slugger stepped up to the plate in his last at bat of his career? Oh, yeah. *Well, Kid, you gotta be loose to hit four hundred.*

Yet Teddy Ballgame's challenge had been easy compared with what he was now expected to pull off. After all, *he* would have to bat a thousand—one for one—or suffer a death he'd not wish on his worst enemy.

He blinked repeatedly at the blur of shimmering white *thawbs* in the lobby, trying to stretch his eyesight, which had deteriorated from the many years of casing jobs. Last month, his pilfering of Van Gogh's *Poppy Flowers* from the Mahmud Khalil Modern Art Museum in Cairo had netted him a paltry million and a half dollars, barely enough to maintain his standard of living for a year. To his great amusement, the museum's board of directors had blamed the missing painting on faulty alarms. In the art world, everybody was trained first and foremost in the art of covering one's ass.

Still, most of the low-hanging fruit had been picked, and he had promised himself that this job would be his last. By next week, he would be retired and ensconced on the white beaches of the West Indies, launched upon his next mission: to beat the Guinness Book record for the most rum brands consumed. He pulled his passport from his breast pocket and smirked at the doctored photo. Walnut-shaded skin. Long black hair. Trimmed goatee.

Damned if he didn't actually *look* like a Hashemite playboy prince.

If all went as planned, he would join the annals of temerity with one of his heroes, Sir Richard Burton, the British adventurer who had infiltrated Mecca in 1883. Maybe he'd pick up a copy of Burton's *Arabian Nights* at the airport bookstore and reread it on the plane out, if only for the rich irony. *Ah, Burton, you magnificent magician. How did you manage to slip past those thousands of fanatics to touch the Kaaba?* He had burned into memory the Englishman's description of the Islam's holiest icon: *The colour appeared to me black and metallic, and the centre of the stone was sunk about two inches below the metallic circle. Round the sides was a reddish-brown cement, almost level with the metal, and sloping down to the middle of the stone.*

He reached into his jacket pocket, checking to confirm that its depth would cover his hand. But then he remembered that he'd be wearing the white garb of the pilgrim. *Come on. Focus.* He closed his eyes a moment to revive them. *Hit the ball out of the park and then give the bastards the bird while trotting back to the dugout.* He opened his eyes again and glanced around the lobby with studied insouciance. The Saudi security police, disguised as tourists, were easy to identify. They always gave themselves away with their looks of boredom, having patrolled their surroundings too many times to care.

He checked his watch. *Game time.*

After circling the lobby one last time to locate the most secure angle, he sauntered over to a bank of computers that were blocked from the view of the reservation desk. At a corner terminal, he typed an address in the browser and pulled up his contact's anonymous Twitter account. All email in the kingdom was monitored, but the Saudis were still clueless about these tweets coded in a hundred and forty characters. The last entry on his Twitter roll—with the prearranged hashtag *#shrimponthebarbie*—said: *NAPOLEON ESCAPES ELBA.* He smothered a preening grin. Half his fee had just been wired to an account in Switzerland. Another quarter would soon be delivered to a safe house in Paris, and the rest would be deposited with a Hong Kong securities house to be laundered into euros.

Satisfied with his aerial surveillance of the mosque, he moved on to the registration desk. After checking in without a hitch, he rode the elevator to his floor. When the gilt doors opened, he walked down the sumptuously carpeted corridor, savoring the cushioning under his Gucci-shod feet. He must remember that feeling; for in a few hours, his ankles and knees would be aching from the punishment of hard pavement. He slipped his room key card through the slot. Cautiously, he entered his suite and checked each room for intruders. Everything looked clear. Chilled by the freon-processed desert air, he retracted a curtain. The inscription on the temperature instructions reminded him that this megalith had been built with the same Saudi Binladen Group construction money that had paid for the destruction of New York City's Twin Towers.

He snorted at the irony. Hell of a world.

He opened his carry-on luggage and carefully removed the neatly pressed garments of his white pilgrimage attire. Shedding his suit, he wrapped the *izar* cloth around his waist to cover his lower body and then draped his shoulders with the *reda*. He finished the disguise with a flowing *ghuta* headdress, affixing it with a circular black cord. He swooshed into the bathroom and looked at the mirror. *Allahu akbar,* he lip-synced to his reflected image.

Somewhere below him, a *muezzin* wailed a call to prayer. He nodded with cold anticipation. All across the city, worshippers were now rising from their beds and moving *en masse* toward the object of their desire. ...

His desire.

Before this day was done, if all went well, one billion believers around the globe would be thrown into mortified chaos.

The next morning, scorched by the rising sun, ten thousand sweating bodies drove him in a counterclockwise whirl around the Kaaba shrine. Nearly suffocated by a miasma of body odors, he elbowed his way through the gyre, moving ever closer to its center. All now depended on his reaching the square eye of this human vortex.

He remembered from Burton's description that the Tawaf ritual required seven circumnavigations. As he shuffled in sandals across the slick white slabs of the Masjid Al Haram, he feigned a rapturous contemplation and waited for the right moment to make his move. He could feel the chanting pilgrims around him becoming consumed with spiritual ecstasy. Behind his shoulder, an English-speaking worshipper kept repeating a prayer using the word *Lightgiver*.

He smiled grimly through the pain, wondering if that name had anything to do with one of the key rituals of Hajj: the stoning of the Devil, when pilgrims hurled seven stones at three pillars that symbolized Lucifer. He didn't plan to stay around for *that* crushing insanity to find out.

A piercing call from the minaret spurred a chorus of labored prayers in response. *"Bismillahi Allahu akbar wa lillahi-hamd!"* Pushed forward, he veered closer to the eastern corner of the giant black cube that held the Black Stone's frame, a silver casing molded into the shape of a *vesica piscis*, the ancient symbol formed by the intersection of two circles with the same radius. A burly Saudi guard stationed next to the relic pushed delirious worshippers away after they kissed or touched it, preventing anyone from lingering at the corner of the Kaaba for more than a few seconds.

Another pass, and he'd be close enough to touch it.

Dehydrated, he was starting to feel a little disoriented. He reached under his robe to make sure the two smoke grenades were still there. In the back pocket of his cargo shorts, he had stored a miniature welding torch whose handle he had configured with a diamond edge, durable and sharp enough to cut steel. Readied, he stole a profane glance at the Kaaba again.

Everything was in place, just as Burton had described.

Keeping his hands hidden under his robe, he continued circling the shrine while assembling, by feel, a syringe whose needle was no longer than a mosquito's stinger. All he'd have to do now was slip a few drops of *botulinum* toxin into the lower back of an unsuspecting pilgrim. If he hit the spinal cord just so, the hapless recipient might feel a sting—moments before falling dead.

With his lethal delivery device constructed, he moved ever closer to the embedded shards of the Black Stone, taking caring not to prick himself with the deadly potion. He brought to his mind's eye the photographs of the embedded fragments that he had memorized. In 1853, Burton had reported seeing thirteen separate pieces, but some of the smaller shards had since been fused together, forming only seven fragments now.

The hum of escalating wails around him was so loud that he could hardly hear himself think. He didn't know how much longer he could endure the noise and heat. This close to the target ... just a few more feet. He palmed the minuscule lancet and worked his hand through an air vent of the *ihram* worn by the worshipper gyrating in front of him.

He stabbed the man's lower back with the syringe. In seconds, his victim buckled and collapsed into the worshippers around him, spawning an undulating wave that reversed upon itself. The throngs began weaving and tottering. Dozens stumbled and fell; others fought the crosscurrent, screaming in terror of being crushed. The Saudi soldier guarding the Stone was swept into the undercurrent.

Now! Go confidently in the direction of your dream!

That's priceless, he told himself. Thoreau, of all people, now comes to his overheated brain. How about a little transcendental anarchy as an homage? Surrounded by mayhem, he dropped the empty syringe and crushed the glass under his sandals. He pulled the first smoke grenade from under his robe and yanked the pin. Green smoke billowed everywhere as he rolled the bomb under the scuffling feet.

The din of panic gave way to an eruption of coughing and gagging. Elbowing closer, he pulled the pin on the second smoke grenade and tossed it into the phalanx of soldiers trying to reach their overwhelmed brother. Red billows blossomed into a multi-colored haze, obscuring every face near the cube. Thousands of pilgrims screamed curses, convinced that some radical Islamist sect had gone off its hinges again. The security police around the plaza stood paralyzed with confusion.

As the vast crowd spun out of control, he threw himself into the red-and-green cloud swirling around the eastern corner of the Kaaba. His hand touched the scorching façade of the silver frame. Grimacing at the burn, he shook off the pain in his palm and reached up, feeling blindly for the fragments.

There they were: rubbed smooth as glass by centuries of caressing hands.

Blinking back tears, he spied the silver nails that held the pieces of the holy relic in place. The obscuring haze would last only a few more seconds. He reached into the chamois bag under his robe and quickly pulled out the small welding torch. Plunging his hands into the depths of the silver oval, he worked with the deftness of a surgeon, and within seconds the seven precious fragments succumbed to the torch heat and pressure of the knife.

The holy remnants of the Black Stone popped out and fell into his free hand like peanuts from a shell.

Unseen in the chaos and smoke, he dropped the torch to the ground, stuffed the fragments into the bag under his robe, and fought his way toward the *masjid's* Fatah Gate.

3

Washington, D.C.

Ishtar Abdallah bin Sultan arrived at the White House by speeding limousine and was hurriedly escorted to the Oval Office. A lean six-foot-two, the Saudi ambassador moved down the corridor with the determined but feline grace that had helped him become one of the highest-ranked handball players in the world. A diplomat in this city for twenty years, he had also earned the well-deserved reputation as a *bon vivant* who was always at the top of the invitation lists for the most august Georgetown dinner parties.

Yet on this morning, despite his natural bronze complexion, he looked paler than George Washington's powdered wig in the Gilbert Stuart portrait on the wall he now passed.

Accompanied by the directors of the National Security Council and Central Intelligence Agency, President Carl Lassen arose from his chair behind his impressive desk and came forward to welcome his old friend with a warm handshake. "Abdallah, it's been too long."

Bin Sultan's voice was hoarse with tension. "Thank you, Mr. President, for seeing me on such short notice."

"You didn't sound yourself on the phone. Are you okay?"

As he firmed his grasp on the one hand that could save his kingdom, Bin Sultan stole a nervous glance at the two intelligence operatives. Meeting the eyes of the president again with unabashed directness, he came right to the point. "Mr. President, the House of Saud is in crisis."

The president's smile vanished. "Please tell me that the royal government has not been shooting protestors again."

The ambassador shook his head, insulted that the American leader thought he had rushed here, hat in hand, for such a trivial matter. "It is, I am afraid, far more dire. And what I am about to tell you is known only by His Excellency and the crown princes. ... This morning, the Black Stone of Mecca was stolen from the Kaaba."

"The Kaaba," the president repeated, as if trying to scour his memory.

Bin Sultan saw that the president was clueless about the global implication of this catastrophe. But the shocked expressions of the two U. S. intelligence officials at the president's side confirmed that they understood all too well the seriousness of the matter.

"You'd better sit down for this, sir," the CIA director told the president.

Bin Sultan suspected the two American spymasters had been expecting him to report on the latest street protests or, perhaps, the escapades of yet another wealthy family prince. But this news was different, beyond the unthinkable.

When they were all seated on facing couches, the Americans nodded for him to continue.

"Mr. President, this theft could quickly turn into a worldwide security nightmare. The Black Stone is held priceless—even more than that—by my fellow believers."

With a hint of pique in his eyes, the president turned to his advisors, as if wondering why he was wasting his time on lamentations about a religious relic.

Bin Sultan moved quickly to explain the significance of the calamity. "Our tradition holds that the Stone was sent from Heaven to show Adam and Eve where to build the first altar on Earth. Originally, the Stone had been dazzling white, but it turned black when mortals became sinful. Abraham recovered the Stone after it was lost in Noah's flood and directed his son, Ishmael, to build the temple in Mecca to protect it. The Prophet Muhammad himself set the Stone in a wall of—" He coughed, struggling to finish.

The president offered the ambassador a tissue from a box on his desk to wipe his dry lips.

Bin Sultan nodded in gratitude. Regaining his voice, he went on. "The Muslim world has long looked upon my family as the protector of the Black Stone. It is a sacred duty. If the loss of the holy relic were to be revealed publicly, well …" He shook his head, fighting back tears.

"You've kept the theft under wraps?" the NSC director asked, clearly shaken that his surveillance officers had missed an event so potentially cataclysmic.

Bin Sultan glanced at the door to confirm that it remained shut. "We have covered the entire Kaaba with a black cloth. The explanation given is that this is meant only as a temporary measure for purification, in preparation for the Hajj pilgrimage in two weeks. This ruse can last only a few days, at most. So far, no one but the King and his immediate family know of the situation."

The president leaned closer. "Do you know who stole the Stone?"

Bin Sultan, nodding, edged to the president's elbow. "We are quite confident that—" He was about to reveal the identity of the suspects when a valet appeared from a side office to place a small silver pot of coffee on the table.

The diplomat accepted a cup and took hurried sips while trying to keep his hands from shaking. When the valet departed and the door closed again, Bin Sultan continued with his report, "We understand the extreme danger now present because we have faced such a crisis before."

"The Umayyad siege of Mecca," the NSC chief confirmed from his memory of being briefed on the region. "In the *hijri* calendar year 756."

Nodding, Bin Sultan wiped the perspiration from his upper lip with a kerchief. "A missile fired by a catapult in that assault smashed the holy Stone. At that time, the Sultan used a special silver glue to put it back together. Two hundred years later, the Qarmatian tribe murdered twenty thousand pilgrims and stole the precious relic for ransom. It was returned two decades later, but broken into seven pieces. In every attack on the relic, dissident sects were found responsible."

"Shi'ites?" the president suggested.

Bin Sultan could feel the tension in the room rising; he tried to wave it away, as if chasing off one of the notorious mosquitoes that plagued the humid summers here. "Iran finances these troublemakers." He caught their smiles. "Of course, we know that *you* know this from the WikiLeaks cables sent by your diplomats ..." He let his critical comments fade.

The president leaned closer to mirror Bin Sultan's candor. "Abdallah, we share your concern about Iran. But our hands are tied. We're already overextended with our commitments in the Muslim world. What can we possibly do to help you?"

Bin Sultan looked directly into the president's eyes to warn, "Sir, if the Black Stone is not returned to its place in the Kaaba by the opening of the Hajj"—his tone turned even more ominous—"our government will not survive the international outrage. The radicals will use this incident to rouse the people to revolution and claim that the House of Saud is heretical and corrupt in the eyes of Allah, praise be upon Him. As you know, tempers already are simmering across the region. The United States will lose its most valuable ally in the Gulf. I don't need to tell you what that will do to the global oil markets, and to every Western economy."

A nettled silence settled over the office. Finally, the president, clearing his throat and tried to reassure his friend. "Your security force is one of the best in the world. I have every confidence that you will track down these perpetrators and bring them to justice, as you always have."

Bin Sultan felt his hackles rise. Having obviously failed to communicate the desperation of the moment, he became uncharacteristically blunt. "Our police can no longer be trusted. Internal sources confirm that the Shi'ites have infiltrated the upper echelons of its command. Underground uprisings, too, have ..." His voice trailed off in desperation.

The president traded alarmed glances with his advisors, only then realizing that the ambassador was seeking the use of American covert forces. "Abdallah, you understand my rather, uh, delicate political situation here. The election is less than a year away. If the Democrats were to learn that I entangled the country in yet *another* Middle East quagmire, well …"

Bin Sultan turned pointedly to the NSC director. "There is another way."

Seeing his NSC chief refuse to acknowledge that veiled suggestion, the president pinned his advisor with a questioning look. "General Buemiller, do you understand what the ambassador is referring to here?"

The NSC director nodded to the president, but then he answered the ambassador's plea with a defiant shake of his head. "Don't even go there."

Bin Sultan refused to be turned away. "General, you commanded a joint subversion operation with us in the 1970s."

"Ancient history," the NSC chief insisted, noticeably uncomfortable with the direction of this discussion had taken.

Bin Sultan kept boring in on the general. "At that time, an operative from your country's own Defense Intelligence Agency task force infiltrated the rebel tribes in my country. He is the only Westerner ever known to have accomplished such a deed."

The NSC chief held up a palm to stop to the suggestion. After a moment's hesitation, he turned to the president and insisted, "Sir, you do not want to hear this." Then, angling back to bin Sultan, the NSC chief added, "With all due respect, Ambassador, that was a long time ago, and—"

"Gentlemen, I will leave you to thrash this out." Taking his NSC chief's cue to remove himself from the discussion for plausible deniability, the president stood to indicate that his participation in the meeting was over. He shook Abdallah's hand and whispered something into his old friend's ear.

After Abdallah was escorted from the office, the president pulled his two intelligence officials aside. "Whatever he needs. If it can be managed without getting the intelligence committees on the Hill involved, I want it done."

4

Malibu, California

Cas Fielding was more pissed off than usual, and usually he was very pissed off.

That morning, the Pepperdine wax boys with their sand bunnies and shiny new foam boards had descended on Nicholas Canyon beach like gulls on a washed-up pile of shit. The old Malibu that had been his refuge for the past ten years was becoming a distant legend, replaced by hordes of tourist buses and Valley riffraff. The traffic on Pacific Coast Highway was now so clogged and dangerous that it was beginning to remind him of the Highway of Death between Kuwait and Iraq. Hell, last week some asshole had even jacked his parked '63 VW bus for the goddamn forty-year-old stereo inside. The whole damn place was going to the crapper. Fires. Mud slides. Earthquakes. Maybe he'd just pull up stakes and head to Indonesia. At least there—

"Hey, gramps!" shouted one of the young pimple faces charging at him atop a wave curl. "How about a little elbow space for me and my bros!"

Cas spun his vintage tri-fin thruster, narrowly avoiding a collision with the brat sweeping by him. He shouted, "Is that a Billabong you're riding, Junior?"

"Bitchin' sweet, huh?"

"Why don't you stick it sideways up your ass and use it for a rudder."

The young wave hogger was so flummoxed by Cas's orneriness that he lost his balance and crashed. He bobbed up spewing, with his board cord dragging him through the froth. When he finally found his breath, he whined at Cas, "Dude! Why so hostile?"

"Get the fuck away from me before I barnie you up for shark bait!"

Cas grumbled curses while he paddled his board back out to catch the next line. He hadn't risked his life working twenty years as a covert Defense Intelligence officer just so punks like that could fritter away their trust funds. *Gramps, my tight ass!* Sure, he was fifty-five, but he could still jazz the glass better than any of these diaper-soiled jagoffs. Hell, he'd been teaching the

House of Saud princes how to surf in the Persian Gulf when these college twits were still swimming in amniotic fluid.

Another wave formed in the distance, and he saw that it wasn't going to be a mere ankle-snapper. He leaned his weight into the oncoming momentum and angled his board toward the shore. Catching the break, he stood up and—

Two more assholes—in black bodysuits and sunglasses—came carving over the waves and hot-dogging next to him.

Bastards! Okay, they wanna play games!

Cas executed a sharp cut-back, turning into the wave and taking on the full power of the line. He flipped his board and landed it on the crest, just above the two intruders. Now they couldn't see him—but they were about to be introduced to the nose end of his sleigh. He timed his leap to land on the back tip of the nutter on the right.

Startled, the surfer peeled into his partner. Both wave trespassers ate it hard, with a side order of fries. Seconds later, their heads bobbed up. They swam toward Cas, who was dragging his board to the beach, having suffered his fill of amateur chonners for one day.

"Hey!" shouted one of the surfers slogging after him. The bald gorilla peeled off of his wetsuit, revealing a shaved strip across his broad hairy chest with a tattoo that read: *Molotov cocktails served here.* "You trying to kill us?"

Cas kept walking toward the dunes. "You'll manage that on your own."

"Hold up, Mr. Fielding!" said the second surfer, a crew-cut human bowling ball with two thumb holes for eyes. "We want to talk to you."

Cas froze. He hadn't heard anyone call him his real name in ten years, not since he had dropped out of sight and assumed a new identity in what the DIA called its burned operatives protection plan. Probably a private dick who had sidled up to one of his old drinking buddies with loose lips. He turned with fists balled at the scumbag who was trying to blow his cover. Maybe the day wouldn't be a total waste, after all. He hadn't enjoyed delivering a good ass-kicking since he had softened up that *paparazzi* who'd been taking photos of his pal McConaughey swimming nude out here a couple years ago.

"They warned us you were crazy," the tattooed surfer said.

Cas swung at the smart-mouthed musclehead, but his blow was deftly deflected. The guy whipped Cas's arm behind his back, bending it until the shoulder socket nearly popped. Cas nodded with a grimace, duly impressed. They didn't teach *that* move in karate classes at the university.

"You gonna calm down now, Mr. Fielding?"

Ballooning red in the face, Cas tried to breathe enough blood back into his brain to come up with a guess who had sent these pro enforcers.

"Beautiful place," the black belt twisting his arm said as he looked around to admire the mansions on the bluffs. "I could see retiring here myself."

Finally released, Cas rubbed his aching shoulder. "Mind if I ask who—"

"Take a little walk with us."

"I'm not leaving my board," Cas grunted. "Those punks'll steal it."

The thug doing the all the talking took off his sunglasses and angled his head toward the parking lot above them. There, two men in black suits wearing wires in their ears stood next to a Mercedes with dark-tinted windows. The lead singer assured him, "Your board will be fine."

The shark knife sheathed on the guy's wading belt convinced Cas to accept his invitation to walk the beach. Suddenly, it dawned on him who these two bounty hunters were. "Look, I told the bank I'd have the payment next month. I'm only three months behind on the mortgage. And they send a hit squad? If you want the damn trailer, take it. You won't get enough for it to pay for the fucking gas you bought coming out here."

"Times are tough, huh?"

"Who are you, anyway?" Cas snapped. "Doctor Fucking Phil?"

"I heard that off-the-books government pension they gave you doesn't quite cover your bar tab. Maybe we can help."

Cas stopped walking. "Help how?"

"Earl Jubal sent us."

Cas backed away, realizing it wasn't the bank stalking him. "Not interested."

"Just hear us out."

Cas spat a wad of briny saliva. "I told that warmongering psychopath years ago that I was done with CrossArrow Global."

"He has another job for you."

Cas snorted. "What's he want me to do this time? Bury one of King Abdullah's butt-licking cousins to his neck and shave him with a lawn mower?"

"You infiltrated the dissident Ikhwan tribe of Utayba in the Seventies."

Cas glanced down the shoreline to make sure no beachcombers were around to overhear. "That operation was classified."

"The Ikhawan were the radicals who seized the holy sanctuary in Mecca."

" Are you trying to blackmail me?"

The CrossArrow messenger turned toward the bluffs, as if to block anyone with a telescope who might be trying to read his lips. "Two days ago, the Black Stone was stolen from the Kaaba shrine."

Cas hesitated, not certain he had heard correctly. "Impossible! What's left of that old slingshot rock is glued into a metal casing and surrounded by the toughest security on the planet."

The mercenary didn't break his glare. "There was a stampede in Mecca two days ago. Not long after the Saudi guards and police restored order, they discovered the Stone missing. Somebody stole it while the police were trying to quell the riot."

"A distraction," Cas said, thinking aloud. "The thieves probably started the fight as a cover. Oldest trick of the oldest profession."

"You think it was the Saudi dissidents again?"

Cas shrugged. "Beats the hell out of me. Maybe, or somebody they hired. Someone the Saudis would never expect. Honestly, can't say that I care."

"The royal family doesn't trust its own secret police, so DOD farmed this recovery mission out to us. All off the books. The Saudis are keeping the Kaaba under wraps for now, but they'll have to uncover it before the Hajj pilgrimage in a week. If the Stone isn't returned by then—"

"I know my Muslim calendar, pal." Cas made a blowing sound to mimic an explosion. "That's just the straw *that* particular camel's back needs. The Saudi regime is so damn rotten, even Fabreze couldn't make its stink go away. But, hey, thanks for the heads up. I'll tune into Al Jazeera in a week, if it doesn't conflict with *Duck Dynasty*."

"You'll be paid two million dollars when you deliver the Stone to us."

Cas's jaw fell open. He stared at the guy, trying to gauge his seriousness. "What makes you think that *I* can get the damn rock back?"

"You're the only American alive who knows the Ikhwans. For some reason, they trust you. And your wife—"

"Fuck you!"

The CrossArrow messenger dropped his gaze. "I'm sorry for what happened to her."

Cas, overcome by a sick feeling, loaded up a punch. Yet this time he held back, having learned from the many last-call bar brawls he'd started over the years that he would only feel worse in the end.

"I can't imagine the guilt you feel."

Cas got into his face. "Guilt? Are you fucking *serious*, man? Guilt?"

The operative backed off. "Easy, soldier. Just scuttlebutt, is all."

Cas stared at the insolent rent-a-thug, wondering what he could possibly know about his Top Secret TDY. Sure, fifteen years ago he had infiltrated and lived among some of the world's most fanatic *jihadis*. He was only doing his job, and he'd been one of the best in the business, too. But he'd never counted on falling in love with the daughter of one of the tribe's leaders.

"Mr. Fielding ..." The operative tried to rouse him from his dark thoughts.

Cas was already spiraling back to that awful time in the desert, when he had become fluent in Arabic and had mastered the differences between the

Shia, Sunni, and Wahabi. But now everyone from Ring C in the Pentagon to Mossad in Tel Aviv to MI6 in London knew he had sworn off his old life because of what had happened. He wanted to scream in the man's face that his wife and son had never been *jihadis!* Just because they'd lived with the tribe didn't mean they believed in all that radical bullshit! From his first day stationed in Saudi Arabia, he had promised himself that he wouldn't so much as peek under the *abaya* of any local talent. Sure, he had bedded Arab women, but that was before he had met …

God had laughed at him, for damn sure, giving him Shada and Farid.

He dug his nails into his palms. Five years of the best intel the Pentagon had *ever* gotten out of the Middle East. And he had nothing to show for it. Not even a promotion. His reward? Losing his family.

Thank you, Uncle Sam and your various and sundry bastards.

God Almighty, Shada had been beautiful. Long, luxuriant black hair and big brown eyes like chocolate drops. He had never revealed his real identity to her. Truth was, she had been murdered without ever knowing anything truthful about him, except his feelings for her and Farid. He had witnessed enough executions to know the terror she must have endured as she knelt in Riyadh plaza with her neck exposed. Nine in the morning, as always. While hundreds of spectators watched, the swordsman in his white *dishdasha* and red-checkered headcloth would have strutted around her like a rooster ready to pounce. One step back, flashing his curved steel in the sun …

And now, just when the pain of those memories was starting to ease, Earl Jubal and his goons had to come along now to stir them all up again.

Cas angled his eyes toward the sun to dry a tear. He had been away on a mission near Bahrain when the Saudis snared Shada and Farid in one of their periodic dragnets for radical scapegoats to distract the populace from the regime's human rights abuses. Before he could rush back to Riyadh to save them, the Pentagon had sent Jubal and his gang of mercenaries to swoop into the desert and extract the U.S. government's most valuable agent in Arabia.

He could still feel the cuffs on his wrists from that night. While he was being whisked back to the States against his will, his son, only twelve at the time, had been hauled off to Ruwais prison, where no one ever walked out. He knew precious little about Farid, but Shada had told him that the boy, born left-handed, was being trained to use his right hand as the dominant one because of tribal customs. It was one of the few things they had argued about. He had harbored a secret hope of one day teaching Farid to play baseball, and a left-handed hitter had a better chance to make it to—

"Hey-uhh." The CrossArrow messenger cleared his throat.

Cas had all but forgotten about the goons. "What?"

"Half the money can be wired into your account by the end of business today. The remainder will be transferred on delivery of the Stone."

"Yeah, and how much is your boss making on this?"

"That's confidential."

Cas returned to his board and balanced it on his head as he walked back toward the surf. "Tell Jubal if I ever see him again, I'll purée his nuts through his helicopter blades."

The operative turned and nodded to his comrades on the bluffs. A satellite antenna rose from the roof of the Mercedes and unfolded. The operative pulled a cell phone from his waterproof pouch and dialed a number. "Mr. Fielding!" He called out, jogging after Cas. "There's a call for you!"

In the water, Cas stopped paddling and turned his board back toward the beach. "Tell Jubal the number he just dialed is permanently disconnected."

"You should take this call."

Now really pissed, Cas paddled to shore and marched back toward the guy. He grabbed the phone and shouted into it, "Hey asshole! Leave me alone!"

A gentle voice on the other end asked, *"Abba?"*

Cas nearly buckled. Only one person in the world would call him that name. Speaking into the phone again, he asked skeptically, "Farid?"

"Abba, where are you?"

Tears of confusion stung Cas's eyes. Had the Saudis allowed Farid to survive all these years? Had they told the boy that he was his father? Why would they do that? He tried to calm the tremors in his voice, "Are you okay?"

"Yes. Praise be to Allah!"

Cas swallowed hard, fearing the boy had been raised in one of those brain-washing radical *madrasas*. "Farid, I have to tell you someth—"

The phone beeped, and went silent.

The CrossArrow messenger nodded to his colleague on the bluffs, and the satellite antenna on the sedan slowly retracted.

Cas frantically pressed keys to redial the last number. No connection. He yelled at the thug, "Get him back."

"You get him back." The hired soldier walked with Cas a few steps closer to the water. "In addition to the two million cash, the Saudis have agreed to release your son."

Cas felt his first frisson of hope in ten years. "I'll go get him—"

The guy shook his head. *"After* you get the Black Stone for us."

"And if I don't?"

The CrossArrow mercenary took a step back, just in case Cas went ballistic. "I don't think I need to tell *you* what the Saudis do with political prisoners who aren't of some use."

5

Dallas, Texas

Bridget Whelan—Goth goddess of Lubbock—was feeling pretty damn potent that morning. Her conjuring spells had finally manifested something useful. After three long years of unemployment, she had actually snagged a gig. She had gotten a master's degree biotechnology and materials technology from Texas Tech because everybody told her those two fields were perfect for a young, single mom needing a steady local job. But the bad economy was still ravaging the state, and the university had been laying off dozens of grad assistants. So, she had finally decided to pull up stakes and come to the big city.

Giddy up, cowboys. There's a new witch in Big D.

The ad in the *Chronicle of Higher Education* had been for a technician with a degree in molecular engineering and nanotechnology. She had written her master's thesis on failure analysis, the science of putting different materials under stress and analyzing what caused them to break, but she had also taken a few classes on the side in mechosynthesis and molecular-scale devicing.

So what if she stretched her resume a little? You try keeping a two-year-old in diapers and pay for day care on a stipend that could barely buy a Happy Meal.

She looked down at the address in her notebook again. Wiping the dust from the bus window, she felt her spirits sink. One morose street after another passed by her view. Her new employer, she now realized, was headquartered in an industrial park. So much for the pleasant work environment that she'd been envisioning in her Transcendental Meditation sessions.

She pulled the stop cable, stood up, and heaved her backpack off the bus. Out on the curb, she looked around for a sign. There it was, in black-and-white lettering, the same as every other bland building sign in the area:

Lightgiver Technologies LLC.

She sighed, tugging her backpack higher up on her shoulder, and headed for the entrance. The money would be a salvation, at least, and the company's health insurance was baby-friendly. But what had really caught her interest in the ad was the mention that the position would involve working with geological specimens and igneous formations.

She loved rocks.

The townies back in Lubbock considered her a little loony, but they were mostly Jesus-Is-Coming types who understood her as much as she understood serial killers. To help cover her tuition, she had opened a small crystal-and-gem store in a section of her mother's grocery. What was it about these Bible thumpers that made them think the Earth began six thousand years ago, when she'd worked with rocks that were millions of years old? Seriously, who was loony here? And so what if she gave the stones names and talked to them from time to time? The mineral world was friendlier—and a lot smarter—than those right-wing blowhards who gossiped about her and tried to exorcise demons from her brain by drawing crucifixes on her windows with purple lipstick.

After scores of employment rejections, she finally had to admit she might not be helping her cause by flaunting her Gothnicity so flamboyantly. Even a Priestess of Doom had to pay rent, and so that morning she had toned down the mascara. She would compromise and look "normal" for her first day, if that's what it took to infiltrate the world of the walking dead.

The entire hiring process for this job had been done by phone, which probably explained why she got it. In person, she had a gift for putting people off. Hey, it wasn't her fault if these rednecks couldn't handle her fem-killer aura. The confidentiality agreement and non-compete clause that these Lightgiver suits had faxed to her at FedEx-Kinko's was pretty scary. The documents even said that her new employer could leech onto her bank account if she mentioned even a word about what she was doing for the company.

Whatever. No biggie. Good luck sucking anything out of that black hole.

Most of the pedestrians around here looked like zombie businessmen and secretaries. Feeling a little nervous, she reached into her purse to caress her favorite green aventurine for reassurance. Quartz always enhanced prosperity and career success, at least that's what the book said. Drawing strength from its polished surface, she could feel her blood rushing through her veins toward the aventurine's magnetism, cleansing her chakras of toxins and negativity.

She was feeling calmer already.

With a deep yoga breath, she opened the door to the Lightgiver Technologies office and walked into a gloomy lobby stocked with rental furniture. Interesting vibe, to say the least. A desk where she had expected to see a receptionist sat empty. Peeking around the corner and down a dark hall, she called out, "Hello?" Now that was just plain ironic. No lights at Lightgiver. *There's a creepy start.* She was all for the whole green-movement thing, but companies that pinched pennies to save a few bucks on electricity seemed like a canary in the bankruptcy coal mine. She tiptoed down the dim corridor and searched for someone, anyone, in any of the mostly unfurnished offices.

"Get your arms up!" shouted a voice behind her.

She froze.

"Turn around."

She dropped her bag and inched her eyes around her shoulder. Two men in military jumpsuits were pointing pistols at her. "I'm here," she said, her voice trembling, "for the new position."

The guards lowered their weapons. One of them spoke into a small transmitter strapped to his upper arm. "Secured."

Seconds later, a stout man in a Stetson and rattlesnake-skin boots marched out with a hitching gait from the shadows. He had a scraggly face as long and droopy as a hound's, with a huge triangular nose and a chin that sloped out like the overhang of a washed-out *arroyo*. Growling in disgust, he took another step forward, sizing her up from head to foot.

"Whelan," she peeped. "Bridget Whelan."

The man motioned his two guards away. Then, alone with her, he broke the sinister smile of a coyote stumbling across fresh road kill. "You can never be too careful in the biotech business."

Her eyes narrowed in disbelief on hearing his deep, grating voice, which sounded a little like the grind of a rusty windmill in a breeze. *This* Lone Ranger was the guy she had spoken to on the phone? She nodded, still trying to force her heart back down her throat.

"So, you're Whelan."

She began calculating the change she'd need to find in her wallet to catch the bus back to Lubbock. "I think I may have made a mistake. I thought ..."

The man reached into his jacket pocket. She flinched, afraid he was going to whip out a handgun and shoot her.

Laughing at her skittishness, the man pulled out a check and pushed it into her hand. "I like to give my new employees a little incentive when they start. There's more where this comes from, *if* you perform as expected."

Bridget's jaw dropped as she looked down at the sum on the check: A five, followed by ... three zeroes.

"Now, Miss Whelan, tell me. Have you been saved?"

She swallowed a curse. Not another one of *those*. If she had a nickel for every time she'd been asked that in her life, she would have been saved, all right—by the bank. But heck, for five thousand bucks, she'd speak in tongues for him. "I come from Lubbock, Mister, um ..."

"Cohanim."

"Yes, sir, I knew that. Folks where I come from believe that Jesus spent his missing years"—she clawed quotes in the air around her reference to the Messiah's life from age twelve to thirty—"they say He was living in Texas, learning everything he taught the Apostles."

Cohanim nodded soberly, apparently not getting the joke. "Use some of that cash to buy yourself a proper outfit. We have a dress code here." He tapped his temple. "You're a smart girl. I know I've made myself clear."

Bridget glanced around for an escape route, until she remembered how easy it would be for him to put a stop payment on the check. So, she resolved to hunker down for the day, at least. "Is there some paperwork I need to fill out?"

Cohanim spun on his heels like a drill sergeant. "Paperwork? You're not signing on with the government. This is Dallas. We shoot first and apply for the gun permit later. Go scrub up. There's a lab coat and a head-band magnifier in the storage closet just outside the lab."

Scrub up? Does this guy think I'm going to assist him in surgery?

She followed him down several long, dark corridors, scurrying to keep up while trying to avoid falling over boxes and binders strewn across the floors.

"You're trained on the newest needle technology for carbon extraction, right?"

At that moment, Bridget was wondering if her bank had a branch in the neighborhood. Getting that check deposited and cleared today would really send her to the moon.

"Whelan!"

His bark jolted her from her fantasizing about a new car. "Yes, sir?"

"We just got a new Magnosyringe Twelve-Hundred unit in. You can drive it?"

She didn't have a clue what he was talking about, but he wasn't going to get that bonus check out of her hands now. So, she lied, hoping she'd be able to wing it, whatever the machine was. "Shouldn't be a problem."

Cohanim pointed toward a changing room. "Press that button on the wall when you're ready. And make sure you've washed up thoroughly. One contamination screw-up, and you're terminated."

F ive minutes later, Bridget, attired in a white smock, was buzzed through another door. She entered a modern laboratory that featured a circular workstation surrounded by a glass bubble. On the far wall was a tinted glass pane that she guessed was a one-way mirror.

Cohanim handed her a stick of gum.

"No, thanks," she said, baring her teeth like a hyena. "I've got soft enamel."

He glared at her. "For the pressure change."

She shrugged, and let him stick the gum into her mouth.

"You'll have ten minutes before the barotrauma kicks in. Signal me if you start feeling any of the usual symptoms. Heaviness in the lungs. Aching in the sinuses. Blurred vision. I'll be in the control room next door."

It slowly dawned on her that this space capsule she was about to step into was an outsized hyperbaric chamber that pumped in high levels of oxygen. Whatever this guy expected her to do in there had to involve handling highly degradable material. She took a step closer to the glass and saw a stainless steel machine on the table that looked like a drill press. A slender needle about six inches long was attached to its neck. The intricate mechanism resembled a multimillion-dollar sewing machine. Next to it sat a Mac laptop connected by a cable.

Cohanim led her around the circular chamber. "Let's go over the protocol."

Being a natural empath—a skill that she had honed in coven training—Bridget was sensing her boss's increasing anxiety, and that wasn't doing her any favors for her own spinning chakras. She faked confidence. "Right."

He was now talking a mile a minute. "The specimen you'll be drilling is an iron chondrite with a mass half the size of a ping-pong ball. You don't need to worry about precise measurements. They've been scanned in and registered into the three-dimensional rendering program on the drill's chip."

Bridget exhaled a held breath in relief. Extracting minerals was no big deal. Heck, she had done that at Tech so many times with the metallurgical syringe needles that she could manage it in her sleep. These new virtual-imaging babies made the whole thing easier than flying a plane on automatic pilot. She looked around for a jar or tray. "Where do you want me to put the deposit?"

Donning surgical gloves, Cohanim walked to a stainless steel refrigerator and carefully brought out a prepared Petri dish. "In here."

Bridget pressed her nose against the glass pane of the hyperbolic chamber and peered over at the drill. Under its tip was positioned what looked like a small lump of coal.

"The secondary layer of the rock is white, like the fruit of a coconut," he explained. "The needle has a nano transmitter in its tip that senses changes in density. When you reach the innermost kernel, an audible signal will be sent to the laptop. That's when you draw the sample into the syringe. Deposit the extraction into the Petri dish and cover it. Leave it inside the chamber, and then get out. Other lab assistants will take over the process from there."

"I don't mind the grunt work."

Cohanim dismissed that teamwork offer an unsettling smile. "Here at Lightgiver, we don't let our Formula One drivers run the lawn mowers."

Straightening with pride, Bridget stared through the glass again at the drilling device. "That's some bitchin' needle." She rubbed her hands together, now looking forward to this little excursion into the mineral kingdom. "Chondrite. Shouldn't be more than a five on the Mohr scale."

"Nine."

She did a double take, not sure she had heard correctly. "That's almost the hardest material on Earth!"

"Almost." Cohanim nodded to the control room on the other side of the one-way mirror. "The needle's tip is crystal diamond. Ten trumps a nine. I hope I don't need to tell you how expensive such a custom-made instrument is to replace."

"The Colin Powell rule, right?"

"What?"

"I break it, I bought it?"

"That's the Pottery Barn rule."

Bridget was about to scratch her head, then remembered her gloves had been sanitized. "Where'd I get Colin Powell out of that?"

"Just get the job done."

Again he ignored her humor, and just like that, Bridget's excitement went up in smoke. She chewed harder on the gum to redirect her nervous energy while she tried to steady her hand. Pressing an elbow against her pocket, she felt reassured knowing that her green aventurine was still with her. And that check for five hundred big ones next to it didn't hurt. She took the Petri dish from him and stared at it. Why would he want to place an inert mineral on a lidded agar plate used to grow cell cultures? Despite his foul mood, she risked another question, "What am I looking for in the rock?"

He wouldn't meet her inquiring eyes. "We've done some infrared scans. These specimens have a protective core in their center. Kind of like a kernel in a nut. Once you're past the blackened skin—"

"Blackened? What caused that?"

His impatience bubbled to the surface. "Look, I am not running a grad school seminar here! Are we clear? Just get the sample and corral the questions."

"Right, boss."

6

Mojave Desert, California

Forced to step out of his air-conditioned kiosk, the guard manning the entrance to the remote CrossArrow Global compound cursed at the vehicle approaching through the dusty haze. The blazing sun threw sparks off the concertina wire fence stretching for miles in both directions, and a sudden blast of heat stole his breath. He peered out at the incoming, but all he could see were drops of condensation dripping toward his nose. Three hundred bucks for non-fogging lenses, and it was like looking through a sauna porthole.

He wiped the shades with his sleeve and then aimed his AK-74u submachine gun at the puke-green VW microbus churning up plumes of dust and acrid diesel fumes. His finger itched at the safety behind the trigger. Before he retired, he'd like to put a bullet through one of these New Age kooks who kept getting lost out here on their way to smoke weed and play Indian vision quest at Joshua Tree. He blasted the warning siren, but the douchebag behind the wheel just kept barreling toward him.

Are you fucking kidding me?

He couldn't make out the driver's face through the sand-scratched windshield, so he fired a warning shot over the vehicle's corroded roof. The sonofabitch didn't even hit the brakes. He sprayed a few rounds into the front right tire, and the van finally careered to a stop with its tie-rods squealing like wounded coyotes.

"Get out!" the guard shouted. "Hands up!"

The driver didn't budge.

The dust on the windows prevented the guard from seeing how many were inside. He aimed his snub barrel at the driver's window. Was this asshole just too stoned to hear him? He knocked out the window with the gun's stock and—

The door flew open, smashing into the guard's face and crumpling him to the ground. On his knees, he cursed and picked shards of glass from his forehead. "Fucking bastard!" He looked up to see his own submachine gun pointed between his eyebrows. He blinked, not trusting his concussed senses.

The man hovering over him wore a Hawaiian shirt unbuttoned to the navel, a shark-tooth necklace, and sandals with flapping soles half-torn from the straps.

Had the ghost of Don Ho just mugged him?

The driver prodded the bleeding guard on hands and knees toward his van's front flat tire. "What size are those radials on your Jeep?"

The guard's head was pounding. "I'm gonna fuck you up so bad you'll—"

The guy in the Hawaiian shirt shit-heeled the guard's nose toward the rim of the van's right front tire. "Fill it up."

"What the hell?"

The van owner drove the guard's mouth to the stem. "Screw off the cap."

With the barrel pressing into the nape of his neck, the guard had no choice but to bite on the tire's stem cap and slowly chew it counterclockwise.

"Now, take her to thirty seven pounds."

"The damn tire's ripped!"

"Then you're just going to have to blow harder, aren't you?"

The guard pretended to puff into the stem, spewing and coughing. "Nobody can do anything like this!"

"Just keep blowing until your dick gets hard," the intruder ordered. "If it reaches four inches, you've hit maximum pressure." He fired a couple of rounds into the sand, inches from the guard's knees. "Damn. These new AK issues are touchy. I barely kissed the trigger. It's like I think, 'fire,' and the mo'-fo' *fires*! Must be some kind of mind-body connection."

The guard was now shaking. "Look, pal, I don't know what you've been smoking, just put down the weapon, and I'll forget what happened."

The van driver slammed his foot into the small of the guard's back, forcing him to crawl toward the rear of the van. "You're gonna take those four tires off your ride and put them on mine. Are those Michelins still under warranty? I'll be needing the paperwork." He shuffled in the sand. "Y'know, damn, it's hotter'n Satan's shit out here. Makes a fella thirsty. You got any brews in that ice-fishing shack?"

"Are you nuts?"

The lunatic fired another dozen rounds into the sky, letting the bullets fall and thump the sand like pigeon droppings. "How come everybody keeps asking me if I'm nuts? I mean, just before I left Malibu, I told this hot little blonde that I had to drive four hundred miles into the freakin' desert to meet with a prick named Earl Jubal, who just so happens to rake in billions of dollars by killing inconvenient civilians for NATO. And you know what she asks me?"

The guard shook his head slightly, too frightened to risk an answer.

"Just like you, she asks the same thing you just did." The van hermit pointed the barrel at his own chest. "And *I'm* the one who's nuts?"

The guard's fingers crept toward the cell phone clipped to his belt.

The van lunatic stepped on his hand. "Don't even think about it. Jesus Christ, can't I just finish my story?"

The guard didn't dare move.

"So, I tell this hottie, right, I say, 'Honey, listen. We-the-People get exactly the kind of government we deserve. We-the-Fucking-People don't give a goddamn that we fritter away our tax money on assholes like Earl Jubal who hire assholes like you to do what we paid our tax money for the goddamn Marines." The lunatic smiled and fired a few more rounds into the distant desert, screaming: "*Semper fi!* Hooah, mothafucka!" He spun in a circle, something of a weird victory dance, as if the heat and euphoria of shooting something really *was* getting to his head.

The security guard kept crouching lower, trying not to draw attention.

The loon's tone turned serious as he aimed the barrel back at the guard's head. "Listen up, *amigo*. The jack is under the spare in the back. You might have a little trouble finding a solid spot around here to crank it up, so you better get started. I hear the sun out here at noon can scramble even shit for brains."

A black SUV, followed by two armored Humvees, flew over the cactus-crenellated horizon and skidded to a stop within a few yards of the van. A tall, leathery-faced man in snappish khakis, leather boots, and dark blue cavalry hat stepped out from the passenger side of the SUV. Four toughs armed with assault rifles clambered out of the Humvees and came aside the head honcho. As the gruff cowboy in charge sauntered up, he spat at a scorpion scampering through the brush. "You're late, Fielding."

Cas shook his head, amused by the flamboyant millinery. "Hey, Robert Duvall called. He wants his lid back from *Apocalypse Now*."

"Still working toward your Scout badge in cleverness, Casbo?"

Cas winced at the nickname. He had seriously messed up the last guy who called him that. He unlocked the clip from his commandeered submachine gun and threw the disabled weapon at the kneeling gate guard, bouncing it off his back. "Earl fucking Jubal. And I see you still maintain the same excellent hiring standards."

The flummoxed gate guard staggered to his feet and, with a large urine stain at his crotch, lurched to attention. "He sucker-punched me, General."

"General?" Cas roared. "What'd you do, Jubie? Give yourself a battlefield promotion when the latest Warcraft game came out for your Sony Playstation?"

Jubal aimed a glare of disgust down his thick red nose at Cas. "Boys, hard as it is to believe, this steaming pile of whale puke used to be one of the best black-ops guys in the business. Former Army Ranger, then special agent for Defense Intelligence. A rare specimen of diamond-studded excrement, this one."

The CrossArrow thugs standing behind Jubal shook their heads and puffed the air in disbelief.

"Mecca in 1979," Jubal said. "A deranged fringe of the Saudi Republic of Fanatics decided to take over the Grand Mosque. That damn fortress was built like one of Saddam's bunkers. The concrete walls were too thick for conventional artillery, so the Saudi king has a dilemma. His army doesn't have the firepower to force the rebels out, and nobody wants American birds dropping bunker-busters from Saudi airspace. Islamic law forbids non-Muslims from entering the mosque. Who you gonna call?"

"I'd call you," said one of his armed sycophants.

Jubal nodded as he circled Cas. "Of course they called me! And I assigned our wonder boy here to the task. Damned if he doesn't come up with a brilliant fucking plan. He and three volunteers from the French GIGN counterterrorism agency offer to convert to Islam for the day. The Saudis buy off one of the *imams* to make it happen, and in go our new Muslim raiders from a hole in the roof."

The CrossArrow mercenaries now studied Cas with newfound admiration.

"The ragheads nicknamed him Cas the Dervish. Wild man of the desert."

"Give it a rest," Cas said.

But no, the CrossArrow warlord was on a roll. "Only, like everything else he did, from eating to screwing, Casbo took things too far. Says he wants to flood the mosque with a few million gallons of water. In the middle of a fucking *desert!* He plans to electrocute the bastards by adding a few thousand kilowatts of high-powered voltage to the mix. Even the Saudis think he's loco."

Cas's temper was rising with the mercury. "Nobody wants to hear about the old times."

Jubal ran his hand under his cavalry bonnet, shaking off the perspiration from his close-cropped head. "But, hey, our hero here goes with a backup plan. He funnels in lethal gas and starts dropping hand grenades day and night for two weeks. It's like rolling out depth charges to catch farmed salmon. Finally, those religious fruitcakes holding the mosque hostage go secular all of a sudden, and damned if they don't surrender. They said they'd rather face God's judgment than the depravities of Casbo the Dervish."

The gate guard who had been cold-cocked now looked thankful to be alive.

Jubal lowered his voice for dramatic effect. "But then ol' Casbo of Arabia here goes native on us. Starts to buy into all of that religious mumbo-jumbo those rug smugglers try to sell you. See, he goes desert diving on what's supposed to be a Top Secret op, but instead comes up with a *family*."

Cas fingered his trigger, itching to bring story hour to a close.

Jubal grabbed a white towel hanging in the guard station and hung it over his Stetson, mocking a Bedouin headdress. "Sure, he collected a ton of priceless intel for us. But in the process, thanks to indigenous *poontang* and—wait for it, boys—even siring a fucking *kid*, he completely loses his shit." He glared at Cas through an ice-cold pause and jammed his finger repeatedly into his own beer-keg chest, now worked up into a spitting rant. "Of course, that's when *I* get called to go in and extract his ass. But, it's already too late. By then, he'd blown every goddamn thing he'd been working for, including, apparently, his American ideals of life, liberty and the pursuit of as much *fucking* wealth as you can accumulate in half a lifetime."

"Happiness, asshole. The Constitution says the 'pursuit of happiness.'"

Jubal exploded in angry laughter. "Semantics! Anyway, from the looks of it, you haven't been pursuing much of either lately."

"That was some nifty history lesson. Now, about the money you owe me?"

"Easy, Casbo. It's good to know those Left Coast commies haven't totally scrubbed the capitalist ethic from your blood. ... Why don't you come back to my office, let me buy you a cold beer. We'll talk things over."

"You've obviously forgotten that I swore never to step foot again in that black hole you call a headquarters."

"Suit yourself. Hell, you always do." Jubal draped an arm around Cas's shoulders. "But humor me, at least, and take a little walk first."

"Make this quick, *capiche*? All I want is the cheddar due me."

Jubal laughed scornfully. "You're kidding me, right? You drove all the way out here to collect on a few bucks?" He gripped Cas's shoulder more tightly. "You must have *way* too much time on your hands."

Cas shook off Jubal's hold. "No, but I have too many of your incompetent wannabes spoiling my afternoons on the beach." Feeling the general's boring glare, he finally admitted, "Okay, and maybe I was a little curious about why you would drag me out here, instead of just calling."

Jubal waited until they had walked out of earshot of the others. "Tell me what you know about this Mecca Stone."

Cas had been wondering when that question would finally rear its head. He shrugged and played dumb. "Now *there's* a rock in a hard place."

Jubal forced a smile, as if humoring his crack in an effort to get information. "You must remember something about it?"

"Not much to tell. Muslims say the rock fell from the sky at the time of Adam and Eve."

Jubal rolled his eyes. "We need a more detailed description."

"Google it."

Jubal pulled a wad of legal tender from his pocket, peeled off five hundred bucks, and stuffed the bills into Cas's shirt pocket. "That ought to make you a lot smarter a lot faster."

Cas detected a hint of desperation in Jubal's nervous cackle. Grinning at winning the standoff, he reached for his wallet and pulled out a folded Xeroxed copy of a book page. After his confrontation on the Malibu beach with Jubal's advance boys, he'd done a little advance snooping at the UCLA Rare Books library. A professor in Middle Eastern studies there had shown him a tome containing the first description of the Black Stone in Western literature, written by two Swiss explorers in the early nineteenth century who had managed to sneak into Mecca disguised as Muslims:

> *It is an irregular oval, about seven inches in diameter, with an undulating surface, composed of about a dozen smaller stones of different sizes and shapes, well joined together with a small quantity of cement, and perfectly well smoothed; it looks as if the whole had been broken into as many pieces by a violent blow, and then united again. It is very difficult to determine accurately the quality of this stone which has been worn to its present surface by the millions of touches and kisses it has received. It appeared to me like lava, containing several small extraneous particles of a whitish and of a yellow substance. Its colour is now a deep reddish brown approaching to black. It is surrounded on all sides by a border composed of a substance which I took to be a close cement of pitch and gravel of a similar, but not quite the same, brownish colour. This border serves to support its detached pieces; it is two or three inches in breadth, and rises a little above the surface of the stone. Both the border and the stone itself are encircled by a silver band, broader below than above, and on the two sides, with a considerable swelling below, as if a part of the stone were hidden under it. The lower part of the border is studded with silver nails.*

Jubal looked increasingly dubious as he scanned the photocopy, apparently not convinced that an encyclopedia entry from a couple of Swiss pacifists was worth five hundred dollars. "How long's the Stone been in Mecca?"

Cas examined the bills, making sure they weren't counterfeit. "No one knows for sure. Long before Mohammed got there, at least. The ground where the Kaaba now sits was once a pagan shrine. It was pretty common in that part of the world for places believed to be blessed with divine power to be marked with an unusual stone. But the Koran says Mohammed himself placed the Black Stone right there at the Kaaba. Some Muslims nowadays even believe the Stone will come alive on the Day of Judgment and speak out against those whose faith is false."

Jubal angled his hat farther down over his face to shield his eyes from the brutal Mojave sun. "Lemme get this straight. Some burnt stone falls outa the sky, and just because of that, it suddenly becomes connected with God?" After mocking confusion, he curled a thin smile, suggesting he knew a lot more than he was letting on. "That would have to be one very special rock, don't you think? One that's different from all the others."

Cas let the silence of the desert wedge some distance between them. Finally, he asked the question that he knew Jubal was waiting to hear. "Okay, clue me in. What are you getting at?"

"In my experience, not that many stones fall from the sky. I can think of only one kind."

"Which would be?"

Jubal plucked the five hundred dollars from Cas's grasp and stuffed the wad into his own pocket again. "If I have to do your job, I'm not going to get robbed in the process."

Cas tried to wrangle the money back, until Jubal unbuttoned the strap on the pistol in his side holster. Cas kicked at the sand in anger. "What the hell are you talking about?"

"I had my analysts do a little checking while I was waiting for you to arrive in your magical mystery tour bus. There's an astrophysicist at Columbia University who specializes in meteorites. She hits our sweet spot. Not far enough up the academic ladder to alert notice from the powers that be, but she seems to know what she's talking about, at least enough to write articles for a couple academic journals." He handed Cas a card with a name and phone number on it. "I suggest you pay her a discreet—and I mean *discreet*—visit. Find out what she knows about strange stones dropping out of the sky."

Cas read the name on the card: Dr. Marly McKinney.

"Worth checking out," Jubal said. "You know the old saying, Leave no stone unturned." He laughed crudely at his own pun.

Cas wasn't following. "What difference does it make if the Saudi relic came from Mars or some slag heap in Arabia? I thought you just wanted it back?"

Jubal shrugged. "I don't care if somebody flushed it from a john on a 747. Right now, we're flat out of leads. And for some reason, my client thinks you're the only one who can retrieve the damn thing. You used to know how to clean up these Saudi messes. Just do us all a favor and don't go making another one."

Cas just stood there, mystified at why the general, who hated pointy-headed university types about as much as he hated Arab terrorists, would want him to go traipsing around gown town.

Jubal turned to leave, but seeing Cas still lingering in confusion, he stopped, exasperated. "Do I have to spell everything out for you in capital letters? If that Arab stone really *is* a meteorite, this Ivy League broad might help you find it in the pocket of some bazaar crier in Istanbul or Cairo who plans to sell it for a hefty profit on the black market."

Cas shook his head at Jubal's naïveté. "It's not as if those Islamist radicals who stole it are going to sell the Black Stone. That's not why they took it."

"You know what, Fielding?" Jubal drawled, mimicking Cas's California twang. "I don't really give a camel's left testicle *what* you think. Just follow it up like I said and see what this university broad knows about tracking down rocks harder than your head. You might actually stumble into some useful information for once."

"And if I *can't* find it?"

"You remember that lone operative we dropped into Pakistan to find Bin Laden two years before we finally got the son of a bitch?"

"Yeah, Billie Conley. Whatever happened to him?"

Jubal's eyes went cold. "If you're captured or outed while you're over there, you know the drill. We deny any knowledge of you. You're on your own."

"Damn. And I was hoping to use you as a reference on LinkedIn."

Jubal wasn't amused. "You might also want to lose that smartass beach-boy attitude for a change. First off, it's not all that charming. Second, things have changed in the Middle East since you rode camels with the Bedouin. These Al Qaeda types have become savvy to even the faintest of American footprints, real ones *and* virtual ones. And this Arab Spring mayhem is causing its own problems for us. Catch my drift?"

"Where do I deliver the package?"

"Don't worry about that." Jubal tapped on his watch as he began walking toward his armored SUV. "We'll send a FedEx pickup. You have a week."

Cas didn't need to be told what would happen if a few million Muslims showed up for Hajj and found their Stone missing. Given the way things were on the Arab street these days, it wouldn't surprise him if the Saudis unleashed some sort of nuclear retaliation for the relic that had vanished on *their* watch. Forget about Tehran and Damascus. And nobody could ever offer a better reason to point a finger—and a ballistic missile or two—at Tel Aviv.

But more to the point, he desperately wanted to get his son back. He longed to tell Farid the truth and make amends for the fact that the man he had grown up knowing only as his father was, in fact, an American spy. He looked up at the sedan and called after his former boss. "Hey, Jubal!" He pulled his wallet out again and pointed at it. "You forget something?"

Before climbing inside the SUV, Jubal glanced at the disabled wreck of a van. He gave Cas the thumbs up. "I'll have one of my men see that it gets towed to the nearest gas station. A whole new set tires, on us."

Cas shook his head at his old boss's attempt to deflect the obvious. "Thanks, but I'm planning on buying a new ride—one of those badass Dartz bitches—with the million bucks you'll be handing over before I leave today." He opened his palm. "Let's have it."

Jubal affected a look of surprise. "My boys in Malibu didn't tell you?"

"Tell me what?"

"I've opened a Swiss account on your behalf. A million dollars, converted to Swiss francs, was deposited into it this morning."

"Sweet. Just give me the account number."

"I'll text it over. But it won't do you any good. Not at the moment, at least."

"Why not?"

"It's a joint account. In your name *and* your son's. Both of you will have to be present to sign and withdraw the money."

Cas reddened. "That wasn't the deal!"

Jubal enjoyed a wicked laugh as he climbed in the SUV and slammed the door. He rolled down the window. "You're losing your edge, Fielding! The operative I trained years ago would have dotted the I's and crossed the T's on *any* arrangement before heading all the way out here to kiss my ring." He blew Cas a fake smooch goodbye. "You'd better get your white scrawny ass back in operational shape before taking on those Arab carpet thieves again."

7

Manhattan, New York

The November rain pattering the windows of Dr. Marly McKinney's third-floor apartment mimicked the throb in her overheated head. She glanced at her watch and saw that it was nearly ten, almost time for bed. Exhausted from six straight hours of work, she uncoiled her long legs and pushed from her desk and her two computer monitors. Even the text of her scientific paper she was reading on her Kindle, which sat near her mug of cold coffee, had become blurry under the dim glow from her desk lamp.

Rubbing her eyes, she glided her socked feet across the lacquered hardwood floors and gazed out at the gloomy night from the wide window that overlooked West 118th Street. These brick walls around her were mostly bare now, with only a few framed posters from MOMA and the Air & Space Museum. She had boxed up all the photographs of Steve, her deceased fiancé, except the one of him in his desert fatigues in Iraq. She looked down at her feet and pressed her toes into the Persian rug that he had managed to ship to her from Fallujah. It had arrived only two days before his remains were returned to Dover Air Force Base. Studying the large collection of rocks that sat on a bookshelf next to her desk, she picked out a beryl crystal and examined it, hoping to find written in its cracks a hidden message.

It was the first gem they had found together.

Steve had been the reason for her love affair with minerals. The summer before their senior year in college, his parents had taken them both on a trip to see a gem mine in the forests near Asheville, North Carolina. The whole experience turned out to be pretty cheesy. She thought they'd be spelunking in some deep, mysterious cave wearing hardhats and headlamps, but instead they had parked outside a trailer park whose grounds were littered with junk cars and drooping clotheslines. There, along a small stream, they had sat together for hours, sifting through the contents in the flume while hoping to find rocks that *might* contain gold. Not very glamorous, but she had loved every second of it.

Only ten bucks a bucket, he had told her.

But what about the *mine?*

That day, Steve had laughed that full-throttled laugh of his. *What about the mine?* He had teased her. *I'm yours and you're ...* She had put her hand up to stop the inevitable.

Outside, the rain became more intense, drawing her back to the present. She so wished he were still here to finish his pathetic pun—and to finish what he had promised her that weekend. Instead, she was forced to find comfort in the hope that his memory still hovered over her shoulder every time she looked at a new rock.

After his death in Iraq, she had escaped to Russia to work with the team studying the remains of the Chelyabinsk meteor, which had injured 1500 people in February of 2013. Some of the meteorites recovered there proved to be more ancient than the Murchison meteorite, the notorious roof-bashing stone in Australia whose fragments were 4.5 billion years old. While on the Chelyabinsk project, she had stumbled onto her life's purpose after engaging in several mind-blowing discussions with other scientists about molecular RNA in space rock. After completing her own doctoral dissertation, "Uracil & Xanthine: Molecular Makeup of Meteorites to Support Panspermia Theory," she had been hired for an ultra-secret follow-up project to the Stardust space probe, which in turn led her to the teaching job here at Columbia. With her plans for a family cruelly dashed, she had thrown herself into the research work, devoting what remained of her life to stalking the answer to one question:

What made us?

Yawning, she poured another cup of coffee, and feeling cold, put on shoes to walk around the apartment. She felt on the verge of a breakthrough, but she couldn't put her finger on it. She was desperate to know the source of the single-ringed uracil and the double-ringed xanthine in the meteorites. Uracil was a component of RNA, and, as everyone knew from Watson and Crick's Nobel Prize-winning work in the early 1950s, ribonucleic acid, along with DNA, formed the building blocks of human life. But how did *those* particular molecules get into chunks of space rock? She rubbed her stinging eyes again and reached to turn off the lamp—

A violent banging rattled the door. She nearly jumped through the ceiling.

Who could *that* be at half past ten? Had that daffy Mrs. Arenson left the building's entrance ajar again while walking her poodle? Sidling up to the steel door with its array of deadbolts and chain locks, she yelled, "Who is it?"

The pounding persisted. "Dr. McKinney!" shouted a man's voice.

She looked around for something to use as a weapon. "No one here by that name!"

The man pounded twice more. "You need to open the door now."

"Go away! Or I'm calling the police!"

"Dr. McKinney, you have information that threatens your life."

She thought about calling a friend who lived down the street, but she couldn't find her cell phone. "Oh, and you happen to know more about what I know than I do."

"You should really update your firewall software."

She was numb with fear. Her techno-geek friends had guaranteed her that her home and office PCs, though networked, would be impregnable, even to those Anonymous creeps who kept hacking global corporations. Virtually everything she knew was on the hard drive sitting under her desk behind her.

"Please, you're going to have to trust me," the man said.

Steve's voice in her head told her to back away, but she unbolted the locks anyway, leaving only the chain hooked. She leaned against the cold steel door while glimpsing the man on the other side. He *was* young, about her age. Tall, lean and pale, with a mop of black hair. He was wearing jeans and a blue hoodie. Probably just a student, she figured. Despite her fear, she put on an air of authority and demanded, "Tell me what you want."

"This is complicated. Just let me in."

"Over my dead body."

The man moved his lips closer to the crack in the door and whispered, "A very dangerous man is coming after you—"

"What's your name?"

"You have two seconds before I blow the door."

She heard a metallic click.

She cracked the door a bit wider to see if he had a gun—

The intruder crunched through the chain with a small cable cutter.

The next thirty seconds passed in a blur. He swept into her apartment, sat at her desk, and manhandled her computer equipment. He reached into the pocket of his hoodie and pulled out a black flash drive. Sliding it into one of the USB ports on the front panel, he banged on the keyboard while keeping one eye on her.

A red light began flashing on the inserted drive.

The man swiveled around to face her and crossed his arms as if waiting to for her to say something. His black eyes and pale face were cold, his silence as icy as winter rain.

"Who *are* you?" she cried, on the verge of tears. "What do you want?" She nodded at her computer. "What could you possibly want from *that?*" Then she snarled at him. "What are you doing to it with that jump drive, anyway?"

"Don't worry about it."

She remained motionless on the futon as the intruder looked at his watch. When a green light on the flash drive flickered, he slid the small drive out of the USB port and slipped the succubus device into his hoodie. She became even more baffled. He couldn't possibly have downloaded all the data in her computer—that would take days. Besides, no removable drive on the market had enough memory to store all of that information.

He stood up, looking even more menacing and talking in an accent she could place. He lunged toward the couch and grabbed her forearm. "We're going to visit a little hangout of mine not far from here."

She tried to scream, but he covered her mouth as he dragged her down the stairs, through the front door, and across the rain-slicked sidewalk. A couple of pedestrians walked by, and he pulled her, struggling, into an alley until the strangers disappeared down the street. She bit at his hand, causing him to curse under his breath.

When the way was finally clear, he yanked her hair back in retaliation for the chomping. "Do that again, and you're gonna need dentures."

"Bastard! Takes a real tough guy to manhandle a woman!"

He pushed her into the passenger seat of a beat-up Hyundai. "If you roll down that window, you'll get more than a mouthful of air."

She hung to the door handle, debating whether to try for the locks, but the kidnapper started the engine before she could get up the courage to escape. They raced the car toward the bridge over the East River. Crossing into Queens, the driver sucked at the blood on the back of his wrist, muttering something that sounded like a curse.

"Where are you taking me?"

He refused to answer her.

"Look, if you're going to kill me anyway, why not let me know why."

Finally, he said, "You are a known expert in rocks."

Shaking with fear, she couldn't stop a smile. *A known expert?* Mysterious people capable of abducting and killing people considered her a "known expert?" She found something weirdly validating about that. Still, she crossed her arms and said, "So what if I am?"

"We get your knowledge. Or we kill you."

"Is the Mafia so desperate these days that it's moving in on the rare stones business?" She found herself talking as if nobody else sat in the car with her.

"You're trying to get rid of legitimate retailers of scientific stones like me to corner the market!"

He sighed heavily, making the same sound she often gave her graduate students who just didn't get it. "Some powerful and dangerous people want something that I must find first. If not, the geopolitical makeup of the planet may be forever disrupted."

Her mouth dropped. "You mean ... like World War *Three*?"

He refused to elaborate.

What could he possibly be talking about? Sure, she knew a lot about rocks from outer space. But why would anybody in organized crime be interested in what she knew about meteorites? The driver's ice-cold intimidation finally pushed her over the edge. She'd seen enough television dramas to know that they would kill her anyway after using her for what they wanted, so why not go down fighting. She began flailing at him. "You murdering sonofabitch!"

The kidnapper recoiled against his door, trying to distance himself from her while still controlling the zigzagging car. "You trying to kill us?"

"You're going with me!" She grabbed for his crotch, but he snatched his pistol from a shoulder holster and jammed the barrel against her forehead. "You hit me one more time, and it's the last."

She stared down the cold cylinder of a gun model that looked familiar.

"This is a Desert Eagle," the man said with an eerie calm. "At point blank, a bullet from this will blow your brains through the window behind you. Have I made myself clear?"

Everything she knew about guns had come from Steve. "An Israeli weapon," she whispered to herself. "My boyfriend—"

"Killed by an AK-Forty-Seven, not one of these."

"How could you know that?"

"You would be amazed by what I know," the man said. "Now listen closely to me. A maniac with half a deck for brains is trying to contact you."

She noticed that he kept checking the side mirror, distracted, as if watching for someone following him. She tensed, waiting for the right moment.

"His name is Cas Field—"

She lunged and scratched at his arm, clawing him and drawing blood.

He turned, trying to avoid her attack, but she jammed her hand into the exposed back pocket of his jeans and ripped out his wallet.

She threw it out the window, hoping to make him stop.

"Now, *that* was not a good move!" He raised the butt end of his pistol to strike her and—

She grabbed his gun hand and slammed it against the dashboard.

The gun went off.

8

Cleveland, Ohio

Walking down the dark corridor, Lenny Kowalski fastened the top button of his starched gray collar and ran a hand through his thinning hair, preparing to settle in for another long shift.

And, as had been the case with almost every night for the past six years, he'd be spending it alone with Lucy.

Not that he minded, not at all. Sure, the boys back home at Okie's Bar in Tulsa kidded him about it. They said he was whipped, head over heels in love, the way he constantly talked about her. Some of them even claimed it was a little weird, given Lucy's age and all.

They were just jealous. After all, how many fellas could say they got up close and personal on a regular basis with the oldest woman on Earth?

Let's see, this was Tuesday, so it had to be the Cleveland Museum of Natural History. He had been traveling with Lucy so much, he tended to lose track of the cities they visited. He reckoned that he had already set the world's record for spending nights alone in the most museums.

Maybe he should contact those Guinness Book people.

He strolled across the Kirtland Hall of Prehistoric Life, checking the locked doors and motion sensors with his Corfams thumping across the earth-tone floors. The T-rexes and saber-toothed cats stared at him with their meat-cleaver jaws open for business. He had to admit that never in his wildest dreams had he thought he'd be with the old girl so long. Six years. When the exhibit consortium offered him this security job, they'd told him it would be a month's assignment at most. But he was so dedicated to protecting Lucy and offering visitors unsolicited tidbits about her life that he became almost as popular as the exhibit. In reward, the museum sponsors had doubled his salary and made him Lucy's personal bodyguard for as long as she stayed in the United States.

Tonight, looking proudly at the glass case sitting at the far end of the corridor, he thought of that haunting song by the young fella from Idaho—

Ritter, his name was. One of the other security guards gave him the CD for Christmas, as a joke, but he listened endlessly to the piano melody about an archaeologist who falls in love with a mummy. In front of him, the display case shimmered in the pale moonlight that pushed through the sooty windows.

There she was, sleeping like a babe.

He walked up to the upright replica of Lucy—a plaster cast of her fragments hung on a wire model of her spine and ribs—and blew her a kiss. "How you doing tonight, hon?"

Man, she had long arms. She had walked with a lurching gait that he found oddly sexy just thinking about it. The lower half of her jawbone was still there, with a few teeth intact. The left pelvic bone was in damn good shape, too. "Yeah, I'll bet you could shake those hips, couldn't you, sweetheart?"

Lucky Lucy ... Mother of us all.

Mitrochondrial Eve.

That's what the highfalutins from the universities called her when they dropped by to admire her bones. Truth was, he never understood what that term meant. Mitochondrial—hell, he could barely pronounce it. As far as he was concerned, she was Eve, the real Eve, *that* Eve from the Garden of Eden, the good girl who'd gone bad with a single apple.

The archaeologists had named her Lucy because the Beatles song, *Lucy in the Sky with Diamonds*, happened to be playing on their radio when they discovered her in the red African clay in 1974. But he preferred her Ethiopian name, *Dinkenesh*. After all, that's where they had found her, in Ethiopia, so it had to have been her home. He didn't see her as the traveling type, moving from forest to forest in search of greener ... not sure what they had for pastures back then. Just getting from one cave to the next would have been tougher than driving through East Cleveland. What with flying predators and giant dinosaurs lurking around every tree, and all.

Anyway, her Ethiopian name meant: *You are amazing*.

He liked that, liked it a lot. Even sang it out from time to time, substituting *Dinkenesh* for *Danke Schoen*, from that Wayne Newton song. Man, he loved ol' Wayne. Saw him way back in the day at the Stardust in Vegas. That boy could croon the chrome off a Chevy. Now he had two melodies noodling in his head, from that upstart Ritter boy and from the oldie-but-goodie. Pretty soon, he'd start serenading her with both tunes at the same time, maybe even waltzing with her, with only the glass case separating them.

Smiling at the thought, he walked over to the controls on the wall and tweaked the overhead halogens, chasing the shadows on the exhibit and putting Lucy in her best light. Next to her reconstructed skeleton on the iron hoist stood a glass case that held her real bones. Forty percent of them, anyway. They were set out like diamonds on a cloth of black velvet and positioned in a two-dimensional representation, from head to toe.

3.2 million years old.

"You don't look a day over two million," he whispered to her as he leaned closer, careful not to touch the glass and set off the alarms.

She had everything a hominid man could want in a woman. Small skull capacity. Long arms for a great hug. Wide pelvis for good child bearing.

A real heartbreaker.

"I'll bet you loved to show off for the boys, didn't you, hon?"

Of course, she did. That's why she came back after all these years—and why the crowds still flocked to see her. He could almost see her preen and pose when the museum patrons came in to gawk at her. One time, when the exhibit was in Los Angeles, one of those forensic-police artists stopped by and carved a clay model of her head and face from her bone structure. Damn, he couldn't get that image of her high brows and piercing eyes out of his head. Reminded him of one of his old girlfriends back when he was in the service.

Sometimes, when he got lonely and bored on the job, he'd imagine what it must have been like living with the queen of all humanity. Knowing her as he did, he figured she probably had the best cave in Africa. He loved to think about how she probably talked to her cave husband so long ago …

Go out and find me some Porterhouse steaks today, Harry! That Tyrannosaurus flank you brought home yesterday was tougher than lizard gristle!

"Yes dear."

And don't let the wind in when you leave. It took me two hours of rock mashing yesterday to get the fire started again.

"See you tonight, dear." He blew her another kiss to say goodbye.

A flash of instinct turned him around. Something about her didn't look right, something that had caught his eye. He hovered over the glass case, studying her bones—the real ones—up close. Was that a tooth missing from her jaw? He counted them again. One … Two … Three … Four.

She'd always had five teeth.

The last molar was missing.

He ran a finger down the bevel between the translucent lid on the glass enclosure and its stainless-steel sarcophagus. He brought his fingertip to his nose. Smelled like the solvent that the curators used to break the airtight seals.

This wasn't making any sense. Every other bone fragment was still in its place. Someone had broken into one of the most secure museums in the world to steal … a tooth?

9

Manhattan, New York

Marly awoke with a splitting headache. Looking around, she slowly realized that she was lying in a hospital room at the Columbia-Presbyterian Medical Center. The last thing she remembered was racing up Queens Boulevard with a black-haired, pasty-faced punk at the wheel. Her left ear felt as if it had been plastered shut with mud. Through the sleep-film hazing her eyes, she saw standing over her a distinguished looking man with a gentle smile and a halo of gray wispy hair. She tried to reach up and touch him, but her hand fell to her head. She felt a thick gauze bandage over her ears and forehead.

"Shhh," the man whispered, putting his forefinger to his lips. "They've given you some sedatives to help you rest."

Her eyes slowly focused. "Paul?"

Dr. Paul Brady, chairman of Columbia University's History Department, was the friend she had almost called when … she tried to work her memory back into focus.

What was *he* doing here?

Not that she didn't appreciate his company. He was a Columbia legend, a fixture at the university ever since the riots in the 1960s. After stepping down from his official government post, he had remained affiliated with the department through the end of the Cold War. But everyone knew that he had never really left his first love. Recruited by the OSS before graduating from Yale, he had worked for the CIA through the McCarthy era. Even while teaching at Columbia, he remained the confidante of presidents and generals, retaining a stratospheric security clearance. Word was that he had friends in the highest—and lowest—of places.

"Yes, it's me." He stroked her bangs away from the itchy bandage. "You're damn lucky, Marly."

"What happened?"

"A cop found you on a gutter outside Nick's Restaurant." He spoke softly into her right ear, continuing to answer questions so that she wouldn't have to ask them. "It's a good thing you were in Forest Hills. The neighbors there always look out for everyone. And at least you chose to pass out near one of the best pizza joints in the city."

She tried to smile, but that hurt, too.

"They ran a rape kit. Good news on that, at least. You weren't sexually assaulted. Somehow, I guess, when you were scuffling, you managed to rip off some of your assailant's skin. NYPD forensics collected a few bits of his DNA out from under your fingernails."

She tried to sit up. Her eyes widened a little, but she felt so drowsy. She reached for the Styrofoam cup on her rolling dinner tray and swallowed some water with a mouthful of crushed ice. She coughed, and felt a bruise around her midsection. Had she been thrown from the car?

Dr. Brady eased into a vinyl-upholstered chair next to the bed. "A colleague at Langley gave me the heads up. He said a certain female professor on campus here had become a person of interest. Anyway, NYPD forensics came back with a genetics match that set off some alarms along the Potomac. Usually when something like this hits their radar, they send an agent to follow up with an interview. But when my contact there told me the name, I assured them that we were friends. He asked me to stop by, talk to you a bit, informally."

She was still trying to catch up. "Genetics match?"

He coughed into his fist, almost apologetically, as if to mask his embarrassment at having such deep connections in the intelligence community. He refilled her cup and asked, "Would you prefer something else? Juice, maybe?"

She shook her head, eager to learn what exactly had happened to her. "The guy had a gun."

"Believe me, if he had wanted you dead, you wouldn't have lasted more than a minute."

She tried to bring back the features of the stranger who had weaseled his way into her apartment. "He also had an foreign accent. I couldn't place it."

He smiled knowingly. "Your kidnapper's DNA profile gave a positive hit for an Israeli national named Avram Isserle." He looked down as he talked, as if to blunt the fact that he was breaking at least a dozen regulations telling her this. "Last I heard, Isserle was a member of an elite unit of assassins known as *kidon*. That's Hebrew for 'bayonet.'"

She lifted to her elbows, stunned. "An assassin? You mean, like some kind of mob gangster?"

He shook his head. "I'm afraid he had a little higher pay grade than Lucky Luciano."

"I'm not following."

"Mossad."

Her eyes flared. "The Israeli intelligence agency? But why would ... ?" She rested her head against the pillow and let her words trail off. She felt the thick bandage around her temple.

"Right. You suffered some hearing trauma in your left ear. I would guess from a close-range gunshot. But you should be out of here as soon as they run a few more tests."

Her memory was slowly coming back. "You said the man's name was ...?"

"Isserle." This time, his smile seemed odd. "But it's a bit more complicated than that. Avram Isserle was born Joshua Silver in Brooklyn, the son of a secular Jewish doctor who was even less, shall we say, religious. When Silver turned sixteen, he launched into a rebellion, I guess you'd call it. He changed his name, turned Orthodox and, more or less, fled to Israel, as if, for some odd reason, to escape his well-heeled upbringing." He looked down at his finely manicured fingers again. "Next thing you know, he joins the IDF and is recruited by Mossad."

"You're saying Mossad was out to kill *me?*"

He patted her hand to calm her. "Nothing of the kind. Isserle is a highly trained killer. He doesn't waste his time on small-time break-ins. Frankly, my sources at the CIA tell me they don't know what he might have been after."

"When I let him into the apartment, he put some kind of jump drive into my computer."

Looking troubled by that bit of news, he thought for a moment. "That would certainly explain taking you to Queens. The police found you not too far from a known Mossad safe house in Forest Hills. Well, it's known to *some* people." His rheumy blue eyes twinkled, and he waved his hand in the air as if to try to dismiss any information he was about to put out there. "Nobody wants to talk about Israeli spies tramping around American soil." He leaned back in the chair and reclaimed his serious look. "My guess is that Isserle was using some sort of high-tech gizmo that connected your machine to a computer in Queens. He was probably planning to take you there while he had all of your data processed and 'go over' it with you." He flicked his fingers in quotation marks.

"He also asked me about Star—"

Dr. Brady put his palms up to stop her from uttering the classified name.

Reminded of her nondisclosure agreement with NASA, she nodded, and suddenly it came to her. She glanced at the door, then lowered her voice. "He must have known something about the top-secret space project I worked on."

"But you told him nothing, right?"

Truth was, she didn't really know much at all about the secret NASA project, having spent only a couple of months among the hundred and fifty hand-picked scientists selected to work on the new, ultra-top-secret Stardust program. "I *couldn't* tell him anything, even if I had wanted to," she said, ruefully, "I was too busy trying to tear him apart." She relived those tense few seconds, then remembered more of what had happened. "This man, though, this Joshua, Avram Isserle guy, or whatever his name is ... he warned me that some maniac was out to get me."

He looked skeptical. "Maniac? There's a lot of those in his business. Did he happen to tell you *which* maniac, by any chance?" he asked, chuckling. "We have such a shortage of them, particularly here in New York."

She rubbed her head, trying to squeeze out another memory. "He said a name. Cas something. Fell ... Feld—"

"Not Fielding?"

"Maybe."

He groaned. "This explains everything."

She blinked, baffled. "Maybe to you it does."

Shaking his chin ruefully, he explained, "Isserle has apparently gone flat-out bonkers. Now he's running from ghosts. It's an all-too-common symptom suffered by operatives. They develop paranoia from the stress. Sad really."

"But why would this Isserle guy choose *me* to warn?"

He tapped his fingers aimlessly on the bed railing. "He must have mistaken you for some hallucinated *femme fatale* in his past cast of underworld enemies. These guys troll the campuses looking for recruits. He may have seen you around, and some disjointed synapse fired in his head. He's really much too young to go to seed mentally, but it happens."

"He seemed coldly sane to me."

"Of course he did. But believe me, this has all the classic symptoms of a mental breakdown. He's definitely got some marbles lose."

"What makes you so sure?"

"The only Cas I know ever in the snoop business was a guy named Fielding. But he was captured and killed by the Saudis over a decade ago. They don't publicize this sort of thing in the newspapers, for obvious reasons. I attended a posthumous ceremony in his honor at the Pentagon at the time. Isserle would definitely have known of Fielding's death. The only sensible explanation is that Isserle has slipped into some sort of delusional fog. ... Of course, I don't need to tell you how confidential all of this is, Marly."

She nodded to reassure him that she'd keep his trust. "What did this Fielding do that would make a man like Isserle hallucinate that he was after him?"

"Fielding had been an operative for us in the Middle East, until the Saudis swooped in and exposed his mission. He probably had a couple of unpleasant run-ins with Isserle. You know, stepping on toes, crossing territories and unwritten boundaries. Mossad isn't exactly a fan of our DIA boys. The Israelis have closer ties with the CIA. It's all one big frat-house testosterone fight.

"Sounds like an academic committee."

He nodded, enjoying a chuckle. "Fielding went by a different name back then. Can't remember it. But he's as dead as the Sphinx now, so you can relax. Isserle's obviously gone over the bend if he's breaking into the homes of American citizens and claiming that Fielding is after them. I'll tell Langley to advise our friends in Tel Aviv that they've got a sleepwalker on the loose around town. They'll pick him up soon enough." He looked inward and enjoyed another private chuckle.

"What's so funny?" she asked.

"Sorry, but I was just thinking about Fielding. I met him only a couple of times. As nuts as he now is, Isserle pegged him pretty accurately. I guess it takes one to know one. Certifiably insane. Loose cannon. A cold-blooded killer." He pressed a hand to her palm to say goodbye. "You get some rest. I promise that Isserle will never step within a mile of you again."

She smiled, and felt the throbbing pain return.

As Dr. Brady walked from the room, he tried to cheer her up with a last salvo, "Lindsey strikes again!"

She laughed, despite the pain in her ribs, and waved him out of the room.

A little private joke between two academic colleagues. They shared a professorial crush on Dennis Lindsey, their favorite chaos theorist. Most people would have seen some nefarious conspiracy in such a bizarre kidnapping so out of the blue. But she took comfort in the knowledge that two objects could easily collide randomly in orbit without there being any intelligent design behind the meeting. This Isserle fellow had simply gone off course, flying around the nucleus of his own paranoia. And she, unfortunately, had been the nearest proton in his path.

10

Manhattan, New York

The Iranian-American waiter sauntered over to the back booth in Tom's Restaurant and angled the front pocket of his pants at Marly. "You've been away for a couple of days, Rock Lady. Fall off a cliff reaching for that stone just out of reach?"

Marly turned the left side of her head away from him, trying to hide the bruises from her run-in with the Mossad loon. "I had a little accident in my apartment. But I'm fine now, thank you."

The waiter lifted his hand from his pocket and opened his fist to reveal what appeared to be a lump of asphalt. "This one is from Mars, Rock Lady."

Marly sighed with exasperation as she looked up again from the article she was trying to read in the *Journal of the Meteoritic Society*. Ever since word had gotten out that she ran a tidy little side business selling meteorite samples to schools and laboratories, the slackers who roosted at this student hangout constantly pestered her with offers for anything from chunks of concrete broken off the curb outside to chondrite shards stolen from the Schermerhorn lab by undergraduate geology majors. Six years of studying astronomy, astrophysics, geology, mineralogy, petrology, chemistry, metallurgy and biology—all to become known as the local street junkie for stone freaks.

"Very valuable." He fondled the asphalt clod lovingly, as if it were the Hope Diamond. "But for you, I give a deal."

She thought about pointing to the cotton ball in her battered ear and acting as if she couldn't hear him, but she couldn't just ignore her favorite waiter.

"Two hundred dollars. My brother sent this precious gem to me from Tehran. My ancestors prayed to it. They were Zoroastrian Fire Worshippers."

"Really?"

"Oh, yes." Holding the asphalt cluster under the table, he rotated it like a craps player about to throw dice. "Your collection is incomplete without it."

"That's astounding," she said.

The waiter's eyes lit up. "This ancient jewel is indeed a rarity."

"No, I mean it's amazing that you're descended from fire worshippers."

He beamed with pride. "My family still tends a temple light in our village. The flame has remained burning for two thousand years."

"Now that's *really* hard to believe."

He looked confused by her skepticism. "Why do you think so, Rock Lady?"

She aimed her mug at him. "Wouldn't such an illustrious descendent of fire worshippers be able to keep my coffee warm?"

His sales pitch deflated, the waiter grinned at her cleverness. "I will return with a refill, and we will complete our transaction, no?"

"Next time, Ahmad. Right now, I'm late for school."

She gathered up her books and threw them into her bag. Waving goodbye to the boys in the kitchen, she headed up Broadway toward Fairchild Hall, where her small, temporary office had, she suspected, been converted years ago from an old janitorial closet. Tuesdays, she hated Tuesdays. That afternoon, she would have to endure another weekly glimpse into the Hell known as Advisor Hours. Part of the extortion demanded for her fellowship required her to counsel sniveling students on all manner of tragedies and emergencies, from missing menstrual periods to muggings in Riverside Park. She followed the drab wave of students through the arched columns of College Walk and climbed the steps past Low Library.

She entered Fairchild Hall. The third-floor hallway was lined with the usual queue of haggard-looking refugees from the dorms. She nodded glumly to them as she passed and glanced at the sign-in sheet on her door. The first name, Malachy Rubenstein, had been crossed out. Over it was written: *Clark Kent*.

Great. A smart-ass to start off the day.

She knew the drill. The jokester would ask her where to find the nearest source of Kryptonite—as if she had *never* heard that line at bars and cocktail parties a thousand times. As the new adjunct professor, she had learned that hazing wasn't limited to the fraternities and sororities. This time, she was determined to make an example of the jerk. If she let one student get the run on her, the sheep would quickly take over the barn. As part of her teaching degree, she had taken Psych 405, Motivation. Shame was the best method for handling these situations, she remembered from a lecture; it functioned as a kind of psychological inoculation against tomfoolery. And forced infantile regression worked wonders, too.

She threw open the door to her office. Without even looking inside, she screamed with insincere alarm, "Help! Oh, Superman, help!"

The students lined up against the wall outside her office traded perplexed glances. They clustered around the door, eager to see what was happening.

She waited at the threshold for this Clark Kent jackass to come out of her office. When he didn't appear, she decided to end the juvenile joke before it had any chance of gaining traction. All she wanted now was to grab the prankster by his ear and yank him out of her space.

A voice from behind the portable chalkboard cried, "I need a phone booth!"

Okay, so it's going to be like this. Turning his nonsense back on him, she went into a damsel-in-distress act. "Oh, no, Superman! There's no phone booth! You'll have to strip off all your clothes and slip into your cape *right there!*"

The other students buzzed with excitement and formed a tighter half circle around her. A few moments passed. Nothing happened.

She knew she had to call the comedian's bluff; time to get to work. "You can come out now, young man. You have already forfeited your half-hour."

A scruffy-looking guy in his early fifties stepped from her closet wearing only a black Speedo. He flexed his impressive biceps for the ogling students, who exploded in laughter.

Before she could recover from the shock, the intruder picked her up in his arms like a super-groom and carried her inside. He kicked the door behind him and yelled over his shoulder to the gawking students, "Don't worry, Lois! Clark was called away on a breaking story! You're in good hands now!"

She thrashed at the brute until he put her down in the seat behind her desk. Red-faced, she screamed at him, "What the hell!"

The man curled an infuriating smile of conquest. "Howdy."

Mortified, she just glared at him.

The guy snapped the elastic band on his Speedo briefs and leaned against his elbows on her desk, his face only inches from her nose. "You must have climbed the affirmative-action ladder fast, getting a large office like this one."

"Get your clothes on! Now!" She fished around in her rucksack for her cell phone. "I'm calling the campus police!"

The man seemed in no hurry to comply. "I'm not sure how *that* would look in the papers. Female professor orders man to strip, then calls the police when he obeys her." He licked his lips. "I might have a lucrative sexual-harassment suit here."

She cradled the phone. "Who are you?"

He looked around the office. "You wouldn't happen to have a wet bar in this penthouse suite, would you?"

Her voice pitched higher. "I know karate!"

"Really? I thought kickboxing was the new fad. But then maybe you're too old for that." The guy settled into the chair across her desk and plopped up his feet. He began picking sand from his cracked toenails. "I'm told you know your way around a meteor. Or is it meteoroid? Or meteorite? I get confused."

She picked up a stapler and threatened to nail the guy's Achilles heel if he didn't move his feet. "I make it very clear on my eBay seller site that I don't accept local pickups for winning bids. You pay for the stones with Paypal. I ship them to a verified address. No exceptions."

The lunatic reached into the rear of his Speedo and fished out a crumpled pack of Djarum 76-16 cigarettes and a rusty lighter. He smacked out one of the unfiltered death sticks, lit up, and filled the room with a clove-scented cloud.

Marly was intrigued by the exotic packaging—of the cigarettes. Recovering her outrage, she insisted, "There's no smoking in this building."

"They're Indonesian."

"What?"

"The cigs. I saw you staring at them. At least, I thought it was the cigs you were staring at." He took a long drag and blew another fragrant whiff at her. "College kids love these things. Forty-some bucks a carton." He tapped ashes onto her desk and leaned back into his chair. "Marly McKinney. Short for Marlene. Your grandmother's middle name. You were her favorite. She used to take you to Mammoth Cave to see the stalactites. Or is it stalagmites? I get those confused. Anyhow, that's how you got so interested in getting your rocks off, so to speak. Then there was that little mine thing with your ex."

"What is this? Some kind of demented *This Is Your Life* stunt?"

He tapped more ashes and whisked them to the floor. "I'm sorry about that, seriously. But you should be proud." His smile cemented his insanity. "Anyhoo, it's no wonder the boys thought you were a little"—he twirled his index finger around his temple—"whoo-hoo. Guess they still do."

She asked him again, this time slowly, as if trying to communicate with a child. "Who ... *are* ... you?"

He switched the cigarette to his left forefinger and thumb and reached out his right hand. "Cas Fielding."

That name hit her like a blow between the eyes. Wasn't that the Middle Eastern agent that Paul Brady said was dead? Her mind raced, trying to make sense of what was happening. Mossad must have gotten word about Isserle's meltdown and sent another goon to shut her up about the break-in and kidnapping. But why would they use a dead American agent's name as an alias? Was every spy in the Israel intelligence brain-sotted? She glared at the guy, this time resolving not to be taken away, even if she had to claw his eyes out. "You'll have to kill me right here. With all those students outside as witnesses."

"Take it easy, Lois. No one's killing anybody. Superman's the good guy."

She glanced nervously at the door. "What do you want from me?"

He borrowed an emery board on her desk and began working on the cuticles around his toenails. "The IRS gave me your name."

"Wrong acronym."

"What?"

"I think you mean 'DIA.'"

He blinked hard, unable to hide his surprise that she knew of his spook background. "I'm a civilian now. I work for a private headhunting firm."

"Really? And after you find the heads, do you shrink them and hang them on your loincloth when you swing around the jungle?"

"Hey, that's cute. I like your style. Anyway, it's nothing *that* serious. These days, I get paid for cleaning up government messes."

Forcing a smile to keep him occupied, she reached under her desk and rifled around in her purse. "Can I confide in you, Mr. Fielding?"

He inched forward, appearing downright exuberant that his charm was having some positive effect. "Why, of course you can."

She whipped her hand up from under the desk and sprayed him with Mace.

Cas flipped backwards over the chair and grabbed at his eyes. "*Awwwggg!*"

She shot up and sprinted for the door.

He dived at her and cut her legs from under her with a football tackle. She fell on top of him, swiping at his pawing hands. Before she could escape, he rolled on top of her.

Their lips hovered inches apart.

With his eyes still watering, he reached down, unfastened her top button, and wiped his tears on her blouse. "There's something I'd like to ask you."

She slapped at his ears. "Get off me!"

"How would you like to make an easy hundred thousand?"

She stopped fighting. "Dollars?"

"Interested?"

Her mind somersaulted. "What would I have to do?"

"Help me find a meteorite. Or meteoroid. I get confused."

Her eyes filled with visions of old American presidents framed in green ovals. Was he *really* offering her three years of salary for a *meteorite*? She had some pretty decent samples back at her apartment. He didn't seem too bright. Maybe she could pawn off one of those igneous paperweights on him. Then, she'd celebrate with a little jaunt to the Bahamas over spring break and—

"Hello? Anybody home?"

Rousted from her daydream, she wiped the Mace from his eyes and purred, "Hey, listen, I'm sorry about that. Sometimes I get a little overwrought."

"I had it coming, I guess. I'm a little out of practice."

She caught him staring at the outlines of her bra. "We should probably discuss this in a more professional manner."

"Right."

Released from under his weight, she stood and arranged her blouse. "What kind of meteorite are you looking for, Mr. Fielding?" She had a hard time meeting eyes, with him still sitting there in just a black Speedo. "Chondrite? Stony iron? Asteroid spectral?"

"One that's been on Earth for a few years."

She spun around to the windowsill behind her, where a coffeepot sat on an ancient silver radiator. She wiped off two mugs from the counter and filled them with sludge that had been burning in the coffee maker. "Shouldn't be a problem. How many years? Old, I mean."

"Since the time of Adam and Eve."

She coughed, spraying coffee across her desk. "You're not one of those, you know, Rapture nuts, are you?" Seeing him staring at the window, she turned to see what he was looking at. A second later, she twirled back in her chair to inquire about what had caught his attention.

He was gone. His wristwatch and gold ring lay on the desk.

Son of a bitch. Had he really ...

He bounced up from under her desk. "Judgment Day."

She caught her breath, realizing that the guy had only been spoofing a divine disappearance. He really *did* belong in a straitjacket. Still, if he were willing to pay what he'd just promised in cash, and preferably in advance, what the hell did she care?

She went into professor mode, putting on her lecture voice. "The oldest known meteorite fragments are from space boulders found in the Tagish Lake in the Yukon. The rocks there survived because they hit the lake when it was frozen. I've got a contact at Brown University, where the fragments are held." She gave him her best poker face. "But I'm afraid obtaining one of them will cost you more than a hundred thousand."

Cas didn't blink at the pricing. "*How* old?"

She fluffed her hair. "It's rude to ask a lady—"

"No, you giddy Gidget! The meteorite fragments!"

She recoiled back into her chair from his rude outburst. Keeping her cool for the money's sake, she said calmly, "They predate the solar system. Four and a half-billion years, give or take a generation or two." She sized him up again, and this time couldn't help herself, adding, "About *your* age, I should think."

"Hysterical. Let's get back to these space boulders. When did they land?"

"Twelve years ago," she said.

"The one I'm looking for has been on Earth for at least two thousand years."

Stunned, she leaned closer. "You're looking for one *particular* meteorite?"

"That's what I said." His intense gaze was jolting. "*Very* particular."

"That being the case, may I ask *which* particular meteorite?"

"I can't tell you."

This was starting to sound a lot like some of the disastrous blind dates she had been on before Steve. "Look, Mr. Fielding, so long as I get paid, I don't care if you're after the Blarney Stone. But you're going to have to give me a little more information if you want me to help you."

"How would you go about determining the age of a meteorite?"

"It's a pretty simple process. We measure the decay of its radioactive isotopes."

"I majored in brewery. Can you dumb it down?"

She rose from her chair and moved to the chalkboard. "Isotopes are atoms of the same element with different numbers of neutrons. Some isotopes are stable. Others are radioactive. The radioactive ones decay into other components called daughter isotopes. Radioactive isotopes decay according to a law of power measured in a unit called a half-life. Take a supernova, for example. When fifty percent of its parent isotopes have decomposed, it's said to have a half-life. Usually the original isotope is held to be extinct after it has run through six half-life revolutions."

Cas rubbed his bleary eyes. "Maybe we should reconvene this seminar at one of the local watering holes." He smacked his lips. "I'm a little thirsty."

She could really use a stiff scotch, but not with a guy dressed only in a black Speedo—and certainly not with a man reputed to be a ruthless killer. "I am sorry, Mr. Fielding, but I do have other students waiting." She returned to the formula she was scrawling across the board:

Rubidium (87Rb)
87Rboriginal = 87Rbnow * (elt)
where, e is the base of the natural logarithm,
l is the rate of radioactive decay,
and t is the elapsed time.
By substituting that in the original equation we get:
87Srnow = 87Sroriginal + 87Rbnow * (elt - 1)

"Let's cut to the chase," he said. "Is every meteorite different in composition?"

"Of course. They all have their own isotropic imprints."

"Kinda like a fingerprint, huh?"

She nodded, trying to remain patient, as if enduring the mental floundering of an unprepared undergraduate student. "Remotely similar."

Cas clicked his tongue against the inside of his cheek, making a popping sound. "Now we're getting somewhere. Okay, tell me this, then. If you had a piece of the meteorite, you could test it and find its fingerprint. And then you could match it against the fingerprints of all the other meteorites in existence?"

"Theoretically, I suppose."

Deep in what passed as thought for him, Cas twirled his expensive silver watch around his index finger while staring at the formula she had written on the blackboard. With a jolting spasm, he threw his feet off the desk and leapt to standing. "I guess that means we need to go fingerprint hunting."

"Go? Where?"

"Pack for a warm climate. And bring a scarf."

Her jaw dropped. "Wait a minute. You haven't even told me why you need this meteorite analyzed."

"That's confidential. You know these corporate paranoid types."

"And if I don't take the assignment?"

"I'll just have to off you."

Her eyes bulged. She reached for the Mace again.

He winked at her as gathered up his clothes. Dressing, he said, "I'm kidding. Come on, Doc. Loosen up."

As her pulse dropped back to normal, Marly tried to square this goofball in arrested development with the cold-blooded killer that Paul had described. She couldn't help but notice his subdued good looks, for a middle-aged guy anyway, with his thick mop of gray-flecked hair and sun-hammered face. Sure, he *could* be a murderous psychopath, but Paul Brady had been wrong about him being dead. And now she was also starting to wonder if that Mossad kidnapper had been as whacked out as Paul had insisted. After all, this Fielding fellow *did* come to find her, just as the Israeli agent had warned her he would.

"Listen," Cas said while he buckled his belt. "I need an answer now."

She debated his crazy-sounding offer. A hundred thousand dollars for analyzing one little meteorite would go a long way toward solving a lot of her problems. What harm could come from it, really? The more she thought about it, Isserle the Mossad, or whatever name he went by now, had probably been working on the side for a corporate competitor in Israel. Yeah, maybe he was trying to keep Mr. Fielding here from hiring her expert services. Made perfect sense. She could really use a professional kick-start in the consulting business. If she made a name on this gig, other referrals might start popping up.

And there *was* that larger apartment with the nice river view coming up for lease in her building next month.

11

Lufthansa Flight 78

After their three-hour layover in Frankfurt, Cas settled into the first-class cabin and ratcheted back his seat on the sprawling Lufthansa Dreamliner bound for the United Arab Emirates. He really couldn't afford these upgrades from economy class, but if that was what it took to get his new business partner, Dr. Rockhead, on board with the mission, then that was the price of doing business. He'd just submit the cost to Jubal on his expense account when the job was finished.

Now, where was that drink he'd ordered with his first step onto the plane?

He looked over at Marly in the window seat and saw that she was already snoozing away. She really was a pretty little thing, if a tad tightly wound. The short strawberry-blond hair, button nose, and occasional dimples didn't square at all with her professorial primness. Her pale skin was as smooth and flawless as Shada's had been—a thought that made him wince—and he knew from having rolled on top of her in their office wrestling match that she had a tight bod.

Now though, having insisted on the view, she had her neck slumped back in slumber land with her mouth open like a baby robin waiting for a worm.

Unable to sleep, he flipped open a cheap paperback and turned to where he had left off, at one of the steamiest scenes.

Marly woke herself with an undignified snort. Recovering with a start, she muttered above the white noise in the cabin, "I'm starving. When's dinner?"

He glared at her. She was hungry *again*? After the lunch on the flight and that one-woman wiener schnitzel festival in the airport restaurant?

"Food is all-inclusive," she reminded him. "That was part of the deal."

He shook his head in astonishment. Apparently the trauma of being nabbed and assaulted just a couple of days ago hadn't dampened her appetite. He put down his novel and reached between his knees for his black-leather rucksack. After fishing around for a minute, he produced a Clif bar. "Don't eat the whole thing. It'll spoil your appetite."

"We get real cuisine on this flight, right?"

"Drinks, dinner, and a movie," he said. "That's why we're on this date. And since all this costs so much—"

"Don't even think about going there, Mr. Fielding."

The flight attendant finally arrived with his cocktail, and he slugged it down. He twirled the gin-coated ice in his drained glass and prepared to brief Marly, vaguely, about where they were going. In exchange, he wanted more details about this mysterious run-in with Avram Isserle that she had mentioned in the cab ride to the airport. He couldn't imagine how such a clueless professor had found out that Isserle worked for Mossad. As best as he had gathered from her semi-coherent babbling about the incident, Isserle had probably managed to install a thumb drive on her USB port.

But why would Mossad want anything to do with a Columbia egghead so low on the academic totem pole? He could only guess that the Israelis were looking for the same crazy SOB who pulled off the theft of the century. There were lots of ambitious grifters around the globe cracked enough to have given it a shot. So, before leaving New York, he had reached out to a former operative buddy freelancing for the CIA in Paris. His contact confirmed that Langley suspected a guest who, on the night before the heist, had checked into a Mecca hotel under the name of Abdul Baith.

His stomach growled, derailing his train of thought. He signaled the flight attendant for a fresh cocktail. Replenished, he chewed on another cube while trying to remember what he had just been pondering. Oh yeah, Abdul Baith. He'd never heard of the guy, but then he'd been out of the game for a while.

Marly stirred. "That ice-crunching? It's honestly rather annoying. But, of course, you already know that, which is why you persist in doing it."

He chomped on a cube again and swallowed the shards. "At least I don't snore. The pilot just went on the intercom to announce that the plane had developed an oxygen leak over Seat 2A."

She looked over at the book on his lap. "You actually *read?*"

He had forgotten about the novel creased open on his knee. "Oh, this? You'd love it." He showed her the book jacket. "It's called *Bruised*—"

"I see what it says," she said with disgust. "I would have pegged you for more of a picture-book type."

"I'll have you know this is some of the best porn lit I've ever read. My only criticism so far is that you have to skip so far ahead to the threesome." He flipped through the gray pages. "That's in here somewhere, I swear. Which is why I bought this particular title."

She crossed her arms. "Do you really have to be reading erotica in public? I mean, right next to me?"

"It's *not* erotica." He acted insulted. "What, you think I'm one of those Fifty Shades of Bullshit groupies? This is a good, old-fashioned, all-American, hardcore pot-boiler." He talked right through her glare. "Lighten up, will ya, Doc. Gee-whiz." He slid the novel under his leg. "Happy now?"

She sighed and rolled her eyes at his empty glass. "I thought martinis went out of style with spittoons and Brylcreem."

"Hey, it may be cheap airline gin, but it *is* a genuine Vesper martini. You should try one of these. Might help you uncoil a little."

She turned away, muttering something about an "ass" that wasn't meant as a compliment on his tight buns.

He whispered to her, "Okay, here's the deal, Miss Manners. We're flying to Jeddah, and then it's on to Mecca. Which, by the way, is off limits to infidels. But we'll manage somehow. Then we—I mean, *you*—are going to scrape up a few shavings from the Black Stone of Kaaba."

She turned so fast that she almost made him spill his drink. "You told me I was coming along to analyze a meteorite!"

He motioned for her to lower her voice. "You are ... but first we have to get some samples."

"*What* samples?"

"We need to know what we're looking for."

"I'm not following."

"The Black Stone of Mecca is a meteorite. That's what we're looking for."

"Looking for?"

"Keep this under your bra ... but the Stone's missing."

She grabbed his wrist to prevent him from taking another drink before he explained himself. "Are you out of your mind? You never said anything about ... Do you have any idea what they'll do to us if—"

"Oh, don't worry about it." He decided not to mention the part about him taking a big leap of faith that the thief had left behind some usable residue from the Stone's extraction. He was actually surprised she knew that much about Mecca's stringent regulations. Still, he shot her a ridiculous grin and jingled his ice next to her ear. "You're such a drama queen."

She slammed the back of her head into the seat. "And *you* are certifiable."

"It's no big deal, really. We're just going to stroll into the Masjid plaza like we're shopping or something. You'll collect whatever rock droppings you can find, and then we're off to the races."

She was half out of her seat and in his face. "And just how do you plan on getting us in to that pilgrimage square to get these ... " She was so flustered, she didn't even know what to call them.

He helped her out. "Sample shavings."

"It's not as if we can waltz right in there."

As wildly different as they were, Cas felt himself, inexplicably, growing fond of her. He had expected her to be bright, but she was so street savvy. He chewed another ice cube, just to watch her squirm, and whispered to her ear, "Don't worry that little head of yours. Waltzing in there is my department."

Twelve hours later, after landing in Abu Dhabi, Cas ushered Marly into the Le Royal Méridien Hotel. Without first checking in, he made a beeline to the Oceans Seafood Lounge and situated her on a stool at the bar, stuffing a few *dirham* into the front pocket of her jeans to keep her stocked in peanuts. "This place is damn expensive, so go easy on the *hor d'oeuvres*."

She slapped away his frisky hand and grabbed the wad of money, secreting it under her blouse.

"One word," he whispered. "Do *not* move from this seat."

"That's six words, even when you slur them."

He nudged closer. "Listen to me very carefully, Doc. This isn't the Upper West Side. If you *even* think about wandering around here—"

"Or what? You'll con me with another one of your spook lies?" She turned away, refusing him the satisfaction of a reaction.

"Just relax and enjoy your munchies. I'll be back in a few. Got it?"

She motioned over the white-jacketed *maitre d'*. "What's the most expensive item on the menu?"

"Tonight, madam, we are featuring a prime cut of Kobe steak that's had more beer and massages than, well"—he looked down his impressive nose at Cas—"your *companion* here."

Cas glared at the snooty headwaiter. "Hey, there's no cause for the attitude."

"Actually," Marly told the *maitre d'*, "I'm already impressed with your judgment. How much is the steak?"

"Six hundred *dirham*.

"How much is that in American dollars?"

Approximately two hundred, madam."

"Make mine medium rare," Marly said. "With a side order of onion rings. And load me up on the bread sticks. There's a big tip in it for you if they have sesame seeds."

The *maitre d'* nodded with a conspiratorial smile and glided off.

Cas was nearly choking. "What the hell?"

Marly turned on her stool and fluttered her eyes at the comely mixologist in the red vest. When the barkeep sauntered over, she asked him, "Where can a girl find a good time around here?"

Cas's jaw nearly hit his knee. "Didn't you hear what I just—"

"Well," the bartender said, returning the seductive glance. "If you're looking for high-end shopping, there's Hermès at the Eithad Towers."

"Great. Oh, and charge my dinner to the room of my assistant here. He goes under Ass H. Fielding" She flirted a bit more with the bartender, then turned and found Cas, speechless, still hovering behind her. "Run along, cabana boy. You're cramping my style."

S till steamed about Marly's spending spree at the lounge, Cas got out of a cab just off Hamdan Street and stood outside an eight-story gray building that looked like a crumbling Russian apartment block. He nearly retched from the cesspool smells of urine and rotting garbage as he hurried through the graffiti-covered hallways into a maze of apartments where Filipino, Bangladeshi, and Thai men slept in heaps.

Turning blue from the lack of breathable air, he finally made it to the basement and found his old Arab friend and CIA subcontractor, Roz the Clipper, a nickname bestowed to honor his skill at shaving off edges of silver and gold coins without detection and selling the harvest for a tidy profit. The handy lowlife kept a meth lab here, along with printing machinery and an office the size of a three-car garage. No cop in the world could stand the smell enough to get anywhere near the place, and besides, the UAE police couldn't have cared any less for the scum who lived around here.

Grinning, the Clipper handed over a packet of documents ordered by phone from New York. "Just like the old days, eh Casuist?"

Cas hadn't heard his spook nickname spoken in years. He nodded quickly, anxious to get back to the hotel before someone from the Dark Years spotted him. After paying the Clipper with a fresh wad of American hundred-dollar bills, he backtracked outside and hailed another cab, gulping draughts of air, as if he had just surfaced from the sulfuric depths of Hades.

A t the hotel bar, Marly kept looking at her watch. No telling what the Fielding of Nightmares was up to on his mysterious errand. Bored and feeling more than a little out of place, she ordered another Cosmopolitan while waiting for her Kobe steak to be served.

The nice young British bartender slid the drink down to her.

She took a satisfying sip and wondered again what this city of Abu Dhabi—more than a thousand miles across the Arabian Peninsula from Mecca—could possibly have to do with the Black Stone and meteorites. Fighting off the questions pounding her brain, she sighed and leaned back on her cushioned bar chair, dogged tired. *Forget about it, Marly, just forget it. Go along for the ride. Then take the money and run.* She started toying with a souvenir book of matches and a handful of those nifty plastic swords used to impale olives. As she sipped her cranberry-and-citrus martini, the weight of the previous seventy sleep-deprived hours began slipping away. A hot bath would be next, and—

She felt a hard jab in her right kidney.

Behind her, a man with a three-day beard and greasy hair pressed something sharp deeper into her flank. "I tell you when to move."

She looked down and saw a pistol, covered by the overhang of the bar.

The man silenced her brewing protest with another jab. "Do what I say," he whispered into her ear. "And *only* what I say."

She couldn't make out his features in the dim lighting. Exhausted, she found just enough energy to clench her jaws. With her brain now as hazy as the smog-cloaked twilight sky outside, she took another sip from her frosty Cosmopolitan, trying to steady her nerves. Despite her terror, instinct told her to act unfazed. She turned on him with as fierce a glare as she could manage. "You know what, mister?" She raised her voice, hoping the bartender would overhear and come over. "You are really pretty annoying. And that poking hurts, too."

But the bartender had his back turned at the far end of the bar.

The man with the gun arched her back by driving the barrel deeper into her flesh. "Pull that little trick again, and you will regret it. You are an American. Nobody here would mind if you were found to have committed suicide in the restroom. Except, of course, the one who must clean up your blood."

A rush of adrenaline sponged her fear. "I could just yell 'gun' and—"

He stabbed his weapon so hard into her ribs that she sucked in her breath. Wincing, she turned on him with raw fury and clenched her fingernails to claw at his face, but the man grabbed her by the forearm. She tried to jerk away, looking toward the bartender in a silent plea for help.

Her abductor tossed a wad of bills on the bar. His silenced purchased, the bartender just shrugged as Marly was hustled toward the exit.

C as dashed through the Oceans hotel lobby and made fast for the restaurant bar. He'd been gone thirty minutes, tops. Not bad, not bad at all. His throat was parched, and his head felt like it was about to explode for lack of sleep. But his long-neglected internal alarm, which had saved his ass countless times, was fully recharged and now blasting warning bells everywhere in his body.

Something was wrong.

As his ears burned from the cheesy American music blasting over the speakers, he scanned the well-dressed tourists and seedy expats in the lounge. Nothing immediately looked out of the ordinary—except that Marly's bar chair was empty. Maybe she'd just gone to refresh herself after so many hours in an airplane. He took the stool next to hers and waited, tapping his fingers on the bar with growing impatience. As the seconds spun into minutes, his anxiety started spinning, too. He wanted scream in Marly's face: *What part of "Somebody will kill you!" don't you fucking understand?* Instead, he waved over the bartender, who was busy folding napkins.

"Yes, sir!" the bartender said. "So sorry. Didn't see you there."

"Vesper martini." Cas cased the joint again, wondering if Marly had really made good on her threat to go shopping. "Make it fast. I don't want the ice cubes to even think about melting."

The bartender smirked. "Glad to have you back, Mr. Bond."

Cas remembered that surly tone from their earlier encounter. "Everybody seems to find my cocktail of choice entertaining."

"We don't get many orders for it, except when the cruise ships come in."

Cas drained the glass and slapped a handful of *dirham* on the bar. "Listen, pal. I gotta ask you something. Damn fine stir, by the way."

"Cheers," the bartender said, clearly not giving a damn.

"What happened to that hot-looking sort-of-blond chick sitting here?"

The bartender shrugged. "We get many female customers in here."

"The one with the steam coming out of her ears."

The bartender enjoyed a tight smile. "She left about fifteen minutes ago with another man."

"Voluntarily?"

The bartender kept polishing the inside of a shot glass, his diffidence way too studied. "She wasn't wearing handcuffs or being dragged by the hair."

Cas reluctantly pulled out more *baksheesh* from his pocket and slid the bills down the bar. "This man with her ... he didn't happen to look like, I dunno, a youngish guy with black hair and a pasty face?"

This time, the bartender couldn't even dredge up a shrug as he picked up the cash and pocketed it. "Maybe. To be quite honest, I didn't notice."

Cas chewed through his plastic swizzle in anger. He had no time for chasing after a ditzy dame. The clock was ticking. Only three days left until the Hajj, and no Stone meant no money, no Farid, and no telling what else. He definitely wasn't in the mood now for a reunion go-round with Avram Isserle. That wiry little bastard and his Mossad toadies had likely been tailing them from the moment they had landed. As he licked the last drop from the martini glass, he announced—to himself—that the outrageous tip he had just plucked down for absolutely no information was coming out of Dr. Rockhead's fee.

12

Dallas, Texas

Bored and tired, Bridget Whelan sighed as she leaned over the microscope for what seemed like the gazillionth time that morning. This boss of hers, Seth Cohanim, was one piece of messed-up work, constantly bursting into the lab and ordering her to recheck the vectors and base pairs on the DNA extracts to make sure her calculations were correct. Anal-retentive buttinski. What had she gotten herself into here? All of this money and time, just to breed a cow that would add a quarter-inch thickness to a Porterhouse steak? She didn't even touch red meat. No way would she risk coming back in the next life as a bovine to be stuffed with genetically altered corn and prodded by electrical jolts into a slaughterhouse.

She adjusted the scope's focus and typed the sequence into her laptop:

ATGCGTGCAATGTTTACGCGTAAAGCGTGCACGTTAGAGTAT
||||||||| ||||||||||||||||| ||||||||||||||||||||||||||||| ||||||||||||||||||||| |||||||||||| |||
TACGCACGTTACAAATGCTCATTTCGCACGTGCAAGCTCATG

Letters and strands … strands and letters.

For the love of Artemis!

She was even dreaming about binaries at night now. She was about to take a break and walk down the creepy dark hall for a cup of coffee when she heard her boss's footsteps on the gray carpet.

Shit.

The lab door flew open. "Whelan! You got those DNA printouts from that tooth yet?"

"Should be finished in an hour, Mr. Cohanim."

The Stetson-crowned *éminence grise* scraped his boot heel across the gleaming white linoleum floor like a bull pawing before a charge. "That's what you told me *two* hours ago!"

"You can't rush Mother Nature."

Cohanim took a menacing step closer to hover over her. "You're not pricking frog's legs for the freshman lab class! This is a business. Time is money."

"Extracting a specimen from that molar pulp was a real bitch."

"That's what you get paid to do."

She didn't know the first thing about veterinary dentistry, but this tooth she was examining seemed unusually small, even for a young calf's mouth. "What are you feeding those poor things? That thing looked like it had been soaked in Dr Pepper for a month."

He ignored her complaint. "How degraded was the DNA?"

"Worst I've ever seen," she said, not exaggerating. "But I did finally manage to scrape out just enough periodontal tissue to do the trick. We got lucky. Usually it's a hundred-to-one shot to find any surviving protein in a tooth from an animal that's been dead for a while. You must have kept it in a climate-controlled environment, huh?"

"We're not amateurs here."

"No, sir."

"I'm going to be out of town for a few days. I won't be around to clean up your screw-ups, so let's go over the cloning protocol again."

"I've got it memorized," she promised.

Cohanim's face reddened. "I don't care if you wrote it in lipstick on that fat backside of yours! I want to hear you repeat it."

Bridget silently conjured up a nasty curse, imagining what her boss would look like with a massive goiter hanging under that yapping jaw of his. If the rent weren't due this weekend, she would walk right out and slam the door behind her. But she vowed to hang on just long enough to get a few more bucks stashed away. Then, she'd show him her ass, all right.

"When you finally have the readout from the tooth DNA in hand," he quizzed her, "what are you going to do next?"

"I'll run it through the database of DNA sequences on the mainframe."

"And then?"

"I'll do a comparative analysis and isolate the one DNA donor that most closely matches the genome from the tooth extraction."

"How many sequences do we have filed?"

She wanted to scream, but resisted the urge. She had known that factoid once upon a time, but now she wasn't sure. Burned by his expectant glare, she finally offered a guess, "Forty million."

Cohanim's eyes flinted with anger. "Four *hundred* and forty million! There are four hundred-and-forty million individual readings collected by the Institute of Genome Study from around the world. Do I have to write it on a Post-it and stick it to your forehead?"

She perked up on her lab stool. "You know, I was wondering about that. Why would a nonprofit want to collect the DNA profiles of so many cattle?"

Cohanim circled her, taking a moment as if trying to recover his composure. "You're just full of questions, aren't you?"

She flipped her head sideways, cute-like. "That's why I went into science."

"That's why I went into science, too," he growled. "But the business of animal husbandry is all about asking the right questions and avoiding the wrong ones. What do *you* think would be the right question right about now?"

Her feelings bruised, she forced herself to submit to his browbeating, if only to get him out of her face quicker. "Would you like me to proceed with the protocol, sir?"

"Good choice," he said with swiping sarcasm. "Now, what are you going to do with the ideal candidate drawn from the Institute's genome database?"

"I'm supposed to fax the specs to the number that you gave me, with instructions to send us the donor egg most closely matching the DNA of the molar."

"Transport method?"

"Medevac jet. Container kept below twenty-two degrees with dry ice only."

Cohanim nodded. "And when the egg gets here?"

"Oh, yeah. I was going to ask you about—" She stopped in time, but she simply couldn't hold back her curiosity. "Why are you trying to create recombinant DNA with the tooth pulp and mineral extracts from that stone we tapped with the needle last week?"

Cohanim stared at her. "What kind of nonsense did they teach you at that football mill down in Lubbock? Every high schooler knows you can't create DNA from an inanimate object."

"I'm confused, then. Why all of this work?"

Cohanim rubbed his fist into his palm, his tic of impatience. "I'm testing a new theory. Some strains of cows have a genetic deficiency in iron. For some reason, this phenomenon is particularly prevalent in the Middle East. It may have something to do with the excess Vitamin D from sun exposure, or the lack of certain nutrients in the grass—or whatever scrub they're getting there. The cattle become anemic and don't thrive."

"So you think injecting minerals into their DNA culture will change that?"

He turned uncharacteristically avuncular, adopting a solicitous tone. "To be perfectly honest, darlin', I don't know. But then, almost all of the important discoveries down through history have resulted because someone was willing to try something outlandish. It may be that the cow genome can be altered by the mere proximity in the genetic soup of the trace minerals that would be deficient when the person—"

"You mean 'cow,'" she corrected him.

Cohanim's face pinched, as if he had made a gross mistake, but he quickly masked it with a forced smile. "Of course. Sorry. I read these sci-fi novels on human cloning, and sometimes I dream of the future."

She nodded. "Yeah, it would be smokin' rad if we could do with people what they did with Dolly the sheep some day, huh?" She noticed that he had turned inward, probably captivated by some deep thought. "So, it kinda sounds like you're doing homeopathy for stem cells."

Cohanim roused from a deep contemplation, and smiled at her.

She felt a shudder. First time she'd ever seen *that.*

"Yes, it's exactly like that," he said. "You're cleverer than I gave you credit for, Miss Whelan. I think you may have a very bright future here at Lightgiver Technologies."

Stunned by the rare compliment, she glanced at him sideways, wondering if he was being sarcastic. But he looked dead serious.

"Tell you what. As soon as we get that test embryo cloned, I'm taking it over to Israel to implant it in our client's test heifer at the Kibbutz Gizan. How would you like to come along? I could use some help in case we get some genetic issues."

She glowed like a redbed firefly, and she began to wonder if maybe she had misjudged the guy. She batted her Goth lashes at him again. "That would be radder than rad, Mr. Cohanim."

13

Abu Dhabi, United Arab Emirates

Marly's abductor—the third in as many days, if you counted Agent Speedo, and she was coming around to doing just that—walked her briskly out of the hotel. In less than a minute, a taxi was rushing them down a broad boulevard bordered by dwarf palm trees. Fighting the brute's grip on her arm, she tried to take in every detail of her surroundings so that she could tell Cas as soon as she escaped.

Fifteen minutes later, the yellow Corolla lurched into overdrive and zipped the few blocks toward the broad avenue that ran along Abu Dhabi's waterfront. They came to a stop in front of what appeared to be a Middle Eastern version of an American strip mall. Tall, latticed windows crowned in sharp arches fronted the facade. The place reminded her of a miniature, cheesy knockoff of a caliph's palace.

Would they really murder her in a place like this?

The kidnapper tossed a few *dirham* at the cabbie and yanked her out of the backseat. He shoved her into a bar that looked like a garden-variety sports dive dropped into a Pizza Hut. The moment she stepped foot inside, the men— mostly Western corporate types, with a few dopey-looking Arabs—stopped talking and stared at her. She felt like Dorothy landing in a hut of overheated, smoke-puffing Munchkins.

"If you think you're going to get away with something," she barked with false bluster at the guy pushing her along, "you've got another think coming!"

The brute just laughed as he whisked her into a dark hallway at the rear of the joint. He punched a series of numbers into a lock screen. A steel door opened, and he pushed her inside, past the slits of a black shower curtain.

In the thick smoke, she saw a half dozen fat men, older and well-dressed, sitting around a large black table cluttered with cocktail glasses, bottles of booze, weapons, and a pair of *shisha* pipes. She could barely breathe in the thick haze. Was that apple-flavored tobacco or opium they were inhaling? The goon at her elbow slammed her into a chair. She wiggled like a worm on a hook as they duct-taped her to the seat.

"So nice of you to come, Dr. McKinney," a thick-accented voice said through the pipe smog. "You are visiting friends in the United Arab Emirates, yes?"

She froze.

Her interrogator enjoyed a cynical chuckle, apparently amused by her sudden silence. "You've come with our old acquaintance, Mr. Fielding."

Her headache worsened. What difference would any answer make?

Draped in a black-and-white *ghutrah* bound with a black cord, the obese man scooted closer and snapped his fingers to regain her attention. "Oh, you watch a lot of American movies, I suppose. You must see many films in which the, how do you say it, 'damsel in distress'"—he held up fingers the size of kielbasa sausages—"keeps her mouth closed. But in real life, the quiet ones pay the steepest price."

Her eyes slowly adjusted to the shadowy darkness cloaked in *shisha* fumes, and she made out the man's yellow-stained smile floating in a face of sweat and oily fat. Was that a line of gold glittering from his teeth?

"We will make this simple." He rubbed his enormous paws across his black *thawb*. "A reliable source tells us that you and Mr. Fielding are on a mission to Mecca. I trust you know that the Saudis do not to look kindly on infidels in Islam's holiest city."

She heard laughter behind her.

"And yet, Dr. McKinney, rules do not seem to apply to you and your"—the interrogator took another drag on his cigarette—"friend?"

She wasn't surprised that the fat slob knew her name. Hell, Avram Isserle had known who she was, and so had the Malibu Screwball. Her popularity seemed to have gone global, for no apparent reason. "First off, mister—"

"Please, call me Aziz."

"I don't give a fuck what your name—" She stopped, surprised by her own spontaneous vulgarity. Fielding was already rubbing off on her, and not in a good way.

The fake hospitality faded from the interrogator's tone. "Be very careful with your language, my dear doctor. The Saudis will not hesitate to arrest a foul-tongued woman."

"Maybe I should give the cops here a try," she said. "Dealing with the Saudi police has *got* to be a hell of a lot better than hanging out with you buffoons."

The men behind her laughed again, this time with more gusto, apparently impressed with her bravado.

But this muttonhead who called himself Aziz didn't appear to be amused. He glanced around the room, cowing his subordinates to silence. "Perhaps we should leave now, if our lady guest here insists on being so vile and unhelpful. She refuses our warm Emirates welcome."

The thugs rustled around their slimy crime boss, as if preparing to leave her sweating in this foggy oven to be cooked into flatbread.

"What is it you want from me?" she demanded.

"Why don't *you* tell us what we want."

She huffed. Couldn't these slimy Arab slumdogs just get to the point? Whatever they were after, it obviously had something to do with Fielding.

Big surprise there.

"I suspect," Aziz continued, "that if we give you some time alone, you may reach an understanding of our needs. If not? Well, then …" He puffed on his pipe and waved toward the door. "We know several customers in the bar who would be very happy to make your acquaintance."

Every creep in the room laughed. Reeling from jet lag, she was damn tired of obnoxious strangers herding her around and then ignoring her. The smart thing to do would be to remain quiet and act dumb, avoiding doing and saying anything that might get her into more trouble, or worse. But she didn't feel particularly sane or compliant at that moment. With no weapon at her disposal but her exhausted mind and strong voice, she exploded into a paroxysm of maniacal laughter.

The goons turned, confused. They squinted at her through the smoke.

She kept shrieking, belting out a long hyena-like cackle. In the midst of this hooting chaos, she pushed one of her taped hands into the left back pocket of her jeans and pulled out the book of Oceans Restaurant bar matches she had kept.

Aziz shook his head and muttered, "Crazy American woman."

The men soon tired of her banshee act, and they walked off to the far end of the room to avoid her decibels, gathering around tables to resume their bantering over the pipes and drinks. One of them leaned his gun—looked like it might be an Uzi to her, but what did she know?—against the wall, about ten paces away from her chair.

While they were distracted with their insufferable male bonding, she struggled against the tape. Obscured by the thick smoke, she finally managed to strike one of the matches. Thanks to the thick, fragrant cloud, she could hardly smell the sulfuric after-breath rising behind her. She kept several matches ignited, dropping them the floor on the carpet behind her. Then she punched her fingers back into her pocket and fingered one of the tiny plastic cocktail swords.

Working methodically but quickly, she punched a series of holes through the tape on her wrist to create a line of perforation that would allow her to tear through the rubber-compound adhesive and the silver polyethylene coating. With just enough wiggle room, she ripped through to the tape's cotton fabric, creating frays that would light up with another match or two. She smelled smoke rising behind her. One of the matches had ignited the rug beneath her chair, just as she hoped.

She couldn't see any flames, but she screamed anyway, "Fire!"

Her exhaustion vanished in a surge of adrenaline. She pushed up from the chair and thrust it outward with her thighs. Swinging her seat toward the men, she leaped up and backwards in the chair, at the same time giving her wrists a violent twist and ripping the hole-punched duct tape. In midair, she grabbed the bottom of the chair and crashed through the middle of the table.

Glasses, ashes, magazines, papers, bottles, water pipes, weapons—a tornado of debris flew everywhere, smashing all around.

She dived for the weapons that the men had left leaning against the wall. She yanked at the biggest one closest to her, hoping it was an Uzi.

Six hundred rounds a minute, you rat bastards! Raging, she aimed the weapon at the ceiling and tugged the sensitive trigger. A rattling burst chattered around the room—her hands felt as if she were trying to control a jackhammer. Casings spewed in undulating arcs as the bullets flailed chunks of plaster and drywall everywhere. She heard glass shatter and felt water spraying from the demolished *shisha* pipes.

Through the haze, shouts erupted. Footsteps pounded for the back door.

She burst through the table's wreckage firing willy-nilly—until she noticed that the carpet had caught fire. Flames danced shoulder-height and raced toward the walls that were draped with flammable tapestries and Palestinian flags.

The smoke dissipated ... the puffing thugs had fled.

She grinned. *Damn that felt good!*

Dropping to a crouch, she duck-waddled through the plastic curtain that covered the door. After popping out the Uzi's cartridge, she jammed the submachine gun into her belt at the small of her back and pulled her shirt over the weapon. She yanked open the door.

Sirens blared down the streets.

She marched through the darkened hallway. The police were already rushing into the bar. Nobody in the roiled sea of drunken men and Asian prostitutes seemed to notice as she calmly walked outside.

She jumped into the backseat of a cab and rolled down both windows, gasping for air. The driver turned on her with a look of fright. Only then, looking at her reflection in the rear-view mirror, did she realize that her hair, face, and clothes were covered black with smoke. "It's Halloween back in the States," she explained to the panicked driver. "I'm going to a party at the Le

Royal Méridien as Fantine in *Les Miserables*. Do you think I pull it off? It cost me two hundred dollars to get to look like this."

The cabbie shook his head, muttering something about crazy Americans as he slapped the meter on and drove off.

Faking a French accent, she gave him directions. "Drop me off at the front entrance of the hotel, will you, comrade? I want to make a statement for the local fashionistas."

While the cabbie raced her through traffic, she straightened her hair, flicking shards of glass and bits of debris from her clothes. Working carefully, so not to alert the cabbie, she quietly pulled the Uzi's cartridge from her front pocket, checking it to make sure that she had kept one round or two for her next target—Cas Fielding's Speedo-girded crotch.

14

Mecca, Saudi Arabia

Marly felt a light buzzing on her shoulder, but the black *abaya* veil she was wearing as her disguise was so heavily meshed that she couldn't see who was pestering her. To chase her worsening vertigo, she tried to keep her eyes closed while she waited on a street corner for Cas to return from scouting the Masjid al-Haram mosque. Her scalp itched like hell, and she couldn't reach it. Had she caught some exotic psoriasis from this desert heat? Then, she remembered: Cas had forced her to chop off most of her strawberry-blond hair and dye black what remained of it.

She wasted a precious breath to curse his name again. After escaping those goons in Abu Dhabi two days ago, she had been adamant about heading home. But Cas had finally convinced her that the dust-up in the bar was just a misunderstanding with some of his old intelligence cronies looking to recoup a little sourcing bribe money. More to the point, she didn't have enough cash to buy a return ticket, let alone cover next month's rent if she didn't get paid for this "consulting" job. So, here she was, playing dress-up in the middle of the holiest city in Islam, where infidels were as welcome as bed bugs.

What could possibly go wrong?

The buzzing on her shoulder became a tapping. Someone was being either incredibly annoying, or desperately wanted her attention. Weren't men forbidden from touching women in public here? She wanted to turn around and give the tapping imbecile one swift kick in the balls with the running shoes she wore under this sun-soaking black tent. At last, fixing her balance, she managed a pirouette in the suffocating medieval getup to confront the jackass.

Nobody was there.

She looked up into the haze and saw that the tapping came from drops of rancid condensation leaking from an old air-conditioner in a window of this abandoned concrete building that Cas was using as their staging base.

Geez, what a shithole.

She didn't even want to contemplate what would happen to them if they were caught here. The last infidel who had managed to sneak into Mecca was a crazy Polish Jew who later converted to Islam and went on to build the fledgling nation of Pakistan. At least she had learned *something* during their eight-hour bone-rattling jeep ride from Jeddah.

Across the street, Cas reappeared from his little sortie. Making a drinking motion, he pounded on a garish Pepsi machine that sat like a calliope under a date palm tree just outside the entrance to a seedy hostel.

Her patience in this heat was draining fast. Just beyond her veil, she heard the muffled rumble of feet shuffling toward the center of the city to get in front of the line for the Hajj, which would begin in a couple of days. Although she and Cas had been in the city for only a few hours, she was amazed at how quickly the dusty city had filled with pilgrims. The sky looked battered with dust and gloomy November clouds, polluted by too many vehicles and residents. Many of the devout who had traveled here were sleeping on thin plastic mats along the streets amid the herds of goats they had brought for sacrifices.

Cas finally convinced the Pepsi machine to cough up a free can. Pleased with having outwitted an inert piece of metal, he walked over and handed the cold soda to her, waiting as if expecting praise for his cleverness.

"Don't they cut hands off for that?" she asked.

"Depends on who catches you. If it's the Saudi security police, they usually aim a little lower."

She licked her parched lips and carefully threaded the can under the cloth until her tongue found its cool aluminum and tasted the sugar water inside. With her poached brain revived, all she wanted now was to get that damn residue sample from the empty Stone frame on the Kaaba—if there was any— and analyze it for its meteorite age and elements. Then, with her fee finally paid, she could get back home and put all this insanity behind her. No more Mossad agents, no more near-naked maniacs in her office, no more *shisha*-fogged thugs armed with rattling submachine guns.

"You just flunked your first test," he told her.

"What are you talking about?"

"If a man talks to you, never turn around and look at him. We're barely supposed to be together in public."

"But I thought—"

"Doesn't matter if we're married."

"You have that fake license, right?"

"Yes, dear. But it doesn't become official until the conjugal night."

"In your dreams."

"Oh, you got that right."

She thought about huffing, but she remembered that the forced exhalation would only bounce off her veil like a hot puff from one of those compressed-air duster cans. "Can we just get on with it?"

"Not so fast, Doc. A well-laid plan ... or is that a well-laid planner? I forget." He slapped his forehead. "Dammit, those impure thoughts again. And on the eve of Hajj. There's just something about a hot chick covered from head to toe in a hot black gown."

"Can we just collect your rock dust and get out of here?" She plucked at her robe, trying to fan air to her legs. "I feel like a broasted chicken in here." Through the eye slits in her headdress, she saw a broad smile crease Cas's face.

"Great idea! There's an al-Bait fried chicken joint right up the street. You've never had wings like they make them here."

She glared him back—as best as one *could* glare through a veil. "The plan? You've got twenty minutes before I start stripping this stuff off."

He paused, as if visualizing that possibility. "Okay, here's what I want you to do. Listen *very* carefully." Circling around to stand behind her left ear again, he spoke just loudly enough for her to hear, but quietly enough for his voice to be lost in the hammering drone of the city. "Go inside the hotel. Alone."

"Alone? What are you going to be doing?"

"We can't go in together. It's an all-female lodging." He pulled another one of those obnoxious Djarum cigarettes from a crumpled pack and lit it, sending nose-clogging clouds of clove smoke around her. "Tell the registry clerk that you're booked for a room for one night, under the name of Busana. I picked that one myself! It's a Chechen name for 'girl of the moon.' Perfect with all this space-rock stuff, right? I figured you might be able to remember *that* one."

Feeling dizzy again, she reached out and found the wall. "Would you mind putting that cigarette out?"

He pulled another long draw and blew a puff of smoke into her veil. "All part of the training. You'd better get used to it, and fast. No Muslim woman would tell her hubbie to stop smoking, Busana Saidullayev."

"What?"

"That's your name, damn it. Come on! Focus! It's on your passport and hotel reservation, if anybody happens to ask you."

She reached into the rear pocket of her shorts and felt a passport there. How did *that* happen? She had no idea ... how *had* he gotten into her pants?

Cas grinned, as if having given that puzzle a lot of thought. "Just so you know, Busana Saidullayev is something of a hero here. She's the very young mother of two teenage Chechen rebels. They became martyrs when they blew

themselves up, along with a few Russian soldiers. She's handy with a submachine gun, too." He winked at her. "I'm just a regular irony board."

"Just out of curiosity," she said. "Tell me again why I should listen to
anything you tell me? You nearly got me killed back—"

"Here's an idea. Next time I tell you to stay put somewhere, stay put."

"It's not like I had any choice. And I'm not the one who ran off leaving me
at a hotel bar."

"Just pretend you're walking into the Times Square Marriott for a special
night on Broadway. Go straight to the front desk and ask for your reservation
in broken, Russian-sounding English. Then get up to your room. Third floor,
facing the Masjid. I got you a great view."

"Why we can't stay in the same hotel?"

"Reason Number One. We shouldn't be seen together until absolutely necessary. Reason Number Two. Men here stay in more plush accommodations. If I
were to bring you along to the Towers, you'd stand out."

"Thanks for being so thoughtful. Once I get checked in, then what?"

"I'll find some grub around here and send your lunch upstairs," he said.
"Along with a bell boy who will bring you a suitcase with some new clothes for
the main event tonight. There'll also be instructions for your makeup."

"Makeup?"

"You're gonna need something more than that mustache you bleach."

"Why do I put up with this?" She shook her head at the lunacy of it all. "And
tell me again why we're doing this at night?"

"Every advantage counts," he said. "The artificial lighting makes it harder for
the cops to see facial features. Besides, you've been bitching for an hour about
the heat. It'll be cooler."

She nodded, her veil fluttering. "Makes sense, I guess."

"You got until eleven tonight to freshen up, so get some rest."

As he disappeared into the masses trailed by a plume of clove-scented
smoke, Marly shook her draped head and wondered how she had managed to
get herself into this mess.

As the Royal Hotel clock tower struck midnight, Cas crawled their rented
black Mercedes through throngs of pilgrims who were surging toward
the Kaaba. Wedged in by the procession of cars, trucks, animals,
vendor carts, mopeds, motorcycles, and bicycles, he felt his adrenaline pumping,
just like old times. The streets here seemed laid out by a crazed spider, with
twisting boulevards and circling rings forming a haven for anyone who relished
the idea of getting lost. He hated every inch of this Arabian Peninsula. Now,

with each breath of stale air, he was pulled back to the searing memories of those Wahabi sonsabitches murdering Shada and taking Farid.

Shaking off the moisture in his eyes, he checked his watch and glanced with concern at Marly, who sat in the passenger seat, staring at the crush around them. As instructed, she had dispensed with the female Arab garb and now, like him, wore a male construction worker's outfit. With her new scruffy beard, geeky black sunglasses, dark construction coveralls, black steel-toed boots, and white hardhat, she looked passable, barely, as a male laborer. He could do nothing now but count on this uptight chick to collect the shavings that might lead him to the Stone. If she came through—and, after watching her in action, he now gave it less than fifty-fifty odds—he would finally be able to return to Malibu and live out the rest of his life quietly with his son.

Maybe, when this was all over, he'd even teach Farid to surf.

Steering with one hand, he grabbed Marly's wrist to stop her from scratching the phony beard. "Some of that stuff might come off."

She repulsed his attempted restraint and itched her cheek anyway. Pressing her nose against the window, she watched with growing dismay as the pilgrims on foot passed them by. "At this rate, it'll be daylight by the time we get there."

"You're right." Without warning, Cas wheeled the sedan off the main drag into an alley, sending her flying into the door. He cut the engine.

Marly jackknifed back upright in her seat. "You're just going to leave it here? What if we get a ticket?"

"I'm not planning on coming back for traffic court, are you?" Cas got out, motioning for her to follow him. With Marly on his heels, he looked down the alley, making sure no one saw them abandon the sedan. Then, he sauntered out toward the main thoroughfare.

She hurried to keep aside him. "Will you slow down!"

"Lose the testosterone vocals, Doc. You have perfect chords for a Saudi Binladen Group engineer." He couldn't see her eyes through the dark lenses, but he saw her hands shaking with nervousness. "Just relax, will ya."

"Oh, yeah. I'll just relax. Speaking of losing, when do we shed these Halloween costumes? Never mind the ridiculous sunglasses. It's dark, you know."

They merged into the crowd that was surging toward the sprawling Masjid.

Cas double-checked the laminated SBG tag on her shirt, complete with bar-coded credentials. He had to trust that the identification cards created by Roz the Clipper for them would pass muster. He leaned into Marly's covered ear and went over the plan with her one last time, "The Saudi authorities and the *imams* have draped the Kaaba with a big black tent, even bigger than the normal black cloth that always covers it. Got me so far?"

She nodded while gripping the tool bag on her waist that swayed with her gait. Everything she would need to collect any shavings would be at her fingertips, along with latex gloves to hide her female hands.

Cas kept his head down while plowing through the crowds. "Binladen construction people have been wandering around here for the last several days. They hire British Muslims from time to time, so the fact that we're not wearing robes and headdresses won't be any big surprise." He adjusted his ill-fitting hardhat. "And don't even *think* about opening your mouth—"

"Sure. No problem. As if I could get a word in edgewise."

Cas's heart jumped when turned the corner and saw the Kaaba, the giant black cube had stood on that same spot for centuries. The Holy Koran said that Adam had first built the structure and that Abraham, father of the world's three great religions, had rebuilt the foundation. The shimmering Masjid stood just ahead, illuminated by high, glaring lights that gave the mosque the feel of a football stadium. Thousands of worshippers milled about in a veritable human cattle drive, all for one purpose—to become one with something ineffable. As if by some habit from his desert days, he began reciting aloud in musical Arabic the 127th verse of the Koran's 2nd Sura. Then, he took a deep breath and pulled Marly closer. "You ready for this?"

She studied him hard. "Is there anything else you haven't told me?"

His eyes darted off. "Such as?"

"Something hasn't been adding up for me about this meteorite job. You don't impress me as a guy who's motivated by money. Especially when your life is on the line. Why *are* you doing this? Really."

"I told you. It's just a business deal."

She shot over to the side of the street, refusing to move until he came clean with the truth.

Cas glanced worriedly at the pilgrims hurrying past them. Finally, he whispered, "Okay, I guess you deserve to know. ... There *is* something else."

"I knew it! What did they promise you? Free women for the rest—"

"My son."

She stumbled for the next words. "You ... have a son?"

"Look, it's a long story. Now's not the time."

"What *exactly* does the Black Stone have to do with your son?"

He forced her to keeping moving by nudging up against her. "I don't want to put any more pressure on you, but if we botch this little operation, I'll never see him again."

"My God."

"Just don't think about it."

He pressed her elbow to hurry her along toward the phalanx of guards standing on high alert around the Kaaba. The Saudi royal police had their hands full keeping the masses from getting close to the shrine and discovering that, behind its big black tent, the silver container for the precious Stone was empty.

Marly still looked shaken by what he had just revealed, but she reluctantly peeled off from him, just as he had instructed. Without glancing back, she made her way toward the far end of the Kaaba tent.

While she took her position, Cas kept an eye on the Saudi officer in charge, the one with that all-important *wasta* influence, one of the guiding principles of any transaction in the Arabic world. Working alone now, Cas bowed to the officer slightly and said with forced confidence, "I understand that you are the man to see here, *sahib.*" He brought his right hand to his heart in a show of respect, and then flashed his SBG badge at the nonplussed Saudi.

The Saudi officer refused him the courtesy of a direct glance. "No authorizations have come for additional construction laborers."

Cas had expected the haughty treatment. Yet his pulse quickened as he saw the officer's eyes travel toward the Kaaba tent and linger a bit too long on Marly, even though she was keeping her chin down. Suddenly, at the officer's signal, the soldiers swarmed them. One of the guards yanked Marly's gear bag from her hip and ripped it open, spilling some of the gleaming technical equipment across the marble courtyard. Thankfully, Marly kept her wits about her and didn't resist. She calmly picked up the tools and put them back into her bag.

Cas whipped a notebook from the pocket of his coveralls and lunged toward the officer in charge. "I will have your name!" He got within an inch of the startled man's face. "Sir Brighton Birdwell has paid for us to come here!"

The officer scoffed. "I do not know who—"

"The president of Binexport's London operation! I am here at the express wishes of the Royal Family, to gather forensic evidence—"

"There will be no more talking!" The Saudi officer glared at him, as if questioning why a British national, particularly one of such low station, would have been told of the Stone's theft, let alone be involved in its investigation. "I know nothing of this matter."

First rule of spook work, Cas remembered, was that the best defense is always a good offense. So, he doubled down on his fake fit and ignored the order to maintain silence. "I suppose, then, *sir*, we will have to fulfill our contract with Binexport the hard way!"

"What contract?"

"Are you going to make me say it in front of all these people? You know very well of the incident about which I was sent here to, how shall I say, *address.*"

The officer hesitated, as if not knowing whether to acknowledge the implication of the Stone's theft, or continue to act uninformed of it. "I need some additional indication of your intent."

"You need *indication*, do you? Perhaps, if I announce my *indication* to all of these pilgrims present, that will suffice?"

The officer's eyes rounded with alarm. He called his junior officers around him, and for nearly a minute, they conferred in private whispers.

"I would ask you one question," Cas said, still hectoring the officer. "Would I have been granted such knowledge if I were not here on Royal Family business?"

"What knowledge?"

Cas motioned the officer back to him, away from the other guards. He whispered into the officer's ear. "I know what is behind that tent. Or should I say, what is *not* behind that tent."

Stunned, the Saudi officer blinked hard. "I have orders—"

"And I will have your name!" Cas shouted. "To report it to Yehia bin Laden, praise be upon him!" He waited until the name of one of the SBG founder's fifty-three sons—of whom thirteen were Saudi Binladen Group board members—sank in. "Then, I will report you directly to—"

The officer put his hand in Cas's face to signal *that* was enough.

"Imam Faisal!" Cas persisted, referring to one of Mecca's chief clerics.

"Cease your talking at once!" the exasperated officer shouted. "I will call in this request to the Ministry."

Cas was about to protest the necessity of that decision when he felt a tug on his coveralls. Bracing for an arrest, or worse, he glanced to his right and found Marly standing aside him, as if glued to his arm. She had the look of a canary that had just swallowed a cat. She nodded, almost imperceptibly, and then shot him a telling glance that was underscored by the faint beginnings of a smile.

Cas forced his eyes back into his sockets. He realized that, in the confusion of his shouting match with the Saudi officer, she had apparently slipped into the tent and harvested the scraping samples. Winking his admiration for her bold move, he returned his attention to the flummoxed officer and barked, "That'll be quite enough indeed! We will return tomorrow with the written authorization!" He threw an arm around Marly's shoulder in a fake gesture of comradeship and, pulling her away, warned the flummoxed officer, "You have not heard the last from us!"

The officer, baffled, watched the two construction workers stomp away.

Stifling grins with their backs turned, Cas and Marly glided off through the sea of oncoming worshippers and hurried for the nearest gate.

15

Shaaba Farms, Israel

Bridget Whelan lugged her suitcase up the metal steps of the drab *kibbutz* barracks and scanned the lodging sheets tacked to the announcements board. Exhausted from her flight and the teeth-rattling drive to the northeastern corner of this maddening country, she staggered down the hall and finally found the volunteer's room that she'd been assigned. The cell, no larger than a walk-in closet, was empty, and its cold cement floor reeked of manure and ammonia. Hebrew graffiti and mold-filled cracks latticed the puke-colored plaster walls. Were those bullet holes above the windowsill?

Too bonked to worry about random gunfire, she collapsed on the lower bed of a double bunk. The flimsy mattress was covered with a threadbare sheet that looked as if it had been once been used for some biblical prophet's burial shroud. She had been in Israel only twelve hours, but already she wished she were back home. She had bribed her mother to take care of the baby for *this*?

Given her boss's obsession with business appearances, she had been expecting to stay in a plush hotel like the King David in Jerusalem. But this wasteland—the locals called it northern Galilee—looked like a war zone set in the scrubbiest part of the Texas Panhandle. At a gas-station stop on the highway from Tel Aviv, a Moonie-eyed Pentecostal missionary from Alabama had given her the proselytizing treatment. Brainwashed into believing that every American was hot-to-trot for the Rapture, the boy had tried to impress her by bragging how Jesus had walked on water not far from here. What *really* impressed her, she had told him, was that Jesus had been smart enough to hightail it out of these miserable boondocks to look for more action in the big city, even if things didn't turn out so well.

Everyone in this neurotic country seemed pissed off or crazy. From the moment she walked into Ben Gurion International Airport—only to be welcomed by scowling soldiers armed with machine guns—she'd been drawing suspicious stares and mumbled whispers. That officious douchebag at Customs had treated her as if she were carrying in the bubonic plague, and some nut job standing next to her in Baggage Claim had started yelling curses at her about the carnal sins of Jezebel.

Apparently they'd never encountered a modern pagan goddess. They oughta take a look in the mirror if they wanted to see weird. The whole bunch of them could pass for gun-toting Amish. And up here, on the northern border of the Promised Land, the Orthodox settlers were the worst of the lot. These aloof Old Testament reenactors packed serious heat, even when they sat at the dinner table, and constantly looking toward the mountains to the west as if expecting a horde of locusts to cross the hills at any moment. They reminded her of those crazy militia creeps that hung around the bars in Lubbock.

And the farms? Ant colonies compared to the ranches in Texas. It was a miracle that anything grew on these scraggy hills, parched as they were from lack of rain and constantly overrun by tunneling Islamist suicide bombers. The Israelis accessorized their tractors with rifle racks and fitted their bulldozers with battering rams. Along the route into here, she had seen a few irrigated fields rowed with cabbage, sorghum and wheat, but she had noticed only a few herds of cattle, and those looked scrawny and swarmed with flies.

The land of milk and honey, my Canaanite goddess ass.

What was Cohanim thinking, coming out here, anyway? This was the last place on Earth she would have picked to develop genetically enhanced bovines. Hell's bells, these *kibbutzim* couldn't even afford to build a decent barn. And yes, she would have asked her boss about all of this, had he been with her. Instead, Cohanim had decided to ride in the ambulance that carried the frozen embryo from Tel Aviv, sending her here separately by hired car.

Her driver, a Palestinian student who attended engineering school on weekends, had jabbered non-stop during the entire six hours, explaining in broken English how the Shaaba Farms—as if she cared—sat in a triangle surrounded by Lebanon, Syria, and Israel. He had also told her that these fields had been fought over for so many years that even the residents now argued among themselves about their own nationality. The nearest town, Al Ghajar, had once been part of Syria before the Israelis occupied it. When the Israel Defense Forces finally agreed to withdraw in 2000, the United Nations left the town divided, half in Lebanon and half in Israeli-occupied Syria. Most residents in Al Ghajar were Alawites, a Syrian religious sect.

When she had asked the driver if this *kibbutz* was ever in danger, he told her with a smile not to worry, that Hezbollah—the Lebanese Muslim militia—fired its rockets over your head here, trying to reach the wealthy Israelis in the center of the country. It all sounded like a big splatter of cow pod, along the lines of the shit parade between the Mexicans in Ciudad Juárez and the Texans across the border in El Paso.

H ours later, stirring in the creaking bunk, Bridget forced open her sleep-caked eyes. She checked her watch. It was nearly nine in the evening. She hadn't eaten since lunch, so she decided to drag her Goth ass out of the bed and walk over to the dining hall to see if the kitchen was still serving.

She staggered from the room half-groggy and walked past the shelves of open mailboxes where letters were left. She noticed that her name had already been taped over one of the nooks. An envelope was inside. She pulled it out and found a message from Mr. Cohanim:

> *I have a dinner meeting with a client this evening in Al Ghajar. Going over the recombinant DNA data and financial arrangements. No need for you to attend. Get some sleep and we'll get to work on finding the surrogate cow candidate tomorrow.*

She shook her head in amazement. How did he do it? A sixty-year-old man who could fly halfway around the world and still be sharp enough without even a nap to discuss complex scientific stuff?

She walked out of the barracks and headed down the main drag. The dingy buildings in this kibbutz reminded her of a dirt-poor community college built in the early 1950s. One new office, though, sat apart from the others. She strode over to check it out and noticed the smell of fresh-set concrete and new paint. There was a sign on the door:

LIGHTGIVER TECHNOLOGIES LLC CATTLE LABORATORY.

Are you kidding me?

Cohanim must have ponied up some serious *shekels* to get a state-of-the-art facility built in this backwater. All so he could play God with a few cows? Man, the boss had to be really rolling in the dough.

She peered through the door's thick glass window. The interior looked downright spiffy. On the wall next to the entrance, a handprint security monitor had been installed. She wondered if Cohanim had already transferred the codes from the Dallas lab. Looking around first, she pressed her hand to the pad.

The door buzzed open. *Sweet!*

Inside, she found an immaculate, brand-spanking-new lab, a stainless-steel heaven. In the corner, some baggage lay opened. Cohanim, she realized, must have dropped off his gear before taking off for dinner. She opened the storage refrigerator. There it was … the Holy Grail.

Four Petri dishes, all marked with their percolating cultures.

She checked them out. The first container held the embryo generated from the DNA of the calf tooth and the rock minerals. She was still convinced that her boss's genetic-homeopathic idea was harebrained. But, hey, whatever paid the bills. Next to it sat the dish with the backup donor egg, just in case the first embryo didn't take and they had to start over. The other two dishes held the remaining DNA from the tooth and the extracts from the iron-rich rock. Hells bells, she hoped the blood of the cow they chose wouldn't react adversely to the embryo and flood antibodies into the recombinant DNA—

Oh, shit! The recombinant DNA data!

The boss had given her that binder to carry in her luggage. If he went to his meeting without it, he'd come off looking like a complete fool to the Israelis. And she'd catch the blame.

She rushed out of the lab and found the dining hall. Hurrying inside, she cornered one of the *kibbutz* students who was cleaning the tables, an Israeli boy crowned with shocks of wild black hair under a *yarmulke* and dressed in a patterned short-sleeved shirt that her grandfather might have worn. "Excuse me. Do you speak English?"

He curled a grin that, roughly translated, suggested there wasn't much social activity here and that he had just hit the jackpot with the new tail. "Yes, of course. Would you like me to show you around?"

She batted her thick black Elmira lashes to reel him in. "Actually, maybe later. But right now I need some information."

"Sure."

"How far is Al Ghajar from here?"

"No more than seven kilometers. I can take you on my scooter."

She did the math: That was about four miles, too far to walk, especially in a foreign land at night. "How many restaurants are there in the town?"

"Maybe five."

"If you were a businessman wanting to impress someone important, which restaurant would you choose?"

"Abu Kamal serves the best grilled lamb and *tabouleh* south of Damascus. The mayor owns it. All the fat cats around here go there to eat."

She debated the risk-reward ratio of accepting his offer to take her into town. Finally, she agreed. "Before we go, I need to get something from my room first."

Forty-five minutes later—and after a promise to go out with Scooter Boy on a date later in the week—Bridget finally convinced him to drop her in front of the restaurant. She wouldn't need him around to take her back. After she saved Cohanim's rich ass, the old curmudgeon would obviously feel obliged to buy her dinner and return her to the *kibbutz*. Besides, she didn't want to have to pay off the horny little toad with some suck-face, or worse.

The village of Al Ghajar looked to be about the size of Seminole or Portales, maybe two thousand souls tops. The restaurant was crowded, just as her new *kibbutz* friend had promised, but she didn't notice any women in the place. Huge platters of mouth-watering dishes that smelled like a spice bazaar sat on long trestles between decanters of wine. On divans in the corners, heavy-lidded men hovered over strange kettles and sucked on pipes attached to hoses.

She scanned the seats but didn't see Mr. Cohanim. That made sense. He was probably in one of the exclusive back rooms reserved for VIPs. Clutching the data binder, she opened the door and entered.

All eyes turned and stabbed at her.

The owner, bald as a cantaloupe and amply girthed, reacted to her appearance as if a swarm of rats had just invaded his establishment. He rushed over to her, evidently dismayed that an unescorted woman—especially an exotic one who didn't bother to cover her face and head—would dare to invade this male sanctuary, let alone wish to eat alone. "I am sorry, madam," he said with a hint of a French accent. "But we have no tables available this evening."

"I'm looking for a business colleague. Seth Cohanim's his name. He's an American."

The owner shook his head. "No Americans have been here tonight."

Damn. Her bad luck just kept pouring down in buckets. Sure, Mercury was retrograde, but come on. Cohanim *would* have to go and choose some obscure joint for his little rendezvous. "Where is the next closest restaurant?"

The owner led her outside, away from the disgusted customers. He pointed down a creepy street that was poorly lit and littered with trash. "The Alhambra is five blocks that way, then turn right. But it is not a safe place for a woman to go alone."

Shit an ancient Holy Land brick.

Could it get any worse? What was she going to do now?

She hadn't changed enough dollars at the airport to pay for a taxi back, even if she could find one around here willing to pick her up. She had no choice but to try the next restaurant down and hope Cohanim was there. She thanked the owner for his patriarchal bullshit and promised to write a scathing letter to Zagat's about the jerky that he was passing off as lamb.

As she hurried past the closed shops, she drew glares from the clusters of cigarette-puffing men who were loitering on the corners. Her heart was racing—and worse, she had to piss like a donkey. She wasn't about to squat over one of those holes like the women here had been forced to do since King David pulled off that stunning upset with his peashooter.

To ward off any lurking demons, she whispered every curse spell she could remember from Harry Potter. The sky seemed to be devoid of stars, and the moon was absent, too, so in the near-total blackness she could barely see where to put one foot in front of other. These cobblestones were chewing up her new Eccos like sandpaper. How many gagging new odors could assault her in one place—smoke, sewage, grilled meat, and human sweat? These old mud walls felt as if they were closing in on her. She could see the headlines on the CNN news ticker now: *Texas woman taken hostage. Terrorists threaten to decapitate her unless ransom is paid.* Yeah, right. Those bastards in Lubbock would probably take up a collection and send a telegram offering to pay double to keep her locked up over here.

She heard a flapping noise, and turned. Was somebody following her? She cocked her ear and tried to muffle her steps to better hear what was behind her. Did that restaurant owner say four blocks or five? She hid the data binder under her jacket. If she were mugged, she didn't want to lose her job, too. Feeling more and more uneasy, she decided to turn right at the next side street and prayed that this was the one.

In the distance, another sound rose and died ... was that a moan?

She froze. Several yards ahead, shadowy silhouettes—she couldn't make out how many—darted across the street. Hoping that they didn't see her, she veered over to a dingy apartment building and pressed her back against the dust-coated stone wall. She sucked in her stomach and straightened her spine to avoid standing out. She heard a man's voice ...

"She checks out as the perfect carrier. Every trait you requested."

"I want her younger than the last one," another man's voice drawled in reply.

Bridget grinned—*that* Texas twang she knew all too well. Cohanim and the client must have finished dinner and were now taking a stroll to discuss the surrogate cow for the embryo implant in the morning. Relieved, she rushed toward the men to greet her boss, but they turned a corner before she could reach them. When she caught up, they had disappeared into the tunneling darkness.

The street was empty.

Alleys and side streets all branched in different directions. She walked as fast as she could down one of the narrow wynds that was circumscribed and arched by towering old tenements. Above her, from the dozens of small apartments, she could hear muted conversations and pots clanging and televisions blaring Arab game shows. At last, the tight warren opened up to another cross street, and she turned the corner.

On the far curb, a neon sign flickered, revealing Cohanim and the other man in the light. They were dragging an unconscious girl toward an ambulance whose headlights had been turned off.

What are they doing?

Wait a minute. Wasn't that the ambulance that Cohanim had taken to transport the frozen embryo? Yeah, she could see the reflective lettering on the vehicle glow in the dim light: *Yeshiva Medical Transport*. She had seen that same sign at the airport pickup station.

Had her boss hit the girl by accident? She couldn't see any damage on the front fender or skid marks anywhere. The prone girl didn't even look bloodied or traumatized. If an accident *had* occurred, wouldn't the ambulance driver have its bubbles flashing? And wouldn't the villagers be out congregating to see what the commotion was all about?

She ducked back behind the corner, into the shadows, and tried to make sense of what she was witnessing. She drew a deep breath and forced herself to inch her eyes around the wall again. She fought a rising tide of paranoia.

The rear door of the ambulance opened.

Cohanim and the other man lifted the girl to a gurney inside.

For a fleeting moment, she saw the victim's face from a distance, illuminated by the overhead light from the open door. The unconscious girl looked to be perhaps thirteen or fourteen years old, stunningly beautiful, with long black hair and perfect olive skin. Her eyes were closed, but her head trembled slightly, as if she were in the throes of a seizure. The man with Cohanim leaned over the girl and dropped a syringe into a medical bag under the gurney. He secured her with two straps, then, realizing that the light was on, clicked the button. The interior snapped into darkness.

Cohanim slowly closed the ambulance door, pulling its lock gently to avoid making a noise. He looked up and down the street and, reassured that no one had seen him, gave a thumbs-up signal to the driver. He patted the rear door as the ambulance began to creep down the street with its headlights still off, until it disappeared into the night. Alone now in the street, he lit a cigar and took several long, rewarding puffs.

Bridget blinked hard. She had never seen him smoke.

Who is this guy, anyway?

She saw him look up at the apartment building, as if studying the address number engraved into the lintel over the door. She squinted to see what he was reading. The lettering was in Arabic; all those squiggly flourishes and dots and slashes looked the same to her. She searched for anything that could serve as a landmark to help her remember this place. The window on the third floor had a flag hanging from its balcony: two red bars surrounding a white bar, with a green tree in the middle. Was that a country? Maybe it was the insignia for a soccer team.

Third floor. Green-and-white flag. She burned that image into her mind's eye.

Cohanim began walking down the street, straight toward her. She pressed herself into a cranny behind a water pipe and prayed to Demeter that her boss wouldn't see her here in the shadows. He walked past briskly, so close to her that she could have touched him.

When he was a block away, she released her breath and dropped her hands to her shaking knees.

16

Paris, France

Wearing safety goggles, Cas looked like an irradiated fly as he leaned over Marly's shoulder and watched her prepare the Kaaba shavings for testing in a Sorbonne University laboratory.

She poured a highly flammable chemical over the mineral residue in a tube and lifted it to the light to examine. The liquid sizzled. She carefully slid the tube into an electrical centrifuge, locked down the cover, and shimmied the contents like a paint can in a hardware store mixer.

"How long until we know?" he asked her.

She nudged his chin back with her shoulder to ease his breath off her neck. "It takes two minutes for the emulsifier to break down the compounds. Then, another ten minutes to settle. We'll have the test results in less time than it takes you to embarrass yourself or piss somebody off."

He had grown used to her pouting coldness, so her newfound willingness to respond with more than a few clipped words threw him, but only for a moment. He checked his watch: almost noon, the prime café hour. It was just his luck that the only testing lab available on short notice happened to be in Paris. He was still a little ragged from the overnight flight from Dubai, but what better time to make his move? "I know a great little bistro in the Marais," he said, risking another try to win her over. "I'll buy lunch."

"Are you actually asking me out on a date?"

"That depends."

"On what?"

"Your answer."

Marly slid off her goggles and returned them to the cabinet. The more time she spent around this man, the stranger he seemed. Here he was hitting on her while the reunion with his long-lost son hung in the balance with these test results. She was starting to suspect that his crass sense of humor and inappropriate comments were just unconscious defenses against the pain of dealing with his sadness and grief. Maybe spooks like him had no choice but to hide behind such personality masks to survive. Still, as oddly charming as he sometimes came across, she wasn't about to get romantically involved with a guy so broken emotionally. She retreated into a formal tone. "I think it's best that we keep our relationship professional. I wouldn't want you to get the idea that my fee is negotiable."

Cas's soufflé of seduction deflated before it had a chance to set. "You call what we've been doing *professional*?"

She kept edged way from him, but he just kept moving closer. Finally, she stopped and turned to confront him. "Look, I don't date older men."

He winced. "Yowze."

"Besides, you're California fusion with guacamole for brains. And I'm Upper West Side Barney Greengrass lox-and-bagels. That's a recipe for indigestion."

The timer went off on the centrifuge.

She sighed in relief, thankful for being saved by the bell.

"Okay, your loss." Cas shrugged off what would have been humiliation for mere mortals. "Just remember. Guacamole can be tasty *and* healthy. And, I swear to god, avocados are an aphrodisiac. The Aztecs called the tree a 'testicle tree,' soooo …"

"You all really *do* think with your dicks, don't you?"

He was surprised again, this time by her coarseness. Maybe he *was* getting to her.

When the test tube had been sufficiently shaken, she pulled it from the rack and stared at its murky contents. "I'm betting we have a positive here."

"What are you looking for exactly?"

"Usually I have the rock itself to examine," she said. "This protocol is a little unorthodox. I have a list I check off. First, does the sample have a black exterior coating that's extremely thin? If so, that's a sign of melting under extreme heat when it passes through the Earth's atmosphere."

"That would explain why the Kaaba Stone is white inside and black outside."

"Could be. Or maybe somebody painted it black to fool somebody. What shape was the Stone supposed to have been in?"

"Seven fragments, held together with some kind of serious cement," he said. "The largest fragment of the original Stone was described as roundish."

Marly brightened. "That sounds promising, then. The pressure on falling meteorites tends to smooth their curvature. How about the texture?"

"Looked like the fragments had bubbles, maybe. At least at one time."

Marly's eyes flashed with rising anticipation. "Spongy. Another good sign."

"I bet you could make a handy little profit selling these on the side, huh?"

"Only if you know what you're doing," she said. "There's a whole meteorite-treasure underworld out there. You have to have contacts who will let you know when one is seen shooting across the sky. Most of them burn up in entry, but about five hundred a year make it to the ground."

"How large are they, usually?"

"Anywhere from the size of a pea to a medicine ball. Most are too small to find. Of those five hundred, half a dozen will be recovered in any given year and make it to market."

"How many hunters are looking for them?"

"Hard to say. Thousands, probably. The odds aren't very good, though. Most of the meteorite prospectors hover around the best impact areas, like Barringer Crater in Arizona and Odessa Crater in Texas. For every one found, you can usually plan on logging in about a hundred hours of searching."

Cas shook his head. "These things must be more valuable than gold."

"The going rate is one-fifty an ounce."

"Whew. For the same jack, you can get some investment-grade silver—or middling weed."

That made Marly laugh. She glanced at the clock on the wall with a mixture of anticipation and trepidation. "Fingers crossed."

Cas braced for the results. "Hey, it's only two million dollars and my son's release from prison. No big deal."

Marly took a deep breath as she printed out the page with the compound results. She scanned the lines of data, giving no hint of a reaction. Finally, she said, "Widmanstatten pattern."

"*Gesundheit,*" Cas joked, leaning closer to her while waiting for an explanation. He tapped her on the shoulder. "Hello? Remember, you're dealing with guacamole brains here."

Marly seemed to be talking to herself. "A series of bands in geometric shapes. Created by the merging of two different iron-nickel minerals formed during slow cooling. Only two percent of all extraterrestrial stones have this composition. It's a pallisite. Very rare."

"So our God Stone *is* from space. Just as the Muslims believe."

She looked more confused than triumphant. "Yes, but that's not all. There's an unusual level of hydrogen and crystallization here, too. All meteorites have crystallization, but this level is off the charts."

"I was afraid of that," Cas said lightly, as if he had any idea what she meant.

"It's the same level of hydrogen found in black diamonds."

His mouth dropped a couple notches. "You're saying that our missing rock once held a diamond?"

"If this is right, it makes the Hope Diamond look like a Cracker Jacks toy."

Cas paced the lab, trying to make sense of the findings. "Y'know, Doc, you might want to show a little more excitement. We're talking major paydirt here, and you *are* a step closer to retirement, after all." When she didn't react to his gibe, he put his hands on her shoulders and gently turned her to face him. "What's wrong?"

She broke off from her examination of the results. "It's probably nothing. This data also shows an unusually high level of carbon and sugar phosphate. It's odd for those elements to survive, especially given the extreme temperatures that a meteorite endures to land here."

"Does that have anything to do with the price of popcorn in Bollywood?"

She shook her head. "I guess not."

"Then, hello, let's focus here."

She took off her lab coat and hung it on a peg. "All right, your Kaaba Stone is a meteorite, just as that CrossArrow creep said it was. Jump for joy. But how does any of this help us figure out where the Stone is *now*? And how does it help us get it back?"

"Pack up that cheat sheet of yours. We gotta get to Gare du Nord pronto."

"Where are we going now?" she asked.

Cas grinned as he played with a Bunsen burner, turning the gas up and down. "To pay a visit to an old flame."

T hree hours later, a statuesque Swedish woman sat on a bench outside the INTERPOL headquarters in Brussels and opened her lunch sack. She took a whiff of the mussels and *frites*, savoring their aroma, and dug in for one of the deep-fried potatoes with mayonnaise. She closed her eyes, having waited all day for this orgasmic moment, and slowly brought the heavenly bite to her lips—

She chomped on air.

Behind her, she heard the sound of someone chewing. She opened her eyes and looked over her shoulder. Startled, she dropped her sack. The mussels and *frites* scattered across the ground at her feet.

Cas, grinning like a squirrel, had snuck up behind her and covertly stolen one of her fries like a magician. Now he was now munching her potato slice.

"You *shitskevel!*"

"Always did love the way 'shithead' sounds in Swedish," Cas said. "Especially coming from one sweet Swede." He kept chewing and blasted a huge smile at her. "I see you still have a weakness for *haute* cuisine. Y'know, Silla, I don't see how you can eat fried crap like that and still be so freakin' sexy."

She leapt from the bench and tried to salvage what the pigeons hadn't taken of her lunch. "What are you doing here?"

"I couldn't get you out of my mind."

She threw the grease-pocked sack at him. "Lying bastard! I'm still paying off that bill you ran up on my credit card in Rome!"

"Matter of fact," he said, "that's why I was in the neighborhood, to tell you that I'll finally be able to pay you back."

The woman saw Marly standing several feet behind Cas, watching their encounter. "Who's *that*? Another one of those high-priced whores I bought for you?"

Cas motioned Marly over. "Dr. Marly McKinney, meet Silla Agardh."

Marly offered her hand to the woman as if testing a pit bull. "You have my deepest sympathy for the misfortune of knowing this jackass."

Silla rolled her eyes. "When I knew this lout, the only doctor he ever consulted was the one who gave him his monthly sulfur injections."

"Closure." Cas reached for an embrace. "You need closure, Silla. And I'm here to help you find it."

Silla shoved his arm from her shoulder. "What do you want?"

Cas looked around to make sure no *gendarmes* were in the park. "Are you still working for the INTERPOL's Satellite Explosives Tracking Network?"

The beautiful Swede shot a glance of suspicion at Marly. She pulled Cas aside and hissed to his ear, "I told you never to mention my work."

"Oops." Cas snapped his finger. "That would be Swedish for, 'My bad.'"

Silla shook her head at him in disgust, as if recoiling from a panhandler. "Nobody's hiring here." She crossed her arms. "Besides, with your background of screwups, I couldn't find enough strings to pull even if I thought anyone around this place would give you a job."

"I'm not interested in sitting in a cubicle going blind while watching circles disappear on a radar screen." Cas paused to wait for an elderly couple to walk past, then he jumped to the point. "Have your infrared capabilities reached the chemical level yet?"

Silla stiffened with alarm. "Where did you hear about that?"

"Come on. Remember what I used to do?"

Silla turned so that Marly wouldn't be able to overhear them. "Since January, we've been tracking weapons transfers using multispectral thermal imaging."

"By telescope?"

Silla surrendered an uncertain nod, not sure why he wanted to know. "We purchased the technology from Los Alamos last year. Images of Earth are collected round the clock on fifteen spectral bands. Visible to long-range infrared."

"What's the resolution?" Cas asked.

"These lenses are the strongest in the world," Silla said. "They'll take it down to fifteen pixels."

Cas whistled. "Impressive. Can you set the spectral bands to pick up specific chemical compositions?"

She dropped her voice even lower. "What in God's name are you up to now?"

Cas's eyes watered, he couldn't help it. "My son is alive."

Stunned, Silla drew closer. "I thought the Saudis had ... you know."

"So did I, until this week." Cas sat on the park bench, momentarily ignoring Marly. The loss of his family in Saudi Arabia had been common knowledge in the intelligence community, so he wasn't surprised that Silla had heard about it. "Listen, I know I left you in the lurch. I'm sorry for that. But I have one chance to get him back. I can't do it without your help."

Silla glanced over her shoulder at a door in the rear of the police headquarters. After a hesitation, she relented. "Meet me over there at midnight."

Inside an office in the INTERPOL building, Cas and Marly stared at a wall-length screen while Silla punched in the chemical components from their test analysis on the Black Stone shavings. The high-definition monitor showed the world splayed out on a two-dimensional grid. Blips of various colors blinked on and off, indicating the location of nuclear and thermal weapons.

Silla asked Cas, "You can't tell me what continent your meteorite is on?"

He shook his head. "I don't even know if the damned thing's still on Earth. How long does it take for this satellite to make a complete pass around our the globe and send back the images?"

"Forty-eight hours," Silla said. "And another week to crunch the numbers."

Cas slumped, defeated. "I don't have that kind of time."

Silla pondered his need for immediate results. "Look, I may be out of line here. But with all of these questions you've been asking about this Muslim stone and meteorites, I'm guessing Islamist radicals stole it."

Cas realized that he'd been a little too careless around her with his whispered asides to Marly. He told Silla, "You would have made a great field agent."

Silla beamed at the compliment. "The reason I'm asking, well ... if they've already stolen these meteorite fragments, they're probably guarding them all in one place, right?"

Cas looked at Marly, assessing her reaction to that possibility. "Maybe."

Silla nodded knowingly, as if sensing his concern that she might blab about their mission to her superiors. "My bringing you into this facility without clearance could land me ten years in prison. Not to mention a conspiracy charge for whatever you've got in mind."

"Right," Cas said. "Mum's obviously the word, then. All around."

With that understanding established, Silla went on to explain the reason for her question. "We keep the images sent from the satellite on the mainframe for a week. I can filter results from those in two hours. If you could narrow *any* location down at all, then I could run the program even quicker."

"Can you isolate cities?" Marly asked her.

"Sure. That would trim the analysis time a hundredfold. We've got thirty minutes before the late-night shift comes in."

Marly turned to Cas. "Don't these *jihadis* feel more comfortable hiding in highly populated areas where they can melt into the background?"

Cas considered her theory, but cautioned, "Not always. Bin Laden preferred cave luxury in Bora Bora, remember?

"Yeah," Marly said, "but then he moved to that compound in Abbottabad."

Cas nodded, conceding she might have had a point. "If this radical Saudi tribe plans to negotiate a downfall of the regime in exchange for the Stone, they're likely holed up someplace where they can't be ambushed in the open when the exchange is arranged." He sent Silla to the task with a wink of confidence. "Karachi, Cairo, Delhi—anywhere with too damn many people. Human shields. Crunch the filter down to cities of a hundred thousand and more."

Silla turned to Marly for the additional data. "The more specific, the better."

Checking her sheet again, Marly read off the rest of the test results that she had earlier thought were extraneous. "Two percent silicate. Iron density of four-point-seven-six grams per cubic centimeter. Nickel point-zero-six percent."

"Anything else of significance?" Silla asked.

"Traces of phosphate and carbon." Cas added, "And look for seven fragments."

"Oh, sure," Silla huffed. "And would you like to see the bevels of their edges?"

Cas watched over Silla's shoulder as she entered the new data points. When she finished, the three of them turned toward the screen to see the blips matching the entries flash onto the screen.

"How many places so far?" he asked.

Silla ran a breakout of the list from the printer. "Twenty-two cities."

His jaw dropped. "That many?"

Silla read them off. "Singapore. Antalya. Naples. Havana. Ulan Bator."

"Gee, what a coincidence," Cas quipped at Marly. "That sounds a lot like our honeymoon itinerary."

Refusing to grace that with a response, Marly walked closer to the wall screen and pointed to one of the blinking dots. "Is *that* one in the United States?"

Cas looked up from the printout. "Dallas? Well, thanks for small blessings. At least we can cross one off the list."

"I'm sorry I can't get it more specific," Silla said. "Several of these may be false positives. And *that* could be for any number of reasons. Museum samples. Smelting furnaces. Chemical factories. The satellite also may be seeing other meteorites out there with the same composition."

Marly studied the screen. "That's odd. Not one hit in the Middle East."

Cas shrugged off her observation. "*Jihadis* know better than to keep it within reach of the Saudi security apparatus."

Silla glanced over at another monitor that showed a closed-circuit camera angle on the hallway leading into the lab. On its screen, the guard was talking to his replacement. She signaled for Cas and Marly to lower their voices. "We don't have much time left."

Cas began packing up their gear and heading for the door with Silla, but Marly hung back, intrigued by the blinking dots on the wall screen.

Cas tapped on his watch. "Uh, you coming?"

Walking closer to the screen, Marly asked Silla, "Can your chemical sensors on the telescope zoom in on the relative ratios of phosphate and carbon in the targets?"

Silla stopped at the door. "Yes, but why?"

"Just a hunch," Marly said. "Let's try it at three parts deoxyribose and five parts carbon. See if any of these cities filter out."

Silla hurried back to the computer and punched in the new data.

Moments later, all of the blips on the screen went out—except for one.

Cas stared at Marly, wondering what ace she had pulled from her sleeve.

Silla zoomed in on the screen's map until the overhead image sharpened into focus. The result looked like the rear parking lot of an industrial area. She called up the address from the coordinates and printed it out.

Cas took the sheet from her and read the address of the filtered location.

He grinned at Marly, amazed at her brilliance. But his elation was quickly tempered by the realization that even if the stolen Stone fragments *were* sitting in some industrial park in Dallas, the clock would nearly run out before they could get there. In less than forty-eight hours, the Hajj pilgrimage would begin, and the Saudis would have no choice but to remove the big black tent that—for a terrifying, all-too-brief moment, at least—was keeping the world from exploding.

17

Northern Galilee, Israel

Bridget awoke the next morning feeling as if she'd been run over by an Israeli tank. The night before, after witnessing Cohanim loading the girl into the ambulance, she had walked the four miles back to the *kibbutz* alone, too frightened to hitch a ride. She had barely slept the few remaining hours until daylight, going over and over in her mind the possible reasons why her boss would be on the dangerous back streets of Al Ghajar, near one of the most volatile borders in the world.

Was Cohanim some flamboyant American cowboy who really should be on a wanted poster for running guns to the Middle East? What had he done to that poor girl in the ambulance? And who was this big-shot client that he was supposed to have been wining and dining? Occam's razor would demand a simple and innocent explanation for what she had seen. After all, she hadn't felt normal since her arrival yesterday. Suddenly she had an idea: she could use the excuse of the data binder he left behind to subtly ask him about his meeting.

Speaking of the binder, where had she left it?

The last thing she needed was another screw-up on her first day of work in the *kibbutz* laboratory. She looked around her room, trying to recall where she had thrown it after stumbling back in that morning. Had she dropped it in her frantic rush into the dormitory? No, she clearly remembered tossing it on the floor with her clothes. She glanced at the window. The pane had been lifted an inch from the sill. She was sure she had locked it before leaving last night.

A chill crawled down her spine. Had somebody been in her room?

What time was it, anyway? She looked at her watch: 9:30 a.m. already. *Shit … I'm a half-hour late.* She threw on a blouse and her blue jeans—sure, Cohanim would throw a fit about those, but this place was a farm, after all— and she slipped into her shoes. She ran a brush through her hair while rushing for the door.

A FedEx envelope had been shoved through the crack.

She stared at it. Did everybody around here communicate by written messages? She opened it and found a page of stationery with the Lightgiver Technologies LLC letterhead:

Dear Ms. Whelan,

Due to the unforeseeable downturn in the extremely competitive cattle-breeding business, the company has been forced to make significant cutbacks in its fourth-quarter budget. Regrettably, these vagaries in the global economy have given us no choice but to terminate your employment, effective immediately.

The confidentiality agreement you signed remains in effect.

We have facilitated this transition for you by exchanging your return ticket for a flight leaving for Dallas this evening from Tel Aviv. An attendant at the United Airlines terminal will have your reissued ticket on your arrival. We have also arranged for a hired car to transport you to the airport, courtesy of the company.

We thank you for your service to Lightgiver.

Sincerely, Burton Smalley,

General Counsel, Lightgiver Technologies LLC

She felt sick to her stomach. Why had Cohanim dragged her all the way across the world to this hellhole if he was just going to cut her loose after a day? The asshole wasn't even giving her a severance check! If he thought she was going to take this like a meek little Texas belle, he had another think coming.

She yanked open the door and marched outside, shielding her eyes from the blast of sunlight. On the dusty dirt road below the barracks, a black sedan sat waiting with its engine running. A man in a dark suit who looked like he could play for the Cowboys stood waiting at the rear passenger door with his hands folded. She walked up to him and demanded, "Where's Cohanim?"

The chauffeur didn't twitch a muscle. "Mr. Cohanim is away on business."

She was about to tell the guy about their boss's nocturnal fetishes with the local girls, but she realized that might not be the best choice at the moment.

"We should be starting for Tel Aviv," he said coldly.

"This change in plans caught me a little off guard. I haven't even packed."

"Make it quick," the driver warned.

Shaken, she retreated to her room and closed the door. Her mind was racing. What was really going on here? She needed something to hold over these jerks when she returned to Texas, something that would force them to cough up some serious walking-away money.

The DNA data.

Where *was* that binder, anyway? Maybe Cohanim had ordered one of his goons to snatch it from her room. Of course! That's *exactly* what happened. He didn't want her taking a match to the binder, figuring she'd throw a hissy. She could think of only one place around here where they would take documents for safekeeping. She sidled up to the window and checked on the sedan thug. He looked as if he was getting a little antsy. How was she going to get around him?

She opened her wallet, checking to see if it was still there. *Oh, yeah.*

She tiptoed into the hallway and settled into the corner, near the communal pay phone. She dropped a couple of *shekels* into the slot and dialed the number that her young admirer on the scooter had given her last night. "Moshe? Hi, it's Bridget. Yeah, I made it back. Thanks for the ride. ... Hey, I was wondering if you wanted to do something together ... like right now ... Listen, I got a problem that I need your help with first. There's an older guy with the company that I work for who's got a little thing for me. ... Yeah, he won't leave me alone. In fact, he's outside the building right now, all dressed up and wanting to take me for a ride. If he were to have, say, a couple flat tires or perhaps a missing alternator, I think we could ditch him."

Smiling as she hung up, she snuck down the steps and positioned herself just outside the back door of the barracks, where she could watch Moshe deal with the sedan driver.

About a minute later, a couple of rifle shots rang out.

She jumped a foot, never dreaming that Scooter Boy would actually fire a weapon. Hiding behind the corner, she saw the driver duck behind the car and drew his pistol, scanning the hills for the source of the shots. Two of the sedan's tires hissed and went flat. The driver looked at the ruined radials and cursed.

Moshe strolled out of the mess hall, whistling with his hands in his dungarees.

The sedan driver, about to blow a gasket, yelled at him. "Did you hear that?"

Moshe looked around. "Hear what?"

"That gunfire, dumb ass!"

Moshe shrugged. "Oh, that happens all the time. The Arabs on those heights over there like to use us for target practice. You get used to snipers after a while. They've got crappy aim."

Exasperated, the driver shook his head as he examined the ripped tires. "Is there a petrol station or garage around here?"

"In town," Moshe said. "You'll have to drive to it. They don't tow."

The driver kicked the wheel rim, jamming his toe. He cursed as he pulled his money clip from his pocket and peeled off a couple of bills. "Listen, a strange-looking piece of American tail happens to be sitting in one of those rooms up there. Keep an eye on her for me until I get back."

"Sure thing," Moshe said, stuffing the cash into his pocket.

When the driver rumbled away on two ruined tires, Bridget ran out of the barracks and gave Moshe a long, wet kiss in reward. "You're my hero!"

Moshe's grin split his face. "What do you want to do? Maybe go to the cinema?" He winked. "Or maybe …" His eyes flashed a lascivious twinkle.

She batted her Goth lashes at him. "I want to show you where I work."

He looked a little disappointed, but quickly got over it. "Okay."

She looked down both ends of the main road through the *kibbutz*, to be sure that Cohanim was nowhere around. Then, she grabbed Moshe's hand and ran toward the new laboratory. At the door, she took a deep breath and placed her palm against the square security monitor. Nothing. Damn, she'd been afraid of that. Cohanim had already removed her handprint from the security pad. She turned, dejected, resigned to packing up and leaving without a fight.

Moshe caught her hand to delay her. "I helped my father pour the foundation for this building."

"That's real interesting, but right now—"

"There's a furnace air duct in the back." He led her around the building and removed an iron grate over a round hole that looked no wider than three feet in diameter.

"We can't get through *that*," she protested.

"Here in Israel, tunnel-crawling is an Olympic sport. And you don't even need to be Hamas." Before she could stop him, he squeezed in feet first and wiggled down. "Meet me in the front."

She replaced the grate over the hole and ran around the building to the front door again. She kept checking her watch, fearful that the chauffeur from Hell would reappear at any moment. Suddenly, the door popped open.

Moshe stood waiting for her inside with a big grin.

She planted another juicy smooch on his lips as they walked around the laboratory. She opened shelves and drawers to search for the binder. Nothing. She was about to give up when she saw a manila folder.

The tab was marked: *Immaculate Deceptio.*

Was that Latin, or some kind of Cohanim-pidgin-English? Intrigued, she opened the folder and found several pages that contained what appeared to be genome structuring. She scanned down the columns, and realized that it was probably just more results from the cattle being tested here as candidates for the embryo surrogate. She started to close the folder when something odd caught her eye.

Moshe looked over her shoulder. "You understand this stuff?"

"I get paid to understand it," she said, shaking her head. "But every day that goes by on this job, I understand less and less of it."

"What's wrong?" he asked.

"This protein reading is too high for cattle. It's more in line with human RNA protein."

"Maybe we have some very smart and muscular cattle here."

She stared at the data, thunderstruck. She had heard a rumor that scientists at Newcastle University in Britain recently fused human DNA with cow eggs for stem-cell research. Was Cohanim also working on some kind of human-bovine hybrid embryo? Human eggs were in very short supply. And finding women willing to submit to surgery to carry an embryo to term was expensive and time-consuming. Never mind that many bioethicists had criticized this new technique for blurring the distinction between humans and lower forms of animals. Could this explain why Cohanim was being so secretive? If his company *was* involved with hybrid cow-human cloning, the bovine DNA in the cytoplasm of the cow's egg would have been stripped out, allowing the human DNA to use the egg as a kind of nurturing shell or container.

She was no lawyer, but she figured that had to be illegal.

She hurried over to the storage refrigerator and opened it. The fertilized embryo and the backup egg brought from Dallas were still in their Petri dishes. She put on a pair of gloves and carefully removed the culture with the embryo that was scheduled for implant once the donor cow was found. She opened a testing syringe and drew a sample from the cytoplasm around the egg. Full DNA tests usually required at least a week, but she was interested in only one aspect: the level of protein. She could determine that with a quick amino acid smear test.

She squeezed a couple of drops of the cytoplasm on a litmus stick. While waiting to see if it would change color, she located the compartment in the refrigerator that held the dozens of DNA samples taken from cows on the *kibbutz*. She drew a sample from one of the cow cytoplasm dishes and dropped it onto a second stick.

Two minutes later, she stood staring at the two test sticks, side by side, in the light. The one stained with the Dallas embryo cytoplasm had turned darker.

"Are you okay?" Moshe asked her.

She required another moment to take in what she'd just discovered. "I can't tell you why, but I'm going to need more time in here. Do you think you could keep that guy with the car delayed another hour in the village?"

Moshe kissed her again and then rushed through the door, off on the next assignment from his new American girlfriend with the dark-shaded eyes.

18

Dallas, Texas

Running on fumes from thirty-six hours without sleep, Cas wheeled their rental car out of the Dallas-Fort Worth Airport and sped down the freeway toward the Lone Star Industrial Park in west Dallas. He really needed a hot shower and some deep REM shut-eye, but he couldn't afford to let the thermal satellite intel on the possible hiding place for the Stone go stale. As the exits flew by, he turned to Marly and asked, "What was the address of those coordinates again?"

She consulted the directions from Google Maps that his old girlfriend had printed out for them in Brussels. "7589 Levinson Hills Drive."

Five miles east of Irving, Cas turned off into a seedy section of the sprawling urban mess and drove down a street lined with rundown convenience stores, iron-barred pawnshops, and gas stations with bulletproof pay windows.

Kicked back in the passenger seat, Marly checked the map again. "This area isn't on our route."

"Right, uh ... I ran out of toothpaste."

"Oh, for god's sake, I've got practically a full tube."

Punch-drunk, Cas peered over the wheel as he crept along and studied the forest of drab buildings, many of them without signs. Finally, he found what he was looking for and turned into a lot with cracks sprouting weeds high enough to bale for hay. He parked in front of a two-story adobe building whose windows were latticed with tie rods and wire meshing and cracked open his door. "Stay inside. And keep the doors locked."

He bolted before she could demand an explanation. Climbing a decaying porch, he entered what looked like a junkyard shack that could have been featured on an episode of *Hoarders*.

A few minutes later, he came out carrying a large paper sack and a used metal detector—vintage maybe 1970—that looked like the handle of a vacuum cleaner attached to a white oval disk and hooked with wires.

Marly flipped open the locks, and he slid into the driver's seat. He squealed off, tracked by the suspicious glares of the scattered loiterers.

When they were back out on the freeway, Marly finally felt safe enough to peek inside the sack that he had placed between them. Her eyes bugged as she pulled out one of two Browning pistols. In the bottom of the sack were five boxes of rounds. "What do you plan on doing with *these*? Saunter on in with both guns blazing like Wyatt Earp at the OK Corral?"

He rubbed his bloodshot eyes. "You've been watching too many Westerns. Wyatt Earp shot the bad guys in the back before they even knew he was coming at them."

Marly dropped the pistol back into the sack, shivering with disgust. After the incident at Abu Dhabi, if anyone had told her she would never see another gun, she would have fallen to her knees in gratitude. "You can just stroll into a place like that dump we just left and buy a firearm as easily as you can pick up a Big Mac from a drive-thru?"

"Down here, darlin', we heart our Second *Amen*-de-ment."

"Isn't this a little overkill? We're just going to check out a few rock fragments. Aren't we? I mean it's not like *narcotraficantes* are going to be staked out *here* to protect a shipment of coke."

"First rule of covert work," he said. "Always prepare for the worst. Al Qaeda has had sleeper cells in this country for years. For all we know, our Saudi friends may have sent the Stone over here to their blood brothers for safekeeping. The last place anyone would think *jihadis* would keep the relic is deep in the heart of Texas."

Marly rolled her eyes as she looked around at the junkies and homeless on the street corners. "I think I'd feel safer in Saudi Arabia."

Cas reached over and pulled one of the pistols from the sack and checked its safety. Satisfied, he pushed the weapon into her hand. "Brownings are lock-breeched and carry a kick. You should practice with it and get used to loading it. Not as much fun as an Uzi, but you'll manage."

She reluctantly took the gun and practiced cocking the trigger, making a series of ominous clicks. She looked at the bullets in the sack and felt a wave of nausea. "You hired me to help you find the meteorite. I got you the location. My job is finished. Write me the check, and I'm out of here."

Cas chuckled at her naiveté. "I've got three hundred bucks in my bank account. So, a wire's not going to work."

Marly's face reddened. "You lied to me!" She gripped the gun tighter.

"A slight breakdown in communication. Happens all the time in my business. You'll get your hundred grand when I deliver the Stone to the Saudis and they pay me. That's how it works in the world of black holes, construction jobs, and off-the-books ops." He reached to the backseat and pulled the metal detector onto her lap. "Now, make yourself useful and fine-tune the settings on this bad boy. Set it for high concentrations of iron and magnetism."

Marly cursed under her breath. Why had she allowed herself to be drawn into this guy's insanity? She could see all too clearly now how this was playing out. Before being snatched away from New York, she had sent a high-priority email to her supervisor asking for an unpaid leave of absence for emergency personal reasons. She was going to forfeit a month's salary, and now this grifter was welching on his promise to pay. Before the year was out, she'd be standing in line at the Riverside Church soup kitchen and dragging her bags of rocks down Broadway in a shopping cart.

Cas pulled off the freeway and drove into a maze of streets that meandered through an industrial park. The hundreds of offices and warehouse buildings all looked the same. Seeing the sign for Littlefield, he slowed down and stopped at the curb. "The seven hundreds are the next block down."

"Aren't you going to call for back up?"

"And just who would I call? Chuck Norris and the Texas Rangers?" He flipped open the Browning's chamber and loaded it with several rounds. He handed her the weapon and mocked a phone call, holding an imaginary receiver to his ear. "Captain McKinney, cover me."

"This isn't funny!"

Cas flipped through several fake business cards in his wallet and finally found the one he was looking for. His voice changed to a west Texas drawl as he donned a pair of thick-framed glasses and shook her hand. "Howdy, ma'am. I'm Hank Beekin, regional salesman for the Kenert Paper Company out of Beaukiss. I'm here for a sales call, but apparently I came to the wrong office. Happens all the time to me. Sorry for the intrusion."

"I'm kind of hoping you take a bullet. Might knock some sense into you."

Cas studied his target down the street, as if looking for signs of life. "Waal, that's downright unfriendly of you, missy."

"Meanwhile, I'm just supposed to sit hear and listen for gunfire?"

"Here's the drill. Give me ten minutes to case the joint. If I'm not back by then, get the hell out of here." He looked at his watch. "Ten after two, on the dot. Ten minutes. Not nine minutes, not eleven minutes. *Comprende, girlfriendo?*"

"I'm not your girlfriendo, or any other endo."

"That's just an affectionate Mexican term."

"For what?"

"Bi-otch."

She thought about using one of those bullets in the sack as a suppository for him. "And if you're not back? I'm just supposed to leave?"

Receiving only a shrug, she nodded uncertainly, hoping in some small way that he wouldn't return. Then, an ominous, even lethal, foreboding shot through her as Cas got out of the car and walked toward the office across the street. She watched him knock on the door and shift from side to side.

Apparently, nobody was going to answer.

Cas looked around the corner.

In a flash, he disappeared down a side alley.

Marly glanced at her watch. Eight minutes.

She heard steps behind the car, and ducked. Waiting but hearing nothing, she slowly peeked over the seat. A man in sunglasses and a business suit was walking toward the trunk.

Damn. She slid her hand into the paper sack and fingered the gun's safety. What if the *jihadis* had been watching them all along from the rooftops or alleys, keeping an eye out for anyone who approached? She might be in their crosshairs right now. This place freaked her out, looking as it did like a modern-day ghost town with steel and glass instead of tombstones and swinging saloon doors. Now that she thought about it, Cas never did explain why a bunch of Saudi dissidents would hide themselves in a Texas business park.

The man in sunglasses walked past her window without seeing her. He was heading for the office where Cas had just been standing.

Shit!

Had the thieves sent a scout to see if Cas positioned someone for backup? She had to come up with a contingency plan fast, or Cas was a dead man. As much as she wanted to just get the hell out of here, she couldn't just leave him. She looked at her watch, but her hand was shaking so furiously that she had to steady it with her other hand to read the time.

Two minutes left.

She looked up over the seat again. Where had the man in sunglasses gone?

Shit squared!

He must have darted into the alley while she wasn't looking.

Holy mother of Shitsville.

Those bastards would carve up Cas like *gyros* lamb. Then, she realized they wouldn't stop until they got her, too. She couldn't just sit here and wait. She loaded the Browning, slid it under her sweater, and leapt from the car. Hopping from shrub to shrub, she stalked the nearest office building and then prowled down the alley where Cas had disappeared.

She pulled out the gun and held it with both hands. Stalking along the alley between the two warehouses, she turned back and forth, the way she had seen detectives do on TV.

The back door of the building was ajar. Cas was going to owe her big time for saving his ass on this one. She peered around the corner. All she could see was a dark hallway. She tiptoed inside. Pointing the gun with her arms rigidly extended, she slid along the wall. What *was* that smell? Something chemical?

Were they preparing to dip Cas in acid? She hurried her pace, feeling her way through the darkness. She felt a doorframe and tried the knob—it turned. Slowly, quietly, she nudged the door open with her foot. In the dim light of a single bulb, the man in the sunglasses stood with his back to her. Struggling to hide the tremor in her voice, she shouted, "Hands up!"

The man started to turn.

"Keep looking straight ahead, asshole! I've got a gun pointed at that bald spot on your Mongolian skull." She felt rattled by how much she was sounding like Cas. "You so much as turn around, I'll pull the trigger."

The man slowly raised his hands. "Lady, you're making a big mistake."

She closed her eyes and squeezed the trigger, firing a shot over the assassin's head. The bullet caromed off of something metallic in the darkness.

"Jesus Aitch Christ!" The hit man ducked. "Calm down!"

Nice try, *jihadi* asshole. She wasn't falling for a fake Christian curse. After her hair-raising experience in Abu Dhabi, she felt downright exhilarated now, and she began to understand why adrenaline junkies like Cas went into this line of work. She'd really love to take out a couple of these 9/11 motherfuckers just for the principle. She aimed the gun toward the lowlife's heart. "Take off your jacket and pants."

The man hesitated. "What?"

"You heard me! Strip! Or the next one will be at your ear!"

The assassin began removing his clothes, throwing them into a pile.

"Shirt and socks, too."

Now he was down to his boxers.

Marly inched closer, crouching, keeping her weapon trained on the nearly naked man and rummaging through his clothes in search of a weapon. When she didn't find one, she knew where it had to be hidden. "Get them off!"

The man, shaking, slipped his thumbs into the elastic band of his underwear and slid them down to his ankles.

"Now," she ordered, trying to keep the barrel steady. "Turn around."

The overhead fluorescents suddenly switched on. Startled, Marly swung around toward the door and fired a shot.

Cas dived into a corner. The door's awning, rattled loose by the bullet, crashed down on him. When the clattering stopped, he peered over his forearm and made an introduction, "Dr. McKinney, meet Mr. Ari Kevan. He's the property manager of Levinson Industrial Park. He was kind enough to take my call and let me into the office." Cas looked at the poor, shaken man. "Sorry, sir. Please feel free to put your clothes back on.

Red with embarrassment, Marly slowly turned and examined the large room for the first time in full lighting. It was rimmed by counters with basins and islands sprouting rubber tubes under shelves of scientific equipment. They were in the middle of a modern chemical laboratory.

The property manager didn't dare move, waiting for the female lunatic to give him permission to get dressed.

Marly carefully lowered the gun to the floor. "I'm so sorry!"

After brushing the destroyed chunks of awning and drywall from his head and shirt, Cas gathered the property manager's clothes and handed the pile to him. "Dr. McKinney here is what we call an idiot savant. She can figure out complex chemical compounds, but she finds it extremely challenging to perform simple tasks that normal people like you and me take for granted. Such as counting minutes on a watch or taking instructions about when to get out of a car."

The property manager needed no convincing that Marly suffered from some severe mental instability. "Why haven't you looked into an institutional setting for her? She obviously needs round-the-clock supervision."

Marly didn't know whether to apologize again or pick up the gun and fire another round at Cas's feet. "I can explain—"

The property manager quickly put on his shoes and tied them. "Take as long as you want to look around." He gave the office keys to Cas. "As I told you, we can offer month-to-month leases, if that is your preference." He glanced warily at Marly as he backed away for the door. "I'll be in my office. The door will be locked. And I will have my fingers on the telephone to call 911, should that be necessary."

Cas delayed him. "Oh, one other question. Who was the last tenant here?"

The property manager inched his head reluctantly around the doorjamb, afraid that he might be shot at again. "A startup biotech company named Light-something-or-other. It must have gone bankrupt. The principals left two days ago without even asking for their deposit back. I guess this has been happening to a lot of these firms lately."

"There's some damned expensive equipment in here," Cas said. "Why would they abandon it so quickly? Some of this could be sold to defray the debt."

The property manager raised his palms, indicating that he didn't even want to know. "Sign for three months, and you can keep the fixtures."

"Just out of curiosity," Cas said. "Who did you deal with at the company?"

The property manager shrugged. "I never met any of their people. Their law firm handled the negotiations on the lease. Our policy is to preserve our clients' confidentiality. We have few if any contacts with them, unless they come to us with a problem about the facility."

"Thanks," Cas said. "I'll drop the keys off when we're done here. And sorry again for my deranged assistant here."

The property manager stole a worried glance at Marly before hurrying off.

Cas shut the door behind him. After an extended silence, he remarked dryly, "I'm sorta new to this whole office-leasing biz, but I gotta think that firing off a round in a prospective property, even in Texas, might be counterproductive to a healthy landlord-tenant relationship."

"Hey! I panicked, okay?" Marly sulked, crossing her arms. "I was worried about you. So sue me!"

Cas walked around the lab trying to figure out what had caused Silla's hi-tech radar in Brussels to hone in on this particular site. "Looks like we might have made a trip to Big D for nothing."

"It was a long shot anyway. What now?"

Cas smelled the test tubes. "What does magnetic iron have to do with biotechnology?"

"Nothing that I know of."

He twirled a tube around in his fingers while thinking. "If you can manage it without sparking a border war, why don't you go out to the car and bring in that meteorite sniffer."

Marly returned moments later with the metal detector.

Cas flipped the switch on the machine and walked around the room again, watching the dials for any signs of magnetized iron. After several circuits, he registered nothing. He shook his head and threw the detector over his shoulder to leave. "Back to square one. Pull the car into that parking lot in the back. I don't want the guy you nearly killed to see us leave. He's probably calling in our license plate to the cops right now."

Marly went out the front door, unlocked the car, and started it up. She drove around the block and headed down the alley that led to the rear of the row of office suites.

Cas was waiting for her. "Pop the trunk." He threw the metal detector atop the spare tire and closed the lid. "You drive. I'm toast."

"Where to now?"

"Airport," he mumbled as he got in. "I gotta sleep on this."

Marly hadn't even put the car in gear before Cas was out cold in the passenger seat, snoring loudly enough to vibrate the plastic grille on the radio speaker. She drove down the alley to look for the exit back to the street. She heard a buzzing sound hummed under the chassis. Finding Cas oblivious, as usual, she elbowed him.

Startled from his snooze, Cas shoved her arm away. "What?"

"The transmission on this piece of junk sounds like it's going bad."

Cas cocked his ear toward the noise. "Put it in Park and gun it."

She pressed the gas pedal to the floor. The engine roared, but the buzzing remained.

"Turn it off," Cas ordered.

She cut the engine, but the buzzing persisted. Pulling the keys from the ignition, Cas opened his door and climbed out. He got on his knees and stalked the sound, crawling toward the rear of the car. He opened the trunk. The metal detector was still vibrating—with its dial pulled all the way to the Positive limit. Doubly baffled, he looked around. The only thing near them was a dumpster. He pulled out the detector and held it over the container.

The needle went haywire.

He motioned for Marly to climb inside the bin and check it out.

"Me? In there?" Marly refused to move. "No way."

"I found the damn place," Cas said. "Now it's your turn to contribute."

Marly pulled a quarter from her pocket. "We'll flip for it." She threw the coin into the air and caught it, covering it with her palm. "Your call."

"Tails."

She uncovered the quarter and grinned. "I thought you spooks were supposed to have a finely honed intuition."

Cas cursed as he climbed into the smelly Dumpster and *thwacked* away at swarms of flies while picking through boxes and sacks of wet, stinking trash.

Marly walked around the bin, aiming the detector at each side. The vibrations grew stronger on the northeast quadrant. "Concentrate here, on this corner."

Cas dived in like a hungry rat. Suddenly, his cursing stopped.

"You didn't suffocate, did you?" she asked, sounding concerned.

Seconds later, Cas popped his head out of the top of the bin. He reached out and displayed one of the Black Stone fragments. Turning the shard to reveal that its interior was white, he threw it to her and dived back into the bin.

Marly's eyes widened. "How many pieces are there supposed to be?"

Cas moled around in the garbage. "Seven!"

Marly stared at the fragment in her palm. Dollar signs began spinning through her head. Sure, millions around the world worshipped this little gem, but at one-fifty gees an ounce, it might be worth a small fortune.

Suddenly, an idea hit her.

Nobody—including Cas—would be the wiser if she took a small commission on the side. And would anybody really lose their faith if one of the seven fragments was returned to Mecca a fraction smaller?

Of course not.

While he was still yapping about each new find, she retreated to the car's open trunk and lifted out the tire iron. She put a corner of the fragment on the frame and gave it a swift *crack*. Five hundred bucks worth of sweet high-density space rock—no larger than half the length of her index finger—sheared off.

"Hey!" Cas shouted from the bin. "A little help over here?"

Shielded by the raised trunk, Marly slid the broken-off shard into her pocket. "Coming, dear!"

She helped him out of the bin. He placed the other six fragments of various sizes and shapes on the pavement. Their interior sides were concave, indicating that they had once been part of a larger round stone. They stood staring in disbelief at their amazing good fortune.

Cas rushed to the car. He reached into his carry bag and pulled out a photocopy that he had packed showing what the Stone's fragments imbedded into the silver Kaaba frame had looked like before the icon was stolen. The shapes of the fragments he now held matched, although one seemed a little smaller. He shrugged off the minor discrepancy and kissed the photo. "Sweet Jee-sus!"

Marly didn't share in his elation. Something didn't quite add up for her. "Why would the *jihadists* go to all of the trouble to steal the Stone, bring the fragments halfway across the world under great danger, and then simply toss them into the garbage?"

"Who cares? You can write a dissertation on it when you get home. We've got what the Saudi government is paying us for. Those ragheads don't need to know how or where we found them. We'll just tell those barbaric pukes that we recovered their precious Stone after a high-speed chase through the Mexican desert. They'll like that, sounds all Wild West and shit." He grinned and settled into the driver's seat. "You got a bag on you?"

She rolled her eyes. "Of course. I always travel with a roll of sandwich bags, just in case I need to put one over somebody's head and strangle him."

"Geez, you'd think your attitude would improve a little with our hitting the dumpster jackpot." He flipped open the glove compartment and found the driver's manual—neatly ensconced in a small plastic cover. He pulled out the booklet, tossed it out the window, and dropped the seven fragments into the pouch, snapping it shut. He slipped the pouch with its precious contents into his inside jacket pocket.

She shook her head. "They'll ream your credit card good for stealing that."

"That's why God made expense accounts. Ol' Jubal will pick up the tab." He leaned over and threw open the passenger door. "What are you waiting for?"

Marly still wouldn't get into the car. "What have you got planned next?"

"I'm hopping the first plane out to Saudi Arabia. Once I deliver these goodies and pick up the cash and my son, it's *Lazy Lay Bon Temperature Roulette*. Come with me. We'll check out our favorite Mecca watering holes before we head back."

Marly was beyond being surprised anymore. A few seconds later, her brow furrowed. "You know what? Maybe we've asking the wrong question."

"You can't be serious," Cas said, groaning. "We just arrived at the end of the rainbow, sweetheart, so quit over-thinking it! Most of these Al Qaeda foot soldiers are boneheads."

"Yeah, it took some real boneheads to bring down those Twin Towers."

Irritated, Cas waved off her worries. "Remember that mental midget who tried to ignite his tennis shoe on the plane. He couldn't even get the lighter to work. Or the numbnuts who tried to blow up his underwear? I mean, everyone knows that C-Four doesn't work that way, but that's another story. Besides, I wouldn't put it past those mopes to have misplaced the Stone fragments in the office, only to wake up the next morning and find that the janitor had thrown them out."

She hesitated, still not convinced.

He gripped the steering wheel impatiently. "In any case, my bet is that these Al Qaeda losers are probably on a plane back to Yemen or some other shit hole right about now, worried like hell that they'll have their heads carved off for screwing this up."

"Maybe you're right."

"Of course I'm right." He patted the seat next to him. "We'll deliver the package and speculate later over fabulously expensive cocktails and dinner. Wear something incredibly sexy." He winked, trying to coax her inside.

Marly looked down the alley at the door to the abandoned office they had just left. "Maybe what we *really* need to find out is why Arab radicals would pose as a biotech company just to steal and then discard the Stone."

"Oh, would you just stop it, please? You know as well as I do that biotech startups are common as bedbugs. Probably makes it easy to explain why they pack up and leave suddenly."

Marly studied the city's skyline in the distance. "That may be true in San Francisco or Boston. But biotech is not that common in Dallas. Why go to all the trouble to build an expensive laboratory if no one was going to be allowed inside of it anyway? And for a rock?" She shook her head and pinched her temples, as if her head might explode with too many questions. "Tell me just one part of any of this that makes any sense? Or does asking *you* that certify me as a complete moron?"

Cas couldn't believe she wanted to continue pursuing something that had no monetary payoff. "You need a mystery to solve?" He handed her a piece of paper. "Here's something to gnaw on while we drive to the airport. Before you showed up in that lab with your gun blazing, I rummaged through the cabinets."

"What is this?"

"Apparently one of our Saudis holing out in there had a speech impediment."

She stared at him, confounded. "How could you possibly know that?"

"I found this inside the office. Looked like it had been torn from some important document. There were a couple of words on it."

She tilted her head. "Which were?"

"See for yourself. It says, 'Stutter band.'"

She blinked hard. "What?"

Cas ran his index finger across his front teeth. "Stutter band. Probably a mouthpiece, or something that stutterers wear to help them talk without the kinks. Maybe you can find a picture in the Post Office of all the wanted terrorists with braces and drop this little piece of evidence to Homeland Security for some extra reward dough. You can work on the case in your spare time between classes. Now, let's skedaddle."

She became silent, turning inward. She fixed her eyes on the paper and bit her lower lip. The line had black-and-white dashes with small rectangles.

"What's wrong?"

Before she could answer, they both turned toward the squeal of a black BMW that had turned the corner and was racing down the narrow lane toward them. She had no room to avoid the car—and couldn't climb the surrounding walls. *It's going to turn me into a pancake!* She screamed at Cas, who was slapping around in the front seat, trying to find the guns. Empty-handed, he jumped back from the car and grabbed her.

The Beemer was picking up speed and gunning straight at them.

She ran with him down the alley, trying the knobs on every door, but every office was locked. She shouted at him, "Give them those stones!"

Cas pressed his hand to his chest, making sure the pouch holding the fragments were still in his jacket pocket. "Like hell I will!"

"They won't do us any good if we're dead!"

Cas hurled himself at one of the office doors. He bounced off like a Slinkie.

Gunshots rang out from the passenger side of the Beemer. The car was now only yards from barreling into them. Staggering and nearly falling, Marly noticed an electrician's ladder leaning against a wall. She jumped on the rungs and started climbing.

Cas followed her and grabbed the edge of the roof, seconds before the Beemer knocked the ladder from under him. He dangled from the ledge. She turned and helped him up before the Beemer skidded into their rental car and pushed it to the end of the alley, crushing it like a giant accordion. The Beemer raced in reverse back down the alley, taking out the ladder.

Marly looked down from the roof and saw two more black sedans parked on the curb across the street. Four men in sunglasses and dark suits jumped out of the steam-puffing car in the alley and looked up at her. She grabbed Cas by the collar. "Just give them the damn stones!"

"Hell no!"

Marly slapped him. Before he could recover, she snatched the pouch from his jacket pocket and ripped it open. Dropping the fragments out into her hand, she selected the largest and gripped it between her thumb and forefinger.

"Give those back!" Cas demanded.

The Beemer thugs jumped from the top of the car to the edge of the roof and worked their way up the ladder. Two more scrambled to the roof and aimed their pistols.

Marly was about to throw a shoulder into Cas to prevent him from snatching the fragments from her. She glanced up and saw that they were surrounded. She and Cas looked at each other, helpless.

One of the thugs motioned for her to hand over the stones.

"Back off!" Marly shouted.

From the corner of her eye, she saw Cas drop his jaw in astonishment. But she just kept retreating, clutching the stone fragments as she neared a large pipe that led to the air conditioner below.

"Lady, just hand them over," one of the goons said. "Nobody gets hurt."

"Take another step," she said, shifting her eyes toward the drainpipe, "and I'll drop them!"

The assailants froze. Their leader lowered his voice as if trying to calm her down. "Don't do anything you'll regret."

"You let us go," Marly said. "You get the stones."

The head thug motioned for her to display the rocks. "I gotta know you're on the up and up."

She flashed the fragments in her fist and counted them for him like a bank teller. "All seven. Now, give me your cell phone."

Cas muttered under his breath, "What the hell are you doing?"

"Just shut up," she ordered him with set teeth. "I'm damn tired of being tossed around like your own personal beanbag."

Cas's eyes rounded. "Do *not* drop those rocks down that pipe."

The head goon pleaded, "Lady, listen to your boyfriend and—"

"You call him my boyfriend again," she shouted in a rage, "and I'm going to send these damn things into Freon Hell!"

"Take it easy," the goon begged, risking a step closer. "I can understand you not wanting to be associated with this dirtbag. You sound like a reasonable businesswoman. Let's talk a deal."

She held the largest fragment over the pipe. "I'm done talking! Giving me your damn phone! Now!"

Convinced that she was just crazy enough to follow through on her threat, the thug reluctantly slid his cell phone across the roof towards her.

Marly kept the largest Stone fragment hovering over the pipe while she picked up the phone with her free hand. She set the phone on vibrate and memorized the number on its screen. She kicked at Cas. "Give me one of your shoestrings."

"Have you lost your fucking mind?"

"Just do it!" she shouted, nearly fumbling the fragment down the pipe.

Shaking his head, Cas unraveled the string from his right shoe and handed it to her.

Marly kept one eye on the thugs while she dropped the seven fragments into the small pouch and tied it to the cell phone. She formed a loose loop around one of the pinions in the pipe and tied the other end of the string to the phone. She pulled out her own phone and punched in the number she had just memorized. She warned their attackers, "I've got your number on speed dial. If I call that phone, it'll vibrate like the San Andreas Fault."

The head goon laughed. "What's a little shimmy going to do to a rock?"

"You take physics in school, wise-ass?" she asked.

The goon frowned. "No, but—"

"Maybe if you had, you'd know that even a slight vibration can break loose the fissures in stones this old. I've got a doctorate in geophysics, so listen up, Gomer. Meteorites have cracks fragile enough to splinter. If this phone starts shaking, your God Stone will go snap, crackle and pop. You might find a few bits and pieces of it, if you're lucky. But most of it will just go poof."

The tough guys traded alarmed glances, not sure whether to believe her.

Marly grabbed Cas's arm and moved him to the edge of the building. They stood directly over the glistening roof of the freshly crumpled Beemer.

Cas suddenly realized what she had in mind. "No way. That only works in the movies."

The gunmen remained deathly still, afraid Cas would drop their phone and set off the vibration.

Marly moved a few inches back from the ledge. "Don't believe for a second that he won't turn those pieces into dust! He's a psychopath!" She stepped back toward the very edge of the roof as if to prove that she, too, was insane. "Now, before he does something crazy that could get us all killed, give him the car keys and drop your weapons."

The thugs reluctantly complied with her demand. With her free hand, Marly caught the car keys. Cas jumped for the guy's gun. Kicking one of the thugs off his feet, he fired a shot at the other man, who dived sprawling across the roof.

Marly reached for Cas and jumped with him onto the roof of the car. She rolled off the hood. While he was distracted with shooting at the thugs on the roof, she untied the pouch and dropped the fragments into another dumpster. She hurriedly snapped the empty pouch shut and tied it to the thug's cell phone.

Across the street from the alley, two other goons waiting in the sedans jumped out and ran toward the sounds of gunfire.

Cas dragged Marly down the alley toward the abandoned Beemer that was still drivable. He fired off another series of rounds into the empty sedans across the street—their tires sank with a loud hiss.

He pushed Marly into the car. The keys were still in the ignition.

He raced the car backwards while Marly held the cell phone out the window, warning the thugs on the roof that she wouldn't hesitate to press the Send button.

Twenty minutes later, when they were safely out of range, Marly leaned back in her seat and took a deep breath. She pulled the thug's cell phone from her pocket and threw it to the floorboard.

The phone began vibrating.

Cas grinned. "That crock you fed those airheads about the phone breaking those fragments apart was Grade A prime bullshit, right?"

"Prime as all the steaming manure you've been feeding me for the past week." She waited another moment for her heart to come back down from her throat. "I did a quick estimate of the aggregate IQ of those apes and figured it wasn't much higher than yours."

He kept his hand raised in triumph. "You've got promise in the spy business, Miss Galore. Okay, let's hug and smooch our million-dollar prize!"

She looked at his upraised palm and shrugged.

Cas untied the pouch from the cell phone and snapped it open. Suddenly, it dawned on him what she had done. "*What?* Are you fucking *serious?*"

She stared straight ahead, her face inscrutable.

He gripped her shoulder. "Where *are* the Stone fragments, goddamn it?"

Receiving no answer, he started the car and whipped it into a one-eighty turn, speeding back toward the industrial park.

"What the hell are *you* doing?"

"I'm not letting those Playstation toons get away with my money!"

She reached her leg over the console and slammed her foot against his on the accelerator. They skidded into the curb and came to a jolting stop. "And I'm not going back there!" she shouted. "I won't get killed for a bunch of rocks!"

"You made a deal with me!"

"This is where I get off! I *never* agreed to this! You hired me to help you find a rock, not ride shotgun on a suicide mission!"

They fought for control of the wheel.

Finally, Cas surrendered, bitter at her betrayal. "It's not your son who's in that prison over there!"

"You're right." Marly's eyes flooded with compassion, despite the adrenaline still charging through her veins. "That's the one thing we agree on. But I can't help you anymore."

Cas's eyes ringed red and moist. "I'm going back."

She wouldn't look at him. "I know you are."

"Where'd you drop them?"

She hesitated before revealing, "In one of the alley garbage cans."

"Did they see you toss them?"

"I don't know. ... I don't think so. But you shouldn't risk it. Those assholes may still be snooping around if you go back there."

Cas waited for her to say something more, but she sat silent, glaring straight ahead. He dropped his chin and muttered, "So, that's it, huh. You're abandoning me?"

She nodded. "Call it whatever you want. I've had my last gunfight."

"We're so close."

"Close to a couple of coffins," She couldn't believe how cold she sounded, but he had left her no wriggle room. "You won't ever be happy until you fulfill that death wish of yours. But I want my life back." She got out of the car and, leaning into the open driver's window, pressed a kiss to his forehead. "I'll call a cab at that Starbucks over there. You go on. You've got a plane to catch."

"What about your part of the fee?"

She stopped, thinking for a brief moment, but then kept walking across the street and disappeared into the coffee shop.

Alone now, Cas looked at his gun, and wondered what its barrel would feel like against the back of his throat. Then he thought about Farid, and realized he still had one thing left to live for.

19

Ghajar, Israel

L ed in shame through her small border village, fifteen-year-old Zaynah Al Homra swiveled her draped head from side to side, searching through her veil for a dagger to steal from the belts of the male onlookers who glared death at her.

She prayed Allah would grant her the chance to cut her own throat.

Her head flooded with the memories of that time, two years ago, when her father had taken her across the line into Lebanon to watch an adulteress from Bastra be stoned. The condemned woman, with her head also covered, had been forced to kneel in the roasting sun while thirty men circled her and casually chose the rocks that would deliver the most pain. Then, finally, they took turns running at her like a cricket player throwing a pitch.

Now, she was being forced to endure that same walk of Sharia justice.

Her father and brothers shoved her down a dirt street. Staggering along, she passed shops where women she had once thought were friends now looked away. The men snarled curses at her and refused to meet her pleading eyes. She hadn't slept for two weeks, afraid that one of her brothers would slip into her room and blind her, or worse. Tired and dazed, she stumbled and nearly fell.

Blessedly, the shaming entourage reached the mosque, and she was permitted to escape the spectators following them. Her father and brothers pushed her into the adjacent office of the local imam, a bearded old man who was always consulted by the town's citizens for the implementation of Sharia justice. The clergyman looked up from his desk with a sad gaze that suggested he had already heard of the scandal and was expecting their arrival.

Tears of anger flooded her father's eyes. "My daughter has brought great dishonor upon me."

The old imam's accusatory gaze traveled from Zaynah's face to her abdomen, as if he suspected Satan to be incubating inside her. "Are you with child?"

Her father answered before she could speak. "The doctor has said it is so."

The imam's eyes pierced Zaynah like stakes.

"I have done nothing," she protested. "I don't know how this happened. I swear—" She then thought better of swearing anything.

The imam scowled at her. "Lying will only bring a harsher penalty."

Zaynah fell to her knees. All she could remember was being asleep one night about a month ago in her family's apartment, and then waking up, hours later, on the sidewalk below her building. "I must have been raped."

Her brothers shouted accusations that she had slithered off that night to fornicate while they had been at the coffee house.

"She became drunk with alcohol!" her father insisted. "Or worse!"

The imam kept tugging at his beard. "Worse?"

"Narcotics! Hashish! Who knows? She is a wanton whore who—"

The imam raised a palm for silence. "You said the doctor examined her?"

Her father nodded. "The virgin veil was found penetrated."

"I've never willingly been with a man!" Zaynah cried, shaking. "Never!"

"When did you discover your daughter in this state of sin?"

"She began complaining of the morning sickness two weeks ago," her father said. "One night, we found her room empty, only a few hours before dawn. She must have slipped out to fornicate with one of the Zionist soldiers who use our women. She tried to cover her sin by claiming that she could not remember where she had been. She also told us another lie."

"Which was?" the cleric asked.

"That strange men were always following her."

The imam turned on her to demand that she identify these men.

Zaynah cried through tears, "I don't know them! I saw only shadows!"

The imam hung his head while contemplating what counsel to offer. Finally, he looked straight at her father. "The Prophet, praise be upon him, said, 'Whoever guarantees me what is between his legs, and what is between his jaws, I guarantee him Paradise.'" With the recitation of the Shia *hadith*—one of the twenty-five ways prescribed to enter Jannah—the cleric arose and retreated from his office to his private study.

Her father and brothers smiled grimly, pleased with the verdict of death.

Zaynah collapsed and caught herself, bracing her hands against the desk to keep from fainting. Her brothers manhandled her and—

"I wish to marry this girl."

The men all turned toward the door.

A young man—Zaynah guessed he could be no older than twenty—had been standing at the threshold the entire time, listening to the case.

"Who are you?" her father demanded.

"My name is Gabir Karam. I am from Halta."

Zaynah's brothers clenched their fists.

The father restrained them. Coming closer to the stranger, he demanded, "Did *you* violate my daughter?"

The youth stole a glance at Zaynah.

She looked at him in confusion, trying to place his face.

"I have never met your daughter," Gabir told her father. "But I have seen her in the village many times. I believe her to be a woman devoted to Allah, praise be upon Him. It would be a privilege to take her as my wife. And to save the honor of your family."

On her knees, Zaynah backed away, wondering who this man was and why he claimed to know her.

Hearing the voices discussing the marriage proposal outside his office, the old imam returned from his private study. He tugged at his beard, trying to assess the young man's unusual offer. "What is your tribe?"

"I am Alawite."

Mollified, somewhat, from learning that he was from his sect, Zaynah's father circled the young man to inspect him. "Your trade?"

"I pour concrete for construction."

"You can support a wife and a child on such a salary?"

The young man nodded. "My father performed the same work. He raised eight children."

The imam motioned her father to his side. After nearly a minute of intense and whispered discussion, the cleric turned to Zaynah. "Will you accept this man as your husband?"

Zaynah glanced at her suitor, still wondering why he had chosen her, especially now. But she knew, given the alternative, that she had no choice but to accept his inexplicable proposal. She nodded her agreement. Her father snatched her up by the forearm and led her toward the door to prevent her from speaking further to her new fiancé.

As they left, her father told the young man, "The wedding will be in one week. Until then, you will have no further contact with my daughter." Her father opened his cell phone and barked orders to his youngest son to drive their family's Citroen to the front of the mosque to pick them up.

Forced to stand on the street curb, Zaynah waited in humiliation, burned by the glares of the townspeople gathered around her. When her youngest brother finally pulled up in the car, her father pushed her into the back seat and ordered her to wait inside.

While the men bickered over where to hold the wedding and how it would be financed, Zaynah, sitting alone in the car, saw Gabir, the young man who had saved her, glance coldly at her from across the street. He walked away quickly, unnoticed by the arguing scrum, and darted into a side alley. He kept looking over his shoulder, as if checking to see whether anyone had noticed his departure, then he motioned another man into the alley with him. Much taller and thick in the waist than Gabir, this stranger joined her new fiancé in the shadows, out of sight of the other men.

She could not identify the large man's features, but she saw him count out what looked to be several bills of currency and hand them to her future husband. The two men shook hands, and then the taller one vanished back into the alley. As Gabir stuff the cash into his pocket, she gasped at the size of her fiancé's new money roll. Was she to marry a rich man? If so, why had he chosen her, a poor girl?

And why had he just glared at her with such shuddering disdain?

20

Dallas, Texas

Decked out in pink sweatpants, sunglasses, and iPod ear-buds, Cas speed-walked down the street bordering the industrial park where he and Marly had encountered the pirates in the Beemers. His jogger's backpack, two sizes too small, cut into his shoulders, but he hadn't had time to properly accessorize. Disguised as one of the neighbors out for a little exercise, he passed the same corner again. This time, he risked glancing up at the utility pole to calculate how many seconds he would need to climb it.

The sun was just now dropping below the roofs of the gray buildings, and the twilight traffic had trickled to an occasional passing car. He could have really used a partner with a pair of eyes scouting the next block, but Marly had followed through on her threat and was on a plane back to New York.

He'd have to pull off this one on his own. The clock was ticking.

Seeing no one around, he sat on a crumbling bus bench and quickly removed his tennis shoes. He reached into the backpack and pulled out the cheap golf shoes he had purchased from the same second-hand store where he'd found his garish outfit. With gaff hooks in each hand, he waddled up the pole, making sure to keep three-point contact with the tar-slathered wood. He whispered the Ranger's rhythmic climbing mantra—"Hand, Charlie, Stroke."

One false grip and the family jewels would be shaved off.

Hovering on the pole, he paused to check his watch. Only twenty seconds to reach the transformer. Not bad for an old man.

Bolted next to the buzzing box of high-voltage death was his target: a police camera hidden to catch speeders and red-light violators. Sucking in a deep breath, he pulled a small screwdriver from his backpack. This close to the transformer, he'd be Colonel Sanders extra crispy in ten seconds if the camera hadn't been properly grounded. He closed his eyes and fingered the camera's casing, bracing for a heart-stopping jolt, and ...

Nothing.

Releasing a breath, he quickly unscrewed the box covering the camera. He lifted it off and read the specs on the label plate below the lens: A megapixel robotic webcam. Pan/tilt/zoom controls with presets. Heater and fan with windshield wiper. This baby was state of the art. Failsafe backup with one hundred gigabytes of archiving—he grinned again—*on the camera's hard drive.*

He had never read words so sweet. The plate indicated that all the video was forwarded to the main capture station every twenty-four hours.

Beat the cam clock by twenty-seven minutes. *Booyah!* He detached the cable to the satellite transmitter, interrupting the connection to the monitoring center, and then pulled a custom-fitted cable from his backpack to hot-wire it to the camera's hard drive. He inserted the other end of the cable, rigged with a USB connector, to his iPod. He opened the video-conversion app on his phone and looked for a new input source.

Bingo! We have target lock.

Now all he had to do was download a few gigabytes of file footage. Should take him, oh, ten minutes, if the iPod didn't burn up first. If he'd only had one of these badass flash drives, like the one that the Mossad agent Isserle had likely used to transmit all that data from Marly's computer, no telling what—

"Hey, pal!"

Cas blinked behind the glaze of his cheap sunglasses. Why was the dusk sky all of a sudden pulsing with the colors of the rainbow?

"Get down here!"

He looked at the street below and saw a police cruiser, its Mars bar flashing, parked right under him. *Damn it.* Sure enough, one of Dallas's finest in blue stood at the base of the pole.

The cop aimed his service revolver up at him, finding the point between his ass and his package. "Did you hear me, chief?"

Cas stole a glance at his iPod screen. *Come on, baybee. Just two more minutes.*

"Lemme guess!" the cop hollered up. "You either escaped from Millwood, or they dumped you out here!"

Cas counted it one small blessing that Marly wasn't there now. She'd probably sign the commitment order to send him to the Dallas psychiatric institution. He glanced at his iPod's screen again—the download was almost finished. Buying time, he yelled at the cop, "Pancakes!"

The cop squinted in confusion. "Huh? What's that you—?"

"Maple syrup!"

The cop shook his head and slipped his pistol back into its holster. "Come on, buddy, let's climb on down. We'll get you back to the hospital and find you some pancakes. If those greedy sonsabitches won't take you in, we can always get you to a shelter."

Still gripping the telephone pole with his legs, Cas disconnected the iPod from the camera, making sure the cop couldn't see what he was doing. He slipped the mobile device into the front of his underwear. He took off his backpack and slung it over the fence into an adjacent lot littered with old car parts. He shouted, "Ough'oh!"

The cop's jaw dropped. "Now, what'd you do that for?"

"New one! I want a *new* one!"

The cop rolled his eyes. This time, he motioned more forcefully for Cas to return to Earth. "Damn right you'll get a new one, friendo. I'm not going over there to get *that* one."

Cas slowly clambered down, careful not to bang the iPod now serving as his hidden codpiece. Reaching the ground, he offered his hands to be cuffed.

The cop laughed. "You've been watching too much late-night tube."

"Book'em, Dano!" Cas raised his thumb and pointed his index finger as if shooting at a bunch of bad guys. "Book'em! Book'em! Book'em!"

The cop led the babbling Cas into the backseat of the patrol cruiser. Closing the door, the cop glanced over to his partner in the passenger seat. "Looks like it's gonna be one of those nights."

His partner grimaced. "You just had to make one more circuit before we took our break, din't'cha? Now we won't get dinner for another hour."

"Hey, whaddya want me to do?" the first cop asked. "Leave the guy sitting on that pole like a pigeon taking a shit? Next thing we know, the papers are running a story about some psych-ward escapee falling on his head while playing tightrope walker on the phone wires. And we get our asses chewed."

"Yeah, I suppose," his partner said. "Whaddya gonna do?"

The cops talked on as if he wasn't there, so Cas slipped the iPod out of his crotch and held the device below the meshed screen, out of their view. He checked the volume: Good, it had remained off. He tapped open the video-replay app to open it.

The cop driving looked at the rearview mirror. "What's your name, buddy?"

Cas hid the iPod from view behind the front seat. "Hilbert. What's yours?"

"Officer Hank."

Hank's partner was chortling.

"What's got *you* so jolly?" Hank asked him.

The cop riding shotgun said, "They shoulda used the name 'Hilbert' instead of 'Forrest' in the movie. Hilbert Gump. Has a better ring to it." He did his best Tom Hanks imitation. "Stupid is as stupid does." He thought a moment. "Or is it, stupid does as stupid is?"

Hank joined in on the Gump-quotes hit parade. "Momma always told me, life is like a box of bullets."

While the two uniformed buffoons continued amusing themselves as they drove, Cas rewound the video he had downloaded from the street camera. He watched the metered time frame speed back the minutes and seconds, praying that he had waited long enough on the pole to reach the point—2:45 p.m. yesterday—when those goons in the Beemers had accosted him and Marly. He blew a sigh of relief when the number hit the target. He stopped the video and zoomed in on the freeze-framed image. There they were … the two black sedans parked at the curb under a light pole when he and Marly were on the roof. The rear bumper of one of the BMWs was facing the camera. He pushed the zoom to the limit, until the resolution of the pixels started breaking up. The Texas license plate came into rough focus. He could just make out the letters and numbers: BA2 A849.

"Hey, Hilbert!" Officer Hank shouted over his shoulder. "You aren't gonna throw up on my seat, are you?"

"Wee-wee!" Cas wailed, hiding the iPod behind his back.

They turned and glared at him through the security mesh. "What'd you say?"

Cas shook and fidgeted, imitating a two-year-old about to do what two-year-olds do best. "Gotta pee!" he cried. "Gotta pee *baaaad*, Officer Friendly!"

Hank's partner flung his head backwards. "Ah, for the love of Jesus, Joseph, and Jerry Jones!"

Hank wheeled a hairpin turn and pulled into to a burger joint.

"Oh, c'mon, Hank, no!" his partner protested. "Let's just get him to the damn shelter, and he can pee his freakin' brains out there. You can't be serious—"

"I'm not taking any chances," Hank said. "You remember that old fart we picked up outside that Irving bowling mart last month? I had to steam-clean the damn floorboards after the mess he made. I still can't get the stink of that puke out of my nostrils."

"You had that one coming. Taking that corner at eighty like that."

Hank parked and popped open the lock on the back door. "Go in there and do your thing, Hilbert. And wash your hands when you're done."

"Yessir. Wash my hands. Wash my hands of crime. I'll come clean. Get it?" Cas cackled like a maniac. "Get it?"

As he leapt out and waddled into the Whataburger holding his crotch, the two officers sat back and scoped the parking lot for potential trouble.

Hank's partner looked up at a giant burger on a sign and smacked his lips. "One of those jalapeño half-pounders sounds damn tasty right about now."

"Uh, no," Hank said. "I'm not punishing my gut with another one of those depth charges. Tonight, I'll be going for my usual. Club sandwich on white toast with cottage cheese. Denny's doesn't cut corners with the cottage cheese."

"Yeah? Since when did you become such an expert on cottage cheese?"

"My uncle used to run a deli downtown. He told me stories about expired cottage cheese that would scare you shitless. Literally. He saw three customers taken to the emergency room for food poisoning." Hank's stomach growled. "Dammit, what's taking him so long?" He rubbed his gurgling belly. "My ulcer is firing up again. If I don't get some cottage cheese in my gut soon, I'm gonna start refluxing like a Galveston gusher. Wouldja just go get him."

"*You* go get him. You're the one that wanted to bring him along."

Hank cursed under his breath and kicked his door open. He walked into the burger joint and found no customers inside. He tipped his cap to the manager. "Slow night, huh?"

The manager straightened to attention. "We do most of our business between five and eight."

"Good to know. Say, did you happen to see a stupid-looking guy walk in here couple minutes ago? Hard to miss. Pink sweats, sunglasses."

The manager nodded and pointed to the restroom.

Hank sauntered over and pounded on the door. "Hilbert! Time's up!" When he got no answer, he tried the knob. Damn door was locked. "Hilbert! Get outta there! *Now!*"

The manager brought the key. Hank unlocked the door and threw it open, itching get his hands on this Hilbert character. The windowless bathroom was empty. Hank glanced up at the ceiling. The covering over the ventilator shaft had been removed with a screwdriver.

Where did that human monkey get hold of a tool kit?

Hank's impatient partner arrived on the scene. "What the hell is—" He looked at Hank, stunned by the dimwitted prisoner's vanishing act.

Behind them, the bathroom door slammed shut.

Hank tried to open the door, but it wouldn't budge. He turned to the manager. "I'm going to ask a question I probably don't want to hear the answer to. ... Do you use one of those rubber wedges to keep this door open while you're cleaning the bathroom?"

"Uh, yeah."

All three men looked down at the baseboards, realizing together that the door had been wedged shut from the outside.

Hank held his churning stomach. "I'm guessing you're the only one holding down the fort at this hour."

"Yes, sir."

Hank put a hand on the manager's shoulder. "Right. Now, I'm going to ask you *another* question that I probably don't want to hear the answer to. ... Do you serve cottage cheese?"

The manager hesitated. "Yes, sir. But I wouldn't eat it."

While the two officers remained locked in the restroom, Cas slithered around behind Hank's police cruiser and crawled into the driver's seat. He searched the hump and found the daily briefing log. Scanning the assignment locations, he located the name of the dispatcher on duty. He picked up the radio transmitter and punched the button, then crooned, "Heather, darling. It must be my lucky day."

The dispatcher replied over the speaker: "Hank? Is that you?"

"All two hundred and ten pounds of prime Texas beef."

"You sound different."

Cas coughed and lowered his voice to improve his imitation of the digestion-challenged cop. "Nasty cold, just crept up on me like a blue Norther. I guess that's what I get for going turkey huntin' naked the other night."

"How's your stomach doing?"

"Fair to middlin'. ... Say, hon, can you run a plate for me?" He powered up his iPod and opened the saved image of the BMW sedan caught on tape by the surveillance camera. "Bravo Alpha Two, Alpha Eight Four Niner"

Seconds later, the answer came across the scratchy speaker: "Registered to a limited liability corporation named Lightgiver Technologies."

Hadn't that property manager back at the industrial park—the poor bastard Marly almost popped—said he rented that abandoned lab office to a biotech company with Light-something in its name? Close enough for government work, considering he had no other leads.

He dropped back into his Hank role and twanged, "Old dawg like me can't keep up with all the new tricks over there in that hi-tech wonderland. Do we still have access to the Secretary of State's database for corporate directors?"

"C'mon, Hank, that's child's play. Let me run it through." Seconds later, she said, "The LLC was registered by a Seth Cohanim over in Llano County."

"That helps," Cas said, though the name meant nothing to him.

"What's the deal out there, Hank?"

"Suspicious BMW near the airport."

After another second's hesitation, the dispatcher asked, "What are you doing clear over there? That's a little out of your pen tonight, isn't it?"

"I've been tailing the suspect for a while. Erratic driver." Cas poked his tongue around his mouth, as if stuffing some chew into his cheek. "Say, Heather," he moaned, his words sounding like mashed potatoes in a blender. "I've been way too easy on you here. Let's see if we can get you to do some serious lifting." He smiled to himself through her confused silence. "We interface databases with U.S. Homeland Security these days, correct?"

"You're pulling my leg now, Hank. You know we are. But the Feds get a little pissed when we make an inquiry."

"Then let's make those stuffed suits in Washington earn their pay tonight, whaddayasay? Drop Mr. Cohanim's name into the hopper and see if he's earned any demerits from Uncle Sam." He unleashed a tremendous belch. "Maybe it's that enchilada I had for lunch, but my gut's telling me we might have a border runner here."

"You're a pig, Hank. Always have been."

Cas could almost hear her tamp down a smile.

"Hang tight, give me a sec," she said.

While waiting for the results, Cas peered over the dashboard and saw the door to the restroom shaking furiously. Hank and his partner were trying to free the wedge that he had hammered into the doorjamb. He expected them any minute now to start shooting their way out of that burger joint's john like Butch Cassidy and the Sundance Kid.

At last, the dispatcher came back on. "Looks like your instincts were half-right. Seth Cohanim has a federal record, all right."

"Transporting illegals from Mexico, *si*?"

"No, selling tainted beef. He's been cited ten times by the USDA."

Cas lurched up, hitting his head on the roof. "Selling ... huh? How's that?"

"Here's something else that may interest you. Mr. Cohanim boarded a flight at Dallas International about an hour ago. He must've left his car there, been in some big fat hurry."

"That, or maybe he was just running late for a flight."

Shots rang out from inside the restaurant. Cas could see the cops tossing the splintered door out into the dining area. He watched them rushing toward the door.

"Were those gunshots?" the dispatcher asked.

Cas ducked behind the dashboard. "Just a backfire there, hon. I gotta get Maintenance on this damn muffler." He sighed. "Heather, real quick, does HSA give the destination of the flight this Cohanim character is on?"

"Riyadh ... Any idea where that is? Somewhere in Mexico?"

No answer.

Long pause, then the dispatcher tried again. "Hank? Hello? Do you copy? Can you read me? You still there?"

Another pause followed, this one shorter.

"Yeah, this is Hank."

"This Riyadh place," the dispatcher asked. "It's near, what? Juarez, Sinaloa?"

"What the hell are you talking about?" The real Hank, now back in his cruiser, yelled into his transmitter. "Who's on this goddamn open line?"

The speaker nearly exploded from the volume spike. "Who do you think? It's Heather, you slip-shoed jackass! Use that kind of language on an open

dispatch line one more time, Benson, and I swear to god I'll write up a harass-
ment complaint faster than you can order a brisket and sides, and then I'll have
your *cajones* deep-fried at Pepe's for happy hour."

The real Hank, grimacing from another shooting burn in his stomach,
clicked off the transmitter. He got out of the cruiser, slammed the door, and
walked slump-shouldered to the speaker in the drive-through lane. He pressed
the button on the order box.

"Welcome to Whataburger," the manager said. "If this is your first time
here, may we recommend our new Down Home Crockett Cobb Salad with
our real Texas bacon bits and fat-free cottage cheese."

"It's me! Look out your damn window!"

"Oh, yes, sir. Sorry. May I take your order?"

"Give me one of those jalapeno cheeseburgers. And supersize it with some
jumbo fries."

"Would you like to try our new red-hot Lonestar barbecue sauce, sir?"

Hank loosened his belt in preparation for the colonic Apocalypse. "Yeah, why
not. Put enough of that shit on those jalapeños to down a ten-point buck."

21

Upper West Side, Manhattan

Marly bolted up on her bed from a nightmare. Clutching her flower-print sheets, she looked around the room in a sleep-fogged daze and slowly realized, to her great relief, that she was not trapped in some smoke-filled Middle Eastern opium den, but safe in her own apartment. The alarm clock said she had slept more than twenty hours, so why was she still so exhausted?

She resolved not to think about the lost week of work. Fortunately, most of the time she had frittered away—thanks to the demented antics of the surfing poster boy for America's Most Wanted—had been office appointments only. Those were easy enough to reschedule, but the semester's end was approaching, and Thanksgiving break was just a few weeks away.

Cas.

She yawned and stretched, promising *again* never to say that name aloud. She calculated what time it would be in Saudi Arabia, and realized that her former partner in crime had blown his Doomsday deadline by four hours. No way he could have retrieved the Black Stone fragments and returned them to Mecca in time for this Hajj thing to happen. The entire Muslim world had prob-ably woken up a few hours ago to discover that their mojo rock was missing.

She glanced at the window. As far as she could tell, the planet hadn't blown up. The only crater she knew existed was the one in her bank account. She waved it off, all of it, anxious to get back to normal and return to South Carolina for the holiday—for grits, cotillions, Gamecock football, and her parents.

She leapt from the bed and padded to the kitchen to put on a teakettle. Hot, finely ground coffee would shake the sleep from her eyes. While her French press worked its magic, she strolled over to her computer and turned it on. She saw a thumb drive inserted into one of the USB ports.

What was *that* doing there?

As the computer booted up, she remembered that Mossad agent—Avram Isserle or Joshua Silver or whatever the hell his name was—had been fumbling with her machine when he busted in.

Had he left it there?

She clicked on the removable drive's icon to view its contents. The menu popped up empty, so she checked its properties. The gizmo contained nearly five hundred gigabytes of pristine memory. Wait, that had to be a mistake. She'd never heard of a flash drive with that much storage capacity. This compact doodad was no bigger than a Bic lighter, but if the specs on it were correct, it could contain more information than was stored in Low Library. She bet the über-geeks on the Stardust project would love to get their hands on this little beauty.

Hmm, that was odd: Only one folder—titled *Exodus*—remained on the flash drive. And it contained only two files, a DAT and an executable program. The entire folder took up less than three hundred and fifty megabytes of space, just a fraction of its capacity. Using a gadget like this would be like taking a commuter flight on the Space Shuttle from New York to Boston.

Uh-oh. The damn thing might have a virus on it.

She clicked on the *.exe* file anyway, and a dialogue box popped up. A status bar began sweeping across the screen. Wait a second. She clicked open the "Processes" folder in her Task Manager. The menu clearly showed the *Exodus* program still running! The software was humming along, even though her computer was shut off. Had this bloodsucking techno-leech been running on her computer the entire time she'd been going down the rabbit hole with Cas?

She crouched to look at the underside of the jump drive. The red LED light was blinking its *busy* state. She yanked the drive from the USB port, and the light went black. She clicked through her hard drive and found a file with a table showing several columns of files that had been transmitted via an FTP transfer protocol from her computer. She looked closer at the file names. All of them were from the Stardust project.

Bastards!

She scoured her memory. Had she inadvertently mentioned the classified NASA project to anyone outside the team? Why would somebody want her private research? She barely understood half of these files anyway. Since leaving the mission, she hadn't had time to sift through the tons of data she had gathered. She stared at the files now flipping across her screen like shuffled cards.

What did they all have in common?

She opened a keyword-mining program that was designed to analyze reams of data. After typing in the names of the first twenty files cannibalized by this *Exodus* software, she searched for any word or combination of letters that appeared most frequently. But then she realized that a scan of the entire computer would take all day. She wouldn't have the time to go through the results before tomorrow morning's class, so she checked-marked the option to email her a copy of the results. She'd have to go over them at the office later.

Suddenly feeling vulnerable, she leapt from her desk and checked the locks on the door. The windows were secure. She had given Paul Brady a set of keys to her apartment. Thank God for that. Maybe she was just being paranoid. This near-fatal intrusion into her life had her thinking like a spook now.

She laughed off her paranoia. The dementia known as Casitis had apparently wormed its way into her subconscious. Aching with fatigue, she decided a hot shower would calm her down. She grabbed her coffee cup and trudged into the bathroom, leaned in to turn on the tap, let the water get hot and slid out of her pajamas. When she stood up again, she caught a glimpse of herself in the mirror. The image of the woman looking back at her appeared ghostly pale, with dark circles under her eyes and *terrible* hair. The dye job Cas had forced on her was sloppy, awful, streaks of black coloring, cropped with the haphazard chopping of a skateboarder.

She rubbed her sides, reminded just how much her back ached, probably from having been duct-taped to a wooden chair and launching herself into a fully armed coffee table. She looked at her wrists. The red welts that had popped up from the tape's nasty adhesive had almost faded. At least, she saw no bullet wound or knife scar anywhere.

Stepping in to the tub, she turned on the shower and lost herself in the rising steam.

Was that a pipe she heard banging outside?

The hot, cascading spray suddenly stopped. *Goddamn landlord!* Didn't he pay the water bill? Or did the stupid pipes get clogged? She stepped out of the tub and, wrapping herself in a towel, marched out to the living room to retrieve her cell phone and call in the complaint when ...

A hand touched her bare shoulder—she gasped.

"Nobody is here to hurt you," said a man's voice beyond the curtain.

She heard the click of a handgun.

"If you give us what we want."

Terrified, she stood motionless, dripping wet and protected only by the towel.

"I'm waiting, Dr. McKinney."

She could think of only one way out of this ... she threw off the towel.

The man's eyes nearly jumped out of his head.

The split-second break gave her just enough time to hammer the stranger with a knee to the balls. The man grabbed his crotch and crumpled over, his head banging with a *donk* on the wooden coffee table as he went down.

His pistol bounced across the carpet.

She grabbed the gun and raced to the kitchen. Yanking open her junk drawer, she pulled out a bundle of yellow garbage-bag zip ties. When she returned to the bathroom, the intruder was just rousing. Still naked as a newborn, she pistol-whipped him.

His lights went out.

She yanked his wrists behind his back and tied them to his ankles. Satisfied that he couldn't move, she reached behind the closet door and pulled out her terrycloth robe.

She marched back into the kitchen and refilled her coffee mug, stopping to open another drawer and pull out an eight-inch serrated knife. She walked into her bedroom and found that the man, dazed, had crawled in from the living room. She plopped into the chair in front of her computer, leaned over him, and slapped his head until he came back to consciousness.

She stuck the knife's tip between his vocal chords. "I'm sick and tired of assholes breaking into my place. I mean, how in the hell do you thugs keep getting in? I've got three padlocks on the damn door!" Her words trailed off while she kept holding the knife steadily with one hand and reached behind her for her coffee with the other. She never took her eyes off the man.

He didn't even flinch.

"You've got five seconds to tell me what's going on." She traced the tip of the blade from the edge of his Adam's apple to a spot just behind his carotid. "The cut doesn't have to be deep, just a nice, clean slice, and you bleed to death. Of course, it would be senseless to do it on this ugly carpet." She sipped her coffee.

The man showed no surprise, nor even a scintilla of hate or fear.

"Five ... four ... three ... two ..."

"Okay," he muttered.

She eased back the knife, just a tad. "You guys are a regular *American Idol* contest of inept thuggery. If one of you jokers doesn't complete the job, do they just call up the next contestant? Who has been sending you and your friends to terrorize me?"

"I have no idea."

"I've been getting a lot of practice lately learning what works best on bungling burglars and assorted other jerkoffs. This apartment seems to be Grand Central Station for scumbags in training. I could easily take this scalding hot cup of coffee and splash it all over your face. Of course, then you'd scream, the super would be here in a heartbeat, and we would have ourselves one hell of a mess. Or, I could do what I really *want* to do, which is to slice you up into chunks and feed you to the Hudson River catfish."

She couldn't believe she was talking like this. Between her quick-thinking ferocity in the Hyundai with Avram Isserle and her violent outburst in Abu Dhabi, she now wondered if she had developed some deep-seated anger-management issues, thanks to the time she'd wasted with the Malibu Mess.

"Listen," the intruder pleaded, trying to talk without severing an artery. "This is just a job for me, see. Nothing else. The bag man gives me half my money and—"

"Oh really? How much am I worth?"

"Depends on what I find in this apartment."

"I'm going to let you in on a little secret." She pressed the knife harder against his neck. "I've got no money. Actually, that's no secret. The entire world knows it. Look around this hovel. Why would anybody want to rob *me? Over and over?*"

The man looked up at her with an almost comical glint of tedium. "I'm suppose to get a stone you're hiding in here."

She looked around the apartment, which was stacked with enough rocks to form a Hobbit den. "You're going to have to get more specific. What *kind* of stone?"

"All I know, it's black and looks sheared off in the shape of a 'V.'"

She could hardly believe her ears. She wanted to retreat to her desk, where she kept the V-shaped shard she had broken off from the Black Stone fragment, but she didn't dare alert the guy. She kicked him in the knee to distract him, and then stole a glance at her favorite paperweight.

It was still there. He hadn't found it ... yet.

Her mind raced. How could this guy possibly know that she had broken off a piece of that seventh fragment? Surely Cas wouldn't have spilled the beans. She played dumb and lied, "I don't have the foggiest idea what you're talking about."

"Sure you do, lady."

"You tell whoever hired you that he's looking under the wrong rock for the wrong rock."

The intruder wiped a trickle of blood from his scalp. "Somebody told somebody that you bought the stone from Abdul Baith."

She shook her head in confusion. "Never heard of her. Is she a collector?"

"Abdul Baith's a dude."

"And who's this, uh, 'somebody' you keep talking about?"

"I don't know. Like I said, I'm assigned a go-between for whoever hires me. All's I know is that somebody says you bought this piece-a rock or whatever from this Baith character, and I have to get it back, or else."

She gripped the knife tighter. "Enough with the lies already. Five more seconds and—"

The intruder's eyes widened. "All I'm saying is all I know, all right? I was given two hours to get what you got …" He chuckled nervously and shook his head again. "You and I don't want to have happen to us what happened to this Baith guy, do we?"

"What happened to him?"

"The West Indies police found his body a few hours ago under a bunch of banana trees."

She couldn't make sense of any of this meth-head's gibberish. Why would someone think she was in cahoots with a murdered thief who stole the Black Stone and got shot up for the effort? She dug the tip of the knife into the burglar's soft palate. "I want you to draw on your vast experience of wise-guying and answer one question for me."

The man nodded.

She got up into his face. "Who do *you* think is after me?"

"Lady, I'm begging you. I don't have a clue. All I know is Baith was shot six times, up close and personal. There was some talk on the street …" He stopped himself.

"What talk!"

"The bullets formed some kind of star in his forehead."

Her face twisted in an expression of utter disgust. "A star? Why the hell did the killers do *that* to him?"

The guy shook his head to plead his ignorance. "I'm just the lowest mug on the totem pole. All I know is, if I walk out of this place without that stone, somebody's likely to give me a similar facial."

She figured it was fifty-fifty he was lying through his teeth. Making sure he didn't move, she edged toward the goon's gun on the floor and picked it up. Now armed to the hilt like Cap'n Jack Sparrow, she prodded him on hands and knees toward the door. "I know some real bad characters in the underworld intelligence business who would love to strap your nuts to a time machine and conduct a séance with your brain."

"I'm not exactly following," the burglar whimpered, his nose now pressed against the door jam.

She stuck the pistol into the back of his neck and angled the knife near the crown jewels for good measure. "Let me make it simple, then, Mr. Bourne-I-

Got-No-Identity. I'm giving you a clear and present choice. You see that window over there? I'm going to pull my chair up there and sip a cup of java. And if I'm not watching you running down Riverside Drive in two minutes, I'm calling in the reservoir dogs."

"Lady, it's a death sentence for me if I walk out that door empty-handed!" He turned his head cautiously. "At least give me something to take to them, so I got a fighting chance."

His fear sounded authentic enough.

She grabbed a worthless lump of black basalt sitting on her sill and stuffed it down the back his pants. "There, go tell your Wizard of Oz to get his rocks off with that!" She threw open the door and kicked him out, then slammed home the bolts on her locks.

22

Riyadh, Saudi Arabia

A customs agent in the processing hall of the King Khalid International Airport motioned Cas forward to the interrogation kiosk and accepted his passport. "Purpose for visit?"

Exhausted, Cas was having trouble keeping his eyes open. After learning that the owner of Lightgiver Technologies was flying to the Saudi capital, he had booked the next flight out of Dallas. He didn't even have a toothbrush or a clean pair of underwear, not that he hadn't gone weeks without either.

Technically, his time had run out to find the Stone. Yet he still held out hope that the Meccan imams who supervised the Kaaba would have sense enough to continue keeping the relic's disappearance under wraps. He couldn't suppress his suspicion that this Texan asshole he was chasing knew something about the recent whereabouts of the Stone fragments that Marly had tossed away. Sure, all he had to go on was a set of license-plate numbers that linked a shady BMW with some mystery man who had just hopped a flight to Riyadh. But as long as there was still a chance, however slim, for him to get his son back—

"Sir!" the customs agent behind the counter said, raising his voice. "Again, the purpose of your visit?"

Cas coughed and answered hoarsely, "Pleasure."

The agent looked at the photograph in the passport, staring at it for nearly a minute. He occasionally glanced at his monitor to compare the photos. He casually reached under his desk, and moments later two officers wearing epaulets and berets emerged from a side door and marched toward the kiosk. The agent ordered Cas, "Please follow these men."

Cas retreated a step. "What's going on?"

"Come with us," one of the arriving officers demanded.

Cas cursed silently. Why had his name been flagged? God forbid, had the Saudis discovered that he and Marly pilfered the Kaaba shavings? No point in resisting these guys—not here, not in public, not now. He had no choice but to be perp-walked past the long expanse of queues, gawked at by the suspecting eyes of the other travelers.

Led into a cold cinderblock room, he was pointed toward a steel table with two chairs. Overhead, a video monitor hung from one corner.

A burly Saudi in a dark suit entered the room with two junior officers. He sat at one end of the table and stared at Cas before lighting a cigarette. "You have no luggage, Mr. Fielding."

Cas found his mannerisms odd for an Arab. Smoking was a rare habit for a Wahabi apparatchik, not exactly conforming to the dictates of the Prophet. "I travel light. I like to support the local economy."

The interrogator held the burning cigarette delicately between his thumb and forefinger, as if contemplating what its tip might do to a man's nerve endings. "You visited the Kingdom a week ago. And left after only one day."

"Last time I checked, staying in a country for just twenty-four hours wasn't a crime."

The agent stood slowly. He walked behind him with calculated steps. "No, but falsifying a customs form is."

Cas was all too familiar with this technique of depriving a suspect of his sightline, the most reassuring of the senses. Most criminals, when denied visual contact, become edgy and less assured. But he slowed his breath to counter the move and summoned an image of the interrogator to his mind's eye. Then, he muttered indifferently, "Yayup."

"Are you on medications for a psychological illness?"

Cas laughed, wondering how the lout had come up with such a question. "Seriously, Columbo?" He couldn't fathom where this could be going. His interrogator didn't move, but Cas watched a plume of smoke blow over his shoulder. He coughed into his fist and played along, "Okay, medication? Yeah, sure, Johnny Walker. I prefer Red, but Black will do. Medicare covers it."

Not amused, the interrogator returned to his seat and leaned forward. "I am going to ask you one more time. Why have you come to our country?"

Cas knew it was just a matter of time before he had to come clean. The sooner he finished toying with these apes and arranged to meet with the superior Saudi *sahibs*, the faster he could track down the man who had paid to have the Black Stone stolen—and now, apparently, was trying to have him killed. "I'm looking for a businessman from the United States named Seth Cohanim. He flew into this airport earlier today."

"Why are you going to so much trouble to find this Mr. Cohanim in Saudi Arabia? It would seem you could conduct your business with an American capitalist far easier at home, no?"

"He has something that belongs to me."

The interrogator nodded to one of his officers, who opened a laptop and punched in a series of keystrokes. The officer slid the laptop along the table to the interrogator to show him the results of the search. "Again, Mr. Fielding, you have lied to us," the interrogator said. "No passenger named Cohanim has entered Saudi Arabia within the past week."

Cas lost his smile. Was this scumbag Cohanim traveling under an alias? Maybe the guy knew he was being followed and was covering his tracks.

The interrogator crushed his cigarette in an ashtray. "My patience is limited."

Cornered, Cas finally admitted, "Okay, here's the deal. I'm working for your government."

"For *whom* in our government?"

"The royal Saud family."

The officer chuckled at the claim, all the more absurd coming as it did from such an unkempt, unshaven, unbalanced American.

"Call your own ambassador in Washington. Tell him that Cas Fielding needs to speak to him immediately. He'll clear all of this up."

The interrogator traded a skeptical glance with his fellow officers. "It is six o'clock at night in Washington. Mr. Bin Sultan is a very busy man. We do not bother him about mundane Customs issues, especially after working hours—"

"I have information he wants."

The interrogator raised an eyebrow. "What kind of information?"

"*That* I can't tell you. Not to be hostile or belligerent or anything, but I've been sworn to secrecy." Cas continued staring at his interrogator, aware that unwavering eyes helped prove he wasn't lying. He also thought about switching to fluent Arabic, but the last thing he needed was a red flag about his past in this country. "Look, here's the thing—if I *am* telling the truth, and you don't make that call, your ass'll get fried like a *falafel.*"

The interrogator weighed the possible consequences. Finally, he walked to a phone on the wall and punched in multiple numbers. "This is the Chief of Security for King Fhalid Airport. May I speak to Ambassador Abdallah?" He waited to be put through, until: "Sir, I am sorry for the imposition. But I have a man detained here who claims to work for you. ... A Mr. Cas Fielding. ... Yes. Yes, I see. I am truly sorry." The interrogator's face hardened as he hung up. "The Ambassador says he knows no one by that name."

"That lying, double-crossing *sonofabitch!*"

The interrogator signaled for his officers to lift Cas from the chair.

Cas tried to fight them off. "Wait! I can prove it!"

The interrogator held his men at bay. "You can prove that Ambassador Abdallah is lying? This I would like to see."

"The Kaaba at Mecca has been covered for a week."

The agent rolled his eyes. "For cleaning. Everyone knows that. But what does that have to do with you?"

Cas knew the confidentiality agreement he had signed for the recovery job would be useless in a Saudi detention facility. So, he told them the truth. "The Black Stone was stolen a few days ago. Abdallah came to my government asking for assistance in returning it. I work for the private company that your government employed—off the books—to work this mission. Abdallah obviously claims he doesn't know anything about me because he can't reveal the arrangement. Y'know, the whole plausible-deniability bit."

Eyes narrowing, the interrogator leaned closer and repeated the charge, "You say the Black Stone is no longer in Mecca?"

"Yeah, that's exactly what I'm saying. And this Cohanim asshole—please forgive my language, *sahib*—this guy who happens to be running around your country right now may have had something to do with its theft."

The interrogator walked to the television monitor and turned it on, scanning the channels until finding the Saudi broadcast of CNN in English. A live video of Mecca at the beginnings of Hajj was being shown on the screen.

Cas took a step closer to make sure his eyes weren't deceiving him. Tens of thousands of Muslim pilgrims were circling the Kaaba—and the ancient black cube was uncovered. After the picture shifted angles several times, he could see the silver oval frame. He lurched closer, rubbing his bleary lids.

The Stone fragments—all seven of them—were clearly visible.

"This is a trick! That has to be an old video clip."

"The cleaning of the Kaaba was completed last night," the interrogator said. "The shrine was reopened to the public this morning. So, as you can see, Mr. Fielding, the sacred Stone has never left our possession. And why *would* it?"

Cas stood slack-jawed. Had this Cohanim character undercut him by selling the seven fragments back to the Saudi government? That must have been why the Texan traveled here last night. But why did Cohanim go to all the trouble to pilfer the damn Stone if only to return it a few days later? The questions kept hammering his brain, until, all at once, the chilly realization hit him: He had been left dangling in the middle of the Arabian desert without a net—just as his son, Farid, had been abandoned here. No one in the State Department or Saudi government had any reason now to confirm his story, let alone admit his existence.

Seth Cohanim—whoever the hell *that* mystery mope was—had just screwed him out of two million dollars.

Two officers dragged him toward the door. He tried to resist, but they battered him with their fists.

The interrogator clasped Cas's chin. "Don't make us use the straitjacket."

"Straitjacket?"

"You appear to be suffering from a severe delusional illness. Our law requires foreign aliens who exhibit mental instability must be detained for seventy-two hours and evaluated by a physician. You'll be taken to the Ministry of Health's psychiatric hospital."

"I'm saner than the whole lot of you Wahabi-brainwashed stooges!"

"You are psychotic. Nothing you just told us has any basis in reality."

Cas's face turned purple with rage. "You wanna hear something real? I'll tell you something real, you ass-wiping son-of-a-whore! You fucking barbarians have held my son in prison for twenty years!"

The interrogator froze at the door. He turned back slowly. "Your son. ... I see. *Now* you claim to have a son here in the Kingdom." He shook his head with apparent regret. "We will get you the medical help that your inadequate health-care system could not offer you in the United States."

Cas struggled against the restraint. "He's in Ruwais! You can check it."

The interrogator hesitated, no doubt pondering the possibility that the transfer to the mental facility would go much easier if he demonstrated the severity of Cas's delusions. He nodded for one of his officers to make a call to test the claim. "Once more, Mr. Fielding, we will humor you. What is your son's name?"

"Farid. He goes by the Arabic name of Farid al-Harbi."

The minion left the room to go check the new information. Several excruciating minutes later, he returned and whispered to the interrogator.

The interrogator nodded, as if having expected the report. "Mr. Fielding, you have no son imprisoned in the Kingdom of Saudi Arabia."

Cas exploded. "Lying bastards!"

"A man named Farid al-Harbi died two days ago in the prison that you named. According to records there, his last testament said he had no family still living."

Cas was too stunned to speak.

"It is all too clear what has happened here," the interrogator said. "You read of this prisoner's unfortunate death in the newspapers and used him for your scheme. Only a profoundly disturbed individual would try to adopt a recently deceased stranger and convince himself that such a man had been his son." He gazed at Cas with keen curiosity. "To what purpose, Mr. Fielding? Have you no sense of decency?"

Cas staggered, blinded by grief and confusion. *Farid is dead?* The officers helped him back to the metal chair. His eyes ballooned with tears, and his throat tightened with inconsolable anguish. He had never in his life felt so profoundly alone. *Two days ago?* What could have happened in … he struggled for breath, for clarity.

Wait, two days ago. That was around the same time those goons got the Stone back in Dallas. Had Cohanim struck a secret deal with the Saudis to return the Stone? The cold, hard realization pummeled him like a haymaker to the face: If all of that were true, the Saudis would clearly have had no incentive for keeping Farid alive.

That sonofabitch Cohanim caused Farid's death!

All of these years, Farid had been alive. And now, he had been taken from him a second time. *Fucking bastards! This time they're gonna pay!*

"Mr. Fielding," the interrogator said, trying to rouse him from his collapse.

Cas sat with his head hung over his knees, mumbling incoherently.

The interrogator ordered his officers, "Keep him isolated until the psychiatric team arrives."

L ocked alone in the interrogation room, Cas sat staring blankly at the monitor showing thousands of pilgrims reaching desperately to touch the powerful Kaaba icon. Now that the fragments of the Black Stone had been returned, he knew Cohanim would be covering his tracks, and fast. The asshole was probably booked on the next flight back to the States.

His fury white hot, he stood and paced, until he spotted a list of numbers for the airport taped next to a paging phone on the wall. It was a long shot, but he picked up the receiver and dialed the number for assistance.

When a woman's voice answered, he spoke first in Arabic, repeating the words in English to be certain they were understood. "Could you please page the representative from Lightgiver Technologies? I need to get an urgent message to him. When he shows up, tell him that his doctor says his diagnosis has come in. He has only a few days left to live. … Yes, that's correct. To *live*. His doctor says it's not medically prudent for him to board an airplane." He hung up, and banged on the door.

A customs officer stuck his head inside.

Cas doubled over on the floor in a fetal position. "I need a doctor! Now!"

"What is wrong?"

"My Demerol! I'm gonna go into seizures if I don't get my medication!"

The officer spoke into his transmitter. "Send the medic to Room Seventeen."

Moments later, a male nurse arrived with a medical bag. Finding Cas convulsing, the medic dug a finger into his mouth and tried to pry his tongue loose to force him to breath.

"He said something about needing Demerol," the Customs officer said.

The medic pulled a syringe from his bag, tore open the sterile packaging, and stabbed the needle into the rubber top of a small glass vial.

The officer dropped to his knees and pushed against Cas's shoulders as the medic lowered the needle toward his patient's neck. Cas grabbed the medic's hand and drove the syringe into the officer's biceps. The officer tried to rise, but the sedative was already coursing through his veins, beginning to render him helpless. Cas yanked the gun from the officer's holster and pointed it at the frightened medic. "Load up another syringe."

The medic was too terrified to move. "Please do not harm me, I beg you."

"Do it! Now!"

With shaking hands, the medic prepared another dose and handed it over.

Cas pushed it back on the medic. "I'm a big proponent of self-medication."

The medic drove the needle into his own arm. In seconds, he became drowsy, and then flopped half-conscious onto the sleeping officer.

Cas leapt to his feet and cracked the door. The officers were gone. He snuck through the anteroom and out through a rear door that led into the airport terminal. Glancing over his shoulder to make sure he wasn't being followed, he walked briskly to the information desk in the central hub and said, "I think I was just paged. Did I hear correctly? Lightgiver Technologies?"

The female information officer looked perplexed. Speaking immaculate English, she said, "Another gentleman answered that page a few minutes ago."

"Really? He must have been one of my fellow sales agents. Did he happen to mention where he was heading today?"

"I think he said Tel Aviv."

Tel Aviv? Why the hell would Texas Hold 'Em being going to Israel? He swallowed back his surprise. "Ah, yes, that would be Bob Hendricks. Gosh, I'd *love* to say hello to ol' Bob." He smiled flirtatiously at the helpful, and quite ravishing, woman. "Say, you wouldn't mind telling me, what gate the Tel Aviv flight leaves from?"

Returning the smile, the woman pointed to a hall connecting two terminals. "Gate Twenty-One."

Before she could ask him about his health, Cas pressed a fluttering hand to his chest, smiling to indicate that he felt just fine except for the patter of excitement she gave him. He blew her a kiss and took off on a determined walk, glancing around for armed security as he hurried past the gates.

Alarms went off throughout the airport. Within seconds, officers armed with machine guns fanned across the terminals.

Cas ducked into a novelty shop and scanned the shelves. He grabbed a pair of sunglasses and a red-and-white checkered souvenir *keffiyeh*, slapped a handful of *riyals* on the glass counter, donned the accessories and sauntered out of the store. As he moved toward the gate, he heard an announcement that the Tel Aviv flight was in final boarding.

One of the men in line wore a Stetson hat and snakeskin boots. *Cohanim, you slimy snake.* That message about impending death apparently hadn't fazed the Texan from risking the flight.

Cas quickly assessed his options. If he confronted him here, all hell would break lose. And besides, he didn't have time with the entire airport now lousy with alerted security. He scanned the other passengers queuing up along the wall, waiting to be called to board. He chose his target, a sleepy-eyed codger who looked like a refugee from an Elderhostel tour.

Shedding his Arab headgear, he walked over and bumped into the man, sending him staggering against the wall. Catching him before he could fall, he whispered to his ear, "So sorry. That's what I get for trying to look at my ticket and walk at the same time. Are you okay?"

The old timer recovered his balance. "No problem, mate. Happens to me all the time."

"Y'know," Cas said, realizing from the accent that his new acquaintance was Australian. "I'm not looking forward to another ten hours on a plane. But I guess it could be worse."

The geezer looked like he might keel over at any moment. "How so?"

"I guess we could have been that poor chap who lost his wallet."

The old Aussie blinked, confused. "Which chap?"

"You didn't hear that announcement just now? Yeah, they found it at the security gate. They're holding it for him in the main terminal."

The Aussie felt for his pocket and turned white. "What was his name?"

Cas thought for a second as the line moved forward. "Uh, let me think. ... Aiden something. I think it was Aiden Rhys ... Rice ... something like that."

"Crikey!"

"That's not you, is it?" Cas asked in mock horror.

"Bloody hell!" In a panic, the elderly Aussie looked at the dwindling line. "I'm bollixed!"

Cas aimed him down the concourse and gave him a supporting tap on the shoulder. "You go push the tit, mate! I'll tell the dollies to hold the bird until you get back, if that's all right with you."

Nodding gratefully, the creaky fellow staggered down the terminal in quest of his wallet.

Cas turned toward the El Al counter and fell in line as the last passenger to board. He reached the gate attendant and handed her the boarding pass that he had just pilfered from the Aussie's jacket. "Life is beautiful. Don't you think, love?"

The cute attendant smiled as she scanned the pass and handed it back to him. "Thank you, Mr. Rhys. I wish all the passengers were as cheery as you."

"I try to bring a little sunshine to everyone I meet." Starting down the ramp, Cas turned back and pulled out a hundred-dollar bill from his pocket. He slipped it into the ticket attendant's hand and whispered, "I know it's not usually done, but I'd be in your debt if you'd ask one of the flight attendants to deliver a double Scotch on the rocks to the gent in the cowboy hat in First Class."

"Is he a friend?"

"Oh, he's a very dear friend. But I don't want him to know I'm on the flight. I'd like to surprise him. Just have her tell him that somebody who thinks about him a lot has more of these surprises in store for him in Tel Aviv."

When she nodded with a smile, he glanced over her shoulder. Dozens of security officers were running across the main concourse with weapons drawn. As the skyway door closed, he waved goodbye to the attendant. Hearing the door lock, his fake smile was replaced by a grim look of determination to make a certain passenger on board to pay dearly for his son's death.

23

Columbia University, Manhattan

Half an hour after sending that bumbling burglar on his scamper across Riverside Drive, Marly hurried down Fairchild Hall's lighted corridors while looking around each corner to make sure no one was lurking in wait. She unlocked the door to her office and slipped inside, hoping the goons who kept breaking into her apartment weren't stupid enough to risk being nabbed by campus security.

The room was frigid, so she cranked up the clanking radiator. She removed her coat and rubber shoes and put on a fresh pot of coffee, then eased into her chair and tried to calm down. She had finally managed to convince the guy that she had never heard of the Black Stone of Mecca. But the lowlife who had hired the even lower form of lowlife might be another story. Lacking any better plan, she had decided to run across campus through a driving snowstorm just to be closer to the university police patrols.

She reached into her pocket and slid out the sliver of the Black Stone that she had grabbed on her way out of the apartment. It seemed to glow in the dim halo cast by the green accountant's lamp on her desk. Why was everybody so hell-bent on possessing it? What could possibly be embedded in this cosmic chunk that would be worth enraging more than a billion people? Glancing over her shoulder into the dim corner of her office, she caught the outlines of the equation that she had scrawled across her chalkboard:

$$87Srnow = 87Sroriginal + 87Rbnow * (elt - 1)$$

She had forgotten to erase the isotopic imprints she had written when that crazed Malibu freak stood here in nothing but a banana hammock. She shook her head, wishing she could take back that moment of lunacy and avoid all of the trouble he had caused her. Desperate to take her mind off her problems, she decided to catch up on her igneous research. She tapped the hibernation-release key on her computer, which was always on. Her side business selling meteorites had been all but dead during these recent weeks. If, as she feared, her teaching job was in jeopardy because of her many absences that semester, she figured she'd better start earning some more money on the side.

She typed into the Google Search box: *Recent meteorite sightings.*

More than nine million results came up, topped by a Wikipedia entry that would tell any layman pretty much all anyone would ever want to know about space chips. The next entry down caught her eye. She clicked on the News link at the left side of her screen.

"I'll be damned," she whispered with a low whistle. She read the rest of the news transcript:

> *LLANO COUNTY, TEXAS (CNN) - Houston's Johnson Space Center confirmed local reports here that something strange lit up the winter horizon last month.*
>
> *"Oh, yeah, we caught a glimpse of that sucker," said astrophysicist Erin Trocker, who told CNN that she was "enthralled, delighted and not a little bit worried" about what she thought she had seen fly across NASA's radar and telescopic screens. "We're not sure, obviously, but the consensus here is that it was a brown dwarf star that soared across Earth's atmosphere somewhere west of Dallas."*

She had been so close to that little star, and hadn't even known. Part of her wished she were still in Texas to track down its leftovers. A meteorite from a dwarf star that visible would probably be worth at least ten thousand bucks. She dropped the Black Stone sliver into her top desk drawer and locked it. Never mind that just about anybody, it seemed, could get into anything any time around Manhattan anymore.

After flipping through her backlog of journals for an hour, she checked her watch. If anybody else *had* been staking out her apartment, surely they would have given up by now. She really needed her bed. Flicking off her lamp, she opened her office door. All the fluorescent hallway lights were out. Strange.

Before she took another step, two men jumped her.

She screamed and scratched at them, but her clawing nails caught only their thick woolen coats. She couldn't get a hold of anything. Blood began pounding her brain, and the contusions, cuts and bruises that spotted her body started throbbing. With her adrenaline drained, and fear and pain over-whelming her, she passed out.

S he came to consciousness on the street. How much time had passed? The muggers her had taken her watch, cell phone, and the new keys that she had recently cut for her apartment. At least she still had her wallet and her credit cards. Why didn't they take those? Rising to her feet, she staggered out of the biological-sciences building and looked down Amsterdam Avenue. The sidewalks were nearly empty except for a few homeless people sleeping in doorways. It had to be well after midnight.

Goddamn it! Now they're assaulting me twice a day?

Did the entire world now have it in for her? Groggy and disoriented, she wobbled up to West 118th Street, determined to get back to her apartment and find out once and for all who the asshole was who kept sending these thugs after her. When she finally reached her six-story walkup, she buzzed the intercom outside for the super's apartment.

"Whaddya? Hey, you have any idea what time it is?"

"Irving, it's Marly from Four-A." Her voice was so feeble, she wondered if he could even hear her.

"Oy, you! Whaddya, *meshuggah?* Out this time a night, cold as it is? D'ja lose ya keys-a somethin', henh?"

"Yeah, Irving, I'm crazy as a bat in a belfry. And, yeah, I somehow misplaced my keys, maybe left them at the office. Had to work late."

At least, part of that was true.

The old superintendent shuffled down the marble stairs and let her in.

"Hey, listen, I owe you," she said, hiding behind her black woolen scarf as if she'd been freezing, to prevent him from seeing the bruises on her face. "Thanks, okay, and tell Mrs. Irving good night for me."

The moment she turned toward the second-floor landing, she could feel something was amiss again. Was she now so paranoid that she heard gun clicks around every corner? Without even taking out the spare keys that the super had handed over to her, she crept up to the third floor and pushed on her door.

It was unlocked.

The door creaked wide open in a terrifying arc. She tiptoed into the dim living room. She had left only her bedroom light on, and she kept the shades open to let in the silver glow from a street lamp. In the thin light pooling over her apartment, she gasped in horror. Everything in the room had been destroyed. Her computer was smashed to bits, and her futon was overturned, slashed with its cotton batting strewn among her shredded books. Her refrigerator and freezer were open, their contents thrown all over the kitchen.

She inched into her bedroom and saw that it had been given the same treatment. Frantic, she found her line phone and called the only person she knew she could trust. "Paul," she said, holding back the urge to cry. "It's Marly. Again." She couldn't catch her breath. "God, I'm sorry! I really am, but—"

"Calm down." Dr. Brady spoke with that same tone of reassurance he had adopted during his visit to her in the hospital. "Just slow down. Take a few deep breaths and talk to me."

She decided against telling him about the break-ins and assaults. Recovering her composure, she said with fake serenity, "Listen, I've run into a bit of a dead end on some research. I've been doing a little freelance work for an intelligence type." She hesitated, trying to figure a way to ask for what she needed without revealing that she had gotten involved with the DIA operative he thought was long dead. "I've lost his contact information. I was hoping you could call in a favor in Washington and find out how I can get hold of him."

"Would this have anything ..." He cut off that question to ask another, "Good God, Marly what are you *thinking*? After that last mix-up in Queens?"

She appreciated his paternal concern, but ignored it. "I need to find him."

"Who?"

She braced for the reaction. "Cas Fielding."

There was a long pause on the other end. "Are you suffering some sort of breakdown? I told you, the guy is dead. And why—"

She was starting to wonder if perhaps Dr. Brady, being so close to the CIA, had been intentionally kept in the dark about Cas's relocation under an alias. After all, she had heard enough small talk from Cas to know that the Pentagon's intelligence operation wasn't particularly keen on trading national security secrets with the CIA. "Actually, I think he might still be alive."

There was another long pause on the other end. "That would be news to my friends at Langley."

"Is there some way you could double-check for me?"

Dr. Brady released a heavy sigh of irritation. "Even if Fielding had somehow managed to escape the Saudis years ago ... Listen to me closely. I'm only going to say it once more. Damn near everybody who ever got close to that lunatic ended up dying. Sometimes in the most excruciating ways. Or they've found themselves rotting in some Third World prison."

"Professor Brady," she said, resorting to a desperate formality. "I'm grateful for your concern, truly I am. But this is important to me." She gritted her teeth. "Please. Just this time. Again. Dinner on me, I promise—soon as I get the chance."

"Okay," he said, clearly annoyed, "I'll check it out, just to put your mind at rest. But I want to know absolutely nothing about any of this. I've already told you I can't vouch for your safety."

"Of course." She was already way ahead of him on that front.

"I'll see what I can do."

Two minutes later, he called back. "Marly."

"Yes?"

He sounded shaken. "I don't know who you've been talking to, but apparently Cas Fielding has arisen from the tomb. He was reported last seen on a plane bound for Tel Aviv. I can't tell you how we know this, but here's a surprise"— his voice rang with sarcasm—"he stole a passenger's boarding pass. The Israelis are planning a rude welcome for him when he lands."

She stifled a gasp. He jumped on a plane as a *stowaway*? Was he *that* broke?

"Hello, Marly? You still there?"

"Yeah, sorry."

"I had my one of my contacts email me the essentials on this guy over a secure account. You really need to know what you're getting into."

"Is it that bad?"

"Here's for starters," he said.

She could picture him sitting at his computer, scrolling through what likely was some sort of encrypted dossier.

"Fielding was a Goat at West Point."

"What does that mean?"

"He graduated last in his class. So did Custer, and we all know what kind of monumental screwup *he* was. Apparently, Fielding still holds the record for cadet demerits."

She had no trouble believing that.

Dr. Brady seemed to be thoroughly enjoying whatever he was reading. "Thinks he's smarter than everyone else."

"That seems to go with the uniform, doesn't it?" She caught herself defending Cas. What was *that* all about?

"Ranger school, then a stint at the Defense Language Institute. He learned Arabic. Flamed out, apparently, after the one very severe solo deployment with the DIA. We already know where *that* took place. His psychiatric debriefing—"

"What?"

"You heard me right. It was filled with more anagrams than are listed in the index of the DSM Handbook for Mental Disorders. Still, he managed to get an honorable discharge. Left the United States Army with a gold-leaf cluster—a major, headed straight for light colonel, maybe even higher-up. Shudder that particular thought."

He sounded like he was shuffling through some papers.

"Anyway, he imploded. So with a doctor's note, four years at the Point and cobbling together the 'right' amount of time served, thanks to pulling a few strings, of course, he managed to squeeze out just enough of a pension to keep him permanently surfing out in Malibu. At least, that's what it says here. I hope that little list of horrors scares you straight."

She was still lingering on the psychiatric briefing.

"Marly, am I talking to a wall here?"

She roused. "Thanks, Paul. I have to run."

"Remember what I said. Don't get within a thousand miles of—"

She hung up and picked herself off the floor. Grabbing her handbag, she angled back down the stairs and raced back down Amsterdam Avenue, praying to get back to her office before the creeps who had destroyed her apartment found her again. Breathless, she turned into the campus and found a security cop. She asked him to escort her to her office.

The guard led her up the Fairchild Hall stairs and brought her to her door. "You sure you're okay, Professor? You seem a little rattled."

"No, I'm fine," she lied, still trying to calm her breathing. "My sister was mugged last week. It's got me a little on edge, is all."

"Understandable," the guard said.

She dug out her keys. She hesitated, then cranked open the door. "Would you mind checking inside for me?"

The guard brought his hand to his holster. "No problem." He turned on the light and found the office empty. "Looks like you're good to go, ma'am."

"Thank you," she said as she stepped inside. "Sorry for the trouble."

"Not at all. You've got the campus security number. Give us a call when you're finished, and we'll send someone over."

She nodded and shut the door behind the guard. When she got to her desk, she pulled her computer out of hibernation again and clicked opened her Gmail account.

Strange … an email from herself.

Of course! She'd forgotten all about it. Earlier that night, she had sent the results of the keyword-mining scan that she ran from her home computer. She hurriedly scrolled down the rotating list. All the files involved test results for chemical and biological compounds found on meteorites.

Phosphate.

Her memory fired. Hadn't Cas's old girlfriend in Brussels told them that INTERPOL's heat-sensitive radar picked up traces of phosphate and carbon on the Black Stone meteorite? She hadn't given it a second thought at the time, but now a major piece of the puzzle suddenly fell into place for her: Those thieves in Dallas didn't give a damn about the Black Stone! What they really wanted was—

Someone pounded on her door.

No way. Not three in one day.

Where was that damn guard? She backed toward the window. The only way out was down the fire escape, three stories of rusty ladders and landings. She moved toward the phone to call—

The pounding grew louder.

She didn't have time for campus security to get back up here. Hell, for all she knew, Mossad could have paid off those damn rent-a-cops to tell them where she was hiding. They sure as hell weren't doing anything to keep her safe. And she couldn't risk calling Brady again, not after she had repeatedly ignored his warnings.

She slid open the window and stepped onto the narrow iron grate. She avoided looking down as she carefully descended the ladder and leapt to the sidewalk.

Above her, a gunshot rang out. A bullet *zinged* past her head.

She sprinted across campus to Broadway and flagged a cab. Pressing a hand to her pocket to make sure she still had her wallet, she shouted to the cabbie, "JFK! Fast!"

24

Tel Aviv, Israel

The EgyptAir plane taxied to the gate at Ben Gurion International Airport, and the pilot cut the engines. Seated in the rear, Cas was forced to cool his heels while an old biddy reeking of cheap cologne struggled to lift her bag from the overhead bin. Cohanim, standing up in First Class, was about to get a big head start off the plane. Cas knew if he didn't catch him before he got to Customs, the Stetson-crowned thief would be out the terminal doors and gone with the wind.

Customs ... hmmm. He hadn't exactly given that one enough thought.

How *would* he get past Document Control? The last name on the ticket he had stolen in Riyadh said *Rhys*, not even close the name in his passport. And this was Tel Aviv, not Mogadishu, so there was no bribing his way in. The Saudis had probably notified Israeli airport security that a notorious free-loader was on board. That's why the attendants had been unusually solicitous. They knew who *he* was but didn't want him to become suspicious. He'd likely be greeted by a phalanx of Uzi-toting Hebrews the second he stepped off.

He moved farther back in the cabin until he was face to face with the prettiest flight attendant, the one who understood English. "Could I bother you for some water?"

"Of course," she said.

He noticed that her hands shook slightly, belying her forced hospitality. The airline personnel were all playing coy, waiting to nab him when the other passengers were gone to avoid a scene. When the attendant turned for the rear cabin to get a plastic cup, he reached for the cubbyhole next to the fire extinguisher and pulled out the crew sheet that he had lifted while boarding from the co-pilot's blazer hanging in the cabin's front closet. He slid the sheet into his front pocket, out of sight.

The attendant returned and handed him the water with both hands to keep it steady. "There you are, sir. Are you here to visit the Holy Land?"

Impressed by her attempt to make small talk to delay him, he flashed her the grin that had launched a thousand one-night stands. "Hon, I reckon wherever *you* are is the Holy Land."

She blushed, apparently forgetting that he was a dangerous fugitive.

He looked over his shoulders and saw that the seats had all cleared. Off the plane now, Cohanim had a good five-minute jump on him. Ignoring the attendant's inquiry if he would like more water, Cas sauntered down the aisle, acting nonchalant as he tried to hustle. He casually lifted the crew sheet from his pocket again, unfolded it, and reviewed the itinerary that would tell him the names of the pilots and all the hotels where they would be staying that night. His only hope to avoid arrest was that the flyboys up in the bubble hadn't been sent a mug shot of him during the flight.

At the exit, he stuck his head inside the open cockpit. The co-pilot wasn't there—likely in the head—but the pilot was finishing up his paperwork. He stepped a foot inside. "Barry? Barry Morris? Well, I'll be double-damned. How long's it been? I thought you flew for United."

The pilot looked up from his seat, confused. "Do I know you?"

"Cedar Rapids."

"Yeah?"

"Oh, man! This is embarrassing." Cas slapped his forehead then gazed at his shoes. "I'd always meant to call and apologize."

"Apologize? For what?"

Cas snuck a glance at the rear cabin. The attendants were loading their baggage to exit the back of the plane. "There's no easy way to say this, so I'll just say it. I banged your girlfriend back when …" He reached for the door. "Do you mind if I close this? Y'know, kind of a personal issue here."

The pilot nodded, as if rummaging his memory for images of old flames.

Cas pulled the cockpit door shut and locked it. "Listen, I felt really bad about this." He put a hand on the pilot's shoulder in a conciliatory gesture.

Wearing wraparound sunglasses and an aviator's cap, the EgyptAir pilot sauntered off the plane carrying his briefcase and nodded to the beret-crowned Israeli soldiers lined up near the exit. He veered over the officer in charge and, with a confident smile, whispered in fluid Arabic that the man the Israelis were waiting for was still on the plane.

The Israeli officer shook his head, unable to understand the comment.

Without a hitch, the pilot switched to English, delivered in a smooth Southern accent. "Your boy's crouchin' down like a scared rabbit in seat Fifty-four C. Gotta say, he doesn't seem all that bright. Give the guy five minutes, and I'll bet he'll walk right out into your arms."

The Israeli officer nodded his appreciation for the heads-up, now understanding the pilot despite his thick drawl.

The pilot strode past the passengers lined up and waiting for their Customs interrogations. He spotted the lane reserved for the flight crew and marched briskly toward a blank-faced matron who was handling the expedited exit. Looking at his watch, he shook his head in a plea for commiseration and muttered, "Can they make these turnarounds any tighter?"

The glum woman glanced half-heartedly at the ID badge on his lapel. With a weary sigh, she waved him through. The pilot tipped his cap in gratitude.

Finally cleared into the main terminal, Cas tossed aside the stolen aviation sunglasses and cap, sparing a guilty thought for the real pilot, who was probably only now coming back to consciousness in the cockpit from the thumb press to his jugular. No need to worry about the co-pilot, either. He was still locked in the john, with the doorknob wedged up against the expandable handle on his carry-on bag.

He saw Cohanim retrieve his passport and walk through the First Class customs stall. The bastard was heading fast toward the doors to the taxi stand.

He elbowed his way through a throng of families blocking the barricades with their insufferable hugging and kissing. He was aching to sink his talons into that arrogant cowboy and haul him to the nearest bank, where he would force him to transfer two million dollars into an offshore account registered to one C.T. Fielding.

He ran outside and shoved his fist to his mouth, gagging under the clouds of diesel fumes. The whole damn airport was log-jammed with jostling rental-car buses and cabs. Security cars raced past with their sirens blaring and bubbles flashing. By now, the pilot he had left passed out on the plane with a pinch to the jugular was probably reviving. With little time to lose, he sprinted down the Departures sidewalk and searched the sea of people.

There he was, that sonofabitch ... across the street, hailing a taxi.

He dashed across five lanes, dodging several horn-blaring vehicles. He reached his target just as the scumbag Cohanim was opening the rear passenger side of a cab. He shoved the stout Texan inside and jumped in next to him. "You don't mind if we share a ride into town, do you, Lone Ranger?" He raised his fist to punch the guy who had caused him all this grief—

The cabbie turned and aimed a pistol at him.

"Do you have anything over two hundred dollars in value to declare, Captain Fielding? Like, perhaps, shit for brains?"

Cas swallowed hard. The guy in the Stetson sitting next to him wasn't the man who had boarded the plane ahead of him in Riyadh.

Bruised from twenty-four hours of the best tenderizing the Land of Zion had to offer, Cas blinked against the harsh sunlight when his blindfold was removed. Two Israeli thugs escorted him into a room surrounded by a wall of glass doors that opened to the Mediterranean. The sea breeze told him all he needed to know. His old Mossad friends, he remembered, loved to situate their work houses in the best neighborhoods, and this one, Neve Tsedek, was the oldest and one of the most exclusive parts of town. His eyes adjusted just enough to make out two figures seated on a garish sofa.

"We're not usually in the business of matchmaking travel companions," one of the Israelis said. "But in your case, we've made an exception. I think you know our guest here."

Cas squinted in an effort to make out another shadowy figure on the couch. He eyes widened in sudden recognition. "What in the hell are *you* doing here?"

For a fleeting moment, Marly looked concerned about his battered condition. Then, finding him okay, she turned angry enough to light a blowtorch. She raised her handcuffed hands and snapped, "Why don't you tell me?"

The man lounging next to her laughed at their bickering.

Cas groaned, recognizing his old nemesis, Avram Isserle. "If it isn't the Wandering Jew. What name you going by these days? Josh? Avi? Camel's Ass?"

The Mossad agent stood up and pushed Cas into his vacated spot on the sofa. "You two troublemakers just can't stay away from each other, can you? At least Dr. McKinney here *pays* for a ticket."

Cas rested his scraped hands on his knees, and everything slowly came into focus. After Saudi authorities tipped off the Israelis that the ex-D.I.A. fugitive was on the plane, Isserle must have planted an imposter in Customs, complete with an outsized Stetson and a suit similar to the one Cohanim was wearing. Damn fine spycraft, that. He nodded with grudging admiration. "I gotta know, Isserle. Where do you find a cowboy hat in Israel on such short notice?"

"We have a vibrant film industry here," Isserle said in a Brooklyn accent for Marly's benefit, just to remind her of the old days back at her apartment. "You'd be surprised how accommodating a production wardrobe department can be when we call."

Marly glared at Cas, her eyes screaming a question: *How could you be so damn stupid?* It hadn't taken her long at all to regret her decision to track him down after learning from Paul Brady that he had conned his way onto a flight to Saudi Arabia. And it had taken the Saudi police even less time to flyspeck her on the Customs manifold and decipher what she was up to.

Isserle walked over to the wet bar and added another ice cube to his Havana Club. "Now, Mr. Fielding, perhaps you'd like to tell us why you attacked an Australian national in Riyadh and stole his ticket, then illegally boarded a flight here and assaulted the pilot?" He flicked his fingers up, as if he were counting. "How many felonies *is* that?"

"Hey, you *do* realize we're on the same side, right?" Cas said. "I happen to know a big-time thief who was on that flight."

"'Zat so?" Isserle said, clinking the ice in his rum.

"Sonofabitch owes me—"

"Us," Marly insisted. "He owes *us*."

Isserle removed her handcuffs. "Owes you what, exactly?"

"Money, for one thing," Marly said, rubbing her wrists. She nodded toward Cas. "And for him, there's the small matter of getting his son back."

Isserle turned to Cas. "She doesn't know?"

Marly glared at Cas, trying to guess what she had been kept in the dark about now. "Know what?"

Cas fought back the tears. Finally, he whispered, "Farid's dead."

Marly looked around the room, wondering if they were all playing a sick trick on her. "But I thought they told you—"

"When the Saudis got their Stone back," Isserle explained, "the young man became expendable. The Saudis are ruthless bastards."

Stunned, Marly sat back against the couch. Forgetting her anger, she stood and came to Cas, placing a comforting hand on his shoulder. She glared at Isserle, wondering how he knew of Farid's death. "How did *you* happen to come by that piece of information?"

Isserle smirked at her naiveté. "Lady, by now, even you should realize that a camel doesn't fart between the Persian Gulf and the Red Sea without our knowing the time and temperature."

She turned back to Cas and whispered, "I'm sorry. I wouldn't have raised my voice at you if—"

"I'm going to get him," he vowed, choking back the emotion.

Isserle heard the threat. "Get who?"

"Yeah," Marly said. "Get *who*?"

Cas hadn't had time to fill her in on his latest theory. "A Texas prick named Cohanim. I think he stole those damn Stone fragments from us. If it weren't for him, whoever he is, Farid would still be alive. Pick him up and put me in a room with him for ten minutes. I'll bet you he's—"

"Seth Cohanim?" Isserle asked, cutting him off. "We know him very well. He's president and chief operating officer of Lightgiver Technologies."

"And just how would *you* know the guy?"

"Unlike you two scofflaws, Mr. Cohanim is here on legitimate business with the Israeli government. He breeds a special strain of cattle for our *kibbutzim* in the northern part of the country."

Feeling Marly's eyes dig into him, Cas shouted, "Oh, that is *such* bullshit!"

"Well, that comes with the cattle now, doesn't it?" Isserle smiled and took a sip of the Caribbean's finest sugar-cane product. "Whatever financial dispute you may have with Cohanim needs to be resolved in an American court." His smile dropped into a malevolent gaze. "That is, assuming the statute of limitations doesn't run out while you're imprisoned here."

Marly leapt to her feet. "So it was this Cohanim con man who was running that fly-by-night lab in Dallas?"

Cas nodded. "I ran the plates on the Beemers those goons were driving after you left me high and dry."

Marly had steaming coming out of her ears. "Then he must have been the guy who originally stole the—"

"The Black Stone of Mecca?" Isserle interjected, amused by their outrage.

"Yeah!" Cas and Marly piped simultaneously.

Isserle shook his head at their ineptitude. "As usual, you two have your heads firmly up your asses. Cohanim had nothing to do with that theft."

Cas staggered to his feet, trying to make his battered posture appear as menacing as possible. "Then why don't *you* tell us more about who *did*?"

Isserle turned to Marly. "There's a bathroom around the corner."

When Marly shot the Israeli agent a quizzical glance, Cas interpreted the order for her. "That's Hebrew for, 'Could you give us a moment alone so that he can share some more brass-knuckle magic on me.'"

Reluctantly, Marly crept down the dim hall, glancing back at Cas and regretting her harsh words about him.

Isserle poured himself another three fingers of the crystal-clear hooch. Alone now with Cas, he said, "Do you seriously think that anything happens in Saudi Arabia without us knowing about it? We've been monitoring this situation in Mecca ever since the Stone was stolen." He sat back on the couch, the fresh cubes clinking furiously. "It's always been in our interest to see Islam's holiest relic protected. If word of the theft had ever gotten out—"

"Muslims around the world would have taken to the streets with their rocket launchers," Cas said. "But yeah, thanks for the freshman world-history lecture."

"If this region is going to blow up in a war," Isserle said, "we want the reward to be worth the cost. Such as the elimination of the Iranian nuclear program. You don't need to be reminded that we would have learned more than anyone ever wanted to know about Tehran's nuclear ambitions if the Stone hadn't been ..."

Marly returned to the living room, looking concerned about Cas. Having eavesdropped the entire time, she shouted at Isserle, "None of that explains why you've been harassing *me*!"

Isserle swirled his drink. "We got a tip early on that your accomplice here was going to be contacting you about meteorites."

"A tip?" Cas yelped. "More like an illegal wiretap on a certain Malibu phone!"

Isserle ignored the interruption. "Taking into consideration his level of intellectual curiosity, we knew he wasn't coming to see you for adult education credit. And given that he has a rather colorful record of erratic mental—"

"Hey!" shouted Cas. "I'm standing here, in case you forgot!"

Isserle nodded to Marly, as if suggesting his point had just been proven. "He has a personal motive for inflicting revenge on the Saudi government. We couldn't take the chance that he might sabotage the Stone's return to Kaaba."

Marly blinked hard, having failed to consider that possibility. "And all that screwing around with my computer?"

"Due diligence, I'm afraid," Isserle said. "Nothing more exotic than that."

"Due diligence? You damn near blew my head off!"

"Don't you think you're being a bit overly dramatic, Professor? I'll admit that from time to time we may get, you can call it, enthusiastic, but we're passionate about our work—"

"Murder!" she shouted. "The word you're looking for is 'murder.'"

Isserle smiled. "We knew from the beginning that your boyfriend here—"

"He's *not* my boyfriend!"

Cas tried to get in on the conversation. "Methinks she doth protest too—"

"You jackass!" she snapped at him. "Two minutes ago, you tell me your son is dead. And now you're cracking asinine jokes again? I swore I was rid of—"

Isserle jangled the ice in his glass to regain their attention. "It didn't take us long to find out that you two were spending a lot of time together. Rock expert and a former Middle East spook who didn't make it through high school. Wouldn't take a Mensa member to figure something was up."

Marly was now even more outraged. "Yeah, well maybe the U.S. District Attorney for New York will be interested in *your* work!" She looked to Cas for support, but he had turned his attention toward the half-empty bottle of rum.

Isserle poured Cas another drink. "Vodka used to be more your calling, if I recall?" He offered a drink to Marly, but she waved it away.

Cas let the effect of his long, satisfying slurp of rum shimmer through his veins. "Okay, riddle me this, Isserle. If this Cohanim con man didn't take the Stone back to the Saudis, then who did?"

Isserle shook his head in mock disappointment. "Come on, Fielding. You're really losing your edge. Don't you remember our old stock-in-trade? Don't trust *anyone* in this business."

"Who the hell have I trusted—" Cas stopped himself, his face blanching.

Marly waited to be clued in. "What?"

Cas clenched the glass so hard it threatened to shatter. "That sonofabitch!"

Isserle grinned. "You bit on Earl Jubal's hook like a blind carp."

Marly turned on Cas. "That militia creep who hired you off the books?"

Cas paced the room in a rage. "The lying warmonger cut us out of our fee! He used me as a bird dog to find the Stone, then he came swooping down to steal it out from under me." He drained his drink. "He took the Stone back to the Saudis and saved himself two million bucks."

Marly was trying to make sense of it all. "You mean those goons in Dallas were your old boss's men? And you've been chasing this innocent Cohanim man the entire time?"

Cas sat down and hung his head in dejection. "I fucked up royally."

Isserle patted Cas's slouched back with obvious condescension. "You retire from the business and cauterize a few too many brain cells at the local *cabana*. Next thing you know, you've lost your touch."

Defeated, Marly flopped onto the couch. "What do we do now?"

Cas felt her eyes biting into him. This time, he made himself at home with the rum, pouring himself an outsized shot, too depressed to think.

Isserle shook his head at the two American screw-ups. "I'm willing to let this one slide, Fielding. Professional courtesy, for old time's sake. And in condolences for your son. If you two poor excuses for grifters promise to catch the next flight back to the States tomorrow and never return to Israel, I'll make the stowaway and assault charges go away. The one-way tickets will be my treat."

With not even a hundred dollars between them, Cas and Marly had no choice. They nodded reluctantly.

"And, believe me," Isserle warned. "We *will* be watching your every move."

Cas got up from the sofa and walked Marly out. At the door, he turned back. "You said Jubal returned the Stone, but you didn't tell us who stole it in the first place. Which dissident Saudi sect was it? There must be a dozen of them now."

"That's way above your pay grade, Fielding," Isserle said. "Just let it go."

"I've wasted a month and lost my retirement and what was left of my family," Cas said. "Some closure on this could help ... a little."

"The thief wasn't a Saudi," Isserle smirked. "Not even a Muslim."

Cas screwed up his face in disbelief. "Who was it then?"

"Johnny Diarmuid."

His jaw dropped. "Johnny D, the Boston Wrangler? I thought he limited his heists to museums and Vegas hotel art galleries."

"He stretched his game on this one," Isserle said. "He used the alias 'Abdul Baith.' Apparently Johnny was this close to pulling it off, but he got a little greedy. Sitting in the West Indies while enjoying the good life for all of twenty-four hours, he became dissatisfied with his fee. As best as we can determine, he tried to blackmail the Saudis *and* Jubal for another million."

"Then how did those Stone fragments end up in Dallas?" Marly asked.

"We think Diarmuid was doing double time for one of the Mexican drug cartels," Isserle said. "Your neighbors to the South have been branching out into other lucrative forms of contraband. Looks like they got a sniff of the Saudi desperation and decided to up the stakes."

Cas connected the dots. "So, Johnny D and the *muchachos* were using Dallas as a mule stop."

Isserle nodded. "Best we can tell, the fragments were being stored in a short-term facility there. The owner of the building probably pitched the rocks into the garbage when Johnny D never came marching home to pay the rent."

The notion had never occurred to Cas that the Stone fragments might not have come from the lab that Cohanim's Lightgiver operation had abandoned. He was impressed by the size of Diarmuid's Celtic balls. "Ol' Johnny must be stocked up with Guinness for life now. What'd he end up getting for the heist?"

"Six shots at point-blank range. In a Star of David pattern."

Marly perked up, hearing confirmation of what the burglar had told her in her apartment about Baith's death.

Cas nodded. "A signature Mossad execution. That would explain why Johnny boy never came back to pick up the Stone for delivery to Mexico."

"You might be right about that," Isserle said with a smile. "Unfortunately, we were a little late in tracing the Stone fragments to Dallas. Jubal got there a few hours before we did. We never did tell the Saudis about Johnny D. Better they believe that one of their own homegrown radicals stole it. That way, they'll round up the usual suspects and put on a head-lopping show—" Isserle caught himself, remembering what had happened to Cas's wife.

Cas took the point. "Sure, let the world think that a Wahabi radical was responsible for the theft. Much more useful to you in future negotiations that might involve, say, occupied Israeli-occupied land for settlements."

Marly admitted to Isserle, "I could probably use that drink now."

Isserle grinned as he poured a glass of rum straight and handed it to her. He opened the curtains wider to expand their view of the gold-banded Mediterranean, and then raised his glass for a toast. "Here's to the last sunset you two will ever see in Israel."

T hat night, with nothing to do but wait for the Mossad cars that would pick them up before dawn and take them separately to the airport, Cas and Marly sat alone in an outdoor café overlooking the sea. Their armed chaperone stood fifty yards away, watching every move they made.

Marly dug listlessly through the bones of her grilled red mullet. She hadn't said a word during the entire dinner.

Cas had tried to dull the grief over his son's death with five rounds of cheap Israeli ouzo, but the effort had only made him more maudlin. Finally, he couldn't take the silent treatment anymore. "Hey, listen, I'm sorry."

"Not your fault," she muttered, picking at her cold dinner. "I should have ordered the risotto."

"No, I mean, about all this hassle I caused you on this wild goose chase." He started to reach across the table, but then withdrew his hand.

She looked up, surprised to hear him sound even remotely vulnerable for once. "I guess it was kind of stupid of me, jumping on a plane and flying all the way over here to find you. Once the dean finds out I've gone AWOL again from my classes, I can kiss that teaching job at Columbia goodbye."

Trying to interpret her facial tells through the ouzo haze, he bored in on her with a puppy smile. "So, why *did* you come looking for me?"

She shoved her plate away. "Doesn't matter now."

"Does to me."

She looked at him suspiciously. "You'll just think I'm wacky if I tell you."

"Uh, hello. You're sitting next to King Wacky. Don't even think of trying to take my crown away from me."

Through a long pause, she managed a half-smile. "I thought there might have been another reason the Stone was stolen. But I was just freaking out from all the stress, I guess."

His brow furrowed in curiosity. "*What* other reason?"

"You remember that piece of paper you found in that Dallas lab?"

Cas squinted to squeeze that bit of information from his brain. "Uh, no."

"The one that said something about 'stutter bands.'"

"Oh, yeah. I'd forgotten all about that. One of Cohanim's employees or whoever the hell was renting that office had a speech impediment. So what?"

She reached into her purse and pulled out a photocopied page from one of her textbooks. "Did that paper look something like this?"

STUTTER BANDS

REFERENCE LADDER

He looked at the copy of the illustration. "Yeah, *just* like this. What is this, anyway? Some kind of puzzle?"

"A DNA sample."

"You mean like *genetic* DNA."

She nodded. "When DNA is manipulated and amplified, sometimes small glitches are created that look similar to the original components of the genetic material. Scientists call these artifacts stutter bands."

"Okay, so somebody was testing DNA in that Dallas lab. Big deal."

"You're right, of course," she sighed. "My imagination just ran wild. Like I said, I've been freaking out recently."

He waited for her to explain more, but she fell quiet again. He tapped the table to regain her attention. "Is there something else you're not telling me?"

"You promise not to laugh?"

"Out with it, McKinney."

"This stutter-band thing got me thinking about an article that I read a few months ago."

"What about it?"

"A colleague at Stanford found uracil and xanthine in an Australian meteorite." She continued through his baffled silence, "Before he died, Carl Sagan suggested something like this was possible, but this was the first hard evidence to confirm the theory."

Cas shook his head. "Sorry, I need the 'Meteorites for Dummies' version."

"Uracil and xanthine are nucleobases. The foundations of RNA. They also may have been stepping-stones to DNA, which is needed to create protein in organisms."

He leaned closer. "Are you saying what I think you're saying?"

She wouldn't look at him directly, afraid of his ridicule. "The raw ingredients for human life on Earth may have first arrived inside a meteorite."

Cas took a slow drink from his ouzo and let it soak his brain. "That sounds like something out of the *National Enquirer*. Look, I flunked science in high school. But how could any living *anything* survive the heat on entering the Earth's atmosphere?"

Marly fiddled with the mood candle on the table. "The theory is that these molecules were protected by a kind of heat-shield shell inside the meteorite."

"So, if I'm understanding this, Sagan said that these space rocks were like seeds that planted *life* here?"

"Pretty much."

"And it was just sheer luck that these surviving DNA strands spawned what ultimately became"—he pointed to her then to himself—"us?"

"You'd have better odds winning the lottery on Mars, but yeah."

Cas looked up at the café's covered awning, as if he could see through it all the way to the solar system. "That means meteorites could have fallen on other planets in other galaxies ... and created life there, too."

"Hard to say," Marly said. "Those other planets would have to have just the right combination of hydrogen and oxygen for the DNA seeds to take root."

Cas swilled the *ouzo*, marinating the idea around his tongue. "You didn't come all this way just to tell me about some new out-there discovery."

She leaned back in her chair and turned away from him, gazing off toward the lapping waves of the Mediterranean.

He sat up and forced her to look at him. "You think there's DNA inside the Black Stone, don't you?"

She flicked a quick glance at him, unable to hold it.

"And now you think somebody hired Johnny Diarmuid to steal the Stone not for the ransom, but for the DNA."

Marly made sure the waiter remained out of earshot. "That old squeeze of yours at INTERPOL told us that the infrared picked up high levels of phosphate." Seeing that she was already starting to lose him on the complication scale, she dumbed it down. "Phosphate is an essential component for life. I considered the idea then, but dismissed it as too ..." She waved toward the stars to indicate that the theory was, as Cas had just said, 'out there.'

"What made you to change your mind?"

She looked guilty. "When you were rummaging around in that garbage bin in Dallas, I broke off a small piece of one of the fragments and kept it."

He pushed out his chair and came standing over her. "You did *what*?"

She glanced over at the guard, who was about to march over, until she waved him away, indicating that all was okay. "Hey, I needed a little something to sell to cover my expenses."

"You were skimming off the top? And you weren't going to even tell me!"

"Sue me."

He sat back into his chair and took another long drink to steady his nerves. "The Saudis don't have their *entire* Stone back. That's what you're telling me?"

"Don't soil your Speedo," she said. "Your Mossad buddy already told us that the Saudis still think some *jihadi* wingnut stole the rock. They're aware it was probably mishandled—"

"Do you have any idea what those Bedouins are gonna do to us if they find out about this? Why are you telling me this now?"

She thrummed her fingers on the table, until finally admitting, "I may have done a little testing on the fragment I saved."

"*May* have done a little ..." He pinned her with a hard stare. "And?"

She turned even more serious. "Positive for uracil and xanthine."

Cas sucked a deep breath, his head aching from trying to understand the possible implications of this revelation. "So you mean that the DNA from all those people over the centuries who touched and kissed it—"

"No. What I *mean* is that I found molecules *deep inside* the igneous."

He took time to think about what she had just said. After the long pause, he shrugged and took bite of fish from her plate. "That makes a great story. Except for one thing."

"What's that?"

"Johnny Diarmuid and those Mexican gangsters and Earl Jubal, or whoever the fuck really stole the Black Stone—they all have two things in common."

"Yeah? What?"

"They were all spawned from primordial pond scum."

She crossed her arms. "And the second thing they have in common?"

"None of them, I can assure you, ever gave a rat's ass about DNA."

She huffed, as if having expected that reaction. "I told you it was a crazy idea. But, no, you just had to hear it. Satisfied now?"

Cas tried to rub the sting of exhaustion from his eyes. "I'll tell you, Marly"— he never remembered having ever called her by her first name; he liked the sound of it—"my brain right now is more fluffy than a twice-baked potato. Too many tokes over the years, I guess. Whatever. I'm actually starting to pay attention to these conspiracy theories."

She just gazed out at the sea.

He couldn't imagine what she could be thinking. Getting no reaction, he called for the bill. After paying, he stood up, staggering from the effects of the booze. After finding his balance, he walked with her down to the beach. For what seemed like eternity, they stood side by side looking up at the Mediterranean stars. Night had fallen, and the November evening had taken on a chill. His flight to Los Angeles was scheduled to leave two hours after hers to New York. They both understood that if either wasn't around for their pickups the next morning, they could count a Star of David pattern being left with bullets on their foreheads, too.

"I guess this is really it this time, huh?" she said.

He wanted so badly to hold her. "What are you going to do now?"

She shrugged. "After this little fiasco? You pretty much guessed that I'm toast at school. The university won't renew my contract. I've missed too many classes. I'll finish out the semester and then start job hunting again."

"You could always come out to California," he said. "I have some contacts at Pepperdine."

She smiled sadly, but shook her head. "I'm an elite East Coast snob. Just a good ol' Southern girl, really."

He moved in, but she pulled away. "Look, Cas … I know you've had a rough time of it these past few days. With the news about Farid, and now this."

"What are you trying to say?"

She kept looking off, as if not wanting to meet his eyes. "I need something a little more …"

"Flexible? Look, I can do my thing and—"

"Stable."

He blinked hard. "*Stable*? Why not just say 'boring?'"

"Boring sounds pretty good right now. There's no easy way to put this, so I'll just be honest. I don't think you're good for me. My friend Paul Brady warned me—"

"Paul Brady? That egghead who has been sucking for years on the CIA's tit? What'd he say about me?"

"It doesn't matter."

"Tell me."

She looked over at the Mossad guard in the distance, wondering if he would pull his gun if things got overheated. She lowered her voice and admitted, "He said you're a train wreck. And that I should stay away from you at all cost."

"I'd like to see him spend a week in the field. See how he'd come out in the rinse cycle."

"Cas, you don't act like normal people."

"Last time I checked, I still have all the normal bodily functions. You mind giving me an example?"

She fidgeted in her chair, looking uncomfortable with the direction the discussion was going. Finally, she said, "Not to bring up a sore subject again … but all along, while your son was in mortal danger, you've been hitting on me like a teenager in heat."

"How long ago did your fiancé die?"

She bristled. "What's that have to do with anything?"

"You've running around the world chasing a prize money while he's still warm in the grave. That sounds pretty callous to me."

She was dumbstruck. "It's not the same at—"

He moved in for kiss, silencing her for an extended moment.

She surfaced, flustered. "Did you not hear me just say—"

He kissed her again, twice as hard and passionate.

She pulled back, gasping. "Enough, okay?" She stood up abruptly and pushed her chair away from the table. "It's over."

For a fleeting moment, he felt his legs go weak—and it wasn't just from the ouzo. He recovered his wisecracking armor and, affecting indifference, quipped, "You mean something had started? News to me."

Marly held a hurt look that suggested she was thinking about answering him, but then she turned away and hurried toward the Bauhaus building where they were being confined. She took the stairs in twos and raced to one of the bedrooms, locking the door behind her.

Abandoned—except for his Mossad guard—Cas shrugged and turned to stumble down the quiet, narrow lanes of Neve Tsedek, trying to come to terms with the hard reality that he would probably never see Marly McKinney, doctor of stones and stony hearts, ever again.

25

Upper West Side, Manhattan

Marly drew an 'X' across the July square on her *Meteoroid Of The Month* calendar, marking off the eighth month since she had escaped Tel Aviv. She hated to admit it, but once in a while, on slow Sunday mornings like this, she actually missed the adrenaline rushes from her crazed adventure into the world of espionage. Ever since that escapade, she had become as sedentary and isolated as the space rocks she studied.

She shook her legs and shuffled to the kitchen for a cold beer. Fired from her teaching job a week after her return, she still had no prospects for employment. Sure, there was that paper, whose deadline she missed, for the *Journal of Meteoritics and Planetary Science*, but she just couldn't get motivated to finish it. Bored out of her mind, she picked up the TV remote and clicked on CNN. Tens of thousands of protestors were chanting for the downfall of some dictator in some Third World hellhole. She didn't even bother to check the news ticker to find out where. Who cared anymore?

She switched the channel, hoping to find an old episode of *Pawn Stars*. She loved that show. Heck, she had even toyed with the idea of flying out to Vegas to sell those guys some of her rocks for a little cash to help pay the rent. Who knew? She might even become their go-to expert on minerals. She paused the remote on an infomercial touting a timeshare resort in Baja.

Suddenly, a face with a California tan flashed through her mind—the face with those same smirking features that she had tried to banish from her memory. Despite her brutally honest smackdown, she now felt an awkward desire, which she was comfortably able to dismiss in a single heartbeat. "Cas Fielding. In the land of brainless mussels, the one-lobed crustacean is king."

She looked up at the clock. It was ten in the morning in California. He was probably up to his armpits in booze right about now. That is, if he hadn't drowned in a surfing binge. She felt horrible, thinking such a thing about a man so broken and violent. Still, she had to admit that he was damn passionate about life and what he believed. Never mind that he'd almost gotten her trampled to death in Mecca. Then, of all the nerve, he had tried to make nice with her on that beach in Tel Aviv. She hummed an old Talking Heads tune that had weaseled into her head.

"Psych—Psych—Psych—Psycho Killer."

He deserved it, sure, but she *had* been awfully hard on him during their last dinner together. Truth was, the more she thought about him, the more she'd come to realize that his insufferable juvenile antics and inappropriate attempts at seduction were probably just a defense mechanism to cover for a deep emotional hurt he held inside. But all that was Freudian water under the psychological bridge now, thank God. The Malibu rock star was long gone.

And she had to be honest: she was no picnic at the relationship beach, either. She had her own head-shrinkable problems. For one, why couldn't she keep a steady job?

"Psych—Psych—Psych—Psycho Woman."

Don't go down that rabbit hole again, Marly.

Anxious for a distraction, she clicked the tube back on and checked out Fox News for high entertainment. Great, another riot somewhere in the Gulf. The whole damn Middle East seemed to be imploding at warp speed.

I wonder what Cas thinks about—for the love of god, stop it!

She sighed, weary of her own internal wrestling. Screw the Middle East. If the Muslim world had discovered the Black Stone was missing, the entire Gulf would now be one giant Scudarama. That whole experience made her wonder how many other scandals had been kept secret throughout history. And why *would* somebody steal one of the world's most conspicuous and highly charged religious icons, only to return it less than a week later?

Come on, get to work.

Driven at last to the task, she plopped down in front of her computer and clicked on the icon to open the document containing her article in progress, an offshoot from her doctoral dissertation on the building blocks of life as they related to panspermia theory. These past weeks, she had been venturing more deeply into her work with the Stardust Project. Truth was, she knew precious little about NASA's top-secret probe, but that didn't mean she couldn't plumb some of its declassified findings for a little journal cash on the side. She took another drink of beer, hoping for inspiration as she stared at the maze of conflicting theories and equations on the screen.

Why can't I forget about that damn Stone?

Nearly fricasseed by the humidity, she decided to try an old trick from her undergrad days to ease herself back into the mood. She scanned the shelves and looked for something interesting to read, something to get the blood flowing back into her brain. She pulled down an old tattered textbook, *Fundamentals of Planetary Science.*

She rubbed her eyes and tried to focus as she sucked in the musty smell of the dull-gray pages. An entry about a British chemist named Charles Edward Howard caught her eye. In 1802, he proved that meteorites contained nickel from outer space; he had illuminated a sample meteorite with an electrical charge that simulated the stone's entry into Earth's atmosphere. According to his report on the experiment, the rock had glowed for forty-five minutes. After that, he never wrote another word about stones from space. She'd always wondered why Howard gave up his avocation and chose instead to run London's biggest sugar refinery. Tragically, he died at age forty-two, suffering heatstroke after he walked into the refinery's oven room.

Something always struck her as fishy about that story. Why would a chemist who knew the dangers of heat take such a risk? Had he really died by natural means? Or had someone murdered him to prevent the exposure of something else embedded in one of his sample rocks?

Geez, listen to yourself, Marly. You're starting to sound like you-know-who.

Flipping randomly through her binder, she finally found the place where she had left off. She noticed that one of the mottled pages in the back had been torn and folded in. Two smears ran across the page. One looked like blood, dried black. She had never seen *that* before.

Maybe one of those Mossad goons who ransacked her apartment had cut his hand on the edge of the paper while rushing to find something inside the binder. The other smear resembled a shoe print. She ran her finger along the edge of the black sole pattern ground into the paper. Faint ruddy lines bordered its outline. She'd been through enough lab tests to know at once what *that* was.

Dirt.

She carefully traced the smudge and felt the roll of tiny granules. Some fell to the floor. She reached down to collect the minuscule grains and rubbed them between her finger and thumb.

Felt like clay.

No, it couldn't be. Indigenous clay of this rusty hue had never been found in Manhattan. She gently laid the binder on her desk and hurried to the bathroom. Snatching scissors and tweezers from her medicine cabinet, she returned to the kitchen and rooted around for a plastic bag. Back at the binder, she carefully snipped the paper that held the reddish smear and dropped several pieces into the Ziploc baggy.

She ran out of her apartment and flew down the stairs.

T wo hours later, after sneaking her way into the biology department lab by sweet-talking one of her former grad students, she returned to her apartment with the test results. She plopped back down in front of her computer and inputted the fresh data into her formula for revealing chemical compositions:

$$(K,Na)(Fe+++Al,Mg)2(Si,Al)4O10(OH)2$$

The sediment was glauconite.

That didn't surprise her. The reddish hue, though, was baffling. Iron potassium phyllosilicate tended to be green and, in its natural habitat, shiny or silvery. Though this sample had many of the same characteristics, there had to be more to this story than what the database was telling her. She typed in more details from her observations, including weight and color. The mineral in the specks originated from the decomposition of potassium feldspar with iron. Most likely in water. These particles had to come from someplace that had once been underwater for eons. No way it was from Manhattan. Or even the Northeast.

But *who* had gotten this stuff on a shoe?

She clicked as fast as she could through the online databases of samples.

Finally, a match.

She scanned the scientific history of the sediment. The grains had been deposited during the Ordovician era, one of the second Paleozoic geological divisions. Greenhouse gases had contributed so much heat to the Earth's atmosphere at that time that much of North America was covered by ocean. Only later in the period, after mass extinctions, did the Earth cool to one of its coldest periods in six hundred million years. And when things began warming up again, the Ordovician era laid the groundwork for one of Earth's most productive, life-giving stages: the Cambrian. There was only one region in the United States where such iron-rich samples with this particular range of color had been found.

She leaned back into her chair, now more confused than ever. This dust had come from rocks that were around a *billion* and a half years old. Even more intriguing, the ruddy smudge had gotten into her apartment ... by way of Texas. She stared through rounded eyes at her scribbled notes: The residue was known as Hickory Sandstone. Found only in Llano County. She punched in Mapquest on her web browser and searched for its location.

Damn. Four hours southwest of ... She pulled at her hair in disbelief. *Dallas?*

Those bastards who broke into her apartment weren't Mossad! That slimy Israeli agent had lied to her! But why would anyone from Texas want to—she froze, the blood draining from her face.

She zippered the plastic bag and slid it with her test results into the top drawer of her desk. Inside, her fingers happened across something smooth. She stared down at the sliver of Black Stone that she had secreted away from those brutes in the Dallas industrial park. She had completely forgotten she still had the Stone sliver. She could never remember where she had put it after cleaning out her office. Some hiding place.

The ancient Meccan meteorite fragment stared back at her in a dare.

She took a deep breath. *Don't do it, Marly*

Despite her better judgment, she typed a few words into Google. When a telephone number appeared, she picked up her cell phone and dialed.

"Malibu Chamber of Commerce," a voice answered.

"I've got a rather strange question," she said. "I'm looking for the nastiest bar in Malibu. One where the lowest form of beach life would hang out."

"That's probably The Fish Tank. But we don't usually recommend it to tourists. There tend to be, uh, altercations there from time to time."

"Sounds like the place I want. Could you please give me that number?"

26

Malibu, California

Cas rolled his swollen tongue across his dry mouth, checking to see if he could still salivate. His upper palate felt like a Bedouin sand carpet, and his teeth were coated with a sticky saccharine glaze. And those were just the first of several worrisome developments now coming to his addled consciousness: Aside from the fact that he couldn't breathe through his nose, his left calf was beginning to cramp and his bladder was sending stinging alarms that it needed draining.

Wiping the sleep gunk from his eyes, he turned to find a young blonde lying next to him. *Oh, right.*

He had met her the night before at the Fish Tank bar, after his third Mai Tai. Hadn't she been blabbering on about being from Indiana or Illinois or one of those lost continents? He also vaguely remembered having convinced her that he was the producer of an upcoming Rambo movie in which Sly Stallone would recruit a bunch of geriatrics to save the world against the enemies of Social Security. Off the cuff, just like that. He always knew that military techno-mumbo-jumbo knowledge would come in handy one day.

He quietly slipped out from under the sheet and stumbled to the kitchen to make a pot of java. Clearing a spot on the counter amid the detritus of empty rum bottles and cigarettes, he found the bag of stale grounds and poured a handful into the Mr. Coffee. A fraying decal of Joe DiMaggio gripping a steaming hot cup stared back at him.

Damn, am I that old? What next? A Baby Ruth candy bar in the fridge?

While waiting for the coffee to brew, he excavated his cell phone from the mess on the table and quietly eased through the sliding-glass door, hoping some fresh air might ease his pounding headache. He settled into a cheap lawn chair on his wraparound deck overlooking the Pacific and lifted his puffy face toward the sun. Shading his cell phone with one hand, he squinted to check for messages. *Nada,* as usual.

Out of booze, he thumb-texted his bartender pal Goobs, who was always good for a free nooner Bloody Mary. Which was helpful, seeing as how his financial situation was getting even grimmer, thanks to that bastard Earl Jubal double-crossing him on the Black Stone payment. If he weren't so hung over, he'd race back to the Mojave Desert and kick that toy soldier's ass all the way from CrossArrow's headquarters to the nearest bank.

His phone came to life, and he covered the screen with his hand to read Goobs' text reply:

Yeah & u got a msg here frm last nite. Smbody who nu yr real name.

He sat up with a start. Who could possibly know to leave him a message at the Fish Tank? His corner stool at that bar was more classified than the bunker under the White House. Hearing the coffeemaker sputtering, he stood with a groan and shuffled back into the kitchen. He poured the new brew into an old thirty-two-ounce Styrofoam cup from some distant Cherry Slushee and coagulated it with a stream of sugar and some questionable milk. Armed with his usual caffeine-calcium fix, he walked outside again, settled back into the lawn chair, and proceeded to work on the mystery at hand. He returned Goobs's text, taking three attempts before finally getting the letters correct:

msg from?

"Hey, baby," a husky voice purred behind his ear.

He craned his neck to see the voluptuous blonde in his men's double-X-sized "Eat It Raw" T-shirt standing over him. Soft, velvety and ... so freakin' young. *Goddamn, please tell me you're at least sixteen! Please tell me that of all the things I could go to jail for ...* Her soft, supple hands massaged his sunburned shoulders, and then he felt the beginnings of a tingle in his groin. He smiled and reached down to guide her hand to ...

"You're cell phone's buzzing," she said, laughing at his disappointment.

He'd forgotten the phone in his lap. So much for *that* loving feeling. He brought the phone screen an inch from his red eyes and read Goobs's answer:

ur call came frm a betty rubble.

While the young blonde pawed at him, Cas punched back a text reply: *wtf?* Then, he looked over his shoulder and told his nubile guest, "Fresh coffee's on the ... uh, hey, listen." He brushed her hands away. "Y'know, I really, uh ... I gotta ... I've got some appointments today, so—"

She got the drift. "Yeah, appointments. No worries. I had a great time. You're weird and crazy, but you're nice, in a kind of fucked-up way."

Betty Rubble? Distracted, he nodded the blonde off and out through the screen door. He scratched his head, baffled by Goobs's texts. Before he could even try to make sense of them, the phone vibrated again with another incoming: *msg sez to call her @ 212-555-9845. sez they r hiring @ llano quarry.*

He tossed the phone across the lawn. For God's sake, what did *she* want?

Dr. Marly McKinney, specialist in petrified hearts. How did she even … geez, those booze hounds at the Fish Tank must have told her where he spent most mornings—late, late mornings, afternoons really.

Betty Rubble? Cute. And *Llano?* What was *that* all about?

What could she possibly want from him? He scratched his head and took another long slurp of his cloying coffee. Hmm, yanking the professor's chain might be good for a few laughs. He dialed the number Goobs had texted.

After multiple rings and a few agonizing seconds of some ungodly Southern beach music, a screaming female voice banged his eardrum, "You think I'm swimming in the Benjamins here? I can barely make my rent, thanks to you!"

He grinned, amused to hear Marly sounding *just* like him now. He was always glad to leave a legacy. "Hey, you're the one who texted *me* to call *you.* I'm not exactly living the trust-fund dream myself." He tried to stifle a laugh while leaving her hanging through a long pause. "Listen, I'm pretty busy. What's so urgent?"

"You're *busy.* That's hilarious. "

"You miss me, don't you?" he said. "You still kick yourself for not letting me come up to your room that night. I knew you'd come around—"

"Shut up for once, and listen!" When he had finally piped down, Marly said more calmly, "I think that Mossad guy was lying to us."

"What Mossad guy?"

"Isserle, you moron! Damn it, take the cotton swabs out of your brain holes!"

"Isserle? Oh, yeah. Gee, a spook lying. You'd better call the Consumer Protection Agency and alert them."

She huffed over the phone, "I don't even know why I'm bothering."

"Take it easy," he said. "It's three hours earlier out here. Most of us don't get out of bed until noon. So just slow down for a breath and tell me what meds you forgot to take this morning."

"That American man you chased to Israel. I think his name was Seth something."

Cas flipped through his memory's rusty Rolodex. "Cohabit?"

"Cohanim! That's the name. Where was he from?"

"Cowboy hat … Texas, I think."

"*Where* in Texas, dammit!"

"Geez, take a Valium, for Christ sake. You're wound tighter than when I dumped you."

"You didn't dump me! Is that what you've been telling people?"

"Yeah, just last night, I happened to mention it to Jimmy Fallon."

"Oh, for the love of God! Cohanim! Where from? Just try to put those two Legos together."

"Hell if I know. Which, I believe, is the next town over from 'Fuck if I care.'"

"Could it be Llano County?"

Cas shrugged as he glanced longingly toward the kitchen table in search of a bottle that might still contain something distilled. "Never heard of it. Listen, I have a black-tie dinner party to prepare for, so, if you're done updating your scrapbook, I need to get back to my life."

"Listen to me! We have to find out if this Cohanim—"

"*Sayonara,* rock lady! Do me a favor, and don't call before noon." Cas pressed the End button on his phone and smiled, imagining the tantrum that Marly was throwing right now.

Yawning, he checked his list for the day. Oh yeah, he'd been meaning to expunge all of his old computer files, a little overdue digital hygiene. With those Anonymous and Wikileaks freaks on the loose, he figured it'd be the better part of valor to clean up some of the classified stuff that he had accumulated on his hard drive over the years. These days, you never knew how or when the damned stuff would be featured on a TMZ segment. The last thing he needed was having a couple of U.S. District attorneys showing up at his door with a cease and fuck-off order.

Feeling a bit more chipper after his shouting match with the Medusa of Morningside Heights, he strolled back inside, moving to the cooler side of the house, and settled into the director's chair in front of his laptop. He hadn't turned it on in a week. Probably a shitload of spam he'd have to dig through. Maybe he'd get lucky and find a Groupon ad for a half-off happy-ending massage.

The computer booted up, and as he tried to focus to see the little icons on his desktop, one caught his eye: a shortcut to an mp4 file labeled *Hilbert*.

When the hell did he put *that* there?

Without thinking, mostly because his head still hurt, he clicked on the file. In the next instant, flickering black-and-white images from the Dallas traffic cam filled the screen. He smiled at the memory of those two bumbling cops trapped in that burger-joint bathroom. Those were the good old days, back when he still had his chops. He shook his head several times, trying to clear the toxins and cobwebs.

The mp4 stopped on an image of a license plate. Under the number ... did that say ... ? He tried to recall what that Dallas dispatcher had told him about the license plate that day when he impersonated Officer Hank. On a whim, he opened his phone again and dialed the LA County Sheriff's Department on Agoura Road, just up the mountain.

"Lost Hills Station. McKenzie."

"This is SAC Emerson," he said, using the FBI's acronym for Special Agent in Charge, and praying the guy wouldn't check the directory online. "Federal ID number oh-seven three-eighteen lima-alpha."

"What can I do for you, Agent?"

"Just a license check. I happened to be up here in your lovely jurisdiction and saw some suspicious activity involving a black BMW with a Texas license plate. Down on Pacific Coast Highway a few minutes ago. Looked like the doors might have been bullet-plated."

"That's not illegal here in California."

"Yeah, I know," Cas said. "Call it a gut feeling, but I'm thinking it might be a target we've been watching for a while. You know, one of those Mexican-cartel types, Texas plate and all."

"Right," the officer said. "Be happy to help. Did you get the full number?"

He remembered that Dallas dispatcher telling him the plate was registered to some mysterious "Light" outfit, but he hadn't thought to ask which county. He leaned into the still shot captured from the mp4 file and read off the license number on one of the sedans that had ambushed him and Marly in the industrial park: "Yep. Bravo Alpha Two, Alpha Eight Forty-Niner."

"Mind if I put you on hold?" Moments later, the deputy came back on line. "That plate comes from Llano. Town's in a county south of Dallas."

"That's a known smuggling route," Cas said, not having a clue whether it was or not. "Can you get anything off IAFIS or NCIC?"

The deputy took a deep breath over the line. Asked to access the FBI's Integrated Automated Fingerprint Identification System and National Crime Information Center databases, he sounded confused. "Wouldn't you have faster access to those directly from your office, sir?"

Cas felt the fish wiggling off the hook. "Man, it's Sunday. You know how hard it would be to get that jackass Mayhue in Washington off his big white butt to help with this?"

The deputy chortled, as if he got the joke about some federal desk jockey that Cas had just made up. "Of course, sure. Lemme see what I can call up." Moments later, the deputy said, "Nothing off IAFIS because, well, it's mostly fingerprints, but ... I *did* get state records here—"

Cas put a hand over his phone to muffle an exhalation of relief. Then, he said, "I'm putting you in for a commendation."

"Aw, well," the deputy said with no small pride, "Says here that the plate and car are registered to a Lightgiver LLC. I'm showing a little activity, but only down there in the Dallas office. Nothing that would mean much here, far as I can tell."

"Activity, huh. Car might be hot."

"Says here it's a black BMW sedan, just like you spotted"—the deputy rattled off the long VIN number—"and the vehicle is considered stolen."

"Any suspects listed in the theft?"

"Dallas had a warrant out."

"Are the perpetrators named?"

"Yeah, it's an Earl ... "

"Jubal?"

"Ayup."

Cas felt his jaw muscles tighten. "You said 'had' a warrant out."

"Looks like it was withdrawn a few months ago. By request of the victim."

He gave the officer his sincerest thanks and clicked off his phone.

Seth Cohanim, again. Why did that Texas asshole keep showing up on his Pinterest board? Did Jubal and his CrossArrow goons really steal those Beemers from Cohanim just to throw everyone off track? If so, why go to so much trouble? And if Cohanim *had* been an innocent victim of a heist, why did he drop the charges only a few days after the Black Stone had been returned? Isserle had insisted that Cohanim had legitimate business dealings in Israel, but something now stank like a fresh, steaming cow patty. He gave the officer his sincerest thanks, clicked off, and called the New York number that he had dialed earlier.

Marly answered. "Asshole! Hang up on me like that one more time and—"

"Listen up. Purchase a couple of ducats for us on the next plane to Dallas tonight. Take me out of Burbank. LAX is a nightmare."

"What? Oh, sure. I'll just—"

"And get me an aisle seat on an exit row. I gotta be close to the john. And if you have any frequent flier miles, upgrade me to First Class. I'll be starving—"

"I swear to everything holy, you've got the balls of a—"

"Easy there, Scarlett. If your hunch is right, you'll get Tara plantation back in no time. And we'll both never have to fly coach again."

27

Ghajar, Northern Israel

Seth Cohanim pulled the thin curtain back an inch and peered across the street into the window of the fifth-story apartment building. This rented one-room tenement perch offered the perfect undetected view of the Syrian family he had been surveilling for nearly a year now.

He smiled, congratulating himself again on having chosen the ideal surrogate for his mission. The family's daughter, Zaynah Al Homra, was coming along nicely late in her third trimester, with no signs of complications. Moreover, she seemed to have accepted without question the marriage that he had secretly arranged for her with the Syrian man on his payroll. The blood tests that he had surreptitiously ordered at the local hospital under the name of the fifteen-year-old virgin's father had come back that week cleaner than Caesar's wife. Blood sugar was stable; normal levels of plasma protein; chorionic gonadotropin hormone well within the range for chromosome normality. He hadn't even bothered with an ultrasound. He already knew the gender of the fetus.

Within a few days, he would be the proud father—no, maybe not the father, but the creator—of a bouncing baby boy.

And soon the world would get a little more interesting. Sure, it would take a few years for the child to grow into his true destiny, but with the birth now accomplished, the hard part was already—

He heard a knock at the door. Drawing his Glock 9mm, he peeked through the crack in the jamb. He opened the door cautiously and, looking both ways down the hall, growled at his right-hand man, "I thought I told you never to come here during the day."

"Boss, we got a problem."

Cohanim motioned him into the small room and quickly shut the door, locking it. "I don't have time for petty financial issues. Just handle it."

"It's the Saudis this time."

Cohanim closed the curtains, making certain no one saw them from the street outside. "What could those heathens want now?"

"They say one of those Black Stone fragments we sold back to them has a corner missing."

Cohanim's jaw dropped. "No one had access to those fragments except ..." He glared at his nervous lieutenant. "You said you got everything back from Fielding and that ditz in Dallas."

"Boss, I swear it. Seven fragments. I counted them."

"Counted? Did you *examine* each one?"

The fixer paled, shaking his head in confession.

Cohanim paced the room. "What would those two losers want with a piece of ..." Struck by a terrifying thought, he bit off a curse. "Drive me back to the lab."

A half hour later, Cohanim rushed into his laboratory at Shaaba Farms and threw open the storage refrigerator. He exhaled with relief. The Petri dish with the back-up embryo was still there.

He laughed at himself, assured now that his fears had merely been playing games with his mind. For a moment there, he thought Fielding and his New York floozie had discovered his plan. He shook his head at his paranoia, and laughed again. Those two freaks couldn't mix a decent martini without screwing it up, let alone pull off a sophisticated genetic sampling. That nerd Columbia professor was nothing more than a rock hound. She probably cut a piece off of the Stone fragment to save as a souvenir or sell on the meteorite market.

"You okay, Boss?"

Cohanim slapped his man on the back. "Just fine, Bolin. Let's go find a steak dinner and a beer. We'll celebrate in advance."

The Texas rancher was about to close the refrigerator door when something odd caught his eye. He picked up the remaining Petri dish and turned it over. The top label showed that the lab plate was the back-up embryo, the one he had brought from Llano in case the first embryo cloning didn't take. But the code engraving on the bottom of the glass was different from the number he remembered.

"What's wrong, Boss?"

"Check the security logs from eight months ago."

The rancher's lieutenant ran the entry data in the computer. "Everything looks okay."

Cohanim stared at the glutinous contents of the Petri dish. Finally, as if fearful of the results, he carefully opened the lid, dug out the embryo, and put it under a microscope. His face turned beet red. "Son of a bitch … *This* is the embryo we seeded."

"That can't be. You planted the original embryo in that girl yourself."

Cohanim stared at the embryo in the Petri dish through the high-powered lens. "Get me the most recent blood test results for the fetus."

The underling ran to the safe, dialed the combination, and opened it. He pulled out a file with the medical information on the Lebanese surrogate and brought it over.

Cohanim thumbed through the pages until he found what he was looking for. He threw the file against the wall in hot anger.

His goon picked up the scattered documents and examined them. "X-X chromosomes. What's that mean, sir?"

Cohanim removed his sweat-rimmed Stetson and ran his hand through his thinned hair, trying to make sense of it all. "This is impossible. That Stone DNA was a mixed X-Y. Somebody would have had to take apart the DNA, reshuffle the genetic contents, and recombine them into a double-X structure. Then they would have had to implant the new DNA into the back-up embryo. I don't know of any technology that can do that."

His fixer scratched his head. "I'm not following, Boss."

Cohanim stammered in full-blown rage. "That Lebanese bitch is about to give birth to a … " He couldn't bring himself to say it.

His lieutenant finally guessed the unthinkable. "This place has been sealed tight. Who could have done it?"

Cohanim glanced around the lab, desperate to find the answer to that very question.

28

Llano, Texas

Cas pulled their dusty Jeep Cherokee into one of the angled parking spots that fronted the Llano County courthouse, a neo-Romanesque tower of faded reddish sandstone that looked right out of a Larry McMurtry novel. He glanced down the street toward the old town's stretch of drab cinderblock buildings, but nothing moved along the sun-baked sidewalks, not even the bluetick hound that lay next to the back door of Charlie's Barbecue Pit. He wiped the sweat from his forehead and muttered, "I'd hate to see the jail here."

Marly dug around in her bag and pulled out the plastic vial containing the dirt specks that she had found in her apartment. She compared the hue of the tiny specimens with the blocks used in the courthouse's construction. "Looks like there's a lot of iron in that stone. I think we're in the right place."

"Go scrape off one of your samples while I do a little reconnaissance."

Before she could protest getting the short end of that deal, Cas got out of the Jeep and walked to a gas station. Catching his breath in the relentless heat, he opened the screen door and found a wild-whiskered codger in bib overalls listening to a Texas Rangers baseball game on the radio. He tipped his imaginary Stetson to the seated fellow. "What's the score?"

The attendant didn't bother to move his boots from their roost on the counter. "If you gave a damn, you'd have it on in that piece of shit you just drove up in."

"It's a rental. Normally I drive Fords, but the Model T production line is behind schedule."

Looking him over with unchecked contempt, the ol' boy spat a black mash of chaw into his RC Cola bottle. "You don't say. I figured that Avis sticker on the bumper was put there for free advertisement."

Cas saw he was getting nowhere fast with this dyspeptic relic. "I can see you're pretty busy, so I won't stick around to fry the grease. Is there a place in town to get a bite without catching a case of *tourista*?"

The surly attendant made a cranking gesture with his chin, as if trying to smooth out a kink in his neck. "Kilroy's garage is three blocks down. The monkeys over there get back at two."

Cas figured the heat must have fused the redneck's ear canals. "Maybe you don't understand my American accent. I don't need a garage."

"You will if you keep driving that tin can on balloons around here. Last guy who came in with one of those Cherokees spent three days at the local motel while his new tie rods were drop-shipped from Dallas. You've been given fair warning. Myrtle only changes the sheets on Mondays."

Cas banged the screen door open again and walked out. "Thanks for wasting my time, *amigo*. I hear they're casting a sequel to *No Country For Old Men*, if you're interested."

Chased off by a flurry of unintelligible curses, he sauntered down the street and found Marly, who had failed to locate a beverage to slake his impossible thirst. "Friendly little *pueblo* we've got here."

"I just saw a place to eat around the corner from the courthouse," Marly said. "Maybe somebody inside will know something."

They made their way across the patchy hardpan that passed for the court-house lawn and entered a diner that looked as if it might have once served Sam Houston. The joint featured a long counter and a dozen Formica tables scattered across a peeling linoleum floor. Cas figured Santa Ana got a more hospitable welcome at the Alamo. Those locals not hovering on stools and tucking into the fried-catfish special were congregated in threes and fours around cups of muddy coffee. The conversation, which seemed mostly about the local high school football team, lowered to a whisper as he and Marly settled into a pair of seats at the far end of the counter. He nodded to several of the suspicious faces, trying to break the ice, but nobody returned the greeting.

The waitress slapped down a couple of menus. "Need more time?"

Cas flashed her his best flirting grin. "My momma always told me a pretty lady will never steer you wrong."

The waitress glared at him. "Your momma was either a fool or downright desperate to get you married off and out of her hair. Now, you gonna sit here and flap your gums, or do you want something to eat? The chicken-fried steak and jalapeño gravy's the special today—"

"I hear the beef in these parts is a little different," Cas said with a wink.

The waitress turned to Marly. "Hon, I'm assuming you're the intelligent half of this road trip."

Marly leaned in closer. "I think what he's saying is, we wouldn't want to get a steak from one of those heifers they raise around here. You know, the kind with two heads and half an ass."

The other customers, overhearing the remark, fell silent.

Cas shot an admiring glance at Marly, impressed by her *cajones*.

The waitress grabbed the menus and slammed them back into the slot. "You gonna badmouth my food, then get out."

Cas smirked a puppy smile at the waitress, having gotten the reaction he had hoped at their mention of the strange cattle rumors. "A person can't be too careful these days, darlin'. We must have been misinformed."

A man in a rawhide hat and ranch duds stood from his table in the corner and came shadowing over Cas's shoulder. "Misinformed about what?"

Cas turned and, seeing a teenage girl with the rancher, tipped his imaginary cap to them. "It's nothing, really, sir. It's just, we've heard talk there's some unusual breeding going on in these parts, is all."

The rancher's expression shifted from suspicion to hostility. "And what business exactly would that be of yours?"

"All due respect," Cas said, "we represent an interested buyer—"

"Next cattle auction's not till next month."

"Our buyer's not interested in an auction, friend. He's interested in a straight and, guess I should say, pretty damned lucrative, trade."

The ranch glanced with grave suspicion at Marly. "And who's this?"

"Oh, her? She's my veterinarian. Know how to keep an Aggie busy?"

Marly picked right up on her cue. "Put her in a round room and tell her to pee in a corner"

The rancher started to walk away, shaking his head at their buffoonery.

"Mr. Cock in Hand," Cas piped.

The rancher turned with a menacing look. "What'd you say?"

"The fella we're looking for. Can't rightly remember his name at the moment. Cock in Hand ... Cockamamie ... Something like that."

"Cohanim," Marly said, playing along with his jestering act.

The rancher's eyes narrowed.

Cas tipped his imaginary cap again, this time to Marly, in appreciation for the reminder. "If you ask me, that's a strange name for a Texas boy. Sounds a little ..."

"Jewish?" Marly suggested.

"I was gonna say Communist. But maybe that's redundant around here."

Several of the diners stood up abruptly and walked to the cash register to pay their checks. The rancher flipped a couple of dollar bills on the counter and nodded for his daughter to leave with him. The young girl glanced pointedly at Marly as she stepped out.

When the place had emptied, the waitress shook her head in despair over the lost business. "Thanks for running off my rent check this month."

"Did we kick somebody's dog?" Cas asked.

The waitress kept a wary eye on the front window. "Seth Cohanim is the straw that stirs the drink in this county. Lots of people here owe him their livelihoods. You won't hear a negative word spoken about him. He's a good Christian man. Does lots of charitable work."

"When you say Christian," Marly asked, "you mean, like, an evangelical, believe-in-the-Bible-literally Christian?"

"Didn't I just say he was a *good* Christian?"

Marly risked testing the waitress's patience. "The patron saint of Llano *does* seem to get around the world."

"Fact is, we ran into him in Saudi Arabia," Cas added.

"He breeds cattle for foreign governments," the waitress said. "That's the word, anyway. Brings in more business and jobs for us. Good for him."

"What about his cattle insemination techniques?" Marly asked. "We heard that he—"

The door flew open, and two local lawmen walked in.

The waitress hurried off to tend the register. "You boys are in early today."

"On business," one of the sheriff's deputies said. "Looking for the owner of a Jeep Cherokee parked in front of the courthouse."

Cas waved to the officers. "That'd probably be ours. Is there a problem?"

"On weekdays, that spot's reserved for the *pro-tem* judge."

Marly came up aside Cas to protest. "There wasn't any sign out there."

The nastier looking of the two deputies pulled out his citation book and began writing up a violation. "City ordinance." He pointed to a bulletin board behind the cash register. "It's posted in here."

Cas knew better than to challenge the shakedown. "How much?"

"Two twenty-five."

Marly was outraged. "That's unconstitutional!"

Shaking his head at the futility of her protest, Cas extracted the cash from his wallet and handed it over to the deputy writing the ticket. "I don't want you boys to take this as a bribe, but seeing as how me and the missus"—he nodded at Marly with a wink—"won't be around for the trial and Supreme Court appeal, how about we just pay the fine now?" He handed the bills to the ham-handed officer. "While we're at it, mind telling us if you got any *other* special parking spots that we should know about?"

The deputy doing the talking stuffed the bills into his pocket and scribbled a 'paid' notation on the citation. "None that immediately come to mind. But just to be on the safe side, you might want to head on down the road."

"Have we got time to sample Margie here's apple cobbler?" Cas asked.

The two deputies walked out, their silence serving as answer enough.

Cas ordered their sandwiches to go. He paid, grabbed the bag, and quickly walked out with Marly. Blasted again by the heat, they hurried toward the Jeep, careful to stay on the sidewalk to avoid a fine for trampling city grass, although they had yet to see anything green for ten miles in any direction.

Safely inside the cab, he inserted the key and turned the ignition. He saw the two deputies parked on the curb a block away, watching them like hawks.

"What do we do now?" Marly asked.

Cas slowly pulled from the space and, flicking on his turn signal, headed out of town, making sure he stayed ten miles under the speed limit. "Looks like Cohanim's got too much juice around here. Nobody's going to talk."

Marly flung her head back onto the headrest. Conceding defeat, she grabbed a sandwich and began chowing it down.

"Is that the one with mustard?"

Marly mumbled with a full mouth, "Oops."

"I should take you back to Andy and Barney and press charges."

A mile outside of town, Marly sniffed something foul. She opened the two slices of bread on her sandwich and looked for blue streaks in the ham. She rolled down the window and spat out a mouthful. "Damn, I think that diner hag may have pawned off some bad meat on us."

Cas's nostrils flared from the stench. "Did you take a shower this morning?"

Marly sniffed the sandwich and realized that it wasn't the culprit. The stench became so intense that she had to hold her nose. "God, that's awful."

Cas stopped the Jeep. "I think it's coming from the back."

They got out and stalked the rear door, not certain if they wanted to open it. Finally, Cas forced himself to release the latch. A calf's foreleg, singed at its burnt edges, lay on the floor of the cargo bay. Tied to its hoof was a note written on a torn piece of lined notepaper. With his sleeve pressed to his mouth, he brought the paper closer and saw a single word written on it: *Slaughterhouse.* What the hell did *that* mean?

Marly picked up the shriveled leg with her thumb and forefinger and sniffed an aroma that smelled like formaldehyde. She brought the carcass part closer to examine, and did a double take. "Do you see *that*?"

Cas's eyes rounded. "Damn, the hide is ..."

Marly was already running to the other side of the highway to flag down an approaching truck.

The driver slowed to a stop. "You folks got car trouble, ma'am?"

"Just need some directions. Is there a slaughterhouse around here?"

"Yeah, Seth Cohanim's stockyards," the driver said. "Two miles up west up there, on the railroad tracks. But they ain't likely to sell quarterflanks to folks just in off the highway."

"Thanks anyway. I guess we'll just have to find another meat locker."

The driver tipped his cap to her and drove off.

Cas waited until dusk fell before starting up the Jeep again. Driving with the headlights off, he crept along the hardpan road toward a cluster of whitewashed pavilions surrounded by mazes of cattle pens and loading ramps, all empty.

"What if those deputies back there set us up?" Marly asked.

"What do you mean?"

She sighed, exasperated at his naiveté. "For a former spy, you can be awfully dense at times. Ten bucks says those redneck gunslingers are watching us right now just so they can haul us in for trespassing. All they'd have to do is just happen to come up on us right now. I would bet they've got cattle prods with our name on them."

Cas searched the cattle pens for movement. "Why would they go to the trouble of incinerating a perfectly good calf and loading it into our vehicle just to bait us down *here?*"

A sharp report cracked overhead—they both ducked.

"Was that gunfire?" Marly whispered from under the dash.

Another crack split the sky above them again.

Keeping his head low, Cas whispered, "Those assholes brought us out here for target practice!"

Bullets *zinged* through the air.

Livid, Cas kicked at the floorboard. "I'll be damned if I'm gonna sit here all night and get peppered like some clay pigeon!"

"Okay, so, what do you—"

He yanked his door open and dived out. He sprawled across the ground on all fours. When the shooting seemed to have stopped, he risked a glance up. Standing over him was a teenage girl armed with a walnut-handled Colt Single Action Army revolver.

Eyes pinched under her broad-brimmed hat, the girl stuffed the pistol into her belt. "You took your time, mister."

Cas slowly rose to his knees, unable to comprehend how such a pint-sized female could pack such big heat. "Lemme see that thing, you little shit."

She debated giving the pistol up. "Don't think I won't shoot you, mister."

"Hand it over, Annie Oakley."

The girl finally flipped the gun and turned the handle toward him.

Cas took the pistol and examined it. "They don't call it a Peacemaker for nothing. This is some fine hardware you got here. Do you always use passing tourists for target practice?"

Before the girl could answer, Marly jumped out of the Jeep and skidded to a stop within a few inches from them. "Hey! You were in the diner."

Cas suddenly made the connection. "Yeah, with that cranky rancher. Is that why were you shooting at us? Did your old man send you out here to give us a scare?"

The girl shook her head with a grimace of disgust, as if trying to imagine how somebody could be so stupid. "My pa don't know nothing about me coming to talk to you. I was trying to get your attention, short of banging on your window and alerting the whole county."

"What's your name?" Cas asked.

"Jennie."

Cas choked back another cough from the peppery stink of putrefied leg in the Jeep. "You think leaving rotten animal parts in out-of-state vehicles is amusing?"

The girl started walking toward the shadows of the slaughterhouse. At a loss about what she intended for them, Cas and Marly reluctantly followed her into the back of a lot. From behind a post, the girl brought out a shovel and dug up several scoops of earth, until she hit something with a *thunk*. She brought up a large plastic gas can that held some kind of liquid. Unscrewing the cap, Jennie motioned them over and held the can's neck to their noses.

Marly took a whiff. More formaldehyde. She looked again and saw something floating inside the can. "What is *that*?"

The girl stabbed at the plastic with the shovel's tip, opening a gash that allowed the preserving solvent to flood out. She ripped open the sides of the can and revealed the charred remains of a calf—with one of its flank legs missing.

Marly and Cas stood frozen, glaring in horror at the carcass. The calf's hide—or what little remained of it—was as red as blood.

"I heard you asking at the diner about strange cattle," the girl whispered.

Cas waved away a couple of flies. "Where did you get this?"

The girl's voice became shaky. "My pa works for Mr. Cohanim."

All of that shooting, Marly realized, had just been a way to get their attention. She pressed the frightened girl for more details, "Yeah ... and?"

"I was with Pa the night he birthed this one," the girl said. "It rattled him somethin' fierce when he seen it come out."

Cas found a stick and poked at the incinerated hide. "Did he burn it like this?"

The girl shook her head. "He called Mr. Cohanim. I was supposed to leave for home, but I circled back on my horse." Her face pinched from the memory of that day. "I wanted the calf to raise. Then I saw ..." She caught her breath, as if the words were going to choke her.

Marly kept digging at her for clues. "What did you see?"

"Mr. Cohanim and another man in strange black clothes come down from his ranch in a helicopter. They cut the calf's throat and burned it on a grill."

Cas took a step back. "You mean, a grill like one your daddy would use for ribs?" Receiving a teary nod from the girl, he swore. "Damn, barbecuing a *newborn?*"

The girl's glances darted nervously around the stockyards. "I don't know for sure *what* they was doing. I'm just telling you what I saw." She looked at Marly, as if for approval, and Marly nodded for her to go on. "Then, Mr. Cohanim and the man in black just gathered up the ashes and took them in a container. All that was left of it was the head, bones, and legs. I saved them when they weren't looking." She pointed to the carcass that she had preserved in formaldehyde.

Marly tried to comfort the girl with a hand around her shoulder. "It's okay, hon. Listen, does your Pa's boss do that with all the new calves at his ranch?"

The girl shook her head. "Just this one."

Cas studied the carcass, trying to come up with a reason why anyone would do anything like that. "What was so different about *this* one?"

"It was red," the girl said. "Red all over."

Cas shrugged. "Calves with red hides are unusual, but they happen from time to time."

"Not like this one, they don't, least not like *I've* seen in my whole life," the girl said. "This calf had eyes as red as blood, too. I got the shivers when it looked at me."

Marly knelt in front of the distraught girl and asked her softly, "Why do *you* think Mr. Cohanim did this?"

Jennie shook her head. Either she didn't know, or didn't want to say.

Marly looked at Cas and wondered what sort of backcountry Twilight Zone they had stumbled into here.

29

Beirut, Lebanon

Under the constant gaze of suspicious men, Zaynah hurried, as fast her condition would allow, down a garbage-littered street, looking for any discarded food that might be edible. Above these burned-out refugee tenements all around her, a thick layer of gray smog hung as heavy as the *abaya* that she had discarded for the loose-fitting Western garb she now wore.

Allah will provide.

God, praised be He, had gotten her this far. She had to trust in His intercession. She had fled from her village three nights ago, panicking after that grimy Alawite coward who had sworn to marry her disappeared without leaving even a note of explanation. Still, no one believed her insistence that she had escaped foreign kidnappers who had somehow raped her more than eight months ago, apparently while she was unconscious. Dishonored beyond redemption, she knew that if her father and brothers ever found her, they would drag her back and mete out Sharia justice.

In her desperation to avoid being recognized on her escape across the border, she had failed to plan for the fact that the clothing switch would dangerously reveal her advanced pregnancy. She feared the child could be born any day now, and she would be left here to die among strangers. During these past horrid weeks, she had suffered through long nights of nausea, all without help, not even from her mother. And now, as the heat of the approaching dusk sucked into her throat, she began to feel sick again. Her eyes were glazed red, and her nose ran from the traffic fumes and clouds of reddish soot rising from the busted sidewalks.

Was that black car following her? Hadn't she seen it an hour ago?

She tried to shake the blood to her brain, no longer trusting her own thoughts. What had those filthy Westerners wanted with her, anyway? She just knew—perhaps because she had lived under the thumb of cruel men— that the stocky one with the big hat had paid the concrete-pouring cretin to save her from the stoning. She had seen him peeling off the foreign bills in the alley that day she was saved. But why? None of it made any sense.

She was about to give up her search for food and collapse when a pink taxi came to a stop aside the curb. With a great effort, she raised her head and saw that the driver was a woman. Was she hallucinating from the hunger?

The woman behind the wheel got out of the cab and helped her to her feet. "Were you left here?"

Before Zaynah could answer, the black car sped by the stopped cab and slowed, as if to see what was happening. She couldn't make out the faces of the men inside. Were they her brothers? Before she could rub the blear from her eyes to get a better look in the dim light, the car sped off.

"Can you hear me?" the female cab driver asked. "Were you left here?"

"Left?"

"By a man?"

Zaynah was too weak to explain.

"Get in." The driver helped her into the back seat. "Where can I take you?"

Grateful for the offer of service, Zaynah muttered, "Haret Hreik." The driver seemed surprised, but Zaynah nodded to confirm her wish, for she had been told that the southern part of the city was less frequented by Westerners.

The driver shrugged and pulled off. "Your first time here?"

Zaynah slowly felt her strength return. "It is that obvious?"

The driver smiled ruefully. "Those blocks you were walking back there were bombed by the Israelis in 2006. Those Hezbollah lunatics bring nothing but trouble upon us! There is only rubble in Haret now."

Uninterested in politics, Zaynah closed her eyes, grateful for the first safe minutes of rest she had enjoyed in three days.

The driver studied her through the rear-view mirror. "Your first?"

Zaynah nodded, the corners of her dropped eyelids moist.

"You were raped."

Zaynah opened eyes suddenly—was this woman clairvoyant?

"Happens all the time here," the driver said. "Tell me your story."

For some reason, Zaynah sensed that she could trust this woman. With fractured explosions of emotion, she explained how she had run away after secretly pilfering a few coins from her father's change bowl. With that money long gone, she had begged for shelter at a home for orphans. But she had been turned away, told that the religious enforcers would make life miserable for any charity that gave sustenance to a woman living in sin.

The driver listened in silence.

After finishing her explanation, Zaynah studied the skeletal remains of Hezbollah's *de facto* capital in the falling darkness. As they sped through several burned-out neighborhoods, tower after apartment tower stood crumbling and stripped. Bombs had ripped the windows, balconies and facades from the buildings as if they were peeled fruit. All that remained were empty cells where squatters now slept.

"You should have gone to Jerusalem," the driver said. "Somewhere safer than here."

That warning snatched Zaynah from her morbid fascination with the exterior devastation that seemed to mirror her own predicament. "Jerusalem is for those with money."

Minutes later, the taxi pulled up in front of a cluster of concrete apartment buildings. The door of one of the offices at the base of the edifice featured a Christian cross that had been spray-painted above the peephole.

Zaynah saw a sign for Karantina, an eastern suburb of Beirut. Only then did she realize that the driver had taken her to the Christian sector of the city. "What is this place?"

"Maronites live here. I cannot promise, but try them. They may be willing to help you."

Zaynah could not imagine asking for the help of Christians.

The driver reached inside the glove compartment, pulled out a pad and pen, and scribbled a note. "Third floor up. Michel Halifi is a good man. Tell him the lady with the pink taxi sent you."

Zaynah hesitated to leave. "I have nothing to give you."

"Allah will bless me. Perhaps you will name your baby Adara."

Zaynah was taken aback, for the name meant 'virgin' in Arabic. "Why do you suggest such a thing?"

The driver smiled sadly. "That is my name, but my family stopped using it for me after a man forced himself on me when I was about your age. And I, too, had a child in shame. But I will always be Adara in my heart. And you must think of yourself always as a virgin."

Zaynah embraced her rescuer, then slid out of the cab.

Zaynah awoke in total darkness. Sore and battered, she rose slowly from the foul dust of the street. Feeling a dried welt over her left eye, she wobbled onto her feet, woozy from the pain and hunger. She looked around for a clock, but found none. Unsteadily, she moved toward the faint light of a main thoroughfare, realizing that she must have fallen unconscious after the taxi dropped her off.

Yes, now it came back to her.

Receiving no answer at the Maronite's door, she had staggered to a nearby shop to beg for something to ease her nausea. The shopkeeper, an old man, had kept looking at her suspiciously, as if he had wanted to despoil what little honor she had left. He had asked about her origins and family, and when she had unthinkingly mentioned growing up in Lebanon, he had shot a knowing look at some men drinking coffee in the shop. Though she was careful not to mention the name of her village, she still felt a jolt from his insistent gaze at her grimy clothes and distended belly. Sensing danger, she had retreated outside, only to find herself surrounded by several toughs. They had taunted her with hisses and had called her a whore, making certain they weren't loud enough for anyone in a concrete building to hear. Then they started pelting her with rocks, delivering vigilante justice.

After that, she remembered nothing.

How many hours had she been lying out here? She reached a hand under her abaya and felt below her extended womb for blood, checking if she had expelled the fetus. Dying from a miscarriage would have been a blessing, she told herself. She wanted nothing to do with what was growing inside her. But no such luck. All she felt were the bruises from the stones.

She lurched toward the entrance to the Maronite apartment compound and heard the *screech* of an iron gate. She tried to make herself invisible by pressing against the shell-pocked wall of an abandoned building, but a middle-aged man who had just opened the gate noticed her.

He approached slowly with his hands up. "I am not here to hurt you."

Zaynah risked a step closer. "A cab dropped me on that corner there."

"Yes, we have been waiting for you. My name is Michel."

Zaynah blinked hard. *He knew I was coming?* Had the kind taxi driver called this man? With a trembling hand, she held out the note the cabbie had written his address on.

The man took the paper and smiled as he read it. He beckoned her to him.

She took a step—and collapsed. Something in her womb didn't feel right. She grabbed her abdomen and moaned in pain. Were these contractions? She was gripped with terror.

The man pulled a cell phone from his pocket, flipped it opened, and dialed a number. He shouted into the phone. "Ambulance!"

While the man assisted her, Zaynah struggled to sit up. She saw two dark shapes turn the corner into the alley. Pushing with all her might, she staggered to her feet and craned her neck in time to see the strangers closing in on her. She cried, "Mr. Halifi!"

The attackers—in black hoods and masks—slammed her benefactor to the street with a blow to the back of his shoulders. They grabbed her arms and began dragging her toward the alley.

She screamed and fought at them, kicking and biting.

An oncoming siren wailed—an ambulance barreled toward her.

Her abductors froze. One of the goons pulled a pistol from under his vest and aimed it at her. The chilling *wop-wop-wop* from a police car followed behind the ambulance.

"Son of a bitch!" one of the masked attacker muttered.

Zaynah was stunned to hear the local religious enforcers speak English. She glared at the man on top of her—he sounded *American*. She screamed at him, "Go ahead! Kill me! May Allah curse you! Death cannot be worse than what I now suffer!"

The second masked man tried his accomplice away. "Let's get out of here!"

Zaynah staggered to her hands and knees. Raging, she crawled after them and cried, "American bastards! What did you do to me?"

The ambulance turned the corner and careered into the alley. Recovering from the blow to his neck, the Maronite Christian man who had offered to help her rose unsteadily to his feet and feebly waved at the headlights.

Illuminated by the beams, the black-clad gunmen backed away and scampered off into the blown-out warrens.

Two paramedics leapt from the ambulance and came hovering over Zaynah.

She felt a needle prick her arm ... an oxygen mask came over her face.

In seconds, she passed out.

30

Mediterranean Coast, Southern Israel

As the flotilla of ferries and small yachts from Istanbul approached the militarized border coast of Gaza, hundreds of Muslim volunteers with the Turkish Foundation for Human Rights surged toward the bows and waved Palestinian flags in support of their oppressed brothers and sisters trapped beyond the coastline near Ashqelon. In the storage bins behind them lay humanitarian aid that included ballistic vests, night-vision goggles, gas masks, and stacks of Turkish *lira*.

The somnolent swish of the lapping waves suddenly gave way to a distant but ominous *whop-whop-whop*. The protestors braced for another round of violence, trying desperately to hide their fear. During their previous attempt to break the Israeli blockade, six of their comrades had been killed and hundreds arrested by the Israeli navy.

A lone scream on the deck was followed by a rush of feet to the starboard side. Five Super Frelon copters swooped down on the lead boat and dropped toward the deck from the gray horizon like hawks targeting prey.

This time, the protestors were prepared for the onslaught. Many of them quickly changed from their lifejackets into bulletproof vests and handcuffed themselves to form a human chain to prevent the Israelis from arresting them individually and take them off the ship to be interrogated or arrested. They began chanting their favorite anti-Israeli mantra from their Friday prayers:

"Go to Jerusalem! Go to Jerusalem!"

Israeli speedboats raced toward the flotilla from every direction.

The protestors loosed a curdling wail of apprehension, sounding like an ancient army just before the first clash of spears. Sirens blared, and the Israeli officers on the speedboats shouted bullhorn demands in Turkish for the flotilla to stop. Hearing bullets whizzing over the hull, the protestors surged forward and waved their fists at the Israeli commandos converging on the lead boat and tossing grappling ropes across its railings. They lurched to the sides and fought to unleash the hooks, but they were too late.

The commandos were already climbing the ropes.

In the midst of this mayhem, two protestors who had neglected to chain themselves to the others slipped away and eased down the ladders leading below deck. They rushed into the cabin nearest the stern and locked the door behind them.

Cas stripped off his khakis and protest T-shirt. He opened the duffel bags they had brought and pulled out the scuba gear and wetsuits he had purchased in Istanbul before signing up for this human-shield mission as a cover to get into Israel.

Marly glared at his Speedo briefs, hoping they weren't the same pair he had been wearing the first time they'd met. "Please tell me those have been washed."

"We don't have all day to visit Memory Lane." He signaled for her to get with the program, but when she crossed her arms, he tried to hurry her up. "What are you waiting for?"

"Turn around."

Huffing at her annoying modesty, he angled away and stepped into his wetsuit. He heard her peeling off her blouse and pants. Just as she got down to her skimpy two-piece undergarments, he spun back around, his wetsuit still at his ankles. He whistled at what he saw. "Smoking bod."

She tried to cover herself. "You jackass!"

He gazed at her, up and down. "Go to the gym much? Da-aamn."

"I work out on punching bags. Want a demonstration?"

He reluctantly returned to the task of pulling up his wetsuit—until the zipper on the back slipped its teeth. These second-rate Soviet-era relics zipped clear down to the small of the back, making it a challenge for someone less flexible than a ballerina—like him—to zip himself up. "Oh, for shit's sake!" he growled, trying to twist himself around to fix the snag, the wetsuit still at his knees. "No wonder half the Russian Navy sank in World War Two."

The commando assault had already put Marly on edge, and now, startled by his shout, she glanced up and saw the bulge in his Speedos. "You have *got* be kidding me!"

"Uh ..." Cas looked down helplessly at his boner, which was also impeding his progress getting into the suit. "I could use a hand here?"

When she finally had her own wetsuit on and zipped, she moved to him, her eyes avoiding his crotch. She stood behind him and tried to re-track the zipper.

Gunfire *pinged* against the ship's hull and railings. Through the overhead deck, they heard muffled screaming that was turning from outrage to terror.

Marly stomped her feet in impatience. "We *have* to get the hell out of here!"

Cas was turning red. "What am I supposed to do about this damn zipper?"

Marly saw that the waistband of his Speedo was caught in the teeth of the wetsuit's zipper. "When did your mother stop dressing you?"

Cas anxiously eyed the door, expecting Israeli commandos to burst in any second now. If *that* happened, his Mossad pal, Avram Isserle, wouldn't stop this time at a garden-variety beating. Seeing that Marly was getting nowhere with the stubborn zipper, he yanked his wetsuit down to his ankles, his Speedo going along with the sweat-slicked neoprene and rubber. "Cut the damn thing off!" he yelled, pointing past his unflagging turgidity.

Marly unclipped a diving knife from the buoyancy-compensator vest at her feet. She stood staring at him—all of him. "Don't tempt me."

He tried to cover his groin like a soccer player waiting for a foul kick as she sliced at his underwear with the knife, splitting the elastic band. Finally freed, he yanked the sliced-up Speedo from the wetsuit, stepped back in, and zipped it up. "Pervert!" He snarled with mock outrage. "Hope you got an eyeful!"

Boots thudded down the metal passageway.

Cas picked up one of the scuba tanks and smashed through the narrow porthole. Then, he slipped the air canister back into the buoyancy-compensator vest. He inflated each BC with some oxygen from the tanks, clipped their masks, snorkels, and fins to the vests, and pushed both sets of gear through the small opening. He helped Marly up to the porthole. After she had wiggled through and splashed into the sea a couple dozen feet below, he followed her through the hole and into the water. They swam to their floating scuba equipment and slipped into the inflated vests and fins.

Thirty yards from the boat, they looked up from the water and saw riot gas canisters rolling off the railings and splashing around them. Near the stern, the Israelis were cutting the protestors apart and herding them down a rope ladder to a waiting incarceration boat.

He pointed for her to put in her regulator and slide on her black mask.

Ready at last, she gave him the "okay" sign.

One of the Israeli commandos on the deck caught the glint in the water from their face masks. He shouted at them in Hebrew, "*Dai! Dai!*"

Shots *whizzed* all around them, slicing through the water. They deflated their vests and sank, turning over and kicking to safety. Seconds later, Marly glided closer to Cas and made some strange hand signals. He was her pointing at him and laughing. What was she trying to tell him? He looked down and bubbled a curse through his regulator. In Marly's haste to cut away his underwear, she had accidentally sliced his wetsuit. The fabric over his crotch hung open like the rear flap on a pair of longjohns.

Marly sneezed and coughed her way through the crowded livestock auction yards at Bet She'an, the largest cattle exchange in Israel. The smells were unbearable, but at least they were keeping her awake. She hadn't slept in two days, not since their swim to the coastal beach and the ride on the local bus inland. Now, as she and Cas passed stall after stall of farting cattle and hovering ranchers checking for signs of disease, she held her breath against the onslaught of knee-buckling aromas. Finally, she exhaled and managed to gasp, "What the hell was *that* one?"

Cas sighed with mock ecstasy. "I'm guessing ammonia. Maybe a little bacterial disinfectant thrown in. Has a bit more fruity bouquet than cow. Not as blowzy, but it certainly outranks urine for the full aftertaste of acidity."

Marly kept scanning the straw-strewn aisles, half expecting Isserle to show up at any moment and drag them off to break rocks in the Sinai. Cas's insane plan to join the humanitarian flotilla in Istanbul had succeeded by sheer luck alone. Yet *this* idea—posing as American ranchers exporting red-heifer meat— took the blue ribbon for lunacy. They simply could have asked representatives of the Israeli Cattlemen's Foundation why anyone would want to develop an all-red cow. But seeing as how they were Americans, that might have raised red flags. So, Cas had to have things his way, working the operation undercover with hyper-discreet surveillance. She stopped and glared at him again. He was having way too much fun, dressed in that damned cowboy hat and swaggering around like John Wayne on weed.

"Howdy," Cas drawled as he tipped his brim to a passing Israeli businessman in a suit. "Huckle Hickabee from Tennessee. Might I take a moment of your time and flint your interest in the newest breed of beef in America?"

The Israeli stared blankly at him.

"Red meat," Cas said. "Now, I know what you're thinking. Well, ain't all cattle beef red meat? This here meat I'm talking about is *real* red meat. And I mean cut from a *red* heifer. That's right, did you hear me? I said a heifer that's red. All over. Even the whites of its eyes are red. Now you might be asking what—"

The Israeli man shook his head and walked away.

"Yeah, this is working brilliantly," Marly muttered. "How many satisfied customers have we scored already? Hmm, let's see. I'm drawing a blank."

Cas pulled his hat farther down over his eyes, more determined than ever. "Somebody in this damn place has to know something about red heifers." He saw that Marly looked distracted. "Cattle prod got your tongue, Doc?"

Roused from her thoughts, Marly whispered, "You know, something's been bugging me ever since we left Texas. If Cohanim is so hell-bent on winning some lottery by breeding red heifers, how does he prevent bulls from being born? Males would be useless to him. They'd be a huge waste of time and resources."

"Beats the hell out of me. For spooks, press 'One'. For science, press 'Two'. You would be in Department Two."

Marly searched the herds of bowlegged men who were migrating past her. "Maybe we should find someone around here who *does* know."

Cas glanced at the nametags passing by until one looked promising: *Baruch Arons, Hebron Technologies.* He nodded to cheer Marly on, "Go do that voodoo that you do."

Given her cue, Marly caught up with the bald man, whose rotund physique and deep-set eyes gave her the impression of a human bowling ball. Swallowing back her revulsion, she twirled her hair flirtatiously at him and tweeted, "Excuse me. Do you speak English?"

Annoyed at the interruption, the man nodded brusquely.

"I wonder if I might ask you a question?"

"Toilets are in Pavilion Three, the next one over."

She resisted the urge to kick him in the rocky mountain oysters. "No, I mean, a question about *cows*. I'm a single mom—don't even get me started on that! Anyway, I'm here with my daughter on her semester abroad from Columbia ... do you have kids, by the way?" When he shook his head, she *tsk'd* her tongue under a charming smile. "The thing is, she's two weeks late on this paper she's doing for science class on cattle breeding."

The cattleman huffed, not the least interested. "What is the topic?"

"Why, thank you for asking. Something to do with how ranchers decide whether they want to have a cow with testicles or one with—" She blushed and crossed her arms, looking as coy and bashful as an embarrassed debutante—"you know ... breasts."

The cattleman couldn't stifle a scorning laugh. "The term you're groping for is 'utter.'"

Cas stood several feet away, trying to look inconspicuous while grudgingly admiring Marly's acting chops and the cattleman's skill with metaphors.

"I grew up in Manhattan," Marly told the cattleman, fluttering her lashes. "So, you'll have to forgive my ignorance of all four-legged creatures."

"Tell your daughter to go online and look up 'semen sexing.'"

"Eww!" Marly put her hand to her heart in faked horror. "Oh, but my, she's only sixteen! I'm just not sure—"

"No, it's completely innocent," the cattleman insisted. "Until last year, ranchers had no way of improving the odds of birthing more heifers—a heifer is a *girl* cow—to increase their dairy production. But scientists recently developed a new technology."

"Did they?" She looked up at him in phony curiosity and reached out to touch his forearm.

"It gets a little complex, so stay with me. There's something called a Y chromosome, which produces male offspring, and an X chromosome, which produces females. Now what we've invented is a dye that is mixed in with the bull's semen and sticks to the X chromosome."

"Kind of like a liquid magnet?" she asked.

"That's a crude analogy, I guess," the cattleman said. "A machine detects the dye and sorts the sperm so that the Y chromosome can be filtered out. Then the semen is frozen and sold to farmers. It increases the production of heifers by ninety percent."

She gasped. "That is *just* fascinating! I can't *wait* to tell my daughter!"

The Israeli rancher reached for her hand and wouldn't let it go of it. "Perhaps we could get together—"

Her cell phone rang, just in the nick. She slipped her hand from the guy's meaty paw to answer it. "Yes, honey. I'm coming back to the hotel right now. I just need to stop at a drugstore and pick up my bipolar prescription." She turned to thank the man again, but he was hurrying off down the aisle between the pens.

Cas sauntered up with his phone at his ear. "Nice work."

She seemed distracted. "I wonder if this semen-sorting works on humans?"

"Should we get started on the experiment?"

Another moment passed before Marly heard what he had just said, and she rolled her eyes. The man just couldn't help himself. He suffered a kind of emotional Tourette's Syndrome, always taking refuge in crass sexual jokes whenever he got nervous or felt threatened. Ignoring the remark, she looked over her shoulder at another Israeli a few steps behind them. "That guy over there has been following us for the last ten minutes."

Bending down to rub some cow shit off his boots, Cas glanced under his armpit at a bearded man who wore black trousers, a white shirt and a long black *rekel* jacket. Cas rose and spat at a bale of hay, mimicking the breeders around him. Then, he whispered to Marly, "You're a world-class actor, but you'd make a damn poor intel op."

"I'm telling you, he's on us like stink on ... on everything in this place."

"He's Hasidic. Ultra-Orthodox. Wing-nut conservative."

"So?"

"He's a religious cop, kinda like a Kosher Columbo. This is the seventh year in the Israeli agricultural cycle. These high-octane Orthodox rabbis try to enforce a Biblical injunction that all farmland should lie fallow every seventh year. These guys snoop around places like this, trying to pick up evidence that the injunction is being violated. They get a commission, like bounty hunters."

Unconvinced, Marly debated a wager. "You really want to sleep with me?"

Cas stopped so fast that his cowboy hat nearly tippled over his nose. "*What?*"

"You heard me."

Cas curled a slow, self-satisfied grin. "Was my little performance on the Good Ship Lollipop that impressive?"

"Don't flatter yourself."

"Well, then why the sudden offer? Especially after all the rejections?"

Marly kept walking. "I'm a gambler at heart. I trade rocks on the open market, remember? I've developed a second sense about motives and intentions. If that man in black isn't tracking us, then I'll be your love slave tonight."

"What's the catch?"

"If I'm right, we split the loot sixty-forty. And I don't need to tell you who gets the sixty."

Cas debated her challenge, his lower anatomy fighting a tug-of-war with his brain. "How are we going to prove his intentions?"

"Just go up and ask him."

Cas howled and slapped his hand against a pen railing, drawing stares from the ranchers and business types. When he stopped laughing, he edged closer and took a whiff of her tantalizing feminine allure, a welcome respite from the acrid odors of the exchange. He whispered into her ear, "Geez, you've got a lot to learn about surveillance work. You don't just go up and ask a trail what they're—"

Marly spun on her heels and walked right up to the Hasidic Jew. "Are you following us?"

The Hasid waited until another auction scrum drew the interest of virtually everyone in the yards. Then, when the bidders were looking in the other direction, he made a quick jerk of his head for Marly to follow him into a room used by the auctioneers to negotiate deals.

Stunned, and more than a little disappointed, Cas skulked into the room behind them.

The Hasidic man shut the door and locked it.

Marly set her hands on her hips. "Well?"

The Hasid turned to Cas and, after a hesitation, spoke English with a thick Semitic accent. "You have been telling people here that you breed red heifers."

"Yeah," Cas said, sounding less than believable.

The Hasid stared at Cas, not buying the claim. "You will not find *here* what you seek."

Cas jerked his head closer. "Oh? And what *am* I looking for?"

The Hasid neither moved nor spoke, letting the silence do the work for him.

Finally, Cas took a step forward, until he was nose to nose with the man. "Let's try this one. Where *will* I find what I'm looking for?"

The Jew pulled a business card from his vest and handed it to him. "Call this number. Tell the person who answers that Reb Chaim Sharon sent you."

Before Cas and Marly could get out another question, the Hasid left the room and disappeared into the auction crowds.

Cas stared at the business card. Incredulous, he showed it to her. While she examined it, he asked, "What are you thinking?"

She closed her eyes and brought her fingers to the side of her head, as if conjuring a clairvoyant vision. Her eyes flashed open, staring at his crotch. "I'm thinking of a number."

Cas grinned on seeing the direction of her gaze, exhilarated with the certainty that she had finally succumbed to his sexual charms. "Eight inches?"

"I'm thinking a little higher."

He straightened with surprise and thrust out his chest. "Wow. That's what I'm talkin' about! A woman who rounds up."

"More like sixty-forty."

"That's not a number!" he protested.

She slapped him on his wallet and walked off. "It will be."

I n the Jewish Quarter of Jerusalem's Old City, a young rabbinical student with a patchy beard led Cas and Marly into a darkened office next to the Hurva Synagogue.

As the door closed behind them, Cas checked the phone number on the Hasid's business card again, perplexed why they had been led here. A single bulb flicked on overhead, and in the hazy light, he could just make out an old rabbi with unruly whiskers hunched over a desk in the corner. The cleric's face, so lean and drawn that he looked like a bent baguette crowned with a yarmulke, bobbed inches from an open tome. He made odd noises through his nose as he traced the lines of what he was reading from right to left. After watching this ritual for nearly a minute, Cas cleared his throat, suspecting that the wizened rabbi was too blind to see them come in.

The rabbi did not look up from his study. "You possess red heifers."

Cas glanced around, wondering if Isserle and his Mossad cronies had set him up with this meeting for a prank. "Maybe. Who wants to know?"

Only then did the rabbi turn from his book. He glared at Cas with currant eyes fierce enough to have turned Moses to stone. "Tell me." He spoke with an ominous, slow pace. "Are you the American who conspires with the Zionists?"

Cas stole an alarmed glance at Marly, wondering what the rabbi was talking about. He was now having second thoughts about following up on the mysterious tip that the Hasid had given them at the auction. But on a hunch, he asked the rabbi, "This American you speak of ... is he from Texas, by any chance?"

"Texans are slant drillers," the rabbi said.

Cas was even more baffled by that enigmatic declaration. "I'm sorry, I'm not following."

The elderly rabbi wrapped his shriveled shoulders tighter with his shawl and motioned them closer to ease the effort on his withered voice. "I once asked our prime minister what he thought of your former President Bush. He told me that Texans are slant drillers. I was hoping you might translate this explanation for me."

Cas shrugged. "Texans will cheat a rock. That's about all I know of the damn bast—"

Marly kicked his boot, trying to silence him before he could offend the rabbi with his coarseness.

The rabbi, taking the inference, nodded. "There are rumors of a man from Texas who has bred a pure, unblemished red heifer."

That bit of information spiked the pulse in Cas's temples. "I think we know just the guy you're talking about."

"You are a commercial competitor with this man?"

"In a manner of speaking," Cas said. "I gotta come clean, Rabbi, you being a man of the cloth and all. I don't breed red heifers. I don't breed anything but a little contempt from time to time."

"Amen to that," Marly muttered.

Cas glared at her, then turned back to the rabbi and went on with his confession. "We've been trying to get our hands on this Texan con man who's apparently breeding red heifers for God knows what reason. We're just trying to find out what he's up to." He hesitated, figuring the story wouldn't be enough to satisfy the cleric. "He cheated us out of some big-time money." He paused again, looked down at his boots and shuffled. "To be honest, I'm not sure why I'm here even talking to a clergyman about cattle-breeding. The guy we're after is named Cohanim. All's I really know is that he's a world-class slimeball. He'll do anything for a buck."

The rabbi poured himself a cup of tea. "Greed is not your Texan's vice."

Cas checked Marly from his periphery, now more confused than ever. He asked the rabbi, "How do you figure that?"

"Are you a godly man?"

"I'd be lying if I said I was."

The rabbi nodded in admiration at the honesty. He reached for his copy of the Torah and opened it to a page. He handed the book to Marly. "My eyes have only a few lines left in them. Would you read from Numbers, Nineteen: Two?"

Marly took the book, which she knew from her bible studies was the same as the Christian Old Testament. She found an English translation of the Hebrew on the margin, and read it aloud: "'Speak unto the children of Israel, that they bring thee a red heifer without spot, wherein is no blemish, and upon which never came yoke.'"

She stole a stunned glance at Cas, and could have hung hangers on his gaping mouth.

Nodding at their reactions, the rabbi explained the passage. "The animal must not have hairs of any other color, it must be in perfect health, and it must never have been used to perform work." He gestured for her to continue reading from the Numbers chapter.

Marly found her place again. "'The Lord said to Moses and Aaron: This is a requirement of the law that the Lord has commanded: Tell the Israelites to bring you a red heifer without defect or blemish and that has never been under a yoke. Give it to Eleazar the priest; it is to be taken outside the camp and slaughtered in his presence. Then Eleazar the priest is to take some of its blood on his finger and sprinkle it seven times toward the front of the tent of meeting. While he watches, the heifer is to be burned—its hide, flesh, blood and intestines. The priest is to take some cedar wood, hyssop and scarlet wool and throw them onto the burning heifer.'"

Falling silent, she reread one of the lines to herself:

The heifer is to be burned.

"Rabbi, let's cut to the chase here," Cas said. "What's all this heifer-burning stuff really about?"

The rabbi bowed his head as if to negate the blasphemy. "The Temple cannot be restored until the ashes of a pure red heifer are again procured."

Marly suddenly understood what that girl in Texas had witnessed.

The rabbi allowed the revelation to sink in. "We have waited centuries for the red heifer to arrive. But while we leave its timing to God, others are not so patient. Some are now trying to *manufacture* this beast—this *precondition* of the Messiah—by artificial means. They who attempt such a thing will produce only abomination and evil."

Cas waited for an explanation, at a loss about what any of this could have to do with Seth Cohanim and his breeding scheme.

Marly couldn't hide the excitement in her voice. "Cohanim wants to restore the Jerusalem Temple. Just as it existed in the Old Testament. He just can't do it without the ashes of a red heifer. Says so right here in the Bible. Now, he has the ashes, and—"

"Wait a minute," Cas said. "Why would a Texas rancher want to rebuild a Jewish temple? The guy's as Christian as the Cross."

The rabbi's bagged eyes became even sadder. "Certain American demonimations believe that your Christ will not return to Earth until King Solomon's

Temple is rebuilt. And only then after a great battle is fought between the Messiah and the Antichrist."

The rabbi's explanation rattled something loose deep in Marly's brain. "That ranch girl in Llano said Cohanim brought along a strange-looking man dressed in black when he burned the calf."

Cas nodded, finally following her line of thought. He asked the rabbi, "Do any Jews in Israel work with these Christian groups?"

The rabbi lowered his head to deliver a shameful admission. "A splinter sect of my faith has sold its soul to them. These Jews now conspire with your fundamentalist Christians for their own ends. They take blood money from these people in the United States to help bring about the conditions for the rebuilding of the Temple. These Christians use my Jews for their own means while all along expecting them to be cast into Hell when the Messiah finally comes."

Cas wondered if Marly was thinking the same thing: What could the Black Stone of Mecca possibly have to do with Seth Cohanim and his obsession to breed red heifers to restore the Jerusalem Temple? Before he could pose that conundrum, the door cracked open.

The student who had escorted them into the office told his superior, "Rebbe, your next appointment is here."

The rabbi grasped the hands of his two American guests in a fretful farewell. "*Zay Gezunt*," he said, offering the traditional blessing for good health. "You must be careful. Such a man who would usurp God's prerogative will stop at nothing to see his demented creation manifested."

31

Galilee, Northern Israel

Leaving Jerusalem with Marly in the middle of the night, Cas raced their rental car up Route 918 along the Golan Heights and crossed into occupied Lebanese territory. Earlier that afternoon, after snooping around Haifa University's science halls, they had picked up on a bit of interesting academic gossip: An unidentified American man with deep pockets had reportedly built a state-of-the-art laboratory in a *kibbutz* near the northern border.

Worth a shot, considering they had no other leads.

As they neared their destination, dawn broke over the ancient Galilean hills, revealing Israeli border guards manning checkpoints in the distance.

Cas slowed down, knowing that a speeding vehicle was a prime target for skittish military patrols. "You sure this is the right place?"

Marly consulted the map again. "Shaaba Farms. Should be just up ahead."

Cas drove through a dusty field of orange groves and pulled into a rocked lane. The entrance to the *kibbutz* was gated and locked. Signs featuring angry stick men armed with machine guns made clear that trespassing would not be dealt with lightly.

"Maybe we should have called first," Marly said.

"Sure," Cas said, sarcastically. "Hello, we just happen to be in the hood. We'd love to drop in and ask a few questions about a total nut job named Seth Cohanim. He's a hyper-religious psycho who's gone global and may be balls deep in some nefarious shit."

"That's not what I meant."

"I'm sure the right-wing settlers around here would be delighted to accommodate a couple of strangers asking about their business dealings."

"Okay, smart guy. What do we do now that we're out here in this giant sandbox?"

Cas looked down the shimmering highway and noticed two hikers with backpacks shuffling wearily along the shoulder. The boy wore blue jeans and a *kippah* skullcap, and the girl wore a scarf and a calico dress that reached to her ankles. They had the confused look of American students just arrived in the country. Going with his guess, he rolled down the window and shouted at them, "*Shalom!*"

The two hikers stopped, their faces set with suspicion.

"You are here to work at the *kibbutz,* no?"

When the boy finally gave up a hesitant nod, Cas snapped his fingers for Marly to hand over her notebook. He got out of the car and pretended to check a roster on one of the notebook pages. "Afrom ... Maschel ... Baruch ... Are you Resnick and Fleischer from New York University?"

The couple looked at each other, puzzled. Finally, the boy said, "No, I am Aaron Katz. This is my girlfriend, Sonia Furst. We are juniors at Stanford."

Cas flipped a couple of pages deeper into the notebook. "Katz and Furst! There you are. A day early!"

Now even more confused, the boy riffled through his travel papers, trying to find his start date. "We were told to arrive today."

"Hey, no sweat," Cas said. "We'll find you bunks. I'll just need to check your personal belongings. You've probably already been told that our security measures are pretty tight here. You understand, of course. Your backpacks and headgear, please. And I'll need your letters of admission to the *kibbutz.*"

The coed didn't look pleased. "How long will this take?"

"No more than an hour," Cas promised. "I'll try to expedite the processing. There's a restaurant about a mile down the road, that way." He pulled a few *shekels* from his pocket and gave them to the boy. "Go have an espresso. Compliments of Shaaba Farms. I'll come pick you up when we get everything squared away."

The students reluctantly handed over their belongings and began walking down the road. When they were out of sight, Cas jumped back into the car and turned down the lane leading to the *kibbutz*. A hundred yards from the entrance, he stopped again and handed Marly the female student's scarf. "You live in New York. You should be able to fake a little Hebrew."

Grinning, Marly babbled gibberish, "*Ye` ikh aroyszogn em zeyer gezunt.*"

Cas tried on the boy's skullcap. "That's my little *siksa.*"

A mile farther down the road, he stopped the car on the shoulder. He and Marly got out, slipped on the backpacks, and walked down the rutted lane to the *kibbutz's* security kiosk. Practicing his *shtick,* Cas offered his hand to her in a mock greeting, "Hi, I'm Aaron Katz. I decided to go back to school and get my degree after 'Nam. This whole Holy Land scene rocks big time, yo."

Marly rolled her eyes and wondered again about her updated life expectancy, now that she had been drawn back into Cas Fielding's dangerous orbit.

Afer passing through the local security with no trouble, Marly and Cas walked down the main street of the *kibbutz* and checked out the barracks. The students and residents had just finished breakfast and were filing out of the dining hall into the clear morning heat. A few gave them quizzical looks, no doubt wondering why a couple of old geezers were here.

Near the end of the main street, Cas spotted a newer building that had a bright red plastic disposal container for biomedical waste sitting near its door. He whispered, "Target locked."

"We'd better wait until night," Marly muttered, covering her mouth.

"That would be a nugatory."

"You mean 'negatory,' you pseudo-Zionist buffoon," she muttered through set teeth. "'Nugatory' is the word that describes your level of intelligence."

Cas shrugged off the Scrabble lesson and led her on an indirect route toward the building, to avoid anyone's notice. As they strolled past the entrance, he jiggled the knob and found it locked. No surprise there. He kept walking around the building, glancing at the windows covered with black drapes.

"Satisfied?" Marly whispered. "Now let's get the hell out of here before someone asks us what we're doing."

Cas kept strolling, as if he didn't have a care in the world. Across the street, he saw a dark-skinned *kibbutzim* boy who was painting a railing. Hands stuffed into his pockets, he ambled over. "Dude, the dining hall is closed? I was seriously jonesin' for a burger."

The boy didn't even look up from his paint job. "That's not the dining hall."

"Looks just like Beckman Bistro at Stanford, only, y'know, smaller."

Keeping his eyes fixed to his spot on the board, the boy pointed his brush at the commissary down the street. "Store hours are seven to ten."

"Word." Cas smacked his lips. "Good burgers there, too?"

Irritated by the interruptions, the boy threw his brush into the bucket and snapped, "Are you here on some special-education program? Like for mentally challenged students?"

"Homeslice, no need to get all up in my grill, yo. I was just admiring your architecture."

"It's the old laboratory, okay?"

Cas blinked. "Old? You mean nobody uses it anymore?"

The Israeli boy glanced around as if making certain no one was listening. "Some rich American built it. He used it for a few weeks and then took off. That's all I know. They keep it locked up now. No one is allowed inside."

He shot Marly a satisfied glance. "Nice work. You an artist?"

"Yeah," the boy grumbled. "I'm a regular Michelangelo. I plant turnips. In two years, I'll go into the Army. Then I'll probably spend the rest of my life hawking cell phones in Tel Aviv. Anything else you want to know about me for your Elderhostel term paper, gramps?"

Cas raised his hands in surrender. "Sorry to bother you, bro."

Sensing an unfriendly vibe around the entire place, he led Marly back down the street until they reached a spot where they saw no one and hoped nobody was watching them. He grabbed her arm and whisked her onto a sidewalk between two beige-brick barracks buildings. Shadowed from the sun and passersby, he whispered, "We have to find a way into that lab."

Marly thought a moment. "I have an idea ... but it's a real long shot."

"I'm a big fan of long shots. Especially when the alternative is *no* shot."

She hesitated to tell him what she was thinking, but his brow-raised glare finally drove her to it. "My roommate in grad school, Rada, told me a story once about her family during World War Two."

"This isn't exactly the time for Masterpiece Theatre."

"Her grandparents were Jews in the Warsaw Ghetto. They survived by living for months in the sewers. The Nazis never did find them."

Cas was growing impatient. "And the Polish sewer system has what, exactly, to do with ... ?"

She frowned at him to drive home her point. "Rada told me that, after that experience, Jews always built escape routes under their houses. In case the Holocaust ever came again."

"You're saying that every *kibbutz* in Israel has a sewer system that can also serve as a bomb shelter and an escape tunnel?"

"I guess. I don't know. Maybe."

He peered around the corner and studied the laboratory's perimeter. "Let's see, where *would* the entrance to a sewer be built?" His eyes followed the slope down a deep ravine, where a wastewater-treatment plant sat. He grinned. "Marly McKinney, you magnificent stone junkie! I knew you'd eventually start contributing to the cause."

"Hell, I've been carrying your wrinkled ass ever since Dallas!"

"How's your tolerance for squeamish?"

Marly narrowed her glare. "What do you mean?"

"This could get a little, uh, fragrant."

I nside the sewer tunnel, Cas pushed up on an iron disc and climbed through the exposed hole. He turned, grinning, and motioned his grumbling partner to follow him.

Covered in filth, Marly climbed up the iron ladder and looked around, amazed that they had guessed the direction correctly. "This looks like the laboratory's maintenance room."

Cas watched her walk into the dim light. "Yikes! Went a little heavy on the makeup there, Fright Girl."

She rushed to the sink and washed the sewage scum from her arms and face. After cleaning herself, she still smelled a foul odor. This one, though, was different: bitter, lingering and deathly. "What is *that* stench?" she asked. "This whole damn country must be rotting."

Waving her to come with him, Cas opened a door and walked around the laboratory, careful to step around shattered glass vials and canisters that had been strewn across the floor. "Look at all this busted-up stuff. I'd say a squirrel must have gotten in here, gone ballistic, then died."

They stalked the smell toward another door, this one in a far corner.

Cas tried the handle, but it was locked. "Must be the office."

"Definitely worth checking out," Marly said. "Cohanim might have left some records."

Cas scanned the shelves until he found was he was looking for—a container of calcium carbide. He took the metal cylinder down and tucked it under his arm. "See if there are any sandwich bags in the kitchen."

Marly returned with a Ziploc baggie.

Cas filled it with the carbide powder and then zipped it up halfway. Striking the pose of a surgeon standing over an operating table, he ordered his nurse, "Your ballpoint pen. Stat."

Marly bit off a curse at his annoying medical act as she searched several lab drawers. At last, she came up with a Bic and tossed it to him. "Do you have any idea what you're doing?"

"Guess we're about to find out." Cas removed the ink injector in the Bic and filled the clear plastic cartridge—the one kids use to shoot spitballs—with water. He pawed through more of the drawers until he found some glue to plug the ends of the plastic cartridge. He stuck the water-filled cartridge into the cylinder of calcium carbide and zipped it, leaving an inch-long opening. He balanced the makeshift bomb atop the doorknob and warned her, "Stand back."

Marly ducked behind a counter.

Cas flicked a lighter and dropped it into the opening of the zip bag. He dived behind the counter with Marly, taking the opportunity to cuddle her. Before she could wiggle from his groping, the room shook with an explosion. When the debris finally settled, they slowly raised their heads over the counter.

The door had swung open, its locking mechanism destroyed.

Cas grinned at her. "And to think I only got a 'C' in chemistry."

They leapt up and walked warily into the office, waving away the smoke from the explosion. Marly was nearly doubled over by the same stench, now even stronger.

"Shit," Cas mumbled.

Marly finally found enough air to take a breath. "What's wrong?"

Cas stood over the decomposed body of an elderly woman whose hands were bound behind her. The ragged nose on the corpse looked as if rats had eaten it. The woman was curled into a clenched repose of agony, as if her last minutes had been spent in excruciating pain.

"What the hell is that on her forehead?" Marly asked.

Cas lifted the rotting head to the light and saw what appeared to be carved letters and numbers: *Leviticus 20: 2-27*

Marly came closer to see what he'd discovered. She turned and dry-heaved.

Cas flipped on the halogen lights to examine the grisly scene. "I'd say she's been here for months. You got any reception on your smartphone out here?"

Marly held a sleeve to her mouth while checking the bars on her phone's monitor. Afraid to take a breath to talk, she nodded.

Cas wrote down the Bible citation in his notebook. He tore out the page and handed it to her. "Search this."

Marly found an online concordance on her cell phone's browser. When the search result came up, she turned pale again as she showed Cas:

> *Whosoever giveth any of his seed unto Molech, he shall surely be put to death. … A man also or woman that hath a familiar spirit, or that is a wizard, shall surely be put to death: they shall stone them with stones: their blood shall be upon them.*

She heard a sizzling sound. Looking down at the floor, she saw what appeared to be cursive script materializing as if by magic. "What the hell?"

Cas touched the floor and retracted his finger, shaking his hand as if something had bitten him. "Damn! That's acid."

She looked up at the halogen lights in the ceiling. "The chemical must have interacted with the ultraviolet rays when we turned those bulbs on."

Cas glanced hesitantly at her, not wanting to confirm what he was thinking. He leaned over the woman's body and examined her chewed-up face. "Her hands are bound. She must have used her nose to scribble a message with the acid."

Marly was trying not to retch. "My Lord."

Cas risked lowering his eyes to the floor. "What does it say?"

Marly could just make out the first word of the harried script. "Looks like … 'Immaculate' something."

Dropping to all fours, Cas studied the letters on the floor from several different angles, careful not to get too close. He pulled out another page from the notebook and carefully placed it over the spot on the floor where the acid-ink message had been written. After several seconds, he pulled the page up, examining the slender lines that had been eaten away:

Immaculate Deceptio.

Baffled, he shook his head. "Is that Latin?"

"I don't know," Marly said. "Does she have any ID on her?"

Cas went through all the dead woman's pockets, but found no wallet. He carefully lifted her flaky hands to check for fingerprints. The tips had become decomposed.

Marly studied the poor woman. "Strange."

"What?"

"Is that eye shadow around her lids?"

"Yeah, so?"

"Slathered on pretty heavy for an eighty-year-old woman." Marly checked a ring that was on the woman's rotting finger. Grimacing at the disgusting task, she finally managed to pull the ring off with a sliver of rotted flesh. Coughing away the stench, she studied the facing on the ring. "A skull and cauldron." She shivered—now that was *really* morbid. "Whoever this was, she dressed and made herself up like a teenager." She looked down at the corpse's feet. "Platform heels. And look, they don't even fit her. Must be at least three sizes too large."

"Hey, everybody's searching for the Fountain of Youth."

"Maybe, but ..." She sighed. "Probably nothing."

Cas heard voices outside. "They must have heard the explosion. That'd be our cue to evacuate the premises."

Marly looked around for a door. "How?"

Cas held his fingers to his snout and said in a nasal honk, "The same way we came in."

As they raced back toward Jerusalem, Cas dialed up an old contact at the State Department. "Mickie! Your patron saint Cas here ... Hold on now ... I swear I left you a note."

Marly didn't even bother to roll her eyes. Age-old story. She didn't need the details.

"*Mea culpa,* my beautiful attaché," Cas crooned. "Listen, darling, despite my past reprehensible behavior, I need a favor. About nine months ago, a certain Seth Cohanim flew from Dallas to Israel. Can you filter out all of the American passengers who flew to Israel from there at around that time, give or take a week? I need to know if anyone *did not* fly back on a return ticket.... Yeah, I can wait."

"Let me guess," Marly said. "You bedded her, too."

Cas was about to defend his honor when he heard the report over the phone. "Really. Only one?" He nodded for Marly to write down what he was being told. "Bridget Whelan from Lubbock, Texas. Can you spell that? ... Great, and do you happen to have her age?" His face fell. "Thanks anyway, but I don't think that's my girl." He hung up, disappointed.

"What?" Marly asked.

"She fits the profile, except for one slight variance."

"Yeah?"

"Bridget Whelan was twenty-six."

Marly sat in stunned silence.

"Cohanim covered his tracks like a pro. I don't think—"

"She was wearing platform heels," Marly said.

Cas took his eyes off the road a moment and looked over at her, utterly perplexed why she kept bringing up the shoes. "Yeah, you mentioned that before. You doing a fashion survey now?"

Marly tried to blink her brain into high gear. "Why in God's name would an old woman risk breaking a hip by walking around in six-inch platforms?"

Cas shrugged. "Maybe she was just crazy. Maybe she liked being tall. Maybe she bought them a yard sale. Maybe the world just doesn't make any sense."

Marly opened her purse and pulled out the plastic bag with the victim's ring. She stared at the jewelry, trying to understand the woman who had worn it. She noticed an inscription inside the band. She looked at the ring through the transparent bag and held it to the light:

Texas Tech, Class of 2009.

Her eyes narrowed with alarm. "How far are we from Jerusalem?"

"A good hour, at least, " Cas said.

"Get me to Hebrew University, Tonto. And fast."

Marly and Cas leapt to their feet when a female lab technician at the university's Hadassah Medical Center strode through the lobby doors. Clutching the requested test results, the technician smiled at Marly. "Good news, Dr. McKinney. We were able to scrape enough DNA from the dead skin on the ring to get a good sampling."

Marly quickly scanned the document. Reaching the end, she closed her eyes, her suspicion confirmed. She thanked the technician, who lingered, as if hoping to be told why the test had been such high priority. But Marly remained silent, until the technician finally got the message and departed through the swinging doors again.

"Well?" Cas said. "You gonna let me in on what this is all about?"

"That dead woman suffered from Progeria," Marly said. "It's a rare syndrome that causes someone's genes to fast-forward the aging process. Children who have the condition age rapidly, to the point that they look like they would in their final years."

"What does any of this have to do with Cohanim?"

"Progeria usually isn't inherited. Something has to trigger the genes to go haywire."

"You mean ..."

Marly had a sickened look. "I think our Doctor Texanstein manipulated that poor girl's DNA and kept her prisoner to force her to watch herself grow old. Happened in a matter of a few days, maybe a week."

"I thought you said the DNA in living humans couldn't be changed?"

She shook her head, still in shock. "That's always been the prevailing scientific consensus. But some biotech companies have been messing around with DNA polymerase to provoke mutagenesis. Cohanim may have stumbled on the process to accomplish it." She pulled out her purse, found her aspirin bottle, and popped a couple into her mouth. "This is why I went into rocks. I don't have the stomach for the living sciences."

Cas paced in a circle. "So, that woman *could* have been Bridget Whelan."

"It's looking that way."

"But why would Cohanim go to all the trouble of torturing a grad-student employee by aging her to death?"

She shrugged. Who could read the mind of a sociopath? She looked at Cas and had to bite her tongue to keep from saying, *Takes one to know one.*

Cas flipped open his phone and called the registrar at Texas Tech to confirm that a Bridget Whelan had indeed been a student there. Informed that her home was Lubbock, he found her listed with an older woman named Livia and an infant, age two. He punched in the phone number listed for the address. Moments later, a woman came on the line with a cigarette-husky voice.

"I'm looking for Bridget Whelan," Cas said. "Does she live there?"

The woman didn't answer immediately. "Who is this?"

"My name is Fielding. I'm with the police. Is Bridget your daughter?"

"Yes, but we ain't seen her for nearly a year. She left her daughter with me. Last I heard from her, she was going overseas for her job."

"Ma'am, did Bridget wear a ring with a skull and cauldron?"

The woman let out a stifled cry. "That was her coven talisman."

Cas shot an alarmed glance at Marly. "Coven? You mean like a witch?"

"She was into all that pagan nonsense," the woman said. "I told her it was the Devil's work, but she wouldn't listen to me."

Before the mother could get another word in, Cas hung up, not wanting to be the one to give her the bad news. He'd let the Israeli police do that when they found the body. Stunned, he looked at Marly. "Why would a Christian rancher from Texas hire a witch?"

"Maybe Cohanim didn't know about her pagan beliefs. Maybe he thought it was just a fad. It's not like the woman would put something like that on her resume. The real question is, why would a modern witch leave her last desperate message in Latin?"

Cas broke a devilish grin. "*Qui quaerit, invenit.*"

"Very funny." Marly stared at him. "Seek, and ye shall find." She touched her temple. "Not just another pretty face, huh? Don't tell me you're going all New Testament on me now."

Cas hurried for the exit, dragging her with him. "All of a sudden, I'm feeling an urge to go to church and confess my sins."

She stopped and dug in her heels, clueless as to what scheme he was hatching now. "You'd have to get an extended work visa here for the time it would take to confess your—"

He was already out the door.

32

Old City, Jerusalem

Marly struggled to keep up as Cas hurried down a narrow medieval street toward the Church of the Holy Sepulcher. When they turned a corner and reached the entrance to the sprawling rotunda built over the site of Christ's crucifixion, Cas ducked into a side alley and pulled a Browning 9mm from a holster under his vest jacket.

Marly saw him slide a magazine clip home. "Where'd you get that?"

"That cop we passed ten blocks back is strapping an empty holster."

"You really think Cohanim is waiting for us in *there*?"

"At the moment, it's not Cohanim I'm worried about."

"Then who *are* you worried about?"

Cas looked around the corner, cautiously eyeing two black-robed Greek Orthodox monks who guarded the arched doors. "You got your Mace handy?"

"Oh, for God's sake, Cas, this is a *church!*"

"Yeah, but not just any church. That nave over there happens to be the most dangerous spot in all of Israel."

She wondered if he had been smoking weed behind her back. "Which would make it the most dangerous place in the world. Yeah, sure."

"I'm as serious as the Pope on Good Friday. Eight different monastic sects maintain the church, and they each have their own little corner of Heaven inside. If one oversteps the borders of the others, all Hell breaks lose. This time of year they do their spring-cleaning. Riots always break out." He leveled a severe gaze at her. "Stay right behind me. And don't look the monks in the eye. They'll attack you for even thinking of invading their space."

Before she could determine if he was just pulling her leg, Cas walked her into the small plaza that led to the main entrance and marched toward the door of the south transept. As they passed through the arched door, she saw a small plaque on the wall commemorating the dozens of pilgrims who had died in a stampede here in 1840. Suddenly, she became a believer.

Inside the old nave, she nearly choked from the smoke and incense that clogged the domed ambulatory. Bearded monks clad in a dizzying array of vestments and headgear glared at them with wariness as they hurried past. The two intruders crossed the steps to an altar dedicated to Mary Magdalene and entered the Chapel of the Holy Apparition on the right side of the rotunda, where a Franciscan friar was saying Mass for a half-dozen worshippers.

Cas plopped down in the front pew and motioned her to sit next to him. A bell rang, and the other congregants stood and lined up down the aisle to receive Communion. Cas waited to be the last in the queue. Turning from the altar to dispense the Sacrament, the friar saw him and dropped his silver paten, spilling the consecrated hosts. Distraught, the friar fell to his knees and hurriedly retrieved the fallen Eucharist. Hands shaking, he hissed at Cas through set teeth, "What are you doing here?"

Smiling like an altar boy at his first Mass, Cas kept his back turned to the other congregants and whispered, "I'd like to take Confession after you take your final bow in your little one-man show up here."

The friar's face drained whiter than his frock. Without answering that threat couched in a request, he stood and walked back to the altar.

When the service was finally finished, Cas put a hand on Marly's arm to keep her seated while the other worshippers walked out into the rotunda. As soon as everyone else had left the chapel, he stood from the pew and shut the doors. Making sure they were alone, he grasped Marly's hand and pulled her toward the confessional.

Marly tried shake him off. "What in the world—"

"Get in here with me." Cas shoved her into the tiny booth and jammed himself next to her on the narrow bench. He pulled the door shut. After an interminable minute, they heard the door to the confessor's adjacent covey open and close. A green light above them blinked on, and the slat that covered the screen between them slid open.

Finally, a voice on the other side of the screen whispered, "I told you ten years ago, Fielding. I am out of the business for good."

"You've got a pretty sweet gig here, *padre*," Cas said. "Not bad for a witness-protection plan. Five years as an informant on Palestinian Christians. I hear the pension and retirement plans are top-notch. Particularly the after-life benefits."

"Part of the deal was I'd never have to snitch again. Another part, specifically, was that I would never have to see or deal with the likes of you ever—"

"Don't piss all over your hair-lined underwear,. I'm not looking to recruit you for another round of Violate Your Vows. I'm done with that nonsense, too."

"Then why *are* you here?"

"I need some theological inspiration."

"You're into Bible study now? A little late, isn't it?"

"How well do you know Latin?"

The friar sounded hesitant. "Enough to fake my way through the old Mass."

Cas leaned closer to the screen. "*Immaculate Deceptio.*" He heard nothing but silence from the other side of the screen. "That ring a bell for you?"

The friar finally admitted, "The Immaculate Deception."

Hearing the friar pronounce an 'n' on the end of the word, Marly asked him, "What does *that* mean?"

"There's a *woman* in there with you?" the friar protested. "Must you bring your debauched proclivities into a holy sanctuary?"

"Forgive me, Father, for I have sinned. All is forgiven. Now, back to the Latin."

The friar sighed. "The 'Immaculate Deception' was a term coined by heretics over the centuries to denigrate the Doctrine of the Immaculate Conception."

Marly leaned her mouth to the screen. "That's the idea that Christ was born without Mary having sex, right?"

"Lay people make that mistake all the time," the friar said. "You're thinking of the Annunciation to Mary. The Immaculate *Conception* refers to the Virgin Mary's birth without stain to St. Anne, her mother. The Blessed Mary had to be free of original sin so that she would not pass it on to Jesus. That's why the Church promulgated the Doctrine of the Immaculate Conception. Of course, various Protestant sects and heretical cabals reject the belief that Mary herself was conceived and born by supranatural means."

"So," Cas asked, "the Virgin Mary was born of a virgin, too?"

"No. It's very complicated."

"Give us the *Cliff Notes* version."

The friar sighed heavily again, as if not wishing to get into this thorny issue. Finally, he explained, "Official Catholic doctrine does not believe that Mary was conceived virginally."

"You mean 'vaginally'? Cas asked, confused.

"No, I mean virginally. St. Anne was not a virgin."

"Wait a minute," Marly said. "I thought you just said that Mary was born without sin."

Through the screen, they could see the friar press his hands together in prayer, as if petitioning the saints for the gift of clarity and patience. Finally, the friar tried again. "The Church teaches that the Holy Mother was blessed with a special, one-time dispensation of sanctifying grace, in order to be preserved from Original Sin during the birth process. Unlike Jesus, Mary was born naturally from a mortal father and mother, but she was free of all hereditary sin. That is what we mean when we pray, 'Hail Mary, Full of Grace.'"

Cas boinged his head back against the confessional wall in exasperation. "The *real* miracle, *padre*, is how you papists have managed to sell this angels-dancing-on-the-head-of-a-pin rubbish for two thousand years."

Marly, still confused, whispered to Cas, hoping the friar couldn't hear. "Why would that murdered girl in Galilee care a whit about some arcane point of Catholic dogma? Bridget Whelan wasn't even a Christian, let alone a Catholic."

Cas thought for a moment. "Mary and Jesus ... both born without sin." He looked at Marly and whispered back to her, "What were the differences between these two biblical pregnancies, other than the fact that one was conjured up without a human father?"

She shrugged. "One baby turned out to be male. And the other female."

"Yeah ... a bull and a heifer."

"Huh?" She pinned him with a quizzical look. "What are you getting at?"

"You remember what that asshole at the stockyards told you about that new semen-sorting technology?"

"What about it?"

"Immaculate Deception," Cas said, repeating the translated message that Bridget Whelan had left in acid. "Maybe our Texas witch was trying to tell someone, anyone, that Cohanim was deceiving the world with what only *appeared* to be an innocent and sinless birth."

"Of cows?"

"You got a better explanation?"

Marly was at a loss. "What possible difference could it make if Cohanim is breeding heifers, bulls, or Power Rangers for the Israelis? He's already got his red heifer ashes to rebuild the Temple. That's what that girl in Llano told us."

"I haven't the foggiest." Cas stood in the cramped booth. "But we need to find out. And fast."

The friar cleared his voice to remind them that he was still trapped in the confessional. "Do you want absolution, or not?"

"That would be throwing pearls to swine. Or to be more accurate, swine throwing pearls to swine. But I'll tell you what I *could* use."

"Yes?"

"You got any extra bottles of Mass wine I could take for the road?"

They heard the friar snap the sleeves of his robes in disgust. "May God forgive you! Now, get out of my confessional!"

Cas didn't budge. "You first, Holy Eminence. Simony before beauty."

The friar bolted and slammed the door behind him.

Still stuffed into the tight box with Marly, Cas snuggled closer to her, but she pushed him away. Pouting, he whimpered, "Now is that Christian love?"

"Just out of curiosity," she said. "Why the hell didn't you tell me you knew a priest here? We could have asked him about Cohanim on the first day we arrived."

"Padre Panhandler out there? He's just a lowlife with a starched collar. I used to know a thousand of his ilk in every hole from Tel Aviv to Riyadh."

"But if he's an informant, he might have heard something on the street."

Cas pointed his forefinger and thumb to his temple and turned them in a signal for her to start up the common-sense engine. "Southern-fried Come-To-Jesus types like Cohanim are a dime a dozen in the Holy Land. They run so many tours here from the States that it's a damn wonder they haven't turned the Temple Mount into an Alamo replica. Our friendly drive-through confessor wouldn't have given the Llano Lightgiver a second thought. Besides, evangelicals think the Vatican is Satan's whorehouse. Cohanim would never cross paths with a papist shill, let alone cross Crosses."

"Well, when you put it so intelligently ... "

"By the way, sarcasm is one of the seven deadly sins. You'll need another forgiveness session." He glanced down at the top button of her blouse. "I've been told I have a spiritual gift for the laying on of hands."

Marly had rolled her eyes so many times since first encountering him that day in her office that she feared it would become an unconscious tic. She threw open the confessional door, desperate for air in the thick incense and ripe fragrance of a man who had gone without a shower for two days.

Cas, shrugging off yet another rejection, followed her out.

An Israeli police officer stood waiting for them.

33

Kiryat Menachem Begin, East Jerusalem

A detective from the Jerusalem District of the Public Safety Ministry entered the interrogation room and pulled a clip credential from his shirt pocket. He slid his laminated ID across the table toward Cas and Marly for their edification.

"Mefake'ah," Cas said with a whistle, repeating the detective's rank in Hebrew. He tried to curry favor with a collegial nod, hoping to establish a mutual understanding of professional courtesy. "Did we violate some kind of a curfew, Inspector? Catholic confessions not allowed during Israeli National soccer games or something?"

The detective didn't buy into Cas's buddy act. He unlocked a storage locker along the wall behind him and yanked out two backpacks for their inspection. "These look familiar?"

Marly burned Cas with a glare that shouted, *I told you so.* Then, averting her eyes from the pilfered bags, she told the detective in a less-than-convincingly voice, "They're not ours."

Cas scooted out his chair, faking an assumption that the meeting was over. "But hey, thanks for thinking of us. We'll let you know if we *do* lose any luggage on the rest of our holiday."

"Sit down!" the detective ordered. "Of course they're not yours!"

"Ease up there, pal," Cas said as he slowly lowered back to his chair. "No need to spike your blood pressure."

"You two find this little crime spree you're on amusing, do you?"

Seeing that they were in it for the long haul, Cas kicked his feet up on the table to relax. "So we borrowed a couple of backpacks for an hour. Good education for those kids. They shouldn't be so trusting of strangers."

"Do you have any friends in Israel?" the detective asked.

Cas glanced at Marly, wondering if she had any clue about the path this oblique line of inquiry was headed. When she shrugged, he turned back to the detective. "Everyone in Israel is our friend. We're just a couple of spiritual seekers trying to find our lost souls in the Holy Land."

The detective sat on the corner of the table next to Cas, near enough to land a punch. "I'm going to ask you one more time. Think hard. Anyone here you ought to reach out to?"

Cas put a finger to his lips in mock thought. "Uh, Uri Geller, maybe? I do have some bent spoons that need refurbishing."

The detective walked over to a glass pane and rapped his knuckles on what Cas had already pegged as a one-way mirror. Seconds later, the door to the interrogation room opened, and a young man with black hair and a pasty face walked in.

Cas lost his smirk.

Avram Isserle, Mossad agent at large, came looming over him. "I thought I'd made clear my conditions for your release the last time we held a reunion. I guess I should have branded them on your dick in English capital letters, so you could remind yourself every time you took a piss."

Cas quickly recovered his carefree façade. "Josh, ol' buddy," he piped, using Isserle's birth name to throw him off his game. "You know, I suggested that very idea to a tattoo artist before I left Tel Aviv. He took one look at my anatomy suggested there was enough billboard space there to translate them into Hebrew and Yiddish, too. I just couldn't decide which text font would be more attractive to the ladies. Arial tends to stretch well, but the serifs on Times New Roman—"

"Same fucking comedian." Isserle swiveled his glare of disgust from Cas to Marly. "I should have known you two grifters were bound to get tired of plane-jumping and petty theft. Murder is more exciting."

Marly leapt to her feet. "Murder?"

Isserle shoved her back into the chair. Motioning for a file from the detective, the Mossad agent pulled out a document that held what looked like ridged ink blotches. He slid the evidence report across the table. "Your fingerprints were all over a body found at a northern *kibbutz* called Shaaba Farms."

Cas scooted the report back to his old friend, not bothering to look at it. "Old news. That girl died months before we stumbled onto her."

Isserle throated a smoker's chortle. "Girl?"

"Yes, *girl*," Marly said. "Seth Cohanim is behind all of this. The victim's name was Whelan. Cohanim somehow manipulated her DNA and caused her to age fifty years in just a couple of days."

Isserle shook his head in disbelief. "You two worms are really scraping the bottom of the Dead Sea for excuses this time. What'd you do, pick up a copy of *World News Daily* and read the freak section on the way over?"

"Just let me get to my carry-on in our car," said Marly, remembering the lab report she had kept from the Hebrew University technician. "I'll prove it."

"And just to make it worth your while, Joshua," Cas added, "I'll stake a thousand bucks on it. If we're telling you the truth, you don't owe us a thing. Just arrange a little meet-and-greet for us with that Texas two-step pirate."

Isserle circled them. "What is it with you two parrots and Cohanim? First you claim he's breeding glow-in-the-dark cows. Now you've got him murdering young women with home chemistry kits. What's next? You gonna claim he's trying to clone Danny Crockett?"

"Davy," Marly corrected him.

Isserle turned on her with threat. "What?"

"Davy Crockett," Marly told the Mossad agent. "If you're going to use American pop-culture references, at least try to get them right."

"I think he meant Daniel Boone anyway," Cas said.

Marly shook her head. "Daniel Boone was from Kentucky, not Texas."

"Actually, he was from North Carolina," Cas said. "Man, I used to have one of those coonskin—"

Isserle slammed his palm to the table. "The body we found at the kibbutz! The one you two jokers pawed over like a couple of necrophiliacs!"

"You saw the platform shoes she was wearing, right?" Cas said.

"Yeah, so what? Maybe she liked the view from up there."

"Come on," Marly said. "Surely you got a better explanation than that?"

"That dead hag was as old as the Judean hills," Isserle said. "She obviously suffered from dementia. We deal with these mania types here all the time. They get a little *meshuggah* and convince themselves that they're the reincarnated Jesus or the Virgin Mary or some—"

"We didn't kill her!" Marly insisted.

Isserle grinned at her emotional outburst. "I know you didn't, Bonnie. I just wanted to get the full attention of you and Clyde here."

Cas was pissed. "Then what *did* happen to this Bridget Whelan, smart guy?"

"These delusional pilgrims always come crashing back down to reality eventually," Isserle said. "And then a lot of them attempt suicide, usually in some grisly manner in a sick homage to some saint's martyrdom. We've had more than a couple of these nut jobs even try to crucify themselves upside down, convinced that they're St. Peter."

"You found a suicide note?" Cas asked, knowing damn well the agent hadn't.

"Suicide note?" Isserle repeated.

Cas realized the corpse must have deteriorated so severely by the time the cops got to it that the Leviticus quotation on the woman's forehead was unrecognizable. He glared a silent warning at Marly not to mention it or the

Deceptio message that they had erased from the acid-etched floor. "Who's the parrot now, Avi? What I *am* saying is that, if your theory's correct, she would have left a suicide note, probably with instructions on where she was going to resurrect herself in three days."

Isserle rolled his eyes. "This isn't Hollywood!"

Seeing that the interrogation was going nowhere, the Jerusalem detective shifted impatiently behind the two Americans. Leaning over their shoulders, he tapped his watch at Isserle. "What do you want me to do with them? I've got other cases waiting."

Isserle glared at the detective for interrupting him, leaving no doubt that he could care less about the local workload. After retrieving his file from the table, the Mossad agent strolled toward the door. "Keep them locked up for the night. I'll send a couple of my men from Tel Aviv in the morning to take them to our detention facility in the Negev."

"Whoa now!" Cas shouted.

Marly protested, "You just said you know we didn't kill that girl! We got a witness here!"

Turning back, Isserle grinned at them, enjoying their reactions on learning that this time they wouldn't be escaping prosecution. He told Cas, "I'm recommending the charges be filed on your little plane fraud fiasco. And your carping co-conspirator here will get the same tour of our judicial system. I'm a man of my word. You should know that by now."

"Let's talk this out, Av."

"What, so now I'm not *Josh*?" He pulled a glossy photograph out of his file and flung it to the table. "Here's something to keep you two 'spiritual seekers' occupied while you wait for your arraignments. Maybe you'd like to meditate on what can happen when you go off your meds." He laughed and walked out of the room.

Marly turned the photograph around and saw that it was an evidence shot of Bridget Whelan's decomposing corpse. She threw it against the slamming door and glared at the city detective, who stood in the corner watching them with smirking bemusement. "That girl didn't kill herself in some imitation martyrdom! She wasn't even a Christian. Why would she go off the deep end after coming over here with a good-paying job to help breed cattle?"

"Cattle?" the flunkie detective said with a dismissive snort. "Whatever that woman was doing in our country, she wasn't working on cattle."

Cas leaned closer to the detective. "Why makes you say that?"

The detective glanced at the door, looking worried about Isserle eavesdropping. He turned off the one-way light on the mirror and then nodded for Cas to continue.

Cas reached into his Speedos, slid out a wad of bills, and laid it on the table. "I probably shouldn't be carrying around this much money in here."

"And here we all thought you were just well-endowed," the detective said. "I guess we need to start doing a better job of frisking suspects."

Cas made his best puppy eyes. "Would you mind keeping the cash in a safe place for me, Inspector?"

Taking the hint, the detective walked back to the table and, with the deftness of a magician, stuffed the bills into his pocket.

Cas cleared his throat, a signal that he was waiting for his end of the barter.

The inspector flicked on the one-way mirror light, making sure no one was watching from the observation room, then he turned the light back off. "We found a discarded Petri dish in the biomedical-waste receptacle at that *kibbutz* laboratory."

Cas cocked his ear to make sure he had heard correctly. "And this is worth"— he angled his gaze toward the bulge of bills in the inspector's pocket—"*how* exactly?"

"The Petri dish held an embryo, all right. Of a human. Not a cow."

Marly slammed her fist on the table, as if having suspected Cohanim was involved in some kind of genetics chicanery. "Anything else interesting show up in your investigation?"

The detective turned his shoulder to shield his next revelation from being heard through the door crack. "Does the name 'Lucy' mean anything to you?"

Cas glanced at Marly, who seemed distracted and disturbed by the detective's question. He shook his head at the detective to indicate that the name drew a blank.

The detective shrugged. "The forensics team found a rather interesting cache of documents at the crime site. They purported to contain data about the DNA taken from a woman identified only by the first name, Lucy."

"I'm not exactly seeing my money's worth here," Cas said.

"I thought it might have some significance. Isserle found it important enough to mark as classified."

Cas dropped his chin and studied his navel, trying to unravel this new knot of mysteries. He looked back up at the detective. "Not that we don't appreciate chewing the fat with you, but why *are* you sharing this intel with us? I mean, aside from my generous donation ..."

The detective sat down in a chair and tied his shoestrings, using the task as an excuse to reveal in a whisper under the table, "Isserle and his Mossad assholes treat us District *politsyants* like parking-meter cops. You just got a sampling of it. They think they run the damn country, barging in anywhere they please and taking over local investigations."

Marly sensed an opening. "Anything we can do to help you?"

The detective came back upright and tapped his fingers on the table, as if choosing his next words carefully. "I wouldn't be all that upset if someone we all know lost a couple of rendition suspects due to his ineptitude."

Cas was all ears. "And how might that happen?"

The detective rubbed a hand over his mouth. "Transfers from our jurisdiction to Mossad's holding pens have to be authorized with a written directive by the agent in charge. Our mutual acquaintance fancies himself as too important to be bothered with paperwork, so he always orders us to do it for him. Of course, a judicial panel investigating the escape of two prisoners would never be told of this abuse of protocol."

"Why is that?" Marly asked.

"It would be quite embarrassing for an intelligence agent to have to admit that he had no transfer documentation to present to the court." He stood up and walked toward the door, but then looked back at Cas with the beginnings of a wink. "I read your background file."

"Pretty boring stuff," Cas said. "You must not be as busy as you let on."

The detective flashed him a grim smile. "You're being way too humble, Mr. Fielding."

Marly's snort of disbelief interrupted Cas's explanation.

"Ignore her," Cas told the detective. "You were saying?"

"For all I know, you may be insane, like most people suspect. But you've got one hell of an impressive record in the field. You're the only Westerner I've ever met who became blood brothers with the Bedouins and lived to tell of it."

Flattered as he was, Cas knew another sandal was about to drop.

The detective put his hand on the doorknob and, pulling its sleeve out an inch, turned the mechanism counterclockwise three times, demonstrating a secret fail-safe release, designed for cops who might find themselves trapped inside without a key. "I like to see our detainees get plenty of exercise. The best time for a stroll around headquarters here is usually around four in the morning."

"I do enjoy evening constitutionals," Cas said, taking his meaning.

The detective hesitated before opening the door. "All I know is, it'd be a damn shame if a man as important as Agent Isserle were to find himself answering negligence charges at a disciplinary hearing for losing a transfer prisoner."

"Yeah, a *damn* shame." Cas tried to control his salivation at his sudden turn of fortune. "And it probably wouldn't help his case if the prisoners he lost had left behind a farewell note wondering why the local detective had been ordered off the case."

"By the way," the detective said. "Just out of curiosity, did either of you happen to smell anything on Mr. Isserle's breath?"

Marly got into the act. "You know, I did detect a rather heavy whiff of scotch. And he was slurring his words so badly, I was afraid the poor fellow might have suffered a stroke."

Smothering a smile of revenge, the detective walked out and shut the door behind him.

Cas pranced around the room. "And you think my karma's run outa gas." He flashed Marly a smug smile. "Hah! Avi boy is going to have—oh, I'm on a roll—a cow!"

While he practiced his *Dancing With The Stars* tryout, Marly sat quietly, troubled by something the detective had said earlier. Rousing finally, she muttered to herself, "Lucy."

"Yeah, how about that. I loved that show." Cas switched to a rumba. "I used to entertain the boys with a killer Desi Arnaz imitation. I even thought about angling for a Guantanamo posting just so I could get to Cuba."

Marly glared at him. "Will you cut the crap for two seconds!"

"What bug's gotten under your buns all of a sudden? We just got dealt a royal flush. You need to stop and enjoy these rare moments of triumph in life."

"A few months ago, I came across a news item in the *Journal of Biological Archaeology.*"

"Archaeology? That's a little far afield for you, isn't it?"

"You'd be amazed what I do to avoid actual work."

"Um, I've got a pretty good idea."

She shot him a warning glare at his crotch, one that might have been interpreted as a reminder that he didn't have any Speedo padding left to protect him from a kick to the groin now. "Anyway, there was a notice in it reporting that someone had broken into the museum where they kept the skeletal remains of the oldest female ancestor of humans ever found on Earth."

"Fascinating." Cas looked around the room for something to entertain himself with until they could escape. "I mean, c'mon. Let's play strip poker or something. Hell, I'd rather look at that corpse photo than listen to—"

"The archaeologists who dug up this Humanoid female named her Lucy. If I remember correctly, the only thing taken from the exhibit on the night of the break-in was a tooth."

Cas was half listening. "Maybe the thief was a fetishist dentist."

She ignored his sophomoric quips. As if speaking to the only intelligent person in the room—herself—she said, "I didn't give it much thought at the time, but then I read somewhere that teeth retain DNA longer than any other part of a skeleton."

That last comment registered a rare brain wave in Cas's head, and he nearly fell from his go-go dancing perch atop his chair. "Wait a minute. And you're telling me this *now*?"

"Hey, you've laughed off all my other theories. Why should I share?"

He leapt down and confronted her. "You think Cohanim—"

"He hired that Boston thief to steal the Black Stone of Mecca around the same time that Lucy's tooth went missing, didn't he? I'd bet this year's pay—which, by the way, happens to equal the amount of money I've earned from this wild goose chase—that Cohanim stole the Lucy tooth, too."

"That's a real stretch. Burning calves is one thing. But breaking into museums and burglarizing famous artifacts?"

"Maybe, but I've got a gut feeling that our detective friend who just left had a reason for telling us about that classified Lucy notation in the murder file. He suspects something, too."

"Suspects *what*?"

Marly took over from Cas's pacing while he sat back down, and she began slapping herself on her forehead. "Why didn't I see this before?"

"See *what*?"

"The Immaculate Deception!"

Cas blinked repeatedly, trying to follow her. "Wait, slow down!"

"This is what that poor girl at the *kibbutz* was trying to say with her acid-etched message!"

Cas was getting dizzy from watching her orbit him. "Dammit, slow the hell down!"

She stopped in mid-step, savoring a lording smile at having bested her spook partner at his own game. "Cohanim's been using this cattle-breeding business as a cover for his *real* work."

Cas didn't know if he really wanted to hear an answer to his next question. "Which is?"

Marly could barely believe she was saying it aloud. "He's mating the DNA from the oldest woman on Earth."

"He's ... what? Did you say *mating*?"

She repeated her theory, slow enough for even him to understand: "He's mating the DNA ... from the oldest woman on Earth ... with the DNA that spawned human life ... on this planet."

Cas's eyes rounded. Glancing at the one-way mirror, he whispered, "Look, we're getting out of here in a couple hours. You don't have to play the insanity card for those bozos."

Marly looked downright possessed. "Cohanim somehow managed to extract the ancient DNA from the Black Stone. That's why he went to all the trouble and expense to have it stolen from Mecca and delivered to him, only to return it a few days later."

Cas fell motionless. The red in his face rose from his neck to his forehead like the mercury in a thermometer. With a sudden burst of anger, he spun and kicked a chair across the room. "And stealing our commission in the process!"

"He must have seen that study back in the late Sixties," Marly said. "When scientists found elements of RNA in the Murchison meteorite in Australia."

Cas was still kicking the chair, cursing and muttering promises of revenge.

"How far back do Muslims believe the Black Stone dates?" she asked.

He halted his raging fit long enough to look at her in astonishment. "From the time of Adam and Eve."

She nodded. "Which means that the Black Stone of Mecca must contain the first building blocks of DNA on Earth."

"You're saying the Stone carried Adam's DNA?"

"I'm not saying it. The Bible and the Koran are saying it."

The two shared a stunned moment of silence.

Then, Cas asked her, "But why would a Texas cattle rancher want DNA that old?"

Marly pulled an imaginary cowboy hat down over her eyes and pawed at the imaginary holstered guns at her sides, as if making a quick draw. "I don't know, pardner, but I'm aiming to find out right fast."

34

East Jerusalem

As the first rays of the Judean dawn flashed against the golden Dome of the Rock, Cas hurried Marly toward a line of taxis that sat waiting beyond the Jaffa Gate. He kept glancing over his shoulder, expecting their old friend Isserle to show up at any moment with a small army of Mossad agents. Finally feeling safe enough to stop running, he pulled Marly into a niche in the giant ashlars that bordered the ancient Roman Citadel. "We're not going another step until you let me in on the rest of this little theory of yours."

She didn't look particularly motivated to elaborate.

"Cohanim puts the Adam DNA and the Lucy DNA in the genetics batter and makes a pancake out of it. I get that. But why? Is he trying to come up with some kind of new, high-powered energy drink?"

After a hesitation, she said, "I think he's trying to clone something."

"Something? Okay, I'll buy a vowel for two hundred, Vanna."

She turned away and mumbled, as if trying to blunt the impact. "God."

He leaned in, waiting for her to finish her thought. "God what? God damn? God almighty? God bless America?"

She braced for the reaction. "Just God … I think he's trying to clone *God.*"

Cas couldn't even dredge up a laugh. "How, exactly, do you figure that?"

"The Bible says that God made Adam in His own likeness and image."

"Yeah, and … ?"

"It's a simple logical syllogism. Adam looks like God."

"Following, so far."

"Adam has DNA."

"Of course he does."

"Therefore, God has to have Adam's DNA, and Adam has to have God's DNA. Get Adam's DNA, and—wala!—you're on your way to spawning the new black sheep sibling of the Trinity. … God the Holy Clone."

His jaw dropped.

"Don't say it."

"That's utterly ridiculous. With the emphasis on 'utter.'"

Marly wasn't laughing. "Apparently Bridget Whelan didn't think so."

"If she was helping Cohanim," he protested, "why would he kill her?"

"Good question."

"Yeah, and one that I'm going to pose to that Texan pickpocket at the point of a shark knife when I catch him." He inched his eyes around the corner. "But I'll bet he's long gone from here by now."

"I wouldn't take that bet."

His eyebrows lifted. "How do you figure?"

"There's one critical element of Cohanim's demented experiment that he'd still have to obtain in this part of the world."

He waited for the punch line.

"A Semitic woman to impregnate with the God embryo."

He cocked his head sideways, still waiting.

"A modern Virgin Mary."

"Damn." Blown away, he circled her, trying to make senses of it all. "You've got this all figured out, don't you. You know, I'm starting to think I'm either rubbing off on you, or you're just a regular mad scientist."

"When was the Black Stone stolen from Mecca this year?"

"Oh, I guess about—"

"Not 'about.' I mean the exact date."

He dug deeper through the ashes of burned-out brain cells. "The Hajj last year was November Fourteenth. The Stone went missing exactly two weeks before. So, November First … but why does that matter?"

"Today is June Thirtieth," she said. "It's been almost nine months."

Suddenly he understood what she was driving at. "Okay, stop for a second. Assuming your Dr. Yahwehstein somehow found a willing local woman to accept some super-holy baby oil into her womb, then you're saying that the birth could be any day now?"

Marly nodded as she slid exhausted against the stones and brought her knees to her chin. "And there's something else you're not going to want to hear."

"Yeah?"

"It's probably too late to stop him. Even assuming his surrogate Virgin Mary could be found, it would take us years to comb through the medical records and track her down. She could be anywhere in the world right now."

Cas became distracted by a passing procession of Christian pilgrims who were carrying crosses on their shoulders down the *Via Dolorosa* in a reenactment of Jesus' final agonizing hours. He watched as one of the wailing women in the group, dressed as the Blessed Mother, fell to her knees and reached for her imaginary Son.

Marly sensed that he was troubled by something. "What's wrong?"

"Cohanim built his lab in Galilee."

"So?"

"You think that was just a coincidence?"

"The Israelis keep most of their livestock farms up there," she said. "Probably just a good cover for his cattle-breeding scam."

"Maybe, but our Stetson-shady fundamentalist impresses me as the kind of guy who doesn't stray far from his Bible."

"You think he's trying to keep all the experimental variables the same?"

"Whatever *that* means in English," Cas said. "All I know is, Jesus was born of an unmarried virgin from Galilee. And scientists are pretty unimaginative when it comes to creativity."

She shot him a wry smile. "Thanks."

"Besides, Cohanim has apparently gotten used to getting the best of everything. If I know him—and we *did* share a plane—I'm pretty sure he'd demand an unmarried virgin from Galilee for his surrogate. If not just for old-time's sake, then to replicate the original God DNA injection as closely as possible."

Inspired with another idea, Marly rose to her feet. "How old was the Blessed Mother when she gave birth in the manger at Bethlehem?"

Cas opened his phone and punched up the Web browser. "Says here that most biblical scholars think she was between thirteen and sixteen. That was the Jewish custom at the time."

"I wonder how many unmarried girls from Galilee in that age bracket would be giving birth this week?"

Cas flashed her that familiar lunatic twinkle. "Maybe we should find out."

R ushing through the Ministry of Health building, Marly briefly flashed her old Columbia University ID card and palmed it back into her wallet. She extended a hand to the young Ministry bureaucrat inside the second-floor office marked Information Services; Cas had already flirted their way past the baffled female security guard in the lightly fortified lobby.

"Hello, I'm Dr. McKinney. Sorry I'm late." She turned to Cas, who stood behind her, and ordered him around as if he were her valet: "Push back my meeting with the Prime Minister to four. And tell the Secretary General that the worst of the situation appears to be contained north of Tiberias."

The medical official, confused, glanced down at her calendar book. "I'm sorry. Did you have an appointment?"

Marly affected an air of indignant authority, "My dear, the World Health Organization does not make appointments. Now, I'll need an office and a computer. The equipment must be wiped down and disinfected. When I'm finished with them, the components should be destroyed. I've been to some rather dangerous hot spots in the last forty-eight hours. No chances should be taken. My life is expendable. But the lives of innocent workers here are not."

The desk official fumbled with her phone. "My boss is away for lunch."

"Of course he is," Marly said with a threatening sneer. "I'll just advise my superiors at the UN that the Ebola outbreak has spread another forty kilometers while your superior"—she swiped a surreptitious glance at the nameplate on the corner office—"Mr. Shechter thoroughly enjoyed his *falafel.*"

The woman reached for a bottle of hand sanitizer on her desk and rubbed a squirt on her palms. "Ebola?"

Marly moved closer to examine the woman's eyes. "Have you been feeling a little under the weather? Itching a lot, as if your skin is being eaten?"

The woman reflexively scratched at her forearm. "I thought I was just ..."

Marly ordered Cas, "Take this down. The potential contactee presents with dilated pupils and labored breathing. She is obviously itching." She turned back to the horrified woman. "Have you been around raccoons or had sex within the last two weeks?"

The woman felt her own forehead. "I ... yes, I met this guy."

"Don't worry. If we can stop this in its tracks, you may yet survive. Now, I'll need to see records of all hospital admittances in Israel during the past week."

The woman began coughing. "But that's confidential."

"Of course it is." Marly turned as if preparing to leave. "It'll take a day to get a court order. Meanwhile, if you start experiencing the least bit—"

"Wait!" The woman glanced around the office, making sure that no one was around. Holding a Kleenex over her mouth, she motioned Marly and Cas down the hall and led them into an empty room with a computer station.

Marly handed her some surgical gloves. "Probably best that you put these on before logging me in."

Gratefully accepting the gloves, the woman punched in a few numbers and letters. A database of hospital admissions appeared on the screen.

"Tell you what," Marly said. "Just to be safe, I'd better let you do the typing."

The woman scrolled down the list.

Marly hovered over her. "We think we've isolated the source of the outbreak to a pregnant girl, age thirteen to sixteen."

"Poor child," the woman said. "Is there any hope of saving her?"

"We're doing everything we can," Marly said.

The woman ran the filter through the admissions-updating database. "Looks like twenty cases fit those parameters."

Marly closed her eyes in despair. "That many?"

Behind her, Cas muttered, "We'll never be able to track down all of them in time."

Marly shot him a warning glance to shut up. Then, she leaned over the woman's shoulder again and studied the list.

The receptionist noticed her kindled interest. "These are not their real names. Our law requires minor girls to be admitted under an alias."

"Who decides what alias to use?"

"The family, or the admitting guardian, chooses."

Marly did not respond to that revelation.

Cas noticed that she kept staring at the woman's neck. "Something wrong, Doctor?"

"You wear a Crucifix," Marly observed to the woman. "You aren't Jewish?"

"I am a Palestinian Christian."

Marly studied the names of the girls on the list again. Having learned a thing or two about how Cohanim's demented mind worked, she tried to remember something that the friar had told them back at the Church of the Holy Sepulcher. She asked the woman, "You wouldn't happen to know who the Virgin Mary's mother was, would you?"

"Of course. St. Anne."

Marly slumped, her hope dashed.

"In Hebrew, she is called Hannah."

Marly suddenly revived. *That* was one of the names on the list. Trading a suspecting glance with Cas, she pointed to the screen. "Could you pull up the file on this admission, the one with the alias of Hannah?"

The woman hit a key and brought up the digital records with a photo of the pregnant girl. "She looks quite healthy to me."

"Does it say where she's from?" Marly asked.

The bureaucrat scanned the chart. "She came from a small Alawite village near our border with Lebanon."

"Wait a minute," Cas said. "If she's Syrian Alawite, why was she brought to an Israeli hospital?"

The bureaucrat studied Cas suspiciously. "Who is this man again?"

"My assistant," Marly said, glaring a silent order for him to play his prearranged part of silent stooge. She turned back to the woman. "But he raises a good point. I thought relations between Syria and Israel were quite strained, especially with the civil war."

"Oh, they are," said the ministry employee. "It is complicated. This girl's home village is situated in disputed and occupied territory. Some villagers in Ghajar have accepted Israeli citizenship. Others have refused. This patient was found in Beirut. The Lebanese Ministry of Health made a determination that she was Israel's responsibility."

"Big surprise there," Marly remarked bitterly. "Who would want to help an unwed pregnant girl?"

Cas whispered to her ear, "This is a dead end. Cohanim wouldn't give a rat's ass about a Muslim girl. Let's get the hell out of here."

Defeated, Marly began backing toward the door as she told the woman, "Thanks for your help." She turned to leave with Cas, but then caught the young woman dabbing at her eyes with a Kleenex. "Are you okay?"

"Poor child," the woman whimpered as she stared at the computer screen. "It says here she had to be brought in constrained and sedated. The admitting physician called for an emergency psych consult. The patient was diagnosed as delusional and taken to the mental-health wing of the Baruch Padeh Hospital in Tiberias. She was placed under psychiatric care there."

Cas was trying to pull Marly out the door. "Happens to the best of us."

The bureaucrat kept staring at the screen. "The girl claims that heavily armed strangers have been chasing her and trying to kill her."

Marly and Cas, nearly through the door, stopped in their tracks.

"I'm sorry," Marly said, turning back. "You said 'heavily armed strangers?'"

The ministry woman nodded with a sigh. "The paranoid hallucinations must have been caused by the strain of the pregnancy." Shuddering with empathy for the girl, she turned to Marly. "Does that help you—"

Marly and Cas were already running for the elevator.

35

Tiberias, Israel

C as and Marly slipped into the basement kitchen of the local hospital and sniffed at the large pots of lentil soup simmering on a long panel of industrial burners.

Spotting them, the head chef barked something unfriendly in Hebrew.

"We were sent by the temp agency," Cas said.

The cook, apparently able to understand English when he wished to, pointed to a notice board above a time-card punch machine. "No jobs today!"

Marly huffed in mock anger. "We drove all the way down here from Tel Aviv! They said you needed food-delivery personnel."

The cook stomped and loosed a flurry of curses. Suddenly remembering that they did not understand him, he switched languages in mid-shout, "Lazy Americans! Come to our country to experience the triumph of Zionism! Then you go back home and get fat on your McDonald's double-cheeseburgers-and-bacon-super-sized! We do not want you fair-weather *goyim*-turned-Jews on holiday here! Get out of my kitchen!"

"You'll have to explain that to the man upstairs," Cas said.

The frenzied cook whirled to a stop. "What man?"

Cas produced a document with the letterhead of the Caesarea Manpower company. As the cook read the letter, Cas stole a preening glance at Marly, proud of the forgery that he had created in just two hours at a local print shop. The requisition order for two new kitchen staffers held the fake but remarkably realistic signature of a Mr. Hiram Beracha, deputy director for the hospital, who just happened to be out of the office that week.

The cook muttered a word that sounded like a chicken hawk screeching.

Cas produced two more forms from his pocket. "If you don't want us, you'll have to fill out this paperwork. We get paid for the day, plus travel expenses."

The lids on the soup pots began popping from the boil. Staffers ran around the kitchen performing tasks as if a drill horn had just been sounded for a raid.

The cook, already behind on lunch, threw the letter and forms into the garbage. "Get dressed! Smocks in lockers! You take tray carts to third floor!"

C lad in green staff uniforms, Cas and Marly pushed their cart of lunch trays onto the hospital elevator and waited with a couple other riders until the doors closed.

"Floor?" a nurse asked.

Cas winged it, hoping they had one. "Psychiatric."

The nurse looked at the trays. "They don't allow silverware up there."

Cas nodded. "Right. Some big *machers* from the Ministry of Health are here today. I guess they're too high and mighty to eat with their fingers, like the patients and we have to do."

The nurse stared at him—and laughed coarsely. She punched in the fifth floor and grumbled, "This country is being ruined by the politicians."

Marly chimed in, "You got that right, sister!"

When the doors opened, Cas and Marly nodded in comradeship to the nurse and wheeled the cart out. An armed police officer stood guard at the desk. They held their breaths and rolled by him and past the security desk. Marly held back a few steps as Cas approached the nurse's station with the cart.

The officer behind the desk glared up at him.

Cas kicked the bottom rung of the cart and sent it toppling over. Trays and food scattered across the floor. Nurses and doctors stopped what they were doing and looked toward the source of the clanging.

Cas stood over the mess, shaking his head. "*Oy vey!* What a *klutz* I am!"

Several angry-looking nurses marched toward him.

Amid the disruption, Marly hovered in front of the fire alarm near the elevator. When no one was looking, she punched it with her elbow.

Red bubbles on the walls began flashing and a piercing blare filled the floor. Those patients who were not restrained rushed from their rooms and began screaming, their ears punished by the sirens. Overwhelmed, the orderlies tried to herd them back. Forgotten in the chaos, Cas and Marly slipped away and speed-walked down another hallway, looking into every room for a pregnant teenager.

Marly realized they would never find "Hannah" this way before the nurses restored order. She stopped one of the orderlies running past them toward a wailing patient. "I have meds for Hannah. Which room is she in?"

Cas glared at Marly, aghast that she would take such a brazen chance.

But the orderly was so preoccupied with trying to corral the patients that he had no time to question her reason for asking. With a huff of disgust at his predicament, he shouted, "Seventy-two eighteen."

Cas and Marly waited until the orderly disappeared around the corner. Then, they rushed to a wall map of the floor plan. The girl's room was across the ward.

They raced down the corridor.

Cas closed the door to the patient's room and quietly propped a chair against its latch to prevent anyone from entering.

Marly approached the bed and found a sleeping girl who looked no older than fourteen. She figured the poor thing must really be sedated to have slept through the fire alarms. Her wrists were connected to intravenous tubes, and her belly was distended. She hadn't given birth yet, but it looked as if the baby could arrive any moment.

Cas tip-toed over to the bed, and whispered, "Is that her?"

Marly glanced at the patient's wristband, and nodded. She stared at the girl's abdomen and wondered what was growing inside. Could this child really be carrying … she couldn't bear to think of it.

Cas quickly scanned the patient's chart, written in Hebrew.

"What's it say?" Marly whispered.

"From what I can remember from my Rosetta Stone tapes, looks like they've got her on a shitload of sedatives."

Marly studied the clear bag hanging from the IV pole. A pump was pushing the liquid into the girl's veins. She read the label, which was marked in Hebrew and English. "Lorazepam. That's prescribed for anxiety. She must have been through Hell and back."

Cas reached across her and turned off the valve on the drip.

Marly gasped, "What are you doing?"

"We need to get her coherent."

Marly watched the door, waiting impatiently for the sedation to wear off. The girl slowly opened her eyes—and recoiled from the two strange faces.

Marly tried to calm her. "It's okay. Do you understand English?"

The girl nodded uncertainly, her eyes straining with alarm.

"We're here to help you," Cas said, trying to calm her. "What's your name?"

Finally, the girl muttered, "Zaynah."

Cas jostled her gently to speed the recovery. "Where are you from?"

"Lebanon."

"Has someone been trying to kill you?"

The girl nodded again, this time with a little more animation.

Marly was relieved that the girl spoke passable English. She grasped her hand in reassurance and whispered, "This is a very personal question. I am sorry, but we need to ask it. … How did you get pregnant?"

The girl's eyes watered with pain. "I do not know."

"You've never had relations with a man?"

The girl shook her head.

"Who brought you to this hospital?"

"A Christian man ... he lives in Beirut."

"Was he your priest?"

The girl looked shocked. "I am Muslim."

Before Marly could get a confirmation of that unlikely claim, the exhausted girl slipped back into sleep. She turned in disbelief to Cas. "Why would Cohanim choose a Muslim girl as the surrogate mother for the God embryo? He's a fundamentalist Christian. There would have been plenty of Jewish or Palestinian Christian girls in Israel for him to target. It doesn't make sense."

Cas looked at the chart again, flipping through several pages until he found a photocopy of a sonogram. He brought it closer to his eyes and studied it closely.

"What's wrong?"

He shook off her question. "Nothing, I guess."

Marly heard voices and footsteps approaching down the hall. "You'd better resume your medical internship *after* we get out of here."

Cas rushed to the bed and pulled the tubes from the girl's arms and throat.

Marly was horrified. "She could go into labor any minute now! After all the trauma she's obviously been—"

Cas lifted the sleeping girl into his arms. "Cohanim and his thugs may be in the hospital right now. They'll kill her. We've got to get her out of her. She's the only one who can tell us what's happening."

"And take her *where*?" Marly asked. "Just how *do* you expect to deliver the baby? I've never done it. And I sure as hell know that you—"

"Bring the chart!"

"Why?"

"We may need to get her more medications." Cas lifted the heavily sedated girl into his arms. With Marly trailing him, he rushed from the room.

36

Old City, Jerusalem

The friar who had said Mass for Cas and Marly in the Holy Sepulcher chapel sat at the admissions desk of the Franciscan Foundation for Unwed Mothers. Attending to his day job, he looked up from his Scripture reading and saw a young pregnant girl standing before him. "Welcome, child. Have you come seeking the mercy of Our Lord?"

She shook her head.

"Why then *have* you come?"

Wiht a weak voice, she said, "I was told to ask you something, Father."

"Of course," the friar said. "God's wisdom is on offer here with lodging and meals. What is it you wish to know? How Christ can be forgiving even when we disappoint Him with our carnal sins?"

She shook her head again.

"What then, child?"

"I was told to ask you … Do you still rat out Palestinians to the CIA for monkfish dinners and bingo money?"

The friar's eyes rounded. "Who told you such a—"

Cas and Marly stepped forward from behind a pillar.

The friar slapped his hands against his tonsured head. "For the love of Mary, Jesus and Joseph. Will I never be rid of you two?"

Cas grinned grimly at his confessor. "We just couldn't stay away from all of that Godly wisdom you dispense. Speaking of Jesus, Mary and Joseph—"

Marly jumped in. "Jesus was in the line of the royal House of David, right?"

The friar frowned, uncertain what these two crackpots were driving at now. Despite his qualms, he risked an answer, "Yes. But what does that—"

"Here's what doesn't compute," Marly said. "If Jesus had no natural father, how is it that his genealogy reaches all the way back to Adam?"

The friar dropped his head into his hands. "Oh, Lord, just send me to Purgatory and be done with it!" Finally, he looked up and warned them, "You think the doctrine of the Immaculate Conception was complicated? Don't even get into this House of David quagmire."

"We're still waiting," Cas said.

The friar sighed. "St. Matthew says the line runs through Joseph."

"That means there was no genetic link," Marly said.

The friar raised his hand for patience. "There's more. St. Luke, on the other hand, says the line runs through Mary."

Marly stared at the friar in stunned silence. "You mean ..."

"Yes, the Gospels are contradictory."

"So," Cas said, "if ol' Luke is right—and I've never known him to be wrong—then Mary *could* have passed on *her* DNA from Adam to Jesus." He thought a moment. "But there's still the problem of the 'Y' chromosome. Jesus was a man, obviously, and He had a Y chromosome. The Virgin Mary couldn't have passed Jesus's Y chromosome to Him, right?"

Marly suddenly paled. "Cohanim didn't *have* to get the Y chromosome from the Marian source. He got the Y chromosome of Adam and the Davidic line from ... the first DNA on Earth.

Cas understood at once. "The DNA that Texas rattlesnake extracted from the Black Stone."

The friar made a move for the phone on the desk.

Cas slammed a fist into the phone cradle. "We need just a couple more minutes of your time, Tuck. Then we'll be on our way."

The friar glared at the pregnant girl. "What have you done to this child?"

Marly supported Zaynah by the shoulders, helping her stay on her feet. "She's carrying a little package you might be interested in."

"Every unborn soul is held precious by the Lord our God," the friar said.

Cas sat on the corner of the desk and fingered a rosary. "Yeah? You and the Pope might want to rethink that policy on this one."

"What do you mean?" the friar demanded.

Marly was equally perplexed. "Yeah, what *do* you mean?

"Something about this whole God-embryo thing has been bugging me ever since you told me your theory about the cloning," Cas told her. "Believers have been trying for years to clone Jesus, taking DNA samples from tombs here in Israel and even from the Shroud of Turin. So, why hasn't it ever happened?"

Marly shrugged. "Probably because no one ever found a DNA sample that was sufficiently preserved."

"Maybe," Cas said. "But even a psychopath like Cohanim would know that God and Jesus could never really be cloned. I mean, come on."

Thinking about it, Marly nodded. "Only the likeness of their spirits in the flesh could be created."

Cas turned back to the friar, who looked totally lost. "Tell us about the Book of Revelation."

"Revelation? What about it?"

Cas screwed his face into a distorted, demonic scowl. "The Antichrist ... where is he supposed to be born?"

The friar edged back in his chair. "Are you back on the hashish?"

"In thirty seconds," Cas said, "I'm going to start yelling at the top of my lungs that you're the father of this baby. The excitement of it all could cause the girl to give birth right here."

Horrified, the friar motioned them into an office and shut the door. After a hesitation, he explained, "The Antichrist is prophesied to come from Assyria. Is that what you wanted? Happy? Now kindly depart and leave me out of your insane spook games!"

"Assyria?" Marly exclaimed. "That's not even a country now."

"The ancient kingdom covered modern Syria, Iran, Iraq, and—"

"Lebanon," Cas piped in.

The friar nodded, not sure where this line of questioning was leading.

And neither was Marly.

Cas kept pressing the friar, "Does the Bible say anything about the mother of the Antichrist?"

"What are you suggesting?" Marly asked him.

"If there's an Antichrist, then there has to be an Anti-Virgin Mary, right?"

Cornered, the friar finally admitted, "The early Church fathers taught that the mother would be an unclean woman." He turned to his library of books and pulled down a volume. "Here it is. St. Hippolytus wrote that she would be polluted, a *supposed* virgin, a Jewess from the house of Dan."

"And who is to be the father?" Cas asked.

"The Devil," the friar said. "But the conception will be unnatural."

"Unnatural in what way?" Marly asked.

"Saint Nilus said the Evil One is to be born of the seed, but ... "

Cas pressed him. "But what?"

"Without man's sowing."

"So, the Antichrist won't have a human father?" Marly asked.

"As the Son of God in His human birth manifested His Divine nature," the friar said, "so also shall Satan appear in human form."

In a whisper, Cas repeated those conditions to himself. "A supposed virgin. Unclean. From the tribe of Dan." He turned a glower of accusation on the pregnant girl. "You're not a virgin, are you?"

Zaynah staggered back a step, stunned by the charge. "I swear by Allah, praise be upon Him, that I did not conceive this child by lying with a man."

Cas closed in on her. "That's not what I asked. You've had sex. Long before nine months ago."

Zaynah darkened with shame. "I could not tell my family. I had to lie."

He grasped her shoulders roughly. "That's not all you're lying about, is it?"

Marly rushed to comfort Zaynah, cradling the distraught girl in her arms. "What are you trying to do to her? Send her over the edge?"

He drove the girl back a step. "Where is your family from?"

"I told you!" she said, sobbing. "Lebanon!"

"And before your ancestors moved to Lebanon?"

The girl's eyes darted. "My grandmother called it Canaan."

"Your ancestors were Jewish, weren't they!"

Zaynah fell to her knees, undone by the exposure of her dark secret.

Cas nodded to Marly. "Cohanim did his homework, all right."

"What are you talking about?" Marly asked.

Cas paced in rising agitation. "Our Texan mastermind hasn't been trying to clone God. You were right about the DNA he extracted from the Black Stone only reproducing an Adam-Jesus facsimile in the flesh. But the Antichrist is a whole other kettle of Galilean fish. The Bible says that the Evil One will resemble the Messiah so closely that the entire world will be fooled."

Marly's eyes suddenly rounded. "Then he is—"

"Trying to spur the Apocalypse by giving birth to God's corporeal body," Cas said. "He thinks Satan will enter the shell of the Messiah and wreak his havoc on the Earth."

All three turned and glared at the girl's bulging abdomen.

"My God," the friar muttered, now realizing what was in his presence. "What abomination have you people brought into this city?" Helpless, he could only bless the girl with the Sign of the Cross.

Zaynah wailed hysterically.

Scolding the friar with a glare, Marly pulled the girl even closer into her arms. "She's carrying a child, not the Four Horsemen of the Apocalypse. Stop with the nonsense."

The friar shook his head. "You have no idea of the evil forces in our midst."

Marly huffed, angered by the friar's attempt to blame the Devil for the work of stupid men. "I got a pretty good idea of the *ignorance* in our midst."

Cas snapped his fingers to stop their argument. "If you two are done convening the Council of Nicaea, can we get back to the problem at hand?"

Marly paced in deep thought, keeping Zaynah at her side while patting her head. "Okay, let's just say if, for some wild reason, Cohanim *is* trying to clone the Antichrist. Why is he now trying to kill *her?*"

Cas stared out at Mount Zion through a cruciform window. After several moments in thought, he turned back and asked the friar, "Didn't the good ol' boys once practice a little human sacrifice somewhere around here?"

"What on earth is going through that demented mind of yours now?"

"Nothing on earth ... yet."

The friar's face fell, as if he suddenly understood the reason for the question.

"Just fill me in." In a bad imitation of Cary Grant's transatlantic accent, Cas added, "And I don't need any morality lessons from *you*, *Ju*-das, *Ju*-das, *Ju*-das."

Pinned against the wall, the friar sighed heavily and gave up the shameful truth. "The Old Testament says that King Ahaz of Judah sacrificed his children born of pagan wives and concubines in a valley below Jerusalem."

"*Which* valley?"

"Most biblical scholars say it was the Kidron valley, the slope that runs right below us. At the time of Ahaz, it was known as the Geenon. Some called it ..." He stopped, as if stunned by his own discovery.

"What?" Marly demanded. "What did some call it?"

"Geenom."

"You mean, like—" she could barely speak it— "a 'genome' of one's DNA?"

The friar looked up at her coldly, as if preparing to dispense an exorcism, and nodded. "The Valley of Abomination."

Cas interlaced his fingers and cracked his knuckles, stretching his arms. "If I were one of those Bible Code freaks, I might find *that* more than just a little coincidental."

Police sirens blared outside, racing closer.

Cas pushed Marly and Zaynah into a corner, out of the window's line of sight. Had Cohanim and his Mossad enablers tracked them down?

He turned to the friar. "Is there another way out of here?"

The friar hesitated, acting unsure about what God would want him to do. Finally, he led them through a series of rooms. "A tunnel runs from the basement to the sewers in the Armenian section. They won't think to look for you there."

37

Old City, Jerusalem

C limbing out of sewers older than King David, Cas lifted Marly and the heaving girl from a drain hole. Exhausted from their underground escape, they huddled under the shade of a back alley to catch their breaths. Cas looked around, trying to orient himself by listening for a distant rumble of traffic. The only sign of life was a stray cat skittering across the lane.

Marly waited for one of his brilliant ideas to surface. "Which way now? Got any nifty secret-agent tricks to get us out of *here?*"

He was getting tired of taking all the blame. "I was thinking of rappelling down the Old City walls using the dental floss I happen to have with me."

Faint from the afternoon heat, Marly was about to lose it. "Lord help us."

"By the way, there's been something I've been meaning to ask you, but just haven't found the time."

"The answer is still no."

"Don't flatter yourself, Doc."

Marly's look hovered between confusion and hurt. "Then ... what?"

He settled down on his haunches to rest against the niche wall. "There's something that's been gnawing at me."

"Probably tapeworms, considering your laundry habits."

He let that one pass. "Why *would* a Bible thumper like Cohanim would want to clone the Antichrist, anyway?"

Marly made sure Zaynah was as comfortable as possible. Then, she tossed her knapsack under her own head to use as a pillow. Finding him still waiting for an answer, she whispered, "Are you really that dense?"

"Guilty as charged. Present and accounted for. All hands on deck—"

"Shut up, for Christ sake!" She huffed at his incredibly annoying habit of taking everything too far. "These fundamentalists think Beelzebub or Lucifer or whatever name they're using for him these days has to show up first before the End Times arrive. Apparently even God Himself can't deviate from the movie script."

He nodded slowly, finally starting to see the big picture. "So, these Rapture crackpots are trying to fast-forward the DVD to Act Three of the story. Forcing the Big Author in the Sky to hurry up and get to the end."

"You'd make a great studio executive."

"And that barbecued red heifer? How does *that* fit into your theory?"

Marly angled her head in a gesture that, roughly translated, suggested he take a look at the gleaming gold dome in the distance. "Just one of the props essential for the big production finale that's supposed to happen right here."

He was still troubled by one missing piece to the jigsaw puzzle.

"Cat got your tongue? Or does the feline species not like the taste of rum-marinated delicacies?"

"This Antichrist is supposed to be a man, right?"

"Yeah, so?"

"It's probably nothing."

She knew that worrisome look of befuddlement. "What's wrong now?"

Cas looked over at Zaynah. She was asleep, out cold. Inching a few feet away to prevent her from hearing, he whispered, "Did you bring her medical charts?"

"They're in my bag. Now that you mention it, we'd better get her some pain medication, or—"

"Take a look at the copy of the sonogram."

Baffled, Marly pulled out the sheaf of documents from the knapsack she was using for a pillow. She waited to hear why he wanted her to look at it.

"When Shada was pregnant with Farid, she showed me her sonogram." He nodded toward Zaynah. "It looked a little different than our virgin's there."

"So? They've probably advanced the technology since the Stone Age."

"I'm not a fake doctor like you, but … something seems to be missing."

Intrigued, Marly rifled through the mess of sheets they had stolen. She found the Xerox copy of Zaynah's sonogram. She stared at the image of a fetus … with no male genitalia.

The blood drained from her face.

Cas nodded, having expected the look of shock. "That cat must have spat out my tongue to get yours."

Marly still couldn't find the words.

"Now, tell me where my logic goes wrong here, Dr. Einsteiness. Christ was a man. The Antichrist is supposed to resemble Christ in all ways. So much so that everyone mistakes him for the Big Kahuna. *Post hoc, ergo proctologist hoc,* the Antichrist has to be man."

Marly's eyes drifted from the sonogram to the sleeping Lebanese girl. Looking at Zaynah's rounded belly, she muttered, "Shit squared."

"So much for *your* theory about Cohanim cloning the Antichrist."

"*My* theory? Hey, you bought in on it, too. ... This can't be happening."

Cas shrugged. "Fifty-fifty chance. We should have thought of it."

Marly stood to stare down at him. "No. It's *zero* chance."

"How could it be zero?"

"That DNA we found in the Kaaba Stone had a Y chromosome."

"Yeah, but Cohanim—*you* think—combined it with the Lucy DNA."

"Doesn't matter," Marly said. "The Y chromosome always passes to the offspring. The God child from the Adam DNA in the Stone *has* to be male." She turned inward, thinking hard. "Unless ..."

"Unless what?"

"That woman in Lubbock you talked to on the phone."

"The dead girl-crone's mother?"

Marly remembered the coven ring she had found on Bridget Whelan's decomposed finger. "Didn't she say that her daughter was into paganism?"

"Yeah, so?"

"Covens and witches. They worship the Goddess, right?"

"Hey, you're the witch expert on this team."

Marly was so focused that she didn't hear the taunt. "A Goddess worshipper who happens to have a graduate degree in genetic engineering. That's a pretty dangerous combination, don't you think?"

"Cut to the chase, McKinney. What exactly are you getting at?"

She glanced again at Zaynah's swollen abdomen. "It's never been done, at least not that I know about. But I've read in the scientific journals that several biotech companies have been trying for years to perfect the process. It's the Holy Grail of genetic engineering for those who hope to see the world populated by women only."

Cas's jaw dropped open to a wide grin. "Sounds like Paradise, as long as I'm grandfathered in to provide the bedroom services."

"The idea is to reshuffle the DNA strands to isolate and remove the 'Y' chromosome. Or, in laymen's terms ... the end of the Patriarchy."

Cas leapt to his feet. "You're saying this Whelan girl sabotaged Cohanim and turned his *God* embryo into a *Goddess* embryo?"

Marly's head was pounding from the heat. "That must be why Cohanim has been trying to kill his modern Virgin Mary here. He probably only found out about the DNA reshuffling by Bridget Whelan *after* the implantation. He wants to eliminate both mother and fetus ... and start over."

"The guy's a ruthless bastard, all right. But why would he do that?"

"No fundamentalist Christian could accept God coming back as a woman. It would defy every prophesy in the Bible. And if the *Antichrist* turned out to be female, well—"

"Damn, of course! The unreliability of God's word would be exposed."

She let that sobering revelation sink in. "Didn't your snitching friar friend say that some of our Israelite forefathers felt it was appropriate to render still-born certain offspring ... " Her words trailed off. She glanced up at him with a stricken look. "Where did the Bible say those abandoned babies were tossed?"

He scratched his head. "I think he said 'Geenon or Geenom.'"

"Which was Hebrew for—"

His eyes rounded. "The Valley of the Abomination."

A stunned silence extended between them.

Her voice quavered. "What the hell are we going to do *now?*"

Cas didn't have a clue. He mumbled something to the brick walls enclosing them, as if they could whisper a way out of this maze. Receiving no oracular guidance, he woke the pregnant girl and led the women through a series of alleys. They passed only a handful of wandering tourists—lost Americans mostly—and moved quickly toward the rising sounds of vehicles and markets.

He stopped at a two-story building that faced a heavily trafficked boulevard. A black-and-white tile on the stone façade of the edifice read: *Patriarchate Road.* "That's promising."

Marly looked around but found nothing unusual. "Why?"

"At least the good friar didn't lie to us about this route leading into the Armenian section." He peered out on the avenue that led to the Jaffa Gate, the closest exit from the walled Old City. A line of freshly vacated tour buses, with diesels humming to keep the air conditioners running, waited just beyond the bustling tourist traps. He noticed amid the bustle of shoppers an Israeli police cruiser and a few heavily armed soldiers standing on a corner. A pair of black BMWs with tinted windows sat parked behind the police car. He signaled for Marly to take the trembling girl deeper into the darkness of the alley, out of view.

"What are you doing?" she hissed.

He motioned them both into a crouch. "Stay here. I saw something I want to check out."

Cas inched his eyes around a corner and studied the man with cropped black hair and a cheap navy-blue suit who stood leaning against the hood of an Israeli patrol car. Likely a detective. Two other muscle-bound apes lingered nearby, enjoying smokes. They wore baggy black cargo pants with their hems stuffed into combat boots. Sig Sauer P226 pistols sat in their holsters, and—

Nah, it couldn't be.

For a second there, he thought he'd caught a glimpse of CrossArrow insignias embroidered on the men's gray Polo shirts. He shook his head, trying to shake some oxygen into his brain. When his eyes jostled back into focus, he inched his head around the corner again and stole a second look at the gaggle of gun-wielding human bloodhounds.

This time, a Semitic-looking young man—wild shocks of black hair, forlorn eyes, slender to the edge of emaciation—was walking toward him from across the street. A synapse of recognition sparked: Was that somebody from his past?

Deciding there was more safety out in the open, he sauntered out from his hiding place and walked straight toward the young man, locking onto his face.

The stranger stopped and stared at him with a knowing but jangled look. After a hesitation, he reached out his hand.

Cas shook it in an awkward grasp. "Do I know you?"

The stranger reacted as if that question hurt him.

Before Cas could ask again, a hand slammed his shoulder from behind. "Of course you know him."

Staggered, Cas spun around.

Earl Jubal stood grinning at him. The CrossArrow chief shoved him into an alcove, out of sight. Another shadow filled the tight space, pressing against him, too.

A drawling voice whispered, "I oughta throw you off these walls."

A blast of sunlight hit that speaker's weathered face. Cas recognized the man who had boarded the plane in Riyadh. "Well if it isn't the Lone Star Frankenstein. I hear you cook up one hell of a red veal barbecue."

Seth Cohanim rubbed the sharp bevels of the impressive Houston Baptist University ring on his fisted finger. "Where's the girl, wise ass?"

"Beats the hell out of me."

Jubal landed a haymaker on Cas's chin. "If that's the way you want it, Casbo. Took us a week to track you down. Lucky for us, that woman you conned at the Health Ministry got suspicious about why an American doctor would have a middle-aged assistant who acts like Mel Gibson on speed. So, she called it in. And we got the tip."

Cas wiped a trickle of blood from his lip. "Mossad."

Jubal nodded. "We used to have prosperous business relationship with those Jewish boys. ... Now, answer my friend here. Where's the Virgin Mary?"

"Have you checked all the mangers around Bethlehem?"

The next fist came twice as fast.

Cas licked the blood from his nostrils, in time to be doubled over with a ham hock of clenched fingers to the gut.

"That was downright blasphemous," Cohanim said. "And in the Holy City, too. You should be ashamed of yourself, son."

Cas spat blood at Cohanim. "You kinda fucked up that whole Second Coming thing, didn't you, Tex? We've already picked out a name for the baby. How's 'Christiana' sound, you murdering cocksucker? Or should it be Antichristiana? We're planning on announcing you as her godfather."

Cohanim purpled. "I'm gonna ask you one more time."

"You owe me two million bucks, you rodeo clown."

Jubal tightened his grip on Cas's neck. "Mr. Cohanim here is a godly man, Casbo. A man of his word, a man of *the* Word. Now, the two million dollars is in the Swiss account, just as I promised it would be at the start of this mission."

Cas slapped away Jubal's hand. "Well, then, I'll just be on my way to Geneva." He glanced at his watch. "I think there's a nonstop flight leaving at two." He tried to walk away—until Jubal clamped his biceps to stop him.

"Aren't you forgetting something?"

"Oh yeah," Cas said. "The account number."

"The deal was," Jubal reminded him, "I deposit your fee in a *joint* account."

Cas lurched to within a bullet's width of his face. "Yeah, well, that's going to be a little difficult now. Considering those Saudi bastards murdered my son!"

Jubal nudged up the young Semitic-looking man who had been cowering behind him during the confrontation. Grinning evil, Jubal patted the hesitant stranger's head. "This is the city of resurrections, remember?"

"*Abba?*"

Cas's eyes bulged. "Farid?"

The young man hugged him, crying and nearly falling to his knees.

Cas fought to hold it together. "They said you were—"

"You really *have* gone soft," Jubal said. "You actually thought the Saudis were going to tell you the truth?"

Cas wasn't listening to Jubal. He couldn't let go of his son. "I'm sorry for everything. I tried to get back, but …"

Farid coughed with emotion. "I know."

That Customs asshole at the Saudi airport lied to me.

Jubal nodded, as if reading Cas's mind. "The Saudis wanted to slice and dice him after we returned the Stone, but I figured I owed you one from the old days. So I convinced them to put him in my custody as part of the bargain."

Cohanim ripped Cas and Farid apart. "This is all very touching. Nothing would warm my Christian heart more than to see father and son reunited. But we have a little business to take care of first."

"I need to tell my son something in private!"

Jubal dragged Farid from the alcove. "All in good time."

Cas fought to reach his son again. "Wait! Your mother—"

Jubal silenced him with an uppercut to the jaw. "Apparently you still have that little hearing problem."

Yanked back, Cas barked at Jubal and the Texas rancher, "You can have the damn money! I don't care about it anymore!"

Jubal tapped his former comrade's face with his palm, each stroke a little harder. "This is what's going to go down, Casbo. We get the Madonna and child, and you get your son back, along with the money. Kind of has a quaint biblical symmetry to it, don't you agree?"

"What about—"

"Rock Lady?" Jubal shook his head. "Nah, she knows too much."

Cas swallowed hard. They were forcing him to choose between Marly and his own flesh and blood. "How do I know you won't put a bullet in *my* head"

"Once a soldier works for me, he's family for life," Jubal said. "You and I have had our differences over the years, Casbo. But I don't abandon men on the battlefield. If I did, and word got out, my reputation would be ruined."

Cas was too ashamed to look his old boss in the eyes. Finally, he nodded his agreement to the deal. He reached for Farid to bring him home.

Jubal raised his pistol to prevent the reunion. "Not yet, pappy. First, you have to get the professor and the pregnant girl out of Jerusalem."

Cas was thrown on his heels. "What ... why?"

Cohanim shrugged. "We've developed a little problem with Mossad."

"Avram Isserle has stopped playing ball with us," Jubal explained. "He's watching every move we make. Seems he got in some hot water when a certain prisoner escaped because of a paperwork snafu. As a result, he's jonesin' to get all three of you back into custody. We're not about to let that happen."

"What are you going to do with the professor and the pregnant girl?"

Disgusted, Jubal shook his head. "Do I need to spell it out for you? Let's just say I always leave the world a better place than I found it, particularly when it comes to witnesses."

Cas had no doubt that these two meat grinders would follow through on their plan to kill Marly and the girl. But if he didn't go along with the trade, Farid would get the bullet, or worse, a return to a Saudi torture cell.

"You get the two women past Isserle's goons," Cohanim told him. "Then meet us at Masada in the morning."

Masada?

He couldn't fathom why they wanted the exchange to take place so far away. Masada was hallowed ground in Jewish history, the rugged rock plateau where hundreds of rebel zealots and their families committed suicide in the First Century rather than surrender to besieging Romans. "Hell, that's sixty miles from here. And the place is teeming with Israeli forces. They go there to train."

Jubal mocked a look of horror. "Right you are, Casbo. Thousands of tourists go there, too. It's the last place Mossad and the cops will expect to find us."

Cohanim grabbed him by the collar to make the plan crystal clear. "Listen closely, you heathen dipsomaniac. I'm only going to explain this once. Two cable cars transport tourists up and down the mountain to the fortress. The first ascent and descent each day are always dry runs to test the cables. Have the women on the first car. It leaves at six in the morning. Don't be late."

"Your son here will be on the car coming down," Jubal promised. "Halfway up, we'll arrange for the cars to stop side by side. You'll get him back when we get the two women. Clean exchange. No one's the wiser."

"And if I can't get them out of the city by tomorrow morning?"

As Jubal checked the rounds in his pistol, he glanced over at Farid. "I have every confidence you will. Let's not contemplate the alternative."

Released from Cohanim's grasp, Cas stared at the two men, trying to determine if they would really go through with the deal. He glanced at Farid and saw tears in his son's eyes. Realizing that he had no choice but to trust them, he nodded and reached to hug his son. He whispered the same promise he had failed to keep years ago, "I'll see you soon. Then we'll go home."

A half-hour later, after cleaning himself up and wiping the blood off his chin, Cas ducked back down into the alley. Marly and the pregnant girl were still huddled there, waiting for him. He signaled for Zaynah to give him some space to talk to Marly alone.

The girl crawled into a corner. She studied him with raw suspicion.

"Where have you been?" Marly demanded. "I was beginning to think ... "

He kept looking beyond her shoulders, unable to meet her searching eyes. "Remember those Beemers in the Dallas industrial park?"

Marly nodded, not certain she wanted to hear the rest.

"Apparently you can fly to Germany now, buy a new BMW, and take it on a Holy Land cruise before returning to the States."

She was about the ram her fingernails into his face. "Just tell me what—"

"Looks like Earl Jubal decided to upgrade his fleet."

Her jaw dropped. "That CrossArrow wacko?"

"He must have tailed us."

"So now we have Mossad *and* those crazy paramilitary assholes chasing us?"

"It gets worse."

"How could it possibly get worse?"

"Jubal's men are talking to an Israeli detective. They're all standing just on the other side of this alley."

Marly pulled at her hair. "Why would Jubal still be after *us*? He knows we don't have the Black Stone now."

"Same thing everyone else is doing here." Cas jerked his head toward Zaynah, who was cowering against the far wall. "Looking for the Blessed Mother."

After a long pause, Marly tugged on his sleeve. "Y'know what, Cas? Let's just go home."

He'd never seen such fear in her eyes, not even on that tense day in Mecca. *She wants to abandon the girl?*

"It's not like there's a pot of gold waiting for us at the end of this bloody rainbow anymore, you know?" She darted her eyes toward Zaynah. "She's only going to get us killed."

He realized that the scientist in her was trying to create some sensible rationale for what to do next. "Are you saying what I think you're saying?"

She nodded. "Go find Isserle and make a trade with Mossad. They get their witness. And we get out of the country."

He couldn't believe it. Sure, to save Farid, he was considering a similar option—not with Mossad, but with Jubal and Cohanim. Yet he was disappointed to see that Marly could be as ruthless and mercenary, and she didn't have a son whose life was on the line. "You know what they'll do to her, right?"

She looked away, ashamed.

"Listen to me." His eyes bored deep into hers. "Do you have any idea what it's like to lose ..." He remembered that her fiancé had returned home in a body bag. "I'm sorry." He brushed at the tears cascading down her cheeks. "I just can't throw this girl and her child to those wolves."

She turned back on him suddenly, as if seeing something now in a new light. "What *happened* to you while you were gone out there?"

"What do you mean?"

"Damn, I've become *you* ... and you've become *me*."

"What the hell are you talking about?"

"The Cas Fielding who stalked into my office at Columbia would have left that girl over there in this alley like a disposable lighter."

He didn't want to admit it, but he knew she had him pegged pretty accurately. "Look, I let my Farid down once. Maybe I can make it up to him if I save this girl."

"You *do* believe in God!"

"Don't be ridiculous."

"No, you're really buying into all of this give-up-your-life-for-another crap."

He snuck a peek into the alcove's cool darkness. Zaynah hovered on her knees, in palpable discomfort. "Look at her. She'll never be able to go back home. What if we helped her out and took her to the States with us?"

Marly fought back tears. "What you're saying is ..." She shook her head in amazement, looking down at her finger, which hadn't worn an engagement ring for over a year. "I've never heard you—"

"Things have kinda changed." Cas was about to reveal that Farid was still alive. Instead, he decided to tell her another version of the truth, one more nuanced. "*You're* my family now. You're all I've got left in this world. And this child that girl is carrying ... Maybe we were brought together to help that baby."

Marly began sobbing.

He held her closer. "Don't you want children of your own one day?"

Heaving against his chest, she looked at him, as if wondering what he was trying to say. Nodding through the tears, she motioned up Zaynah to them.

The girl became frightened when she saw Marly's tear-puffed eyes.

Cas's heart soared as he pulled away. In the next instant, he wiped his eyes and deliberately calmed his pulse, switching back into operative mode. Had he just lied to Marly? No, he really did love her. That much he knew for sure. But what was he going to do? Save the woman he loved? Or betray her and this girl to save his son?

He didn't have a clue.

Never make a decision until absolutely necessary. That was the one lesson he had learned after thirty years in the field. He had bought more time. If he could just, for once, see Farid again and look into his eyes. Maybe *then* it would all become clearer to him. He pulled Marly closer. "Listen up. It's time we get this show on the road. Here's the plan, okay? I'm going to head for the BMWs and—"

"The hell you are!"

"You are going to steal the tourist bus and drive it out of the Jaffa Gate."

"The hell I am!"

"If we can get to Masada—"

"Masada? Isn't that where everybody killed themselves?"

He nodded. "It's the perfect place to hide until we can shake off their tail. Caves and tunnels all around—"

Marly cut him off. She shifted her chin, angling his attention toward the girl. "She could give birth at any moment!"

"Mossad and the cops know that. They will have every hospital and clinic staked out. No one will expect us at Masada. Thousands of tourists go there every day. If we can get the bus there, we'll be able to merge into the crowds."

She studied him hard, as if not quite knowing what to believe. "Oh, for a minute there, when you talk about us and ... I thought that you really *hadn't* lost your mind."

He pointed her toward Patriarchate Lane. "When you steal that bus, try to do it quietly. Wait until the driver steps out for coffee or something. Then get the girl into the bus with you and just drive off, with no one the wiser."

"Of course," Marly said sarcastically. "No problem. And where do you plan to be during all this, once we supposedly drive off with no one the wiser?"

Cas winked at her. "Save me a window seat. I hear the scenic drive down to Sodom and Gomorrah is spectacular this time of year. The pillars of salt are just turning white."

Before she could utter another word of protest, he motioned the pregnant girl over to him and nodded for them both to get ready to run again. With a collective inhale for courage, they all leapt out of the alcove and headed into the crowds.

Cas crossed the alley first and slid along the buildings until he returned to the corner. The police car was still there, but one of the BMW sedans was gone. The two CrossArrow men were still leaning against their black car. The Israeli detective had returned to the patrol vehicle and was sitting in the passenger seat. He could tell by the anxious looks on their faces that they were about to launch a manhunt.

From across the street, he motioned Marly and the girl toward the coach.

Taking a deep breath, Marly put her arm around Zaynah's shoulders and led her to the bus. They took a peek inside, and then boarded it. Moments later, the driver tumbled out the bus and fell into the street. The doors slammed shut—and the *whoosh* of the hydraulic brakes set the bus into motion.

Cas nearly pissed his pants. *Dammit, Marly! I told you to wait until he got off first!*

Bewildered tourists returning to the bus shouted for it to stop. Alerted, the detective jumped out of the cruiser. Unable to flag down the bus, he opened his passenger-side door for a shield, but then realized it wouldn't offer much protection. He clambered to the roof just in the nick of time.

Marly flew past and sliced the cruiser's door off its hinges.

Another cop car sped down the street from the opposite direction and flashed its bubbles, trying to stop the bus.

Watching from behind the corner of a building, Cas pumped his right foot nervously against the cobblestones, pressing an imaginary accelerator.

Go, Marly! Don't stop now!

But there was no way for her to drive the bus around the second cruiser.

The cops pulled their weapons.

Cas leapt out and fired a couple of rounds at the approaching patrol car. Blood and brains sprayed against the shattered windshield. The detective's body slumped into the steering wheel—the cruiser slammed into cars parked along the avenue.

Sirens blasted as Cas sprinted for the bus.

Marly didn't see him. Picking up speed, she miraculously avoided hitting pedestrians as she snaked down the curving streets toward the Jaffa Gate.

Dozens of cops ran after Cas and the bus. They had to hold their fire because of the terrified crowds converging around them.

Cas veered off the street and dashed down the sidewalks, looking for a short cut through the irregular blocks. He glanced over his shoulder. More police cruisers were flying toward him. Lungs burning, he darted into a side alley, praying it wasn't a dead end. Seconds later, he came out the other side.

The bus was hurtling down a hill—straight at him.

He tried to wave Marly down. Looking demon-possessed, she didn't see him. He dived out of the way and landed in a pile of refuse. Struggling to his feet, he brushed himself off and ran for the rear of the bus. With bullets *pinging* all around him, he reached the ladder and finally grabbed the middle rung.

As the bus sped through the Jaffa Gate, he pulled himself up and scrambled to the roof. Sprawling atop the bus cab's roof, he came face-to-face with an Israeli Defense Force helicopter swooping down from Mount Zion. He fired a few token shots toward the helicopter's bulletproof windows.

The gunner responded by leaning out of the helicopter and aiming a fifty-caliber weapon. Slugs ripped into the coach, shattering its windows.

The bus weaved wildly through the heavy traffic on the Ma'ale HaShalom highway that bordered the Old City walls. Barely hanging on, he crawled to the front of the roof and managed to drop his head over the cracked windshield.

Seeing him suddenly appear, upside down, Marly nearly crashed.

He pointed to the door. When the panels finally screeched back, he grabbed the rim of the roof and flung himself into the coach.

Marly was clutching the wheel for dear life.

He peeled her hands off the wheel and pulled her out of the driver's seat. "My turn! I need eyes in the back!"

The bus nearly caromed off the highway as he turned onto an exit for Ein Gedi and the Dead Sea.

Dead Sea. *Just perfect.*

Zaynah, terrified, clutched her seat three rows back, trying not to throw up.

Marly ran down the aisle and stationed herself in the rear of the bus to watch for the police. She shouted at Cas, "That helicopter is still buzzing the Jaffa Gate! I think we've slipped them."

He enjoyed a manic grin of triumph. But he knew this window of opportunity wouldn't last long, so he wheeled the smoking bus into a parking lot of an archaeological dig park and yelled for the two women to get out.

Marly froze. "What are you doing?"

He shoved them off the bus. "Get in that Peugeot over there!"

Marly and Zaynah staggered across the lot and climbed into the backseat of the empty sedan.

Running behind them, Cas spotted several drivers standing at a coffee bar, waiting for their tourist passengers to return. He shouted, "I need a bus driver!"

The men stared at the bullet-ridden bus, and ignored him.

He pulled a wad of bills from his front pocket. "Three thousand *shekels* to drive it to Haifa!"

The men just looked at each other, until one shrugged and took up the offer. "What do I do with it when I arrive?"

Cas pushed him toward the bus. "I'll be in touch."

The baffled Israeli climbed into the bus, shut the door, and chugged off. The approaching police helicopter veered off and followed the bus.

Cas rushed to the Peugeot and slid his head under the wheel. He yanked out a bunch of wires, flipping open his pocketknife to cut them. In the back seat, Marly and Zaynah watched in disbelief as he rearranged the wires to jump-start the engine. They glanced at the market stalls across the street, expecting the car's owner to arrive at any second.

Cas threw the gearshift into Reverse, spun out of the lot, and sped off in the opposite direction of the departing bus.

Seconds later, a dozen police cars came flying over the hill with bubbles flashing. No doubt alerted by the helicopter pilot, the cops on the ground slammed their brakes and, screeching into U-turns, pursued the bus heading north, in the opposite direction from the road that led to Masada.

C as drove the steaming Peugeot into the Masada parking lot just as dawn broke over the sweeping desert horizon. He searched the gates. Eight long hours had passed since their escape from Jerusalem, but fortunately no cops had shown up, not even after they had pulled off onto a remote maintenance road to hide during the night.

Hearing the car churn to a stop, Marly roused from her slumber in the back seat. The girl, still asleep, lay on her lap. Marly looked up at the ancient fortress on the desolate mountain. "And just how are we going to get up *there?*"

Cas checked his watch. He had fifteen minutes until the tram made its daily dry run, always an hour before the first tourists were taken up. There wasn't another soul around. He had to give it to Jubal and Cohanim. Those bastards knew what they were doing, all right.

He leaned over the seat and shook Zaynah awake. She gazed up at the looming fortress and rubbed her swollen eyes, as if caught in a strange dream. He climbed out and nearly dragged her, still groggy, out toward the cable station at the base of the mountain. His hands were shaking. He usually got cooler when things turned nasty, but right now he felt like a nuclear reactor spiraling toward a meltdown. Without a word, he herded the two women into the gondola terminal. A lone kiosk manager nodded as if expecting their arrival.

Marly looked around at the station. The place was empty except for the tram manager in the glass ticket booth. "I thought you said there'd be hordes of tourists here. Where is everybody? How are we going to hide now?"

Cas avoided her questioning glare. "I guess we're the first to arrive."

The tram manager pushed a button to open the cable car door. He pointed for them to step inside.

Cas knew the guy was probably one of Jubal's men, substituted for the real operator. He rushed the girl to a seat. Seeing Marly holding back, he tried to spur her along. "What's wrong?"

Marly held her stomach. "I'm not good with heights."

Cas rushed out and pushed her inside. "How are you with foreign jails?"

Before Marly could escape, the door *whooshed* shut behind them. She sat with her arms around the girl, trying to comfort her and working hard to dampen her own fear. The car began moving up the cable, and Marly shuddered as she looked down at the desert floor.

"Just keep your eyes closed." Cas stood at the front of the car and watched the terminal at the top of the mount. "We'll be up on top in no time."

Exhausted and dehydrated, Marly was losing the battle to focus her brain. "We didn't even pay for the ride? Did that man know we were coming?"

Cas had to think quickly. "All reservations have to be made in advance."

"When did you call them in?"

"While I was casing those cops yesterday."

Marly blinked hard. Nothing was making any sense. In the hazy distance, another gondola appeared, descending toward them.

Cas glanced at Marly, and a vision of Shada suddenly came to him. Had his dead wife had returned in spirit to be with him in this moment of his permanent reunion with their son? As the descending car neared, he searched its windows. Three men stood in the gondola. That had to be Farid, between Cohanim and Jubal, with his face pressed against the glass.

His heart was nearly beating through his chest.

He turned to Marly. "Get ready."

"Get ready for what?"

Cas waved at Farid in the distance, and his son waved back at him with his left hand. Cas dropped his hand and looked to the floor, thinking.

The two cable cars moved side by side, and slowed to a stop.

Marly had turned even greener. "What's going on?"

He didn't answer her. Standing just inside the closed doors, he tensed every muscle as the panels on the other cab opened. He could see Jubal pushing buttons on a remote-control device.

The doors on the ascending gondola slid open.

Across the gap, Marly saw Cohanim and Jubal for the first time. "What are *they* doing here?"

"Just stay put!" Cas told her.

Jubal motioned for him to jump into his car, ten feet away, with nothing but air and a deadly drop between them.

Cas hesitated—and then leapt across the gap. He landed with only a few inches to spare. Farid grabbed him and pulled him inside.

Jubal punched another button on the remote device to shut the doors of both gondolas. "Nice job, Casbo. You may have a future with *Cirque du Soleil.*"

Cas snuck a glance over his shoulder at the cab he had just left. Marly and the Lebanese girl, now frantic, stood at the closed door, banging on the window and trying to get his attention.

He turned to Cohanim. "What now?"

"Jubal and I will cross over and take that one up. You stay here with your son. Once we're off on atop the mount, we'll send you down."

"You'll be on your way home," Jubal said. "You can leave the rest to us."

Cas noticed that they had brought a wide plank with them, apparently to use to bridge the two hovering gondolas. He turned and locked eyes with his son. "Did they teach you to write in prison?"

Farid frowned, confused. "Of course, *Abba.*"

"I want you to write a goodbye note to my ... friend ... for me. Her name is Marly."

Annoyed with the sentimental delay, Jubal motioned for Cohanim to give Farid the pen that the Texan kept in his front pocket.

Farid found a tourist brochure in a slot on the cable-car wall. "What would you like me to say for you, *Abba*?"

"Write that there was something I forgot to tell her when I had the chance."

"Yes, *Abba*?"

"That I love her. More than anything in the world."

Farid hesitated, not expecting to hear such a message, but then he scribbled it quickly. He was about to give the note back to Cas when—

Jubal intercepted the note. "I'll be happy to deliver it."

"Okay, then." Cohanim inched toward the door. "Everybody ready?"

As the cab switch was about to be made, Cas kept his eyes fixed on Farid.

Suddenly, he wheeled and slammed his shoulder into Jubal.

Jubal flew against the car's wall—the remote sailed across the gondola.

Cas pounced on the control device and pushed madly at the buttons.

Marly's cab began ascending toward the fortress.

Jubal struggled to his feet and watched in horror as the two women moved out of his reach. Glaring at Cas, the CrossArrow general reached for his gun. He turned pale, reminded that he had checked the weapon at the station before entering the scanner. "You fucking screw-up!"

Cas backed away. "Little fly in the ointment."

Circling Cas withs fists balled, the Texan snarled at Jubal, "I told you we couldn't trust him. We should have put a bullet in his head back in Jerusalem."

Jubal switched into his benevolent-uncle act. He inched closer, trying to bring Cas back into the fold. "What's the problem here, Casbo? Something else we can do for you?"

Cas reached for Farid's hand. When Farid reached back, Cas grabbed his son and spun him around. He twisted Farid's arm behind his back, until the young man let out a yelp. "Little family history you may not know, Jubal. My son was born left-handed."

Jubal glanced worriedly at Cohanim, as if not following the import of that detail. "I think I recall hearing something about that."

Cas edged Farid toward the door, forcing the two men to back off. "Here's something you may *not* have heard. Just so happens, the tribe I infiltrated doesn't allow boys to grow up left-handed."

Jubal watched his every move like a hawk. "We're all fascinated with your camel stories, Casbo. But we're a little pressed for time."

"He just wrote that note with his left hand."

"Yeah?"

"In my wife's sect, the left hand is considered coarse and impure. So, she trained him to become right-handed."

Cohanim turned and glared at Jubal for having failed to turn up that detail.

Cas cranked the imposter's shoulder to its limit. "Alridey, then, Farid the *Fakir*. What's your real name?"

"Diyah! Diyah! They made me study prison files of your son!"

Cas wrenched the imposter's arm until his shoulder was nearly disjointed.

Jubal glanced at the other gondola slowly making its way up to the fortress. "Well, you've really outsmarted yourself this time, Casbo."

"Is that so?"

"In about three minutes, the woman you love more than anything in the world"—he spat those words out mockingly—"is going to smash into that mountain up there."

With the terrified young man still in his grip, Cas began frantically pushing buttons on the remote device.

Yet the cab containing Marly and Zaynah kept rising.

His plan to send her to safety atop the mountain while he took care of these lowlifes had hit a snag ... the damn buttons wouldn't work!

"Don't bother," Jubal said with a grin. "You have to punch in a code first."

"Couldn't be more perfect," Cohanim said. "Pregnant teen and American woman killed in tram accident. Really makes our job a lot easier."

He couldn't get the damn buttons to function. And without an operator to press the brakes, Marly and Zaynah would crash into the stanchions on the face of the Masada. That tin can they were in would collapse like an accordion.

"Now," Jubal taunted him. "Why don't we go get some popcorn and watch the fireworks."

Cas grabbed the crossing board from the floor.

Jubal motioned for him to drop the board. "Easy there, cowboy."

Cas leaned down, as if planning to release the heavy plank.

Instead, he threw it into the large viewing window behind him.

Jubal and his two companions recoiled with their elbows to their faces, dodging shards of flying glass.

Before they could stop him, Cas climbed through the open window and scampered onto the cab's roof.

Careful to avoid cutting their hands on the jagged remnants of the pane, Jubal and Cohanim stuck their heads out the window. They laughed at him.

"You planning to jump, Fielding?" Cohanim yelled. "Long way down!"

Cas looked up. Marly's climbing gondola was only a hundred yards from the cliffs. He searched the roof. A brakeman's rod rested in a slot.

Still reeling from the discovery that Farid had been dead all along, he levered the rod out of its sleeve and rushed to one of the two roller arms that held the cab suspended. He wedged the rod into the cable slot and heaved his chest against it. After several desperate shoves, the slot finally broke—

The cable slipped out of one of its two tracks. The gondola lurched, now hanging by one metal arm.

Jubal and Cohanim lost their smirks. They realized that Cas was serious about hurling himself to his death with them.

"Hold on!" Jubal yelled. "Let's talk about this!"

Marly's gondola now looked to be only thirty seconds away from impact.

Cas pressed the iron rod into the slot that held the remaining cable arm. "You got five seconds to punch in that code and stop that tram."

Cohanim and Jubal turned ashen as their gondola swung violently.

"Four ... three ..." Denied a vantage, Cas could only hope that Jubal was now punching in the code.

Above him, Marly's gondola suddenly squealed to a halt.

Cohanim poked his head through the window again. "You satisfied now?"

Cas lifted his eyes to the cable above him. He shoved his full weight against the rod—the track split open.

The cab dropped. He leapt and caught the cable.

Dangling a thousand feet above the rocky ground, he heard the plummeting tram hiss through the haze below him. Seconds later, the car holding Cohanim, Jubal, and their stooge crashed into the foot of the mountain. The screech of metal slamming against rock slowly faded into a deadly stillness.

He looked up. Marly was sobbing and frantically waving at him through her window. Her gondola swayed just a few feet from where the ancient Romans had once broken through the walls of the Israelite rebels.

He threw his legs over the cable and, with his hands burning from the friction, slid toward the lift station that sat hundreds of feet below.

Zaynah's screams broke the brittle stillness in the stifling gondola. Drenched in sweat. Marly tried to comfort the terrified girl, whose blood-curdling yells warned that the baby was on its way.

The gondola's door slid open. As Cas flung himself head over heels into the cab, Zaynah howled another series of shrieks. Marly burned him with a glare that made him wonder if she might kick him to the desert floor to join Cohanim and Jubal.

"Look, I can explain," he said.

Marly crouched between the girl's legs to deliver the child. "Come over here and hold her shoulders!"

Clearly, she wasn't in the mood to hear about how he had heroically cold-cocked the tram manager and had hot-wired the maintenance tram on the ground to ride it to the top of the mount and save her like Superman. Hey, now there's a story to tell back at the Fish Tank. He first met Marly as Superman, and now he had returned to—

"Dammit! Get over here!"

"I don't know nothin' 'bout 'birthin' no babies, Miss Scarlett!"

"Shut up for once and help me for once!"

He threw himself behind the seat where Zaynah was groaning in agony. He put his hands on the wailing girl's shoulders, at a loss what to do.

Marly tore off Zaynah's drenched cotton skirt and ripped it in half, discovering that girl had rid herself of underwear somewhere along the way. "Oh! My! God!" She gasped as the mother's spasms pushed out a child.

The infant's cry echoed through the tram.

Cas pressed a hand against Zaynah's dripping forehead, trying to soothe the girl, who had collapsed in exhaustion.

Marly wrapped the baby in the remnants of Zaynah's skirt. "Now help me with the umbilical cord!"

"What should I do?"

Marly pointed at his shoes. "I need a string."

He yanked off a shoe and quickly pulled out its string. Following her directions, he snatched the umbilical cord and tied it off.

Marly cradled the infant, easing its cries into silence.

Cas wiped his hands on his pants legs, stunned at what he had just accomplished. While Marly held the squirming bundle, he moved behind her and grinned at the infant girl, still not quite able to believe that they had managed to birth it. "Wow, talk about a high-wire act."

Marly pressed her ear against his lips, unable to find the words to express her overwhelmed emotions. She looked down at his hands and for the first time saw the burn marks from his escape down the cable. She pressed his scabbing fingers into her palms, trying to nurse him now.

Shrugging off the pain, Cas leaned over to wipe more sweat from Zaynah's forehead with his sleeve, making sure the mother was okay. "You did great," he told the girl. "She's got your eyes."

The cab jerked dangerously—and Marly screamed, clutching at him with the arm she was not using to hold the baby.

Caught in her embrace, Cas grinned, knowing it was just the wind. "Don't make me fall for you, Dr. McKinney."

"Stop it with the puns." Marly watched him coo at the baby, amazed how he was turning to putty. "You never cease to amaze me, Agent Fielding."

"Agent?" Cas shook his head to reject that old rank. "Unh-unh, no more of that spook mess for me, missy. I'm retired." He breathed a heavy, satisfied sigh. "Broke, but retired."

She looked into his liquid eyes. "I'm sorry."

"For what?"

"Your son. I wish … "

He pressed a kiss to her lips to prevent her from saying what she was thinking. Surfacing, he whispered, "He's with his mother, where he belongs."

His mystical turn surprised Marly. "You really believe that?"

He winked, making a poor attempt to mask his disappointment and sadness at having discovered that Farid was dead, after all. "I never make a decision about the really important stuff until absolutely necessary."

Marly looked over at Zaynah, who had fallen asleep on the bench next to them. "Maybe God *does* work in mysterious ways."

Cas trailed her gaze and realized what she was suggesting. "You'd have to sell a lot of rocks to support all four of us."

Marly was about to say something else, but raw emotion choke off her words. She looked down, and the baby's squished lids flickered. When its tiny eyes flashed open, she thought she caught a glimpse of … No, she was a scientist, for Christ sakes. All of this God cloning and Antichrist nonsense was just that. Shaking her head wearily, she looked down at the baby again and muttered to herself, "Slouching towards Bethlehem to be born."

Cas roused from his own dark thoughts. "What'd you say?"

She could never offer him a logical explanation for what she was feeling. Instead, she answered him as best she could, with another verse. "That twenty centuries of stony sleep were vexed to nightmare by a rocking cradle."

Cas stared at her, wondering if the strain had pushed her over the edge.

Feeling his perplexed gaze, she admitted, "I don't know why that came to me just now."

"Was that a poem? What was it from? Maybe I've heard of it."

She smiled at his attempt to pretend that he'd ever even cracked a book of poetry. "*The Second Coming* by Yeats."

"Right." He snapped his fingers. "Didn't he play tailback for Notre Dame?"

She laughed. "Let's go home, falconer, and maybe …"

"Maybe what?"

Hanging a thousand feet above the land of miracles, Marly kissed him and whispered, "Now that you understand how chromosomes and shooting stars work"—she looked down at the mysterious child in her arms—"maybe we should think about building a little lab of our own."

Taking the hint, Cas brushed away a tear, but he quickly dismissed the idea as impractical. "I'm too old to start over."

She rested her head against his shoulder while she swayed the baby in her arms. "I'm not giving up on you just yet, Fielding. If a three-million-year-old rock can become a father, there still might be a second chance for you."

A Note on the Front Cover Art

With the generous permission of his daughters, the front cover incorporates a painting titled *the money lenders* by **David Boyd** (1924-2011). Boyd was a distinguished Australian artist who began his career as a ceramicist and transitioned seamlessly to paintings. As the fourth child of four generations of artists, he and his four siblings grew up in a creative environment in which pottery, drawing, painting, poetry, and music were encouraged as intrinsic to daily life. On the family property, Open Country, at Murrumbeena in Victoria, Australia, each Boyd family member developed a personal artistic response to the Australian environment and their family life. Boyd was honored by the Australian Government with an Order of Australia in 2008 and in August 2012 an exhibition celebrating his enormous contribution to art and culture was curated by Eva Breuer Art Dealer and held at the S.H Ervin Gallery Sydney Australia. A commemorative book, *David Boyd: his work, his life, his family*, was published by Eva Breuer Art Dealer to mark this exceptional exhibition.

About the Authors

A graduate of Indiana University School of Law and Columbia University's Graduate School of Journalism, **Glen Craney** practiced trial law before joining the Washington press corps to cover national politics and the Iran-contra trial for *Congressional Quarterly* magazine. The Academy of Motion Pictures, Arts and Sciences awarded him the Nicholl Fellowship for best new screenwriting. His debut novel, *The Fire and the Light,* was named Best New Fiction by the National Indie Excellence Awards and an Honorable Mention winner by *Foreword Magazine* for its Book of the Year in historical fiction. He lives in Malibu, California.

A graduate of Columbia University's Graduate School of Journalism, **John Jeter** has worked as an editor and reporter for the *Chicago Sun-Times*, the *San Antonio Express-News,* and the *St. Petersburg Times.* He is the author of two nationally published books, including *Rockin' A Hard Place* (Hub City Press, 2012), a memoir of his years owning and managing one of the South's premier music concert venues. A television series based on the memoir is currently in production. His first novel, *The Plunder Room,* was published by St. Martin's Press/Thomas Dunne Books in 2010. This is his first major collaboration. He lives with his wife in Greenville, South Carolina.

Also by Glen Craney

The Fire and the Light
A Novel of the Albigensian Crusade

As the 13th century dawns, Cathar heretics in southern France guard an ancient scroll that holds shattering revelations about Jesus Christ. Esclarmonde de Foix, a beloved Occitan countess, must defy Rome to preserve the true path to salvation. Christianity suffers its darkest hour in this epic saga of troubadour love, monastic intrigue, and esoteric mystery set during the first years of the French Inquisition.

The Virgin of the Wind Rose
A Mystery-Thriller of the End Times

While investigating the murder of an American missionary in Ethiopia, State Department lawyer Jaqueline Quartermane discovers an ancient Latin palindrome embedded with a cryptographic time bomb. Separated by half a millennium, two espionage conspiracies dovetail in this breakneck thriller to expose the world's most explosive secret: The true identity of Christopher Columbus and the explorer's connection to those now trying to launch the Apocalypse.

The Yanks Are Starving
A Novel of the Bonus Army

Mired in the Great Depression, the United States teeters on the brink of revolution. And as the summer of 1932 approaches, a charismatic hobo leads twenty thousand homeless World War I veterans into the nation's capital to demand their service compensation. Here is the epic story of political intrigue and betrayal that culminated in the only pitched battle ever fought between two American armies under the same flag.

The Spider and the Stone
A Novel of Scotland's Black Douglas

As the 14th century dawns, the brutal Edward Longshanks of England schemes to steal Scotland. But inspired by a headstrong lass, a frail, dark-skinned boy named James Douglas defies three Plantagenet kings and champions the cause of his wavering friend, Robert the Bruce, leading the armies to the bloody field of Bannockburn. Here is the thrilling saga of star-crossed love and heroic sacrifice that saved Scotland and set the stage for the founding of the United States.

More information at www.glencraney.com.

Also by John Jeter

The Plunder Room
A Novel

Moments before Edward Duncan dies, the colorful World War II hero leaves a mandate for his grandson Randol--to safeguard the family's proud Southern legacy. Randol, paralyzed and in a wheelchair after a car accident, buries his grandfather, and learns that his father, a Vietnam veteran, is running an illicit empire with Randol's half-brother, Jerod.

A wise-cracking music critic, Randol already has his hands full with his pot-smoking Goth son. When Jerod brings the gorgeous Annie down South and parks her in their South Carolina home, the family maid Volusia, "quick to ram a bar of soap into any foul mouth," sizes up Annie in short order. Jerod, his father, and Randol, are blind to what Volusia sees so easily, making it that much harder for Randol to bring the family together and salvage their dignity. A powerfully compelling story about one man's mission to preserve his family's ideals of honor and loyalty.

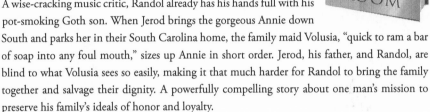

Rockin' A Hard Place
Flats, Sharps & Other Notes From A Misfit Music Club Owner

John Jeter was a burnt-out journalist living in Florida when his younger brother, who once saved Jeter's life by donating one of his kidneys, telephoned with life-altering news: he found the perfect spot in Greenville, South Carolina, for the concert hall they always dreamed of opening. This is the story of The Handlebar, an intimate listening room that has presented thousands of artists—John Mayer, Joan Baez, Zac Brown, and Sugarland among them—and hosted a quarter-million fans since its opening in 1994. A promoter's memoir of a naive plunge into an industry that Hunter S. Thompson once called a cruel and shallow money trench, a long plastic hallway where thieves and pimps run free.

More information at www.johnjeter.com.

Made in the USA
Charleston, SC
16 April 2014